I·Shall AWAKEN

I·Shall Awaken

KATEŘINA ŠARDICKÁ

Albatros

ISBN 978-80-00-06347-8

Dedicated to my grandparents,
Anne and Jan, one of whom awoke in me the passion
for storytelling, while the other supported me in it for years.

And to anyone who has ever been afraid to look underneath
their bed before going to sleep.

THE NIGHT BEFORE

I t was a winter that would be talked about for many years to come. A winter that came so swiftly and abruptly that there was hardly any time to adequately prepare for it. But what was to be etched in people's memories wasn't the frost and the cold—no, it was those twelve nights, on the cusp of the New Year, that ended up changing everything.

As dusk fell, Dora Lautner had to press her cheek against the window to even see the scenery passing by. And when the train suddenly hurtled into such pitch darkness that it seemed as though it had left the ground below and was moving through nothingness, Dora turned away to face the train compartment.

Apart from her and the conductor, nobody else was left sitting in the old diesel train. The brown leather upholstery on the seats was torn and the door wouldn't shut properly. Dora sped along the single-track railway in a Hurvínek train car, which had been used abundantly in the past on regional lines with fewer passengers.

She couldn't believe that these old models could still be found on the tracks. Dora had spent a substantial part of her childhood near trains, whenever she would stay at her uncle's place near the upper side of the valley for the summer, and even back then, he used to tell her how they'd soon be replaced by wholly new trains. But things hardly ever changed here, so it didn't surprise her all that much. Most of the inhabitants put down roots here for good, becoming so entwined with the village that they couldn't leave even if they wanted to. Whatever took root here eventually ended up dying here too.

But Dora was glad there was even a train to take. It stopped here only three times a day by sheer force of habit. Back in the day, a supply route used to pass through here for passenger trains going over the mountains to the borderlands. But that had fallen into disuse a long time ago, and it was only a matter of time before the train station would be closed down for good.

Dora often found herself feeling disdain for her village. She hated its inhabitants for what they had done to her. She despised them from the bottom of her heart. But she suppressed these feelings just as quickly as they took hold of her. The village was her family. It was all she had.

Dora was on her way back from school. Class let out a bit earlier due to the beginning of winter break, but she'd gotten held up by her shopping in town.

She let the train rock her, feeling the gaze of the conductor upon her since the moment they were the only two people left sitting in the train. *Don't look him in the eye, for goodness' sake.* She wasn't in the mood to talk to him.

"Last stop," he announced suddenly. The two hours had flown by unusually fast.

He always said it in the same tone, in that impersonal, definitive voice of his. *Last stop.* Nothing more.

The train stop was in the middle of nowhere, the station

building having been torn down right after the war. Dora got off and set out along the Black Forest toward her village.

She didn't like the cold, and here, in these parts, it was always cold. Or at least it was cold in the winter and cool in the summer. Not her cup of tea. The inclement weather only intensified the feeling she had of returning to the brink of hell itself.

Dora trudged northward through the snow-covered fields. She knew the way by heart. Despite the hunger, cold, and her frozen limbs, she refused to let up. If she were to stop now, she wouldn't be able to muster the strength to go on. She suddenly wished that she had never been born in this godsforgotten land, this secluded little stretch of wasteland.

After several minutes, Dora spotted her house through the trees. Judging by appearance alone, few people would think someone actually still lived there. Her family never did have much money, but once they were on their own, everything began falling into ruin much faster. As always, whenever she came back, an uneasy sense of dread overcame her. In the city, nobody knew her—she could be anybody. But here, everybody knew everything.

Dora arrived home just in time for dinner, the clinking of plates in the kitchen reaching her ears.

"Where were you all day?"

It wouldn't be like Pa not to start admonishing her before she had even stepped into the house. His head popped into the hallway just long enough to give her a once-over.

"Sorry."

"Git to the kitchen. Move it!"

Dora hung up her things in the hallway and obeyed. Her younger brothers were just setting the table while Grandpa sat in the rocking chair by the window, dozing off. The kitchen was cramped. Dora rolled up the sleeves of her blouse to avoid getting dirty. Her exposed forearms revealed her tattoos—traditional symbols of protection. A pot of soup was already bubbling on the stovetop. Pulling out some semolina, eggs, and milk from the pantry, Dora began to make dumplings, just like her mother used to do. The smell of the soup brought back childhood memories. As she sunk spoonfuls of dough into the boiling water, she wished she could go back in time. Back to when her mother was still alive, or when she still had friends. A time when the entire village didn't think she was crazy.

Twelve years ago, four children vanished. Dora Lautner was the fifth child, who hadn't. The child whose bed was in the middle. The child who, for years, couldn't utter a single word about what had happened to the others.

"Done?"

Pa's sudden presence in the kitchen pulled Dora out of her reverie. He gave her a fright, as she didn't hear him coming in. Ever since the accident she'd had as a child, she was deaf in one ear. Whenever somebody would talk to her on her left side, she had trouble understanding them. She was never allowed to use her injury as an excuse, though. Wordlessly, Dora cut the flame under the pot and grabbed two dishtowels to carry the hot soup to the table. Her twin brothers were already primly sitting side by side, awaiting the food eagerly.

"Grandfather, sir, please come take a seat. Dinner is being served."

For generations, they had always upheld the deep-seated tradition of addressing elders, even family members, in a proper, formal manner as a show of respect. Dora leaned down to help her grandfather get up. He was all frail and withered, barely able to stand on his own two feet. Clutching Dora's wrist in a viselike grip, his long, yellowed, dirty fingernails dug into her skin. She tried to hold her breath to avoid smelling the mustiness and sickness surrounding Grandpa, and was ashamed of herself for feeling repulsed by him.

Grandpa sat down at the table with difficulty, with Pa already at the head of the table. The seat on his right was empty. It had belonged to her mother, and nobody was allowed to claim her spot. Dora took the ladle and began to serve the soup, while the others looked on wordlessly. After she too sat down, they all held each other's hands and said grace together.

Pa was the first to start eating. When he swallowed a bite and didn't object, the others began to eat as well. He was the head of the family and everything was always done his way. They ate in silence, and only the clinking of cutlery on plates echoed through the kitchen.

After dinner, Dora dutifully cleared the table, washed the dishes, and stored the leftover soup in the chilly hallway. In the meantime, her brothers took a bath and got ready for bed. She had promised her father she'd read them a bedtime story tonight and put them to bed. In doing so, she hoped to avoid having to help bathe Grandpa. Pa didn't object, but she could tell from his expression that she wouldn't be getting off so easy tomorrow.

The twins were lying in bed, their covers pulled right up to their necks. Dora reached for a storybook and began to read right where she'd left off the night before. She didn't pay much attention to the story, her mind wandering, but her brothers didn't seem to mind.

"One more," Oleg pleaded.

"That's enough for today. It's late."

She set the book down on the bedside table between the twins' beds. In unison, Oleg and Anton stuck out their arms from underneath their covers.

"Now I lay me down to sleep, and I shall awaken, for the evil spirits cannot reach me," Dora whispered, her fingers tracing the tattoos on the boys' forearms. At the age of five, all the village children underwent the tattooing ritual. The tattoos served as protection and warded off all evil.

"At this nightly hallowed hour, we call upon the ancient powers," all three siblings recited in unison. "Protect us till the light of day from Notsnitsa's evil sway." They completed the prayer by crossing their index and middle fingers and placing them first on their brow, then their lips.

"Sweet dreams," Dora bid them good night.

Pausing in the doorway, she made sure they were both properly covered before shutting the door behind her. She had a quick wash and headed to bed. After she lay down under the covers, she kept the lamp in her room lit.

It took Dora a long time to fall asleep. It was only after an hour of tossing and turning that she finally began to drift off. Her mind was wandering somewhere between the realm of dreams and the conscious world, when all of a sudden, she felt somebody touch her.

"Dory!"

Jolting awake, Dora shot up in her bed. She pressed the palm of her hand against her cheek where she had felt somebody's touch just a moment ago.

"Astrid…?" she whispered into the empty room.

Dora felt as if her friend had just left the room and closed the door behind her. She had no doubt that it was Astrid who had visited her in her dream. The girl had always had a peculiar, unmistakable aura surrounding her.

Astrid had been Dora's closest friend. That is, until she disappeared twelve years ago without a trace, along with the others.

The seventeen years she'd been in this world had taught Dora one basic rule. It wasn't zoning plans and walls that made up the village she lived in, but the inhabitants themselves. At one end, mountains separated them from the rest of the world. At the other, a river cut through the valley and, if followed downstream, would lead to several smaller villages and settlements. In other words—words that would cause her father to scold her, at the very least—it was a dump. Dora was a little ashamed of herself for thinking it. But she couldn't think of a more fitting description. It wasn't the remoteness of the village that was to blame for the lack of progress here. It was the locals.

Pa had always taught her to blend in, to make do according to what the village wanted. So, Dora conformed. What she had never come to terms with, however, was the locals' shortsightedness. She couldn't think of a better expression. The events that had transpired at the cemetery that very morning only served to further convince her.

Once a week, Dora would visit her aunt, Valeria Hattler—her mom's older sister. Dora did it secretly behind her father's back, as he had never really liked his sister-in-law, and after Dora's mother died, he had completely shut the woman out. He forbade Dora from seeing her aunt. Nevertheless, Dora would sometimes help her out with stuff, and every month, they visited the cemetery together to honor the dead.

Dora genuinely liked her aunt. In some ways, she reminded Dora of her own mother and took on her role, to some degree, during those days when Dora felt all alone. But what the teenage girl liked most about her aunt was the fact that she had never been angry with her about what had happened. With her, Dora never felt as though it were her fault that her aunt's son—Dora's cousin—had disappeared... while Dora herself hadn't. Every time she visited her aunt, her stomach churned at the guilt she felt toward her father for lying to him, but also toward her aunt for being afraid of someone spotting the two women and telling her father about it.

Two days before the winter solstice—or Korochun, as the locals called it—Dora headed out to the cemetery with her aunt. That time of the year was approaching, when—according to the villagers—the barrier between the world of the living and the dead blurred, and both benign ancestors and the malevolent undead appeared among the living. This time of year, it was custom to pay due respects to the dead.

An unpleasant feeling overcame Dora as soon as she walked through the cemetery gate with her aunt. As they rounded the corner, they spotted a cluster of people, huddled together among the tombstones: the Foreths. The family belonged among the poorer inhabitants of the village, even though Mr. Foreth slaved away at two jobs from dawn till dusk. They had many children, each and every one of them incredibly pale and quiet.

Poor, sickly little things, people called them. Every day, their mother would shoo them like a flock of chicks to the chapel. A few feet away from them stood old Mrs. Kober, the biggest busybody in the entire village. She was endowed with incredibly good hearing, eyes like a hawk, and the gift of always appearing wherever something was happening. From afar, it looked like she was in the middle of an argument with the Foreths.

Auntie Hattler noticed the unusual crowd, too, and tried to pull

Dora in the opposite direction before anyone noticed them. But Mrs. Kober had already spotted her and began to call her way.

"Mrs. Hattler, good day to ye!"

With great reluctance, they turned around and joined them. Despite the bone-chilling wind whipping all around them, the arrival of Valeria Hattler caused an even icier, sharper chill to set in.

"G'day," she acknowledged them.

Dora simply nodded in greeting to the oldest children she knew from school.

"We were just talking about how it feels like it were only yesterday that the tragedy occurred," Mrs. Kober explained. "Twelve years it's been. Goodness me, how time flies! Like it were only yesterday, indeed. I can see her right in front of me, that little pig-tailed girl, running across the yard."

She clearly hit a sore spot. Mrs. Foreth bowed her head and pressed her two youngest children more closely to her body.

Mr. Foreth could no longer conceal his irritation. "Yes, sadly, we must all submit to time's passing."

"Such a scrawny little thing she was," Mrs. Kober sighed. "What a terrible tragedy, just terrible."

"We pray for our sister every day," one of the children piped up.

"That there won't bring her back," the old woman snapped icily and turned to face Dora's aunt. "Planning to light a candle for yer boy?"

"No. Unlike others, we didn't leave our Tom for dead," Mrs. Hattler replied.

Mrs. Foreth let out a soft gasp, quickly crossing herself.

"Surely there's no need to dredge all that back up again," Mr. Foreth gritted through his teeth. "We already said what needed to be said back then—"

"I feel sorry for you," Valeria Hattler interrupted him. "You buried your own child. You gave up on her!"

"Shut up!" Mrs. Foreth lashed out at her. "Don't you dare speak that way in front of my kids! You don't know—you can't know—what it was like!"

"I can't know? How can you say that? My son vanished, too—remember? My little boy!"

Both women began tearing up. Dora wanted nothing more than to run away or let the ground swallow her whole.

"It's been twelve years, Valeria. With no leads! Deny it all you want, but you can't keep ignoring the fact that our children are long de—"

"*No.*"

Valeria Hattler looked like she was about to launch herself at the Foreths in a fury.

"There are wounds that keep on hurting, even after years," old Mrs. Kober interjected.

"You be quiet, Mrs. Kober. This is on you," Valeria Hattler rounded on her in anger. "It was you who provoked the quarrel."

The old woman, however, feigned innocence. "Me? Whatever are ye talking about, lassie?"

"Of course. Innocent as always. You make me sick. Let's go, Dora."

Auntie Hattler barely said a word the rest of that morning. Dora left her with a hasty goodbye and set out for the village to get her grocery shopping done.

The teenage girl exited the bakery with a fresh loaf of bread and stood outside for a little while, like she always did. Since the break of day, the local boys had been gathering wood into a large pile by the town hall for a bonfire that was to be lit during the

Korochun festivities. It looked like this year, the bonfire was going to be the tallest one yet. Dora fixed her eyes on the ground before her. The events from twelve years ago were marked only by a small memorial plaque underneath the oak tree on the village green, bearing the names of the vanished children. Dora had tried to avoid it for many years, though her gaze seemed to fall upon it almost every time. Perhaps it was the vivid dream from last night that made her come right up to it this time.

Sonya Foreth. Tom Hattler. Astrid and Max Mahler. Her friends—the only four friends Dora had ever had. And she lost them all in a single moment. It was a memory she had long tucked away. She'd been trying to suppress it for so long in vain. All these years, she had wished for it to have been only a bad dream. The whole village had forgotten about it, or pretended that it didn't remember what had happened.

If only Dora could have prevented it somehow. If only they could come back.

If only she could…

"Sparky, heel!"

A large black dog was running toward her. Dora barely managed to jump out of the way just as it hurtled past her like crazy, barking at everything in sight. A little boy was hot on its heels.

"Wait for me!"

Dora set off to the butcher's for some cuts. What with the holidays approaching, they deserved to treat themselves at least once a year. But a long, winding line had formed at the butcher's, one that wound all the way outside. Dora took her place at the end of it, hoping there would be at least a small lean cut of meat left. She'd already promised her brothers a roast, and she couldn't bear the thought of their disappointment if she came back home empty-handed.

With time, Dora had learned to ignore the chattering women as they stood in line. After the tragedy, when she had stopped speaking for three years, she learned to blend in with her surroundings. It was easy. Dora gradually became invisible. Sometimes, she even felt as if people were looking right through her. As if she weren't there at all.

Lately she'd been wondering more and more often whether she, too, hadn't vanished all those years ago.

The line was edging along at a snail's pace. Endless minutes later, Dora was grateful to escape the freezing cold into the shop, warming her bones. She shook out the snow from the lapel of her coat and stood on her tiptoes to peek over the others. Luckily, it looked like there was still some meat left. In that moment, snippets of a conversation from the front of the shop reached her ears.

"…I'm just sayin' what I heard is all. They says they let him out…"

"So soon? Wasn't he in for longer?"

"Old Mrs. Kober said he'd been doin' time in the madhouse. I'd think they don't just let somebody outta there like that…"

"May the gods protect us. We oughta start locking our doors at night and looking out for our young'uns."

"Ye don't think he'd come back here?"

"And where else would he go? He never known anything else."

Dora felt a shiver run down her spine. This couldn't be true… The women couldn't possibly be talking about…? Or could they? She pushed her way to the front so she wouldn't miss another word.

"Thank goodness old Mrs. Linhart didn't live to see this. If it was my son, I wouldn't dare step outta my house for the shame… Who knows who the father was, that he was born with a screw loose…"

"That family's always been a bit feebleminded. Old Linhart shot himself with a bolt gun. Was my old man who found him."

"You don't say!"

"Ladies, come on. Next in line!" the butcher interrupted their gossiping. "I ain't got all day!"

In that moment, the door to the shop swung open, icy air rushing inside. Dora assumed it must've been an impatient customer who didn't realize the line extended outside, or someone who wanted to make sure there was even enough meat left to go around for when their turn came. She only realized something was wrong when the entire shop fell silent, everyone turning around. Dora looked over her shoulder.

In the middle of the shop stood Lena Mahler—or rather what remained of her. She looked unkempt: an unsightly rash adorning the sides of her face, her hair all tangled and matted. She stood there, shivering, her gaunt frame lost in the thin fabric of her nightgown. The customers were looking her up and down—some with curiosity, some with open disgust, a few with pity—while the woman ran her fingers through her hair with jerky movements, mumbling incomprehensibly.

Dora wasn't sure how long the moment actually lasted, but it seemed like an eternity. She felt mortified, as if it were her standing there in front of the others. But she wasn't brave enough to step out and help the woman.

"Whaddaya want?" the butcher asked cheerily.

Lena Mahler did not react. It looked like she had no idea where she was.

Before anyone could intervene, the door to the shop opened once more. And in strolled Hedda Mahler. The old white-haired lady, who had always given Dora the creeps ever since she could remember, wordlessly grabbed her daughter-in-law by the hand and started pulling her outside.

"Nothing to see here," she angrily snapped at the onlookers.

Once both women were out of sight, it only took a few moments for the quiet shop to turn back into a buzzing beehive.

"Poor woman."

"To lose two kids like that, I'd go crazy too…"

"Imagine if she knew they'd just let out that sicko who's to blame for it all…"

The last sentence hung in the air. Dora wanted nothing more than to run away, but she was frozen in place.

Don't stand out. Try to blend in.

Like Dora's, most of the families in the village celebrated the holidays and upheld traditions and customs according to the old faith, just like their fathers' fathers had done. Even though faith in the old gods was waning, and more and more skeptical voices were emerging, claiming the old customs were barbaric and outdated, it was not unusual for the entire village to gather in the town square on the day of the winter solstice. That year, the shortest day of the year fell on December 21st.

Long ago, this holiday was for worshiping Dazhbog, the Sun God. Their ancestors believed that it was during the winter solstice that Dazhbog was born a babe in the underworld, grew up in the spring months, and achieved his prime during the summer solstice, before slowly weakening and dying on the day of the winter solstice, when he was resurrected. Between his death and birth, right on that magical night of the solstice, when the earthly realm existed outside his sphere of protection, the barrier between our world and the underworld disappeared, and dangerous beings were free to cross over into the mortal realm.

When Dora was little, her mother used to tell her scary stories of vampires, werewolves, and fairy folk that roamed the earth at night. To protect against these creatures, the village would light a protective bonfire at sunset, which had to be maintained all through the night as well as the following twelve days and nights, during which their world was in danger.

Taking a break from preparing the solstice feast, everyone donned their festive dress and began to gather outside at the first signs of the sun setting.

"Good evening, Mr. Lautner!"

"And to ye!" Dora's father greeted a neighbor of his.

Crowds had always frightened Dora more than anything. She kept her brothers close at either side as she clutched their hands and strolled, her head and gaze cast down, from their house to the square, avoiding meeting the eyes of the other villagers. She had been right—the bonfire was going to be a bit taller than the year past.

The youngest children gathered around the firepit, jumping in a circle around it as they danced and sang loudly. The adults gradually settled around them, and then, the time had come for the prayer.

"Dazhbog, our mighty ruler,
All-seeing and all-knowing bearer of light."

While the prayer was being recited, the bonfire pile was approached by four men, representing the four seasons and four stages of life. One by one, they lit the bonfire, chanting:

"May your unwavering flame burn on,
Imbued by your might.
May it protect us from the dangers of night."

Dora watched as the fire grew in size, the orange crackling blaze rising higher and higher toward the sky. The band was playing an upbeat tune on drums and horns, and several young women burst into dance. It was believed that evil spirits would balk at the merry-making and flee.

"Dora, look!"

Anton tugged hard on her sleeve, pointing somewhere into the crowd. It took Dora a while to realize what he was looking at. A few people over, it appeared that some sort of dispute between neighbors was occurring. Some of the villagers had huddled together and begun to shove at each other.

"Oleg!"

Dora's other brother wrenched himself out of her hold, the crowd immediately swallowing him like the water's surface settling over a drowning man.

"Oleg!"

Dora rushed after him without a second thought, dragging Anton with her. Nobody made way for her; people were rooted to their spots and refused to move. It was a struggle for Dora and her brother to push through the crowd. At one point, they found themselves straitjacketed in between the villagers, Dora's body suddenly touching more people than she'd have liked. People were singing loudly and bumping into each other. She bluntly elbowed her way out of the crowd, pulling her brother along with her.

"You okay?"

Dora glanced at him to make sure he was still in one piece, and then began to look around for Oleg. As she went to call out his name, she suddenly realized they were now smack in the middle of the conflict they'd spotted from afar moments ago. In those few minutes, the situation had escalated. It wasn't a scuffle, as Dora had initially mistaken it to be. It was a whole group of people against one.

"Go back to where ye came from!"

"Did they let ya out, or did ya break out?"

Some poor wretch was standing in the group's midst. Hunched over like an old man, he obviously hadn't shaved in days, and his clothes were wrinkled like those of a vagabond who'd just crawled out of a ditch. In his hands, he was clutching a scrungy hat at least two sizes too small for him. He kept pivoting in place, looking from one face to another, as if unable to understand what they were trying to tell him.

"Wack job!" some child shrieked.

Dora realized in horror that it was her brother's voice. And that this oddball whom people were starting to shove around was Loony Gusto. She hadn't seen the man since she was a child, and even then, he had terrified her. But the dozen years he'd spent in the madhouse had done a real number on him.

"What did you do to our children!" Dora's aunt, Valeria, screamed, lunging at the man.

The crowd shifted. Dora immediately located Oleg, grabbed him by the collar, and backed away from the chaos with her two brothers.

The ceremony had been disrupted, and a good half of the villagers were now looking on as the local madman was harassed. Dora led her brothers as far away from the angry mob as she could, where she proceeded to tell them off.

"I told you to stick close to me! What were you thinking?!"

Oleg, used to the sudden and menacing anger of their father, bowed his head.

"I'm sorry. Please don't tell Pa."

Dora couldn't stay angry with him for long. She knew that if she told on her baby brother, he'd get a beating.

"Come on then," she said forgivingly.

They found their father among the others and joined him. The communal lighting of the fire always ended with every family carrying off a flame from the bonfire in the form of a lit candle, which they could then use at home to light whatever they needed in order to protect the household. Dora was the one guarding their candle the entire way home to make sure it wasn't extinguished—something that was regarded as a bad omen.

They had almost made it home when Pa stopped in his tracks, pricking his ears up.

"What's wrong?" Dora asked cautiously.

"The dogs are restless," he replied.

She paused to listen as well. Their house stood a short ways beyond the village on a hill, and they could hear the barking of dogs echoing all around them—as if something was continually setting the animals off.

"Let's get a move on," Pa hurried them along. "The demons have already set foot upon the land. Best to keep out of their way."

Sometimes, the certainty with which her father believed in the village lore truly fascinated Dora. But when, as a child, she had tried to explain to him what she'd witnessed, he hadn't believed a word she said. Dora had never mustered the courage to ask him what it was he actually believed in.

After what happened on the village green, the families dispersed to continue the celebrations in their own homes. For years, old Mrs. Kober had been living on her own in a tiny cottage in the very heart of town. Ever since her husband left her, she had occupied just one room, the rest of the house remaining empty.

After she came back, the old woman prepared a modest dinner for herself, eating it in the kitchen unhurriedly. Once she was done, she cut an apple in two and was pleased to see, by reading its core like a fortuneteller, that another year of good health was in store for her. Old Mrs. Kober was used to going to bed early, but today, an immense fire was burning a mere dozen feet from her window. She drew back the curtain and peeked out curiously at several young lads from the village guarding the fire. The bonfire was always lit at sunset in order to soak up the very last remnants of Dazhbog's power.

Old Mrs. Kober filled up a washtub with water and took a quick bath, changed into her nightshirt, and lay down on the plank bed in the kitchen. She read a newspaper for quite a while. It wasn't today's edition, but as she'd never learned to read properly, getting through longer texts was always a struggle.

Today, though, she just couldn't concentrate. Her neighbor's dog was barking like crazy. She lay in bed, leafing through the paper more than actually reading it. Her thoughts kept returning to what had happened on the village green. *Who would've thought Loony Gusto would be stupid enough to come back here?*

At first, it was the silence that made her pause. The dogs had finally gone quiet.

After she extinguished the lamp by her bedside, it took her a long time to realize what was unsettling her.

It was the total darkness that the room was plunged into. The bonfire had gone out.

The Foreths sat down to dinner unusually late.

Mr. Foreth was forced to run around the yard, chasing the sheep that had mysteriously escaped their pen while they'd been gone. It was taking him a long time, the animals refusing to yield and listen. And as was the custom, the others couldn't start dinner without the head of the family being present.

"What the hell's gotten into those damn sheep?" he complained when he finally made it to the kitchen. "Never seen 'em act like that before."

"Maybe they're scared," their youngest daughter piped up. "Teacher said the boogeyman comes out when Korochun is over."

Mr. Foreth slammed his spoon against the tabletop impatiently. "Enough. Your teacher ain't got no business telling you things like that."

"Honey." Mrs. Foreth looked at her husband pleadingly.

"Don't *honey* me, Zoya. I told you once and I'll tell you again, I don't like all this nonsense they're feeding them at school. A teacher's supposed to teach our young ones, not confuse 'em."

His wife nodded wordlessly. "Whatever you say. Let's go eat."

Tension had been reigning between the married couple for the second day in a row, and their unpleasant encounter with Valeria Hattler at the cemetery was to blame. It had reopened old wounds.

Dad got dinner underway with a toast to bless their home with good health, good fortune, wealth, and prosperity, as well as an invitation for ancestral spirits to join the meal. The children would come to see this as a great injustice, once they got old enough to understand the painful irony of it all. It was all right to pray for the souls of their forefathers, but believing in ghosts and boogeymen stalking from house to house after dark... *that* was forbidden. Who was Dad to decide what was real and what wasn't?

They ate their fasting meal, consisting of several courses that, while meatless, were filling enough. Once they were finished, their mother cut a round loaf of bread—symbolizing the sun—into as many slices as there were members of the household, and as was the custom, left aside one slice for the ancestors.

They hadn't yet finished eating when there was a knock on the windowpane. The chatter at the table broke off as everybody turned to the window. But nobody was there. Another knock echoed through the room, this time coming from the front door.

Zoya Foreth slowly got up from the table. Her husband growled his disapproval.

"Where are you going? We're still eating."

"Today is a day when we're supposed to open our home to anyone who should arrive," she reminded him. "In case our forefathers should appear."

He didn't argue further and continued cracking the walnuts in front of him. Zoya opened the door leading to the hallway. Another knock came.

"Yes, I'm coming!"

Taking advantage of not being under scrutiny for once, the children wolfed down the last of the apple slices. They could hear Zoya unlocking the carefully bolted door. The muted sounds of her voice echoed into the kitchen.

"Zoya, who is it?!" Mr. Foreth shouted over his shoulder.

In that moment, a shriek filled the house.

It was just a gut feeling.

Dora shot up in her bed in the middle of the night. It took her a few seconds to get her bearings. Her room was pitch dark, even though she couldn't remember turning the light off before she'd gone to sleep. She switched it on immediately as she tried to calm her shaky breath, her nightshirt drenched in cold sweat.

Throwing the covers off her legs, Dora slipped on her slippers and slowly rose from her bed. She could navigate their tiny house blind, but she opted to turn on the light as she left her room, walked down the creaking stairs, and found herself in the kitchen. Pouring herself a glass of water, she drank from it greedily.

She stilled. Was that movement she just saw outside the window? A feeling of unease took hold of her again as alarm bells went off in her head. Something was wrong.

Dora entered the hallway. All too suddenly, loud pounding on the front door filled the room. She stared helplessly at the blank expanse of the door, as if it could reveal what it was concealing.

Her heart beat to the rhythm of the rapid knocking. "Who is it?" she called out tentatively.

There was no answer. All she was met with was silence. Dora stood in the hallway, at a loss as to what to do. She began to suspect she'd just been imagining things. Even so, she crept closer, placing her ear against the door. Still, silence.

Without quite understanding why she did it, Dora reached for the key hanging on the wall. She turned it in the lock and pressed down on the door handle, certain there would be no one behind the door.

A young woman stood there, drenched from head to toe in mud. It covered her hair and every inch of her naked body, as if she'd just crawled out of the deepest recesses of the earth. She was visibly shaking.

Dora couldn't breathe. She wanted to scream and run away. She wanted to slam the door in the stranger's face. But she did neither.

"Who are you?" she yelped. "Wh-What do you want?"

For a long time, the woman didn't respond, and just fixed her with a stare. Dora wasn't all that sure she had understood her. When she finally spoke, it was in a whisper.

"I'm Astrid," she introduced herself. "Astrid Mahler. Don't you recognize me?"

THE FIRST NIGHT

Old Mrs. Kober could hear her own heavy breaths as her heart raced. Her wrinkled hand wiped at the windowpane and she peered outside again. The village was doused in inky darkness. Muffled shouts reached her ears.

She was quick to throw on her coat, tuck her hair under her scarf, and wrap a shawl around her neck. Under no circumstances could she let anything that was happening out there escape her notice.

The old woman stepped out of the house, the snow crunching beneath her boots. For the first time in her life, she could feel the gloomy side of aging—she felt frail, capable only of slowly trudging along. She wanted to get closer and she wanted to get there first, almost tripping over her own feet in her eagerness.

"Light it up, hurry!"

"I'm trying!"

One of the Firekeepers was scurrying this way and that with lit lantern in hand, while two others were kneeling by the smoldering pile of wood, trying to relight it as if their life depended on it.

"I'm trying! The wood's all wet!"

"How can it be wet when it was on fire just a minute ago?"

"How should I know? Light it yerself, smartass!"

Mrs. Kober drew nearer, crouching behind a tree so as to not draw any attention to herself. Windows across the street began to light up. Clearly, she wasn't the only one who had noticed the noise.

"What's that in there? Can ye see…?" one of the men suddenly asked.

Mrs. Kober leaned forward to see better. One of the Firekeepers dug his hands deep into the lifeless firepit.

"Are you crazy? You'll knock it over!"

"There's something… Something's stuck in there. Come 'ere with that lantern."

It took them a while to pull that *something* out of the woodpile. The man held it in his hands, but Mrs. Kober was too far away to recognize what it was.

"What is it?" the third Firekeeper asked, still trying to light the fire on the other side of the pit.

"A dead cat," they replied. "A black one."

"A cat? How on earth did it get there?"

"I guess… Guess it froze to death…"

"Froze to…? In the middle of a blazing fire? Have you gone nuts?"

After a moment of deafening silence, one of them said aloud exactly what Mrs. Kober had been thinking all this time.

"Dead animals in fires are a bad omen."

All their grandparents had believed it to be true, and old Mrs. Kober had heard it said as a little girl. It didn't bode well.

The oldest Firekeeper snorted. "Already got bad luck. The fire didn't even burn past the first night. We won't have peace till the New Year."

In that very moment, the village bell suddenly began to toll. All three Firekeepers, along with old Mrs. Kober still crouching behind the tree, turned to look in alarm. It was a couple minutes after midnight, and there was no reason for the bell-ringer to be sounding the bell right now.

Dora didn't know how long it took her to overcome her initial shock, or whether she even managed to. She was clutching the door handle so tightly her fingers started to tremble, and she was at a complete loss for words.

In the dead of night, a young woman had come to her door, claiming she was one of the children who had been missing for twelve years—Dora's best friend, whom they'd mourned and buried long ago. It couldn't be true. It didn't make any sense. But still, there was something about the poor girl that urged Dora not to shut the door in her face.

"It's cold. Come inside," she forced out eventually.

When Dora saw how much effort it took the young woman to take a hesitant step forward, she offered her arm, like she was used to doing with Grandpa. Before shutting the door, she looked left and right, in case someone might spot them here at the edge of the forest.

From the coatrack in the hallway, Dora grabbed her grandpa's sweater and her old coat that she wore whenever she tended to the animals and did housework. She led the woman as quietly as she could into the kitchen, closing the door behind them so they wouldn't wake up the rest of the house.

"Here you go." She held out the clothes. "That's all I've got down here. If I went upstairs, I could wake up Pa, and…"

Dora didn't finish the rest of her sentence. It seemed the woman didn't understand her words anyway. She was eyeing the offered clothes suspiciously, even though she was visibly shaking with cold. Dora waited patiently, and as the adrenaline began to wear off, she started to realize her own embarrassment at seeing a naked body.

Dora sat the stranger down at the table, flitting around the kitchen quietly. She set a pot of water on the stove to make tea—afraid to use the kettle, as its whistling would awaken the sleeping house. While the water was slowly heating up, she filled a small washtub with warm water and set it with a clean dishcloth in front of the woman so she could clean herself. But she just sat there, still as death.

Dora decided to do it herself and, wetting the corner of the dishcloth, she brought it up to the woman's face. The mud on her skin hadn't managed to dry yet. It didn't make any sense—the ground outside had been frozen for weeks and was blanketed in snow... Where on earth could she have come from that she was covered in dirt from head to toe?

Silently, Dora used the soapy hot water to clean the woman's face, neck, and hands. She couldn't get the dirt from under her fingernails, though—that was a job for a proper bath and a thorough scrubbing. Neither of them uttered a word the entire time Dora was dunking the cloth in the water, which only got dirtier and dirtier.

Eventually, Dora decided to take matters into her own hands. She gestured to the woman that she would help her with the clothes. The woman didn't protest and allowed Dora to pull the sweater over her head and help her with the sleeves. The clothing was so large that it fell mid-thigh. After wrapping her in the coat, the woman's trembling subsided a bit.

The water on the stove began to boil. Dora poured it into two mugs full of herbs she'd picked and dried herself in the summertime. She placed the larger mug on the table in front of the woman and kept the smaller one for herself.

"Thank you," the stranger spoke in a raspy voice.

Now that the woman's features were washed clean, Dora could examine them better in the light. She had huge eyes, her gaze reminding Dora of a wounded wild animal. Dark, untamed, shoulder-length locks framed her pale face. It wasn't anyone from the village, she was sure of that. She knew all the girls, especially those around the same age as herself. She could have come from one of the settlements nearby, but in that case, how would she have been able to walk dozens of miles in such freezing weather? And without any clothes, in the dark? At the same time, she couldn't shake the feeling that the person in front of her reminded her of someone. Dora bit back a myriad of pressing questions to eventually settle on asking her the most banal question of them all.

"Do you feel any better? Feel warmer?"

The woman wrapped her numb fingers around the mug and nodded. "Yes, thank you."

An endless silence engulfed the room once more. Dora listened to the rhythmic tick-tock of the clock on the wall, and at times, she swore she could hear Grandpa's snoring coming from the top floor. She had no idea what to do or say. She was afraid the door would come flying open at any moment and her father would barge into the kitchen. What would she tell him? How could she justify her actions?

As if the woman could read Dora's mind, she gazed at her for a long time and said, "You have many questions for me."

"Why do you say that?"

"Because I can see them mirrored in your eyes."

Dora didn't stop to ponder the woman's peculiar reply for long. Her curiosity was stronger. "Who are you? What happened to you?"

"I've already told you," the woman whispered. "You don't believe me?"

Dora shrugged uncertainly. She wasn't sure how to respond so she wouldn't hurt the woman's feelings. Her face felt hot as a noticeable blush bloomed on her cheeks.

"It's me. Astrid."

"Don't be mad, but... that's not... that's impossible."

"How come?"

She hesitated. "Astrid is... dead."

"For Perun's sake, what on earth is going on here?"

Old Mrs. Kober stepped out from behind the tree, and the trio of Firekeepers didn't look at all surprised to see her there. The whole village knew that nothing ever got past her anyway. As one, they looked up at the belfry of the chapel, where the bell was still ringing like mad.

"An omen," the oldest Firekeeper whispered, immediately pressing his crossed fingers against his brow and then his lips. "May the gods protect us," he added in a low mutter.

The others parroted his gesture. In between two peals of the bell, they could hear raised voices behind them, soon turning into full-on shouting.

"STOP! I SAID STOP!"

A figure appeared between the bakery and the old barbershop. It was running straight at them like a madman. Right on its tail was Mr. Kowalski, the baker, shouting his head off.

"THIEF! CATCH HIM!"

The unknown figure probably had no idea he was headed straight into the midst of the Firekeepers. He didn't spot them until two of them left the bonfire to block his path. He froze for a moment before pivoting without a second thought and rushing in the opposite direction. But that led him right into the path of the third one, and before he could react, all three Firekeepers toppled him to the ground.

"Let me go! I didn't do anything!"

He was wildly thrashing this way and that.

By then, Mr. Kowalski, the baker, had caught up to them, and old Mrs. Kober had hobbled up to them from the safe distance of the tree for a closer view. She was expecting to see some brawny thief, maybe the butcher's brother, who had the stickiest fingers around. But instead, a young man, barely grown up, was rolling around in the snow—and what's more, he was wearing a pair of ill-fitting pants and a grubby shirt. He looked like a beggar.

"You thieving brat!" the baker shouted. "I caught him stealing in the bakery!"

"That's not true!"

"Why, he's just a kid!" one of the Firekeepers chuckled. "What could such a rugrat have stolen from you? The boy's barely out of his diapers!"

"He broke into the bakery! Wanted to make off with my fresh-baked bread!"

The young man managed to slip out of the Firekeeper's clutches and kicked him with all his might.

"Hey! Calm down!"

"You little twerp!"

But the insults and brute force did no good, and the stranger fought like a trapped wild animal. Old Mrs. Kober thought he might've run away from one of the cottages up in the mountains where wildlings and odd folk had lived since time immemorial. During his next attempt to wrench out of their clutches, the lad's shirt tore open, revealing a half-boyish, half-manly chest full of old scars.

"Start talkin'!" the baker growled in anger. "Tell us who your family is so I can settle this with your father, or I'm calling the cops!"

Everybody knew it was just an empty threat. The locals never got the police involved in village affairs if it wasn't a serious crime. Smaller conflicts were always settled by those involved, without the help of outsiders. Or they called the Firekeepers, or Guards, in. They were in charge of keeping peace in the streets.

"I wasn't stealing!" the young man shot back. "I thought it was a different house! I was looking for the Hattlers' cottage!"

This time, old Mrs. Kober got a word in. "And, pray tell, why exactly were ye looking for it, ye scoundrel?"

When the stranger stayed silent for too long, the baker snapped at him, "Answer the question!"

"I live there," he finally blurted out. "I'm Tom. Tom Hattler."

Everybody froze in surprise, gaping at each other. In the meantime, the bell had ceased its chiming, and people were starting to emerge from the surrounding cottages, woken up by the noise.

"This is it," a Firekeeper mumbled. "We've brought bad luck upon the village."

The Foreths had married twenty years ago, and since then, they had been through a lot. The loss of their first-born daughter was the worst thing that could've happened to them—every parent's worst nightmare. After a year of fruitless searching, they had decided to file for a death certificate. Some of their neighbors and friends began to look down on them for this decision, while others turned their backs on them completely.

Some people might have thought it immoral, insensitive, and inappropriate that they had buried their own child without a body having been found, but the Foreths were plagued with the thought of their daughter never finding peace—of her soul flitting about, lost. And they had other children to tend to, bring up, take to school, and care for.

They hardly ever spoke of Sonya in their family. It was as if she had never existed. But come Sunday, Zoya Foreth would always take all her children, dress them up in their Sunday best, and after Mass, lead them to the cemetery, where they prayed for Sonya's soul over her empty grave. It had become second nature to them, no longer feeling strange at all.

The Foreths might've been trying to forget the past, but the village wouldn't let them. Whenever they least expected it, the unpleasant truth resurfaced out of nowhere, hitting them like a well-aimed slap to the face—their daughter had disappeared and they had had her pronounced dead.

And now, the person who everyone claimed was responsible for her disappearance was sitting in their kitchen.

The food on the table had long gone cold. Zoya Foreth was

cowering in the corner, pressing her children into the wall behind her defensively and sobbing bitterly. Her husband stood in the opposite corner, aiming his loaded hunting rifle at the head of Gustaw Linhart.

"I… I-I-I…" the village loony stuttered.

"Silence!" Mr. Foreth warned him. "Who gave you permission to step into my house?"

Gustaw's face was twitching. His head was jerking to his left shoulder in a tic, and one corner of his mouth was drooping. He was protecting his face with both hands, anticipating a blow, and kept rocking from side to side.

"I… I-I-I… didn't want to anger…" he forced out with effort.

Mr. Foreth shoved the barrel of the rifle right in the man's face. "I told you to stay out of my sight! To keep away from my family!"

Gusto began to make braying noises.

One of the children started to cry hysterically. "Mommy, I'm scared."

"Me too," another one piped up.

"Quiet, children," Mrs. Foreth pleaded with them in between her own sobs.

"Give me one reason," Mr. Foreth threatened Gusto, "one single reason why I shouldn't just shoot you on the spot!"

Just then, a sharp knock on the door pierced the tension. The Foreths wordlessly exchanged a look of terror. Who on earth could it possibly be at this hour? Could the neighbors have spotted Loony Gusto entering their house? What would they think if they found him sitting here?

Before they could figure out what to do and who would go answer the door, the kitchen door opened, revealing their neighbor. He couldn't hide the excitement from his features.

"Have ye heard? The Hattler boy's been found!" he shouted. "He's alive!"

She heard the rustling of butterfly wings.

It was as if they were constantly fluttering around her ear. She kept rubbing at it. Her hand snapped up involuntarily a few times, but she always came up empty-handed. They had to be inside, however crazy that seemed. She could feel them inside her head. Astrid rubbed at her temples. It did nothing to help.

She couldn't remember anything. Even wide awake, she saw flashes of vague memories in front of her, but when she tried to zero in on them, they evaporated and vanished forever. She was beginning to panic.

"Astrid is… dead," Dora said.

Astrid didn't understand what she was talking about. Dead? Couldn't Dora see her sitting here in the flesh, right in front of her? She felt weird and uncomfortable, in the here and now, in this adult body. Something was wrong. Maybe everything was. Every sound in her ear was like a train slamming on the brakes, every source of light burning deep into her retinas. Her now grown-up body hurt, and it felt as if it had forgotten even the basics—like breathing.

"You have to believe me, Dora," she implored her friend with urgency in her voice.

"How do you know my name?"

That rustle again. She batted her hand around her ear. It didn't help.

Astrid had to convince her friend somehow. She had to recall some memory.

"Your name is Dorota Lautner and you've lived in this house your entire life. You hate dill sauce and you still suck your thumb before you fall asleep. When you were four, you fell into the lake in the winter, got pneumonia, and it damaged your hearing. You're deaf in your left ear."

Every memory she was struggling to pull from the recesses of her mind was causing her physical pain.

Dora paled. She was clutching her mug with such strength it looked like it might crack.

"What else?" she whispered.

"You had a cat," Astrid suddenly remembered. "She gave birth to a litter of kittens in the spring, but you were terrified your dad was going to chase them away and beat the cat to death. He didn't want to allow you to keep it in the first place, you had to beg him, and he only allowed it under the condition that it would just be the one. We took the kittens out back, to the backyard, and threw them all into the well to drown them. Your grandpa caught us doing it. He screamed at us and gave us a beating. He thought it was my idea and forbade you from being my friend, but you didn't listen. I never told anyone it was you who threw all those kittens into the well, while I just held the cover open."

Dora was wordlessly staring at her with wide eyes. Her expression was morphing—from incredulous in the beginning, to ashamed during her friend's recounting of the incident with the kittens, to one of a sudden epiphany.

"Astrid...?" she whispered in shock. "It really is you!"

Without warning, Dora jumped up from her spot and flung her arms around the young woman's neck. Astrid just remained sitting, rigid, and didn't think about what she was feeling. She just was, here and now.

"How did you get here? What happened?"

Astrid blinked. "I... I don't know..."

Astrid's vision turned black, her mug slipping out of her weakened grasp. She heard Dora calling out her name before she slipped into unconsciousness.

A good third of the villagers were awake and had begun to gather in front of their houses. One by one, they craned their necks, trying to figure out what was going on.

"If you're lying"—the baker raised his hand menacingly to strike the thief—"then you'll be sorry!"

"We can easily find out if it's true," old Mrs. Kober butted in. "Go wake up one of the Hattlers!"

The youngest Firekeeper hastily nodded and dashed off toward the house that was right next to the bakery. Meanwhile, the other two released the stranger and helped him to his feet. Old Mrs. Kober was observing him curiously. Maybe the teenager wasn't making this up after all—his sharp cheekbones did remind her of the Hattler family a bit. If there was any truth to what he said, though... She couldn't imagine what sort of consequences it would mean for the village.

An almost tangible tension was hanging in the air. After all these years, nobody dared hope for any sort of headway in the case of the missing children. It wasn't long before the Firekeeper reappeared on the pathway between the houses, this time accompanied by Valeria Hattler. As the duo approached, the woman increased her pace.

"Stand back, make room!"

Valeria almost broke into a run the last dozen feet. She stopped mere steps away from the young man claiming to be her son. They stood looking at each other for a long time.

The man was the first to break the silence. "I didn't mean to… It was an accident, I didn't break the window. You have to believe me."

Old Mrs. Kober didn't understand what he was trying to say. He was babbling nonsense. So he is crazy, after all, she thought.

Valeria shrieked, her hand flying up to her mouth. The young man took a few uncertain steps toward her and kept repeating, over and over again, "Mom… You have to believe me, Mom…"

Mr. Kowalski, the baker, apparently didn't understand what was going on either. "So is it him or not?" he asked.

"It's me. Mom, look at me. Look me in the eye."

Valeria was now so close to him, their noses were almost touching. Tears were streaming down her cheeks. She clearly noticed his torn shirt and his exposed chest full of scars. A painful moan escaped her lips this time. Her fingers touched the scars ever so lightly, as if she were tracing their long-forgotten shape by heart.

"Tom," she finally choked out. "Is it… Is it really you?"

"Yes, it is. It's me."

She hugged him close as she began to weep. They stood in their embrace for a long time, mumbling things to each other not intended for anyone else to hear.

Old Mrs. Kober just stood by the baker and the Firekeepers, observing the reunion. They couldn't believe what they'd just witnessed. More and more people began to shuffle up to them as the news that something extraordinary had occurred was spreading like wildfire.

"Is it really him?"

"It's Tom Hattler!"

"It's a miracle!"

"Where's he been all these years?"

"It can't be…"

It was a miracle indeed. For a brief moment, all those present forgot about the extinguished bonfire and the dead cat the Fire-keepers had found amongst the charred chunks of wood.

"I can't…" Valeria sputtered. "I gave up on ever seeing you again, my sweet boy…"

The crowd was jostling old Mrs. Kober farther and farther away from all the action, and she didn't like that. The mayor pushed his way to the front and started shouting all around about what a joyous day they had been blessed with. Even the Foreths came rushing with all their children, expecting it all to be some cruel joke. But when they spotted the young man with their own eyes, their blood ran cold.

Tom pulled away from his mother for a moment. He looked around, as though he were searching for somebody.

"What? What's going on?" Valeria asked in a worried tone, perhaps afraid to lose her newfound happiness again.

"Where are the others?" Tom asked.

"The others…?"

"Who do you mean, son?" the mayor added.

"Where's Astrid? Where's Sonya and Max?"

His eyes didn't stop flitting in confusion from one face to another. Valeria stood there, her mouth agape with surprise.

"You came back together?"

The exuberant atmosphere suddenly disappeared without a trace, replaced by a tense silence.

"Speak, young man." The mayor shook Tom's shoulder.

"I think…" he hesitated, as if fishing something from his memory with difficulty. "I think so…"

"Are they alive?" someone asked. "Are they all alive?"

Tom nodded. "Yes."

Zoya Foreth's legs buckled. If it weren't for her husband catching her in time, she'd have crumbled to the ground. A murmur of excitement swept through the crowd.

"Well, what are you waiting for?" the mayor thundered. "We have to find them! Men, split up!"

When Astrid came to again, the first thing she saw was Dora, who was leaning over her with an expression of genuine concern.

"Are you okay?" she tried to make sure.

Astrid couldn't answer. She tried to sit up with a groan, but after her fall from the chair to the floor, she felt as if someone were pressing a hot wet sponge to the back of her neck. She wanted to throw up.

Dora helped her back onto the chair. It was admirable how much strength such a slip of a girl could possess.

"I'm sorry," Astrid forced out after a moment. "About the mug."

Dora reached down for the broken pieces and picked them up nimbly. "Don't worry about it…"

Pain unlike anything Astrid had ever felt before was splitting her head open. She couldn't focus on a single thought, even though a myriad of them were swirling through her mind. As if it were somewhere there, within arm's reach, but she was grasping at it in vain as it kept slipping through her fingers.

"Astrid." Dora's voice brought her back. "What happened to the others?"

"The others…?"

Dora was staring at her expectantly, but Astrid didn't know why, or what, she was waiting for. She felt her eyebrows scrunch in confusion.

"I don't know… I don't know how much you're actually aware of," Dora tried again, "but you should know that it's been twelve years since you vanished."

"What?"

One piece of the puzzle suddenly fell into place, but the whole picture was still just out of reach. The image of the cracked ceiling in their kindergarten class suddenly flashed through Astrid's mind.

"Twelve years…?"

"Yes. I know… I know it's none of my business, but where were you, Astrid? Can you remember?"

The pain returned. Astrid pressed her fingers to her temples and hung her head between her knees. Dora was at her side in a flash, saying something, but the words didn't reach Astrid's ears. All she heard was a muted murmur.

"Everything's going to be okay… Try to take a deep breath."

Astrid attempted to follow the advice, but her lungs were constricted and she couldn't breathe. She felt like she was about to faint again when she finally managed to gulp down a deep breath of air. The excess of oxygen made her head spin.

"Max!" Astrid suddenly shouted. "Max, Tom, and Sonya!"

In her shock, she sunk her nails deep into Dora's forearm.

"Yes." Dora nodded in agreement. "Max, Tom, Sonya, and you. You all vanished at once twelve years ago. Something…" She obviously wasn't sure how to finish the sentence. "Something terrible happened to you…"

"I have to go," Astrid suddenly decided. She didn't know why, but she felt like that was the right decision.

"What? No, Astrid, listen. You're tired, disoriented. You should rest."

"I have to find the others…"

Yes, the others. She had to go. Now.

"Astrid!"

The young woman shot up from her chair. Her vision swam, but this time, she managed to find her bearings fairly quickly. Dora was trying to stop her, but Astrid didn't pay her any mind, heading straight for the door.

"Wait!" Dora said, her voice an urgent whisper.

They both found themselves in the hallway. Before Dora could stop her, the light on the stairway flickered on, the sound of hurried footsteps drawing near.

"Dora, what's going on?"

A man's voice filled the room. Dora, who was clutching Astrid's wrist, froze in terror. Astrid took advantage of her paralyzed state and slipped out of her grasp. All it took were two steps to open the front door and she was back out in the freezing cold.

"What's the meaning of this?"

As she left Dora behind, Astrid heard her trying to explain something to her father.

It wasn't easy to find her bearings in the dark, but the moonlight reflecting off the fallen snow created at least a semblance of light. Instinctively, Astrid set out toward the village.

A thick fog began to roll in from the forest, quickly spreading in every direction and stretching all the way down to the village. It was a biting, chilling sort of fog, which soon engulfed everything in sight.

The snow was freezing the soles of her bare feet, reminding her of its existence with each step—like millions of tiny needles piercing her skin simultaneously. Astrid was quaking from the cold so much, the abrupt sound of her own teeth chattering startled her. She placed one foot in front of the other, and she kept going, even though she felt like she couldn't go on anymore. She didn't stop, and she didn't think about the freezing cold spreading through her veins. She didn't allow herself to think that each breath she took could very well be her last.

Astrid could already make out the village in the distance when she suddenly stumbled, a snowdrift collapsing underneath her feet. She lost her balance, falling to her knees, then face first into the snow.

"She's coming to! Sit her up!"

Astrid hadn't even opened her eyes before someone's hands were already forcing her into a sitting position. She suddenly began to cough, tasting blood on her lips. She must've bit her tongue when she fell. A harsh light was blinding her.

The metallic taste of blood hit her with a wave of nausea. She could taste the bile rushing up into her mouth.

"I'm... I'm gonna throw up..." she wheezed out, her eyes squeezed shut, unsure if anyone could hear her.

"Just get it all out," a comforting voice told her.

Astrid threw up. Someone brushed back the hair from her forehead and handed her a glass of water. Feeling completely parched, she gulped it down greedily.

"I can't open my eyes," she mumbled in a panic. "My head... It's killing me..."

"Lie down for a bit and rest. The doctor's on his way. I'll make you some poppyhead tea to calm you down."

Astrid wasn't sure if she fell asleep or fainted again. Maybe she was conscious the whole time. She could make out voices, footsteps, someone touching her forehead. She didn't know where she was, what had happened, or how long she'd been left lying in the snow. But from the sounds and snippets of conversation, she gathered that the doctor was near.

After some time, Astrid finally dared to open her eyes. She was surprised to find herself staring into a familiar, kind face she hadn't seen in ages, but at the same time, it felt as though it had been with her this whole time. She recognized him immediately, despite his now adult features.

"Tom," she breathed out.

The young man immediately squeezed her hand. "I'm right here, Astrid. It's okay. You're safe now."

His words caused a pleasant, warm feeling to spread through her chest.

Someone interrupted the silence. A woman dressed in white appeared behind Tom's back and tried to lead him away. He didn't budge.

"The others?" Astrid asked.

"They found Sonya right before they found you," he hurried to answer her. "She's still unconscious, but the doctor said she'll survive. She's in the room next to you."

"And Max…?"

Tom didn't answer, but his face was an open book.

"Boy," the woman insisted, "you shouldn't be here. Get back into your room, right now."

She grabbed Tom by the arm and began leading him away.

"What happened to Max?" Astrid called out in despair.

She felt like a whole eternity passed before he replied.

"Astrid, Max didn't make it. He didn't come back."

When Astrid was little, her mother would often berate her for being a careless child. She would tell her that she didn't appreciate her toys enough since she didn't put them back in their place at the end of the day. Astrid never really gave it much thought, but to appease her mother, she started picking up her toys every day, right before dinnertime, and chucking them thoughtlessly back onto the shelf. There was no system to her tidying, but her mom couldn't complain—before they would sit down to eat, not a single toy was left on the carpet.

One evening, and Astrid remembered it well, she was in the middle of washing her hands before dinner when she heard her mother's raised voice coming from the children's bedroom, asking her what was the meaning of this. Astrid was confused—she had cleared away her toys like she always did, but now, they were all scattered across the floor. Someone had even dumped out all of Max's building blocks, which he hadn't played with in forever, and had completely turned the room upside down, including their beds. Her mother first asked her in a calm voice to explain why she had done this, but when Astrid denied having anything to do with it, she got angry. She gave her a sound spanking and kept asking her who had done it, then, if not her.

The only thing Astrid kept repeating the whole time was: "I don't know."

The feeling of helplessness and injustice had stayed with Astrid for years. And now, she felt it come back in full force as she spent the past few hours being bombarded with endless questions she couldn't answer. Everyone she had come into contact with since last night kept asking her things, and everyone was clearly expecting answers. But she had none.

The door to the cramped room she was staying in opened again. It almost seemed like they were on some sort of rotation schedule: *It's my turn now, you're up next—just make sure not to leave her alone for a single moment.* Not once did anyone from her family walk through the door, though. It was all just unfamiliar faces. She was starting to get worried. Something was wrong.

"Astrid?"

The doctor she'd spoken to several times today was standing at the foot of her bed, glancing at what looked like her medical chart. She wasn't even in a real hospital but in a regular house. Astrid was starting to doubt whether this man was actually a doctor. They kept forcing all sorts of concoctions and drops down her throat, which tasted so bitter her tongue grew numb. Her mind was a total mess. She had a million questions, but couldn't put a single one of them into words.

"Based on the results of your first tests, you're completely healthy," the doctor started off generally, holding a file in his hands, but not opening it. "Your body is just weakened and fatigued. You'll have to be on bed rest for a couple days."

"I don't remember anything," Astrid said. "I… I don't know what happened."

The doctor gave her a long, scrutinizing look. Before he replied, Astrid felt like she nodded off for a few short seconds. Her head was spinning. Was she really this tired? Or were they putting something in her water? Why couldn't she focus?

"There's no apparent physical cause that led to your amnesia. People who've suffered from a brain injury connected with loss of consciousness can often experience post-traumatic amnesia—a state of short-term memory loss which manifests shortly after the injury occurred or after regaining consciousness, when patients are unable to fully orientate themselves in time or to recognize where they are or the people in their lives, and their short-term memory is damaged."

The doctor spoke like a living dictionary. He must've been the only one out of all the people who'd come to her room that day who didn't speak the local dialect. Astrid realized he must've studied for years to be a doctor somewhere. Why return to their town? Why here? To these forgotten parts?

"I… I don't understand what you're trying to say," Astrid admitted.

"You've probably suffered a bout of amnesia. You're able to reconstruct your life up until the incident, but you don't remember anything that followed—specifically, the past twelve years. After some time, your memories of this period of time may return completely, or you may at least remember certain fragments."

Until the incident… Astrid quickly caught on to the fact that everyone was trying to give what happened a name.

"Hopefully, it's just a question of time," the doctor added.

"I want to talk to Tom," she blurted out.

He was here. She remembered. They had spoken. *Hadn't they?*

"I want to talk to Tom and I want to leave."

The doctor kept looking at her as if she were some sort of anomaly. "I can't discharge you until the Elders say so."

She had no idea what he was talking about.

"Where's Tom? Is Sonya okay?"

In reality, she was afraid to ask why nobody was talking about Max. *Did something bad happen to him? Where is he? Where is my baby brother?*

"I cannot tell you any information until the Elders say so."

She was starting to panic. "Then tell me when I can leave at least."

"From a medical point of view, there's nothing more I can do for you at this time. The Guards are in the hall and they want to talk to you."

Astrid considered her options. The sooner she got away from the doctor, the better. Even at the cost of having to talk to more people, and having to keep repeating that she couldn't help them.

"You can let them in," she finally told the doctor.

What she would actually tell them, though, she had no idea.

"Let's start with what happened last night."

Tom gazed out the window at the unkempt garden, as though he could find the answers in the snow-covered trees. It should've been easy—to remember. So why was he suddenly unable to?

"I thought it was our fence, so I climbed over it, like always. It was dark and terribly cold. I got inside through a window in the back that was cracked open. I didn't want to steal the clothes, but I needed something to wear…"

Two men sat across from him at the table. They had introduced themselves as the Guards—the self-proclaimed government of the village. Their rank was recognizable by their simple brown uniform and badge. One of them was incredibly tall and lanky, the other stocky.

One of the Guards scribbled down a few words in his pocket notebook. "You weren't wearing anything?"

In spite of himself, Tom felt ashamed under the man's scrutiny, as if he had exposed himself in public on purpose.

"No." He shook his head. "I grabbed the first shirt and pair of pants I found. I wanted to get out right after, but the fresh bread smelled so good..." He could feel the blush creeping up his throat. "I was hungry. It was just a small piece, I swear. Then the lights came on all of a sudden, and the baker appeared in the doorway. He started yelling that I was a thief, so I ran."

The Guard was nodding along after each sentence. "Nobody is accusing you of breaking into the bakery. What happened afterward?"

"They stopped me at the square... I didn't recognize them, dunno who they were... They started asking me who I was. I tried to tell them, but they didn't believe me. They sent for my mom and she confirmed it was me."

Though it had only been a few hours since the incident, to him it felt like ages.

"There were so many people there... They went to search for the others. Sonya was found in the school gardens, she was chilled to the bone, and Astrid was lying in some field behind the village. They didn't find Max."

The Guards exchanged a look.

"Max Mahler was with you?"

"I... I don't know. I guess. That's what they said. They said that four of us had disappeared."

"But you don't specifically remember Max being there as well yesterday?"

Tom watched as the string of words in the Guard's little notebook steadily grew. "I don't remember anything," he admitted.

The Guard decided to try another angle. "How did you find yourself at the bakery?"

"What?"

"What were you doing before you broke in through the window?"

Tom thought hard. *What was I doing?*

He was running. He recalled his heaving breaths. Tom had been running for such a long time—chilled to the bone and surrounded by darkness. But before that, he had no idea. Maybe he'd run up from the river? Out of the forest was more likely—or it suddenly seemed probable, at least.

"I'm not sure. I think I was in a forest…"

"The Black Forest? Outside the village?"

Tom shrugged. He could barely remember it was called the Black Forest. How was he supposed to know that? A canopy of tall trees sprung to mind. It could have been the Black Forest. Damn it, it could have been any forest for miles and miles around.

"Anything else? What happened before the forest?"

Tom was starting to feel a bit like an idiot. "Sorry, but I really don't know."

"That's all right."

The Guard's tone, however, suggested that everything was definitely not all right. He wasn't satisfied with Tom's responses. And Tom wasn't either. If he'd stayed silent the whole time, it would've amounted to the same thing.

"Take your time, Astrid. We understand the whole situation is very emotional and still fresh. There's no rush."

Astrid felt conflicted. On the one hand, she was dying to figure it all out for her own sake. To find out what had happened. To fill in all the blanks. Answering the Guards' questions wasn't that important to her. She hoped her expression didn't make it too obvious. On the other hand, the pain induced by each attempt to remember was so piercing that Astrid was consciously rebelling against herself. She couldn't shake the feeling that although the Guards had told her to take her time, they were impatient.

They entered all the way into her room to see her. She sat on the edge of her bed while they lingered by the window and took turns questioning her. Of the two Guards, she liked the shorter, baby-faced one much more, as he occasionally threw a kind smile her way. He made her feel much safer than his companion—a tall, surly man—did. They spoke to her as if they all knew each other. But Astrid didn't remember them.

When she stayed silent, not knowing where to start, the shorter, pudgier Guard spoke first.

"You might be interested to know that Tom Hattler is all right, according to the doctor," he said, forcing a smile. "They're letting him go home."

Astrid nodded. She wondered what Tom had told the Guards. But she knew that any questions she may have were of no use. They wouldn't tell her anything anyway.

When that didn't get a reaction out of her, the Guard pressed on. "Sonya Foreth is still unconscious. The doctor fears she's in a deep coma."

Astrid didn't know what to make of that.

"Twelve years ago, you, your brother Max, Sonya Foreth, and Tom Hattler disappeared from kindergarten in broad daylight. Astrid, do you remember what happened?"

Instead of replying, she looked over their heads out of the window. "The doctor said it could take a long time for my memories to come back. That it's most likely due to trauma."

"Do you feel as if you and the others experienced trauma?" the Guard pressed on.

He was the one who asked the questions, apparently, while the other one stayed quiet and jotted down notes.

Astrid shrugged. "Everyone says so."

"What about you? What do you think?"

The question infuriated her. She was running out of patience.

"I think everyone around me knows what happened to me better than I do. I don't remember a thing... My childhood seems so far away, as if someone else lived through it. And then there's this... gap. A blank darkness. Something's missing, a big part of myself is missing. Other than that, all I remember is last night, and it's unclear and confusing. And you all claim I've been missing for twelve years and want answers. But I don't have any, there's nothing. And I don't see why I should even trust you. For all I know, I could've been walking down the street yesterday and just slipped and hit my head..."

Tears began to roll down Astrid's face. She was upset with herself for showing weakness. But the more she tried to hold back, the more tears streamed down her cheeks.

"We don't want to upset you, Astrid. We understand it's difficult—"

"You understand?!" she cut in. "You understand what it's like to go to sleep as a six-year-old one day and wake up twelve years later as an adult? Really? Excuse my frankness, but I doubt it. Nobody knows what it's like. Even I don't know what it's like. I can't describe it, because my head—my brain—has a meltdown whenever I try to remember something. I've suddenly found myself in this adult body that I don't recognize. You're trying to get answers from the wrong person. I barely know anything about Astrid Mahler!"

Silence cut through the room. For a long while, it was broken only by her sniffling cries. Astrid hated herself for showing weakness in front of strangers. She shouldn't have let them see her crying.

"I can send for the doctor to give you something to calm down," one of the Guards offered.

Astrid quickly shook her head. Her arm still stung after her last shot. Who knows what they'd already injected her with since she got here. She didn't want any more medication.

"We can continue this another time."

"No!" Astrid protested with a sudden intensity. "I... I just want to get out of here."

The Guard nodded. "I understand. Let's circle back to yesterday then. They found you on the outskirts of the village, lying in the field."

Astrid wondered if she would get Dora in trouble by telling the truth, as she recalled the furious voice of her friend's father. She'd definitely have to go apologize to her later on.

"I was... I remember a forest," she said, her voice unsure.

The Guards exchanged a glance Astrid couldn't decipher. "The Black Forest?" The other Guard spoke up for the first time.

"I'm not sure," she confessed. "Could've been, I guess... I saw tall pine trees. I think they grow there. Or... at least they did when I was a kid."

"What else?"

"I spotted a house, the one where Dora Lautner lives. I knew she lived there. I suddenly had this feeling... I don't know how else to describe it. Just this feeling that I had to talk to her. But before I even managed to knock, she opened the door herself."

"She was expecting you?" one of the Guards asked in surprise.

"I don't think so..." Astrid tried to recall the details. "She didn't even know who I was. And she didn't believe me. She let me in, gave me some clothes, and washed my face..."

"You were brought in here completely covered in mud. Do you remember how that happened?"

"No."

Even now she could almost taste the bile in her throat. She had thrown up—last night! She had thrown up from all the blood in her mouth because she'd bitten her tongue. And Tom had been there... It couldn't have been a dream. If only she could talk to him!

"Dora made me tea to warm me up. We talked. I had to prove to her that it was really me."

"And did she believe you?"

Astrid nodded. "She did, eventually. I told her something that only the two of us know."

"And what was that?"

"Something stupid." She shook her head. "A stupid, childish thing we did as kids. It's... personal."

The Guard narrowed his eyes, but thankfully let it slide.

"All of a sudden, I started to feel sick and I fainted. Dora had just told me what happened. That we had disappeared and were gone for so long... I couldn't wrap my head around it. I still don't... understand."

"How did you end up in that field?"

"I'm not sure... I remembered the others. I thought of Max, my little brother... I wanted to find them. But I have no idea which direction I ran in. Then I just remember being here."

"What's your relationship to Gustaw Linhart?"

Astrid was about to answer that she had no idea who he was talking about, but a long forgotten memory suddenly came to the forefront of her mind, its very intensity surprising her.

Loony Gusto.

"Like everybody else in the village, I guess..." she admitted. "All the kids were scared of him."

Just then, the door opened and a woman entered the room.

"Excuse me... The doctor sent me. I brought some clothes for you to leave in."

The woman was speaking to Astrid as if she would know who she was. But she didn't.

"It's fine. We were wrapping it up here anyway," one of the Guards replied.

The woman left the garments on the bed and hurried away.

"That's it? Have you found out anything about my brother? Are you looking for him?"

"Patrols are combing the surrounding villages and questioning potential witnesses. We're doing our best, but so far it looks like nobody saw anything. Don't get your hopes up, Astrid."

These were the men's parting words as they headed to the door. As one of the Guards reached for the doorknob, Astrid called out to them.

"Actually, there is a favor I have to ask," she realized. "Could you take me... home?"

At first, the Guards' faces betrayed their surprise. Astrid hoped they wouldn't start asking her why nobody from her family had come to pick her up. Why nobody was here with her.

It would be embarrassing to admit that it was yet another question to which she had no answer.

Dora couldn't recall a time when there had ever been such a palpable mix of excitement and tension in the village. Since dawn, nobody had spoken of anything else but the strange events that had occurred the night before. When Dora came into the village to help out in the store where she worked a few times a week, she was met with an unusual number of people standing outside—idling in front of their houses and not even trying to feign any activity as they just chatted amongst themselves.

Dora quickly walked past them without stopping. Once inside the store, she donned her work clothes and spent most of the morning restocking the aisles. While stacking canned goods and sorting out decaying fruit and vegetables, she overheard snippets of conversations. Dora tried not to pay it any mind, but that was easier said than done.

Around noon, the teenage girl had already put together a complete picture of what had transpired last night and in what order—everyone contributing their own piece of the puzzle. Sometimes, the individual accounts differed from one another in the details, but Dora could easily decipher which ones were true. If only the villagers had any idea what had really happened. But none of them knew that it was Dora's house where Astrid had first appeared.

Apart from Dora's father, of course, who flew off the handle when his daughter confessed to who exactly she had let into the house in the middle of the night. Dora wasn't sure if he was angry because she had let someone in without his permission, or because it was Astrid. He had never approved of their friendship when they were kids. Dora even suspected it might've been a relief for him when Astrid vanished all those years ago.

Dora had been scared he'd give her a beating like she was a little girl, but he just ended up shouting at her while she meekly agreed to everything thrown her way. Dora was unable to fall asleep after that—she was just too agitated. The closer to dawn it got, the more distant her lost friend's strange visit seemed to her.

Dora had long dreamed of her friends' return. It would've even been enough if their bodies had been found and the case had been solved. Anything that would have proven that back then, she had been telling the truth, that she wasn't crazy. As young as she had been, she hadn't made it all up.

She needed to make sure.

And Astrid and the others were the key—the answer to her questions.

"Dora," Mrs. Lesovska, the shopkeeper, interrupted the teenage girl's train of thought. "Go grab the shovel and clear away the snow out front. There's been a flurry of it since morning."

Dora wordlessly entered the storeroom in the back. She threw on her coat, scarf, and gloves, taking the shovel with her. This winter, the wooden tool in question had become one that Dora had wholeheartedly come to hate, being forced to shovel the snow several times a day until her back ached.

Making way for a few customers entering the shop, she stepped outside. The sharp afternoon sun reflected off the snow, blinding her momentarily. Then Dora began to shovel the snow-covered sidewalk. A foot-thick layer of frozen snow lay beneath the fresh snowdrift, and whenever she struck it, the handle of the shovel dug into her collarbone. Within a few minutes, she broke into a sweat.

As yet, the Firekeepers had been unable to relight the bonfire on the village green, and nobody understood why. They kept at it all morning, trying to kindle the fire. Dora tried her best not to look in that direction so they wouldn't suspect her of knowing something. If she wasn't careful, each look, each movement, could potentially incriminate her.

Dora was almost done when she noticed the two Guards on

patrol. Her heart skipped a beat. Paranoid, she immediately thought they were there for her. As if she'd aided and abetted a criminal, the guilt she felt completely froze her in place. But she hadn't done anything illegal. She had just helped her friend.

But you didn't even report it to anyone, said a bold voice in her head.

That's not a crime, though... Is it?

Dora was torn. She'd already cleared away the snow obstructing the sidewalk. What she should do is return to the store, get back to work, and keep out of sight of the Guards. But a part of her was genuinely curious to see what was going to happen next, and so she pretended to keep shoveling snow, though it had stopped falling. The patrol was going door to door. Asking questions. They had even let loose their sleuthhounds. What were they looking for? Max?

Dora wasn't the only one whose curiosity was piqued. As people sauntered back and forth over the village green, most of them stopped for at least a moment. But she didn't get away with it for long.

"Dora!" Mrs. Lesovska flung the door open, her voice echoing over the entire square. "What're you still doing out here? Your work's gonna get done all by itself, is it?"

"I'm coming. Sorry," Dora whispered, feeling ashamed, and quickly followed her boss back inside. "My ear, ma'am. I didn't hear you..."

"I don't pay you to dawdle!" the woman reprimanded her in front of the customers. "Business in my shop's not stopping for three foundlings! Stop trailing snow everywhere and get behind the cash register. You pretend to be deaf only when it comes in handy! I know your kind! Pshaw!"

Dora could feel the eyes of everyone present in the shop on her. A blush bloomed on her cheeks. She quickly shed her coat in the back and took a seat at the cash register. Her hands were trembling so much it took her several tries to pull out the change from the coin trays whenever she had to. All she could do was apologize, again and again, for her clumsiness.

Not even an hour later, the Guards showed up at the storefront. Dora couldn't help but throw a surreptitious glance their way. The tracking dogs were running back and forth, sniffing every inch of ground. But it seemed they didn't catch any scent, because within the next few minutes, they were gone.

Around three in the afternoon, business was wrapping up, and Mrs. Lesovska sent Dora home early, perhaps so she wouldn't have to pay her for the last half-hour. Dora didn't argue. She was tired and klutzy after a sleepless night and looked forward to finally having some alone time. Not that there weren't chores waiting for her back home. But at least at home she could hide from the outside world.

On her way from work, she passed by the house where Astrid's family lived, but it seemed empty. It looked like Dora wouldn't be getting her answers just yet.

Tom was leaving the doctor's office in the afternoon in the company of his mother. She'd had to wait outside of his room for all the administered tests and his talk with the Guards, even though he'd heard her shouting at the doctor that she had the right to be present, because she was not only his mother but also a nurse. The doctor hadn't budged. But whenever the doctor or the Guards left, she would appear right by his side to hold his hand, as if afraid her son would vanish into thin air.

The fluorescents lit up the cheerless building with unpleasant, intermittent flashes as their footsteps echoed down the empty hallway.

"Do you know where they're keeping Astrid?" Tom asked his mother.

"No, but I'm sure she's fine. The doctor will take care of her."

Tom tried to hide his disappointment, but he must've failed, because his mother spoke again, her tone encouraging. "You'll see each other soon, okay? Now we have to focus on getting you home."

As they slowly set out toward their house, Tom couldn't help but wonder why his father hadn't come as well. But he didn't ask. It seemed to him that his mother was purposely trying to steer their conversations away from the subject.

Tom didn't recognize anything specific, but looking out at the hills and tall trees looming over the houses stirred up within him a feeling of home—a home once distant but now recovered. The doctor lived at the very edge of the village, by the river. When they finally arrived at their house, it was already getting dark.

His mother clung to him and supported his frame as though he couldn't stand on his own two feet. Tom soon realized why— huddles of villagers were standing in front of their houses, gaping at them shamelessly.

"Some things really haven't changed," he spoke for the first time since leaving the doctor's house.

Valeria nodded, her expression sullen. "People don't change… Let's go inside."

She ushered him in. Tom was surprised to see that everything in their home had stayed the same—the chipped paint, the creaky floorboards, the familiar smell.

"Come on. Are you hungry? I'll cook you whatever you want. I'm not used to cooking for others anymore. Do you still like porridge? Of course you do, everybody does."

As they walked from room to room, Tom's mother kept talking while he took it all in.

"There ain't much to eat here, but I'll think of something. What do you want to eat? Our neighbor knocked off a pig last week, and he gave me a cut of pork, but I've been saving it for a special occasion. Not that this isn't one. You're home, my sweet boy. Thank gods, you're really home!"

They stood in the kitchen—a cramped room with an old bench covered with ripped faux leather set by the table.

"Mom?"

"Yes?" She tore her gaze away from the hopelessly empty pantry. "Truth be told, I haven't had time to get groceries yet, but there's still bread left over from yesterday…"

"Mom," Tom pressed her.

"I'm listening."

"Where's Dad?"

Her expression suggested she'd been dreading the question this entire time. He patiently waited for her to find the right words. But the silence stretched on.

"Mom?"

"It was a trying time for us, sweetie," she spoke in a motherly tone. "When you… When we lost you, we couldn't handle the emotional strain. I want you to know, though, that it's absolutely not your fault."

Tom felt as if someone had dumped a bucketful of icy water down the back of his neck.

"Your father and I… We got divorced ten years ago."

Tom hadn't heard of anyone ever getting a divorce in their village. It was unthinkable, and even apparently dysfunctional families stayed together until the end. Marriage vows were something only death could sever.

"Where is he now?"

His mother looked dejected. She probably didn't imagine this was what they'd be talking about.

"Mom, where is he now?"

"He lives by the old mill. He repaired the house there for his new family. I know it must be hard for you to accept..."

Tom collapsed onto a chair. If he'd had trouble grasping his twelve-year absence before now, the reality of it suddenly struck him, clear as day.

On her way home, Astrid had to force herself to keep going and not turn on her heels and flee. The closer she got to her house, the greater the dread that settled on her chest, winding around her organs, suffocating her. She couldn't explain its presence, or rather pretended not to know its cause. Because if she did, if she let only half of those reasons out of the safely locked box tucked away deep in the recesses of her mind, she'd end up going crazy.

As Astrid had been leaving her room in the company of the two Guards, she had run into Mr. and Mrs. Foreth. They had just stepped out of Sonya's room at the end of the hall. Mrs. Foreth had looked broken, barely able to stand on her own feet. If her husband hadn't been holding her up, she would've most likely found herself crawling along the floor on all fours like some animal. The mental image had captivated Astrid to such a degree that her eyes had locked with the woman's for a second, which turned out to be a big mistake.

"Why? Why?!" Mrs. Foreth had broken free of her husband's grasp and flung herself in Astrid's direction. Astrid had unconsciously taken a step back, the woman's fingers slipping down her arms. Mrs. Foreth had begun sinking down to her knees, but her husband and the Guards had caught her in time. She had managed to grab hold of Astrid's wrists, however, with no intention of letting her go.

"What did you do to my little girl?" she had cried out. "Why isn't she waking up?"

Astrid had stood there in total shock, not knowing how to react.

"Zoya, calm down," her husband had urged her coldly as he tried to tug her away from Astrid. "Don't cause a scene."

"Why is she unconscious and you aren't? Wake her up!"

Astrid didn't have the answer to her question, and she started to shake once she was outside on the street. She didn't know whether it was because of the confrontation or the fear of what awaited her at home. Maybe everything at once.

"It's nice to be back, right?" the Guard broke the silence once they had all set out.

Astrid didn't respond. She didn't find anything nice about it at all. *Frightening* was more like it. The streets seemed both familiar and unknown—as if she were seeing these houses, gardens, and corners for the thousandth and first time all at once. What if the doctor was wrong? What if she never got her memory back? What if she stayed like this forever—half-empty, not even recognizing herself?

As they walked down the streets, more and more people got out of their way. Some of them stopped, pointing at her and whispering to their neighbors. Others observed her with ill-concealed interest. She wasn't sure if it was caused by the presence of the Guards and their authority, or if the whole village already knew who she was. It just made her need to escape their gaze all the more urgent.

Astrid recognized her house immediately. And not even the twelve years away could erase the emotions she associated with it. She wanted to thank the Guards, but all she managed was a nod. Her stomach flipped with every step that brought her closer to the door.

Okay, let's get this over with, she told herself.

Astrid sharply knocked on the door. Nothing happened. For a moment, a false sense of relief spread through her as she thought of turning on her heel and running somewhere far away. But where would she go? Did she even have a choice? And so she knocked again.

She was punishing her—Astrid had no doubt whatsoever. She must've spotted her. She always saw everything—nothing ever escaped her. She was sure to be staring at Astrid through the walls, leaving her there in the dark out of spite, enjoying her misery. She wanted Astrid to keep knocking and pleading. *She* was capable of it.

Finally, Astrid heard shuffling steps approaching the door. She faltered, feeling like a little girl again. Had the feeling ever really gone away? She wasn't sure.

The door opened. On the threshold stood a woman who, apart from a few new wrinkles, looked as if she hadn't aged a day, let alone twelve years. As far back as Astrid's memory reached, those piercing gray eyes hadn't ever been capable of anything but this very gaze that was currently freezing her in place—scornful, full of repulsion and hatred. A gaze that made her flesh crawl.

Astrid decided to break the silence first.

"Hi, Grandma."

THE SECOND NIGHT

They wordlessly stood in the doorway. An eternity must've passed and not a single muscle twitched in her grandmother's face. She looked like a statue. Astrid knew the woman had recognized her even before she greeted her. The silence was driving her crazy.

"You're back," the woman eventually said, her voice chilling Astrid to the bone. She couldn't have imbued the words with more disappointment if she'd tried.

Astrid took a deep breath. She could do this. She was eighteen, she was not a little girl anymore. But how was she supposed to act like an adult when someone had robbed her of her entire adolescence?

"I have nowhere to go," Astrid got right to the point.

"And so ye came *home*," her grandmother emphasized the last word, her lips pressing into a thin line.

Astrid had nothing to say to that. They continued to communicate nonverbally, their expressions saying it all. After a while, her grandmother finally stepped back. She opened the door all the way and let Astrid come inside.

It couldn't be seen as a complete victory, but it wasn't total defeat either.

The house had changed. Someone had tried to brighten the interior by repainting the walls white. A parquet floor had replaced the old one. It didn't change any of its dreary atmosphere, though, which resided in its inhabitants, Astrid thought, not its walls. Something a new coat of paint or retiling could never fix.

Astrid took off her shoes by the front door, like she'd been taught to do, and followed her grandmother into the kitchen. Her aunt was standing in front of the stove cooking dinner. As Astrid walked in, the woman turned her head to look at her. Her aunt had always reminded Astrid of a fox—thanks to her close-set eyes, long, narrow nose, and ginger hair. She also had a sly tendency to snoop around.

"So you're back," she declared, as if Astrid had merely gone off to the corner store and had gotten held up. Astrid nodded.

Her aunt dried her hands on her apron, walked right up to her, and brushed away the hair from Astrid's brow. "Let's get a look at ya! Well, well, well… Almost a full-grown woman now. You've been the talk of the town since the morning."

"Where's Mom?" Astrid interrupted her.

A shadow flitted across her aunt's face, and Astrid noticed she was trying hard not to glance at Grandma. Instead of answering her, she turned back to the stove and resumed her cooking.

"Where is she?" she asked again, this time looking at her grandmother. In the meantime, the old woman had sat down at the table and started shelling walnuts, which is apparently what she'd been doing before Astrid's arrival.

"Ye have only yerself to blame," she answered her cryptically. She took another walnut, placing it into the nutcracker. It produced a loud crunch.

"What d'you mean?" A terrible feeling of dread overcame Astrid.

Grandma lifted her eyes from the walnuts to look at her. Astrid glimpsed the tattoos adorning the woman's forearms. "She lost her mind. It's your fault. She had a nervous breakdown."

Astrid didn't press for more answers. Instead, she rushed into the hallway and headed straight for her mother's bedroom, as if she'd never been gone from this house at all. She knocked on the door, but upon hearing no response, she entered the room.

Astrid soon realized there was no point in knocking. The room was unkempt and messy, stinking of stale air, mildew, and something unidentifiable. Her mother was half-sitting, half-lying in an armchair. With a blanket tucked around her frame, she looked even more petite and frail than Astrid remembered. Her arms hung limply over the armrests as if she were a rag doll someone had simply set aside, just waiting to be picked up again. The woman didn't turn around at the sound of the opening door and she didn't move when Astrid entered the room either.

"Mom...?"

Astrid rounded the armchair, gazing at the perfectly blank features in front of her. It seemed as if someone had erased all her mother's emotions and expressions she knew so intimately.

"Mom." She reached down to grasp her mother's face in her fingers, angling it to face hers. "Mom... It's me, Astrid."

The young woman's voice broke halfway through the sentence. Her mother was staring right at her, but there was no recognition in those eyes. She might as well have been staring at a complete stranger.

It was in that moment when Astrid finally fully realized, since her return, what had happened. She'd been relentlessly denying the truth everyone had been trying to get her to accept all day, as if there was no proof of it. Well, the proof was right in front of her.

The individual puzzle pieces were starting to fall into place. She and her brother had disappeared without a trace. As a result, their mother had suffered a breakdown and was left imprisoned here in this house. With *her*. For twelve long years. Astrid couldn't even begin to imagine what her mother had been forced to endure. And now, she was back, while Max... her baby brother hadn't come back. But why? Why did she return while he didn't? What had happened? Where had they been the past twelve years? Why couldn't she remember anything?

Why did she feel as if someone had erased a part of herself?

Astrid clutched at her head, which had started to throb in unbearable pain. She beat at her temples with her fists in hopes of jumpstarting her memory like an old out-of-tune radio one only had to whack in order to get the right station. It wasn't working. Her legs gave out underneath her and she fell to the floor, curling into a ball. Astrid sobbed, right at the feet of her mother.

She sobbed for a long time, until she found herself gasping for air. She sobbed until she had no more tears to cry, her throat hurting from the dryness. She proceeded to wipe her cheeks and stood up on shaky legs. Her mother looked through her with apathy.

Astrid stepped out of the room back into the hallway. Closing the door softly behind her, she found herself standing face to face with her grandmother. Astrid wasn't sure how long she'd been standing there and whether she'd heard her crying, but her puffy eyes were a dead giveaway.

"Dinner's at seven, when the men come back from work," her grandmother announced. "Ye'll be helping yer aunt out with all the household chores. Ye can sleep in yer old room. My house, my rules. Understand?"

Her grandmother turned on her heel and walked back to the kitchen. As she stepped over the threshold, she made sure Astrid heard her next words. "It's yer brother who should've come back. Not you."

The worst part was that right then, Astrid wished for the same thing too.

Astrid spent the time remaining till dinner in the kitchen. Wordlessly, she helped her aunt prepare the meal—chopping the vegetables, basting the roast. She felt like a klutz, partly because she could feel the incessant stare of her grandmother's all-seeing eye on her back, but mainly because she didn't know her way around the kitchen. Unsure where to reach for what was needed, Astrid was more of a burden than a help to her aunt.

Right before seven, her uncle and the younger of her two cousins, Kristian, walked through the door. Kristian was actually a good three years older than Astrid, and over a foot taller. Along with his older brother, who had apparently already moved out, Kristian used to torture her when they were kids. Astrid still hated them for it.

Now, Kristian was an adult, and so was she. He didn't look any more pleased to see her than all those years ago.

"So it is true," he boomed out in the doorway as he looked Astrid up and down. "I told the guys they had sawdust for brains from all the logging they're doing. But they were right, you're really back. Well, I'll be damned…"

"Watch your mouth," his uncle admonished him, barely sparing Astrid a glance. He ignored her as if she were invisible. Even that hadn't changed. "Is dinner ready?"

"Yes," her aunt hurried to answer him.

Both men left for the bathroom. Probably to wash off the dust and dirt, Astrid assumed. She didn't ask, but her uncle had always worked at the lumber mill in the mountains, and his son had clearly followed in his father's footsteps. Astrid remembered that as a child, she had always been afraid of those large, callused hands full of splinters and sticky with resin.

She quickly rushed off to set the table for six.

"Can't ye count?"

Her grandmother's gaze pierced through her like an x-ray. Astrid waited with her question until she'd set all six plates out on the table.

"I thought..."

"Lena eats in her own room," her aunt replied quickly. "She doesn't sit with us at the table."

They were shunning her mother. Just like they had done back then—only now, she couldn't fight back. They were reminding her that she wasn't their flesh and blood. The thought of staying longer at the doctor's suddenly seemed much more pleasant than it had in the morning. Astrid shouldn't have been in such a hurry. She should've stayed there. What did she think would be awaiting her here?

Mom. She desperately needed her mom. But instead, it was her mom who needed her.

Dinner turned out to be one of the strangest moments of her life. To an outside observer, Astrid thought, this might've appeared to be a random gathering of strangers speaking in different languages at each other, either ignoring the others' words or trying to hurt each other as much as possible.

Astrid had never liked being the center of attention, but if she had been sharing a table with someone who went missing for twelve years, she could imagine wanting to ask a few questions. Or engaging in at least some kind of interaction. Like it had been with Dora.

But in this house, Astrid felt like she'd found herself in the middle of a game to which no one had explained the rules. Her uncle spent most of dinnertime wordlessly staring into his plate. Occasionally he would respond to some question directed at him by his wife—he curtly mentioned work at the lumber mill and the weather that was hindering their plans. Whenever his eyes landed on Astrid, he pretended her chair was empty. But Kristian kept staring at his cousin throughout the meal, as if she were prey he'd been lying in wait for. His sly gaze was making Astrid uncomfortable, along with how conspicuously silent he was the whole time. Her aunt was the only one to acknowledge Astrid's presence at the table—though only in order to check she wasn't turning her nose up at her meal.

"Eat up. You look terrible," she urged the young woman.

"Yeah, Astrid, eat up," Kristian echoed, observing her with that pig-eyed stare of his over the rim of his glass of beer.

Astrid picked at the meal with her fork, trying to swallow at least a few bites as she cut off bite-sized chunks to chew. But the food kept coming back up. She felt like one of those geese they used to raise, when her grandmother would shove food deep down their throats to fatten them up properly. Astrid recalled how she had to help catch the birds and look on as they struggled in Grandma's clutches. In her mind, she could still hear their desperate honking.

Everyone had finally finished eating. Her uncle downed the last of his beer and let out a mighty belch.

Then, his voice cut through the silence. "I'm not taking care of another mouth to feed."

Astrid froze. She didn't know what to say.

"She just came back," her aunt unexpectedly stood up for her, placing her hand on her husband's forearm in an effort to calm him down.

"You didn't see what it's like in the village." He gestured with his head toward the window. "Guards were everywhere. They turned half the forest upside down. I don't want any problems."

"Where would she go?" Kristian butted in. "Back to where she's been for the past twelve years? Wherever *that* was," he cackled. "Maybe it was with Czernobog himself…"

"Enough!" Grandma slammed her palms down on the table. "His name shall not be taken in vain in my house."

Astrid recognized that even Kristian harbored enough respect for the old matriarch as he lowered his gaze and fell silent.

"She'll stay here until the New Year and help take care of the house and that madwoman," Grandma decided. "She'll have to find work after that."

The old woman decided on Astrid's behalf as though she weren't there. As though she didn't even deserve to express her own opinion. As though she actually wished to be in this house.

It was madness. She wasn't going to last a week.

After dinner, Astrid attempted to feed her mother. But even though she mashed the potatoes with a fork and cut up the meat into tiny pieces, her mom spit most of it back out onto the plate. It was like feeding a child. When Max was a baby, Astrid had enjoyed feeding him. He was like a doll come alive that she could play with. She felt a stabbing pain in her chest. It seemed to her that Mom's glassy eyes were focused wholly inward—on a war she was waging somewhere far away from the real world. Somewhere Astrid couldn't follow.

"Maybe it's for the best that you don't know…" Astrid whispered into the silence of the room as her mom spit out another mouthful of food. "Maybe the gods have shown you mercy."

It was just a false justification she used to comfort herself. Her mother had been through a lot. She had lost her husband, for years she'd been living in this house, enduring the day-to-day terror dished out by her mother-in-law, and then she had lost both her children. That's more suffering than the average human mind could take.

"I'm sorry I didn't come back earlier, Mom. I'm sorry that…"

There was no use finishing the rest of the sentence. Astrid felt silly, but there was such turmoil in her mind that the only thing she wanted right now was for someone to embrace her and tell her everything was going to be all right. But she had no such person in her life.

Why is she unconscious and you aren't? Wake her up!

Astrid didn't feel as though she had much more of a grasp on reality than Sonya did.

She helped her mother to bed and went to lie down too. Opening the door to her old room, she switched on the light. Her family must've turned it into a storage space over the years. Boxes full of stuff that didn't belong to her were stacked in the middle of the room. Everything else was just the way she remembered—two twin beds, a wardrobe, shelves full of toys, a desk, and an old, broken piano that had belonged to her father. As she shut the creaking door, it fell into place with a familiar click.

Astrid looked around. The residue of some scribbles in white chalk was visible on the door from the inside. At first she thought it was from when she and Max had been playing and doodling, but the markings were too high up for such small children to reach. As Astrid began to discern a certain pattern in them, she realized they were old symbols of protection. Mom must've drawn them there.

Now I lay me down to sleep, and I shall awaken, for the evil spirits cannot reach me, Astrid recalled the words of the prayer they always used to say before going to bed every night.

Her fingers made as if to trace the individual lines of the symbols. She was probably doing it wrong—she couldn't remember where it began and where it ended. It was so long ago.

She stepped over several boxes toward the beds. The one on the right belonged to Max—really still a child's bed; an adult would've fit only with their legs drawn up to their chin. The teddy bear that Max always used to haul around everywhere lay tucked under the striped comforter. Astrid couldn't bring herself to approach the bed and pick up the toy, even though she wanted to. She wanted to hug the teddy bear close and somehow bring her brother back.

Instead, she opened the window to allow some fresh air into the room. Almost immediately, an ice-cold gust of wind blew inside, causing goosebumps to break out all over her skin. Astrid sat on the edge of her old bed, listening to the absolute silence outside. For the first time that day, she was finally completely alone and could let loose all that was rushing through her mind. But it was hard to know where to even begin. Even though she wanted to get it over with, she also felt a terrible fear. Fear of what her memories would actually reveal if she tried hard enough to get them back. At the same time, the possibility of not remembering anything at all didn't frighten her any less.

Astrid closed her eyes. She took in a deep breath, then exhaled. It was easier than she remembered. She didn't even have to make much of an effort—all it took was a few seconds of concentration and her mind yielded, just a tad. Astrid's memories were swirling around in her head like dyes dancing in a glass of water. They touched and bounced off one another in a colorful entanglement. She wove her way through the memories, searching for the right one—the one that would be the key to opening up all the others.

Nighttime. The rustle of butterfly wings. Max's scream. A tall, faceless, and eyeless figure.

Her heart started pounding. All it would take was the slightest pressure, one wrong move, and her entire consciousness might shatter into a million pieces. Unbearable pain exploded behind her eyelids, and she felt her legs start to tremble. She quickly willed herself to return.

Astrid's eyes shot open. She felt guilty for breaking a long-kept promise. But what troubled her even more was the fact that it didn't get her anywhere. Maybe it was still too soon to try. *But maybe she's forgotten even how to do this,* it occurred to her. No, that can't be. What she needed was more time. She was sure of that.

Astrid tried calming her heartbeat by taking deep breaths, letting them out slowly. Her fingernails dug into the palms of her hands, and she focused on the pain. It helped when the physical sensations drowned out the mental ones. As soon as she calmed down, she got to her feet.

Astrid closed the window, the air being more bearable now. She was asking too much of herself. The doctor had said it would take a while for her to remember, for her to recover. But what if she never did? What if... Astrid tried to recall all the medical terms, but her mind wasn't capable of retaining those either. What if her memory was damaged permanently and it would never come back? How would she ever know?

Let it run its course—don't push it, Astrid thought to herself. Easier said than done.

But Max is who knows where and might not have much time left.

Astrid simply couldn't accept that. She almost couldn't bear the thought.

She had to speak with Tom and find out what he remembered. She decided to go see him first thing in the morning. Which meant she'd somehow have to make it through the night.

Despite her impaired memory, Astrid was sure of one thing. It wouldn't be easy to fall asleep. It never had been. Nightmares had plagued her since childhood.

She'd have to prepare for it in advance.

If her family had really left the room untouched all these years, it meant she'd find everything she needed inside. Astrid tiptoed across the room softly, pushing boxes out of her way, searching through the wardrobes, proceeding as cautiously as a thief expecting someone to burst through the door at any moment and catch her in the act. She got down on her knees, groping around under her bed.

Astrid's courage faltered as her arm disappeared deeper and deeper into the pitch dark. She fumbled around, not knowing what was beyond her reach, coming across only dust balls. She had to lie down on her stomach and push both her arms under the bed.

Lying there helplessly, she hoped nothing would reach out of the darkness to drag her who knows where. Finally, her fingers collided with a cold metal object. Astrid wriggled back out into the light. It was a broken fireplace poker. One that she'd used as a makeshift crowbar for a long time.

Astrid sat back and lifted the old moth-eaten rug from the floor. She shoved the small rod between two floorboards, prying one of them deftly open.

Twelve years ago

"Astrid, what're you doing?"

"Shhh, be quiet!" she silenced him.

Max tried again, his voice an urgent whisper. "Astrid!"

The girl didn't pay her baby brother any mind as he peered down at her fearfully from under his covers tucked all the way up to his chin. She had the edge over him, anyhow. After all, she was the older sibling. Whatever she told him to do, he would do. Max even liked repeating things after her that he didn't have to. Her brother wouldn't give anything away—not to a living soul.

Astrid pried out the floorboard quietly, lifting it up and pushing it aside. Her hands fumbled beneath the floor before pulling out a small wooden casket. She examined it in awe in the glow of the lamp, as if it contained all the treasures of the world.

"What is it?" Max mumbled.

"Something that'll help us," she answered cryptically. "Do you trust me?"

Max's eyes twinkled with the promise of a shared secret. "Yeah."

Astrid opened the casket, which held several valuable objects. First, she pulled out a stubby beeswax candle, placing it on an empty plate on the nightstand and striking a match to light it.

Next, she pulled out two bulbs of garlic. She took one and shoved it under her pillow, handing the other one to Max.

"It stinks like hell, but do it too."

He lifted his pillow without objection, tucking in the garlic.

Next in line was a cloth sachet. Astrid untangled the drawstring and scattered its contents, first along the door and then the window-sill, in neat straight lines from corner to corner. Max looked on silently as she completed the task.

At last, she took a piece of white chalk.

"Come here and help me!"

Doubt clouding his features, Max threw off the covers and got up from the bed.

"We gotta push the beds together as quietly as possible, okay?"

First they pulled Max's bed from the wall into the middle of the room. He pushed from one side while Astrid pulled with all her might from the other. They tried to be quiet, but even so, they felt like each inch they covered must've been heard for miles around.

"That should do."

Astrid's critical eye assessed there was now enough room along the walls. The first phase of the plan was complete.

"Now mine."

The other bed was heavier, though, and took up more room. It wasn't as easy to move from the wall, and blocking it from the other side was the piano, which was impossible to move at all, leaving them with little room for maneuvering.

"Shhh... Wait!"

They both froze. It sounded as if someone was walking down the hallway. Astrid saw the look on Max's face. She was scared too, but she couldn't show it. She was older, after all. Max depended on her. Astrid pressed a finger to her lips, indicating the need to keep quiet. They strained their ears, but nothing happened.

"Hurry up, push."

But Max was too weak and Astrid could barely move the bed on her own. They were at it for way too long, making way too much noise. After a while of grappling with that *damn old piece of furniture*, as Astrid called it in her mind—though she had no idea what *damn* meant—she had to accept the fact that she wasn't going to achieve her desired goal.

"It'll do right here... I hope."

"What're you doing?"

"Drawing a circle of protection," she answered, as if that had been obvious the entire time.

Max stood there with teddy bear in hand, watching his sister with a confused look on his face. Vaguely aware that her accuracy was rare for a six-year-old, Astrid pressed the chalk to the floor and began drawing a huge circle in which she tried to fit both beds and the nightstand, with her brother in the midst of it all. She held the chalk carefully, making sure not to falter even for a second as she drew the circle without pause. Max lingered behind her, curiously craning his neck to see better.

And then several things happened in such quick succession, it almost seemed as if they had happened all at once. Something slammed into the window. Both of the children's heads jerked up in alarm, just in time to see a bird's wing sliding down the windowpane. All it took was one second of inattention for the chalk to snag between two floorboards and break in two. Astrid, whose full concentration had up until then been on drawing, lost her balance and took a step back, crashing right into Max, who had been standing right behind her on top of the bed.

"Astrid!"

She lunged at him, but it was too late. Max fell between the two beds, pulling down the lit candle from the nightstand with him. There was a terrible bang, followed by a stifling silence.

"Max!"

The boy's eyes were nearly popping out of his skull as he gasped for air, clearly winded from the fall. The candle had fallen onto the blanket, which caught fire within seconds. Astrid shrieked. The door was flung open, their mother appearing in the room.

"For Perun's sake! WHAT'S GOING ON HERE?!"

Her eyes flitted from the fire to her son, and she instinctively rushed over to the boy. She lifted him off the floor and began massaging his chest to help him catch his breath.

"Astrid, get away from that fire!"

In that moment, Grandma appeared behind her, a stony expression on her face, as if there was nothing wrong, grabbing a pillow and putting out the flames. Max got his breath back and started to cry—tear after tear rolling down his cheeks.

"It's okay, sweetie," Mom soothed him. "It's all right."

Grandma managed to extinguish the fire. She quickly opened the window to air out the smoke, which was stinging their eyes. Then she grabbed Astrid's wrist, forcing her to stand up.

"What did ye do?!"

She was still in shock and couldn't answer. Max was crying harder and harder in their mom's arms. The woman rocked and shushed him, kissing the top of his head, not sparing her daughter a single glance.

"What were ye up to in here?!"

This time, Grandma squeezed Astrid tighter until it started to hurt. "What's all this?" She pointed to the candle and the surrounding mess.

"I-I..." Astrid stuttered in a shaky voice.

"Speak!"

Astrid had never seen her grandmother this furious.

"I was trying to... I wanted... It was supposed to protect us..." Astrid's voice broke. She began to cry.

"From what?"

The tone of her grandmother's voice betrayed that she already knew the answer. She just wanted her granddaughter to say it out loud.

"Well?!"

"From the d-demons," the girl confessed.

What seemed like an eternity of silence followed. Grandma was pinning Astrid in place with her piercing gaze, and she didn't dare move, let alone blink. Suddenly, the old woman tugged on her sharply and dragged her out of the room. Astrid's worst nightmare was coming true. The girl began to panic. She knew what was about to happen.

"No! Grandma! Grandma, don't! Please!"

But Grandma could muster an unbelievable amount of strength when she wanted to. It was as if the old woman didn't register the girl's weight hanging off her arm at all, nor the way she was desperately digging in her heels.

"Mom!" Astrid shrilled in hopes that her mother would stop Grandma. But this time, she didn't.

"I told ye to stop with this nonsense! Did I not make myself clear?" Grandma growled in the hallway. "But ye disobeyed me! Ye little liar!"

Astrid knew it would be smarter to stay silent. But she couldn't deny something she was certain was true. Why didn't anyone believe her?

"I'm not lying! I know what I saw! It-It was there!"

"Ye saw nothing! Ye're just making it all up, seeking attention."

"No, Grandma, that's not true, I swear!"

The old woman grabbed Astrid by the collar of her pajamas and dragged her to the staircase. The entire house was up by then, and Astrid spotted her cousins peering over the banister, laughing at her.

"Ye see ghosts, girl? Let's find out how ye fare with them!"

"No! Grandma, no! Not the cellar!"

But Grandma was already opening the door, pushing the girl inside. Astrid's feet slipped on the first step and she fell on her butt, sliding a few stairs down. She quickly grabbed at the banister to keep from falling all the way down, her shoulder emitting an unpleasant crack. Before she could stand up and run back up the stairs, Grandma slammed the door in her face, locking it. Astrid found herself standing in complete darkness.

"Grandma! Let me out, please! Let me out!"

"QUIET!"

Terrified, Astrid fell silent. Her hands, which had just been banging against the door, slid down to hang at her sides. She could hear the pounding of her heart all the way in her head.

"Ye're gonna stay there until ye stop with this nonsense, ye hear me? And I don't want to hear another sound out of you!"

Astrid felt betrayed. Why didn't Mom take her side? She hadn't done anything wrong. And why did Grandma hate her so much? Petrified, she slid down the door and stayed on the floor, leaning her forehead against the wood. She refused to turn around, hoping to avoid facing whatever was hiding in the dark.

The present day

Full of trepidation and excitement, Astrid pulled the casket out of its hiding place. She opened it and, to her surprise, found it full—still containing the stub of a candle, garlic, a sachet of fennel, and the remains of chalk. She couldn't believe her old talismans were still intact.

Without any hesitation, she set out repeating all the old customs she'd been taught as a little girl by her mom. Astrid sprinkled the dried fennel along the door and windowsill, placed the garlic under her pillow, and lit the candle on the nightstand. Not having enough chalk, and unable to move the bed for all the boxes cluttering up the room, she would have to make do with drawing a few symbols of protection on the wall by the bed. They were much smaller than the old faded ones on the door, but still better than nothing.

Exhaustion suddenly hit her. It was as if all her vital signs were suddenly giving out. It got worse with each passing second, and though Astrid would kill for a hot, relaxing shower, she was sure she'd pass out in the hallway on her way to the bathroom. Sleep would have to do.

Astrid struggled to pull off her clothes. Only seconds separated her from relaxing slumber, from the dreamless nothingness that welcomed her with open arms. She fell into bed wearing only her underclothes, her eyes fluttering shut.

It didn't take long, a mere few dozen seconds. A feeling of something twisting in her stomach, like she was about to throw up right then and there. Astrid shot up in bed.

She resigned herself to going to sleep with that old, familiar feeling of panic. How many times had her mother tried to get Astrid to go back to sleep, after she had slipped into her mother's bed in the dead of night, or after finding her daughter sleepwalking through the house?

The night embodied all of Astrid's greatest fears. It was the one thing she genuinely wished she could forget. But as it turned out, luck was not on her side. The fear persisted.

After several minutes of taking deep, calming breaths, Astrid relaxed enough to lie back down again. This time, though, her eyes stayed wide open as she stared at the wall. Maybe it would be better if she didn't fall asleep tonight. A few sleepless hours during which she could try to remember what had happened? It sounded much less dangerous than sleep itself.

The first thing Astrid noticed was the immense pressure pushing down on her chest. It felt like someone was pressing their entire weight onto her torso. She wanted to scream, but not a single sound escaped her throat. Astrid was paralyzed. Her body was asleep, but her mind was wide awake. A tingling ran through her arms and legs, small electrical pulses—not unlike what she imagined amputees experience when their brain refuses to accept the absence of a limb. The eighteen-year-old poured all her concentration into shifting at least a finger. Nothing. Her muscles remained unresponsive.

Astrid fixed her eyes on the door. She couldn't blink, even though she clearly felt the tears pooling in her eyes.

The candle had gone out. She was surrounded by darkness in

which the objects in her room—the furniture and the boxes—began to move, as if the darkness itself had come alive.

Astrid wasn't alone. Someone was in the room with her.

A shadow appeared by the door—a more perfect version of a shadow, as tall as a person. A dark figure that began to take jerky steps in her direction.

Astrid focused on the fact that she needed to move. She needed to escape—right now! Or at least call for help. But she was unable to do anything. She just lay there, at the mercy of whatever was to come.

The figure had already made it to the foot of her bed. Strange buzzing vibrations and noises surrounded Astrid. She didn't know where the sounds were coming from—the figure had no mouth. But the closer it got, the more certain Astrid was that she was hearing the sounds of hell itself.

Astrid had never been this terrified. She had never felt such evil emanating from anyone or anything. Though it was eyeless, the figure was observing her. It could see right through her, piercing her very soul.

The figure's hands reached for her and Astrid suddenly knew it wanted to rip out all her organs, knew it wanted to steal her soul. She began to fight back.

The hands drew closer and she felt fingertips grazing her face, thumbs just about to press into her eye sockets.

Astrid's jaw started to tremble, her teeth chattering. And then her entire head started to vibrate. Something grabbed her from behind and yanked her backward.

Finding herself back in control of her own body, Astrid shot up in bed. The room was empty, the figure gone. She sat there, knees drawn up to her chin, gulping down air greedily. A sheen of cold sweat covered her back. This time, it took her a long time to calm down.

Astrid experienced one of the longest and worst nights of her life. Just like all those years ago, when her sleep paralysis first began to emerge, it was impossible for her to fall back asleep. She sat in bed, curled up in the corner, for hours. Her fingers traced the symbols drawn on the wall as she kept repeating her mantra: *Now I lay me down to sleep, and I shall awaken, for the evil spirits cannot reach me.*

The deafening silence oppressing the room genuinely terrified her. Once in a while, she'd shift a bit to make the bed creak under her weight, just to interrupt that sinister quiet for at least a brief moment. It was as if time had come to a complete standstill, as if it were mocking her waiting and despair.

Astrid welcomed the first rays of sunshine with open arms. The thought of a new day, including the few precious hours unmarked by fear, made her immediately feel so much better. Her entire body was sore from the constant sitting. She got up and stretched a few times, cracking her neck.

Astrid went to open the window, noticing several dead moths lying belly up in a peculiarly symmetrical row, side by side on the windowsill. Reaching for them, she changed her mind right before she touched the tiny carcasses.

She flicked the table lamp switch on and off a few times, as it had gone out during the night. Probably a burned-out lightbulb.

Astrid quietly washed herself in the bathroom, getting dressed in the clean clothes her aunt had presumably picked out for her from her own wardrobe—a pair of pants, which surprisingly fit, and an unflattering blouse, its sleeves stretched out. But appearance was the last thing on her mind right now. She had been gone for twelve years, anyway. What could she possibly know about current fashion?

For some twisted reason, the idea genuinely amused her. Astrid grinned at herself in the mirror, but the smile melted off her face as soon as she took a closer look at her reflection. The corners of her eyes were bruised purple. At first glance, it looked like the result of exhaustion, but when she gingerly pressed down on the skin, she realized it hurt.

Astrid recalled the fingers of the shadow figure, which had touched her face during the night. In that moment, the mirror reflected the scene back to her. A piercing, stabbing pain in her eyes. For a fraction of a second, she saw the shadow directly behind her. Astrid whipped around, but nobody was there. She looked back into the mirror, but the apparition had vanished. Quickly gathering her things, she decided it would be best to return to her room.

Astrid didn't dare go to the kitchen until she heard the house beginning to stir as the others woke up. Upon entering, she automatically muttered a "Good morning" in greeting, but the only reply she received was from her aunt. Astrid was starting to warm to the woman a bit more than to the rest of the family. If a devastating fire were to break out in the house right now, her aunt might very well be the only one to offer her a helping hand. Astrid was convinced that her grandmother, cousin, and uncle would not only leave her in the burning house, but would chuck in a couple of gas canisters to get rid of her even faster.

Astrid sat down at the table.

Her uncle didn't eat breakfast with them. She'd spotted him through the window in her room just a moment ago walking across the yard, feeding the animals. Kristian was engrossed solely in his food, while Grandma read the newspaper.

Astrid poured herself a cup of tea, her noisy slurping cutting through the silence.

Breakfast transpired much like dinner last night, with the slight difference of Kristian and her aunt talking this time around. They had a curt exchange about the approaching Koleda and everything that had to be arranged and prepared before then. Astrid silently finished her tea and ate a thin slice of buttered bread with honey. She was pretty hungry, but when she noticed Grandma staring at her, she decided to avoid any potential conflicts—like any aggressive insinuations of her wanting to eat them out of house and home.

After breakfast, Astrid cleared the table and went to take care of her mother. She helped her get out of bed and wash herself. Today, she was doing noticeably better, which meant she did everything Astrid asked her to do. She cooperated when Astrid got her dressed and ate all of her breakfast without spitting anything out. Otherwise, though, she sat in the armchair in her bedroom, looking out the window. Or at least Astrid hoped she was really looking at something out there.

"I'll be back as soon as I can," Astrid whispered to her mother.

She exited the room and headed for the hallway. No sooner had she pulled on her shoes than Grandma appeared by her side.

"Where do ye think ye're going?"

"Out," she snapped.

"This is my house."

"You have no right to keep me here. I'm not your prisoner."

Astrid quickly laced up her shoes, grabbed her coat from the coat stand, and headed out. For a brief moment, she was scared Grandma would grab her wrist and keep her from leaving, but she didn't. Astrid wasn't sure if the woman's inaction didn't terrify her even more than if she had barricaded the door with her body to prevent her from leaving.

It was only when Astrid was outside that she finally took a deep breath, realizing she was awake and alive. How easy it was to forget such things in that house. It wasn't snowing today, but the village still looked like it was covered in a big white blanket. The reflection of the sparkling snow blinded her eyes and she had to shield her face, as if it were a hot summer day.

It was such a strange feeling to be back. Even though Astrid had no idea where it was she had come back *from*. She walked through the village uneasily, seeing it with both old and new eyes. Some small things had changed—several of the houses had gotten a new paint job, others had fallen into disrepair. The trees on the village green appeared taller to her, and the gully through which a small mountain stream had flowed years ago was now nearly dried out. Astrid could feel the stares of passersby. Some did a double-take after walking past her, while others gaped at her openly the whole time.

She's back, Astrid heard the whispers from all sides.

The young woman automatically headed for Tom's house. She remembered he lived right next to the bakery. As she was passing the storefront, the baker nearly toppled over the counter in his rush to see her better. It was strange how little it took for her to remember what it was really like to live in a small town—where everyone knew you better than you knew yourself. As a child, she had never really given it much thought.

Astrid knocked on the door of the Hattlers' house, hoping they'd let her in fast enough for her to escape the nosy stares of the villagers. Thankfully, Valeria Hattler appeared in the doorway almost immediately.

"May I help you?"

"Hello," Astrid's voice faltered. "I… I came to see Tom. Is he in?"

The woman looked her up and down with distrust in her eyes. "Sorry, but now's not a good time…"

She was about to slam the door shut when Astrid grabbed it with force.

"Excuse me, Mrs. Hattler, I know it's an unpleasant situation. But it's me, Astrid… Astrid Mahler."

In that moment, the woman's expression changed—any traces of animosity gone, replaced by surprise.

"Oh, Astrid, it's you… I'm sorry. It's just that since yesterday, there's always someone trying to get inside. The neighbors, the Guards, the snoops. I thought…" She waved her hand in a dismissive gesture, as if to indicate what she thought about it all. "So it is you! Come inside, quick."

Astrid made her way into the narrow hallway. She couldn't help noticing the hateful look Mrs. Hattler threw at the neighbors standing across the street. Almost as if they were unaware that they could be seen, that they were making them uncomfortable.

"Everyone in this town's always done nothing but stick their nose in other people's business," Mrs. Hattler sighed in frustration as she finally shut and locked the door. "Let me see you." She grabbed Astrid's hands, taking a good look at her. "Perun's beard, it's really you… You look just like your mother…"

As if just realizing that Lena Mahler's condition was far from good, the woman let go of Astrid's hands uncertainly. "I'm sorry. You must be overwhelmed by everything at the moment."

Astrid attempted a smile. "It's a bit… crazy."

Mrs. Hattler laughed. "You're right about that. Can I offer you anything? Tea? It's cold out there. Have you eaten breakfast yet?"

Her concern and motherly tone were touching. For a second, Astrid wanted to ask her for a hug.

"I... Don't worry about me. Really."

The woman looked right at her as if she could read her mind. She could clearly tell Astrid was lying, but she didn't call her out on it.

"I'll bring you some tea and oatmeal with apple slices, okay?" she said instead. "You're both thinner than a stick. You need to eat."

Astrid tentatively shifted from foot to foot. She didn't want to be rude, but oatmeal was the last thing on her mind right now.

"Oh, silly me." The woman shook her head at her tendency to stray from the subject at hand. "Tom's in his room. At the end of the hall, the last door on the left."

"Thank you."

"Just..." Mrs. Hattler hesitated, visibly unsure whether to say more. "You might be expecting the impossible, dear."

Astrid didn't think twice about the woman's peculiar words as she walked toward Tom's room. She couldn't very well admit to Mrs. Hattler that she'd already been inside their house once, years ago. Tom had let her in one afternoon, in secret, when they were all supposed to be playing in the Foreths' backyard. They hid here from the other children and lay sprawled out on the carpet while Astrid read aloud from a book of fairytales.

Reading had been her favorite activity—one that she'd learned unusually well for a six-year-old. That day, Tom had listened to her attentively, only interrupting her halting and jerky reading to ask a question or to suggest his own version of where the story was headed. Most of his ideas were so off-the-wall crazy that Astrid had to laugh, and when he joined in on the laughter, they forgot about the book altogether as they tried to one-up each other by coming up with the best ending. The memory warmed her heart like a gulp of hot chocolate on a chilly day.

Astrid knocked on the bedroom door, her stance jittery. Tom called out a "Come in" almost immediately, and the eighteen-year-old was quick to enter, lest she change her mind.

The young man was standing by the window, tugging a sweater over his head. His dark hair was tousled every which way, sleep lines evident on his face, as if he'd just woken up. He was tall—a good two heads taller than Astrid. A slightly confused look appeared on Tom's face. Clearly, he'd been expecting his mother to walk in. It was him. It was really him who Astrid had spoken to that first night. She hadn't been dreaming.

But now that Tom saw it was Astrid, he froze, and so did she. Even though Astrid had been unable to think of anything else but seeing Tom, she suddenly didn't know what to say.

Hey, I'm that girl you probably last spoke to in kindergarten. We both disappeared at the same time. I don't remember anything and I was thinking that maybe you would? Yeah, probably not a great start.

"Astrid," he spoke first.

Her name wasn't spoken as an uncertain question or assurance—but with utter conviction. He had recognized her.

"Tom," she replied in kind.

He smiled and, crossing the distance between them in record time, hugged her. And there, right in the middle of his childhood bedroom, Astrid returned the hug with feeling, unafraid and unhesitant. She didn't stop to ponder whether it was right or appropriate. They both poured so much understanding and support into the gesture of friendship that no one else had been able to give them. Tom and Astrid had gone through this together—maybe they didn't know the full scope of what had happened to them, but the shared horror had forged a lasting connection between them.

"Take a seat, please."

Astrid accepted Tom's offer and they both sat on the old rug. Pulling her knees up to her chin, she glanced around the room. The walls were decorated with drawings scrawled by a child's hand, while a model train, toys, and stuffed animals littered the floor. Without breaking their gaze, Tom answered Astrid's unspoken question.

"Yeah... Mom left everything the way it was. It's still the room of a six-year-old boy, except I'm eighteen now."

"It's weird."

"Yeah, super weird."

They both smiled hesitantly. There was more pain in their expressions than any other emotion.

"Does your room look the same too?"

"It's been turned into storage."

"That sucks."

"It's... just a room." Astrid shrugged. "Doesn't matter."

"I guess you're right."

There was a knock on the door, and Mrs. Hattler peeked into the room. As promised, she was carrying a tray with breakfast for them both. The smell of oatmeal wafted through the air and Astrid could hear her stomach growling.

"I'll just put it here, okay? If you need anything, let me know." Tom's mother placed the food on the floor next to them. For a moment, she stood there looking at them, as if she couldn't get used to the sight.

"If only you knew... what it was like..." she whispered, her voice breaking. "It was an unimaginable nightmare..."

"Mom," Tom interrupted.

"Goodness me. I'll leave you two alone. Eat up while it's still warm!"

Mrs. Hattler left the room, closing the door behind her. Tom picked up one of the bowls of oatmeal and handed it to Astrid.

"Watch out, it's hot."

She gratefully wrapped her cold fingers around the bowl. Even though the food smelled delicious, she couldn't bring herself to pick up her spoon and start eating.

Tom fixed her with a look as he took his first bite, acting as if it were the tastiest oatmeal in the world.

"I'm not hungry."

"I know." He nodded. "I'm not really hungry either. But you need to eat. Come on, at least one bite."

Astrid put a spoonful of oatmeal in her mouth. She chewed on it for a moment before swallowing. "Happy?"

"Barely."

What Astrid saw in this mutual teasing was a need for some semblance of normality—proof that they could talk to each other normally; confirmation that one day they'd both be okay again.

"Tom, I—"

"Finish your breakfast first," he interrupted her.

Astrid frowned. She didn't like his domineering tone.

"I know what you want to talk about, what I want to talk about, and what we probably *should* talk about," he said, searching for the right words. "But I also know that in the past twenty-four hours, everyone's been treating us as fragile, damaged goods who can't think for themselves and will break down under the slightest pressure. I'm sick of it. And so are you. But it's not gonna disappear. It's a stigma we'll be carrying forever, and that scares me. I just…

I don't know, I just want to eat breakfast with my friend like a normal person."

Astrid looked at him for a long time. "And are we? … Friends?"

"What do you mean?"

She shrugged. "We used to play together as kids. Climbing trees, building water trenches. We haven't spoken in twelve years…"

Astrid suddenly realized it sounded like she was trying to push Tom away, though that was the last thing she actually wanted. "You don't even know what we're like. You don't know our personalities. And how do you even know what *stigma* means? That's hardly the vocabulary of a six-year-old!"

Tom angrily jabbed his spoon into his oatmeal. "Exactly, Astrid. I don't know how I know. I just know the word. And there's more. But the thought of having to figure it all out right now terrifies me. I don't know about you, but I'm scared."

"I am too."

"Okay. Then let's eat first, all right? It's not like someone will crack the mystery instead of us in the next five minutes."

Astrid let out a choked laugh. He was right. She slowly began to eat her breakfast. Wordlessly, they ate side by side for a few minutes, observing one another. Astrid didn't find it strange or uncomfortable at all—on the contrary, it felt like the most natural thing she'd experienced since coming back.

When they finished eating, Tom was willing to start talking. It really was easier on a full stomach.

"I'm trying to remember, but it's hard. It's so hard."

"So you don't remember anything either?"

Tom shook his head. He looked genuinely sorry. "Hardly a thing. Just the night we came back… and then childhood memories. There's a huge gap in between. What about you?"

"The same. It's as if somebody had ripped that part straight out. I know that there's something... *there*, but it's just a missing piece right now. Somebody took it out and didn't put it back in its place."

"Yes. That's exactly how I feel. The doctor said that it could return in time, that my memory is just damaged as a result of trauma."

"Yeah. Maybe."

"You don't believe him?"

"I don't know what to believe. How can I come to terms with being gone for twelve years, when no one knows where I've been, myself included? Or, even worse, maybe I do know but just can't remember?"

Tom nodded. "My mom wishes she could just forget the whole thing."

"The less you talk about it, the faster you'll heal," Astrid mumbled into her mug of tea. "That's what my mom used to say. When I... When Dad... That's what she believed in."

"Hmm, sounds to me more like denial and pretending your problems don't exist."

The corners of Astrid's lips turned up into a slight smile. "Yeah, it's not exactly brave, is it? And I don't want that. I don't want to pretend that nothing happened."

"Could you even? Doesn't seem like an option to me."

"Tom," she hesitated, but his kind expression compelled her to go on. "I want to figure out what happened. I know... I know that we might find out terrible things and that it won't be pleasant. But I need to know the truth. I need to know what happened, because only then will we be able to figure out where Max is. And I was hoping you'd help me."

Tom raised his eyebrows. Clearly, her speech, full of urgency, surprised him. "Of course," he replied. "You really think that I'd be fine ignoring all this? That I'd be content with the fact that I'm back but unable to remember anything? No way. Of course I'll help. And we'll figure it out. Together."

Astrid let out a sigh of relief. "Together. All three of us," she added. "Maybe Sonya will remember something," she thought out loud. "Maybe her memory's a bit better off."

It sounded more like a naïve desire for the simplest solution at hand than an actual game plan. They both knew it was wishful thinking. If they didn't remember anything, it was doubtful that Sonya would.

"Maybe. Do you have any update on how she's doing?"

Astrid made a face at the thought of yesterday's scene at the doctor's. She doubted the Foreth family would come to her house to apologize for their behavior, even if Sonya were to wake up.

"Nothing more than you already know."

But Tom wasn't about to give up. "We could try to visit her."

"Later," she agreed. "But until we figure out how to get back our memories, we'll have to make do with what everybody else tells us."

"What do you mean?"

"We have to reconstruct what happened on that day twelve years ago. We'll question all the witnesses, try to put together a timeline, and figure out, for instance, why Loony Gusto was a suspect."

"They asked you about him too?"

Astrid wondered if Tom also remembered how they used to laugh at him and make fun of him.

"Yeah, and he was even put on trial for it, but ended up in the mental asylum. They didn't release him until a few days before we reappeared."

"Are you saying you believe he had something to do with it?"

"I'm saying that we have to take everything into consideration. That means the Guards' investigation too. If they came to the conclusion that Gusto had done it, they must've had a lead. And these leads are important for us."

She looked at Tom expectantly, waiting for him to agree. He didn't leave her waiting long before he nodded.

"Okay," she breathed a sigh of relief. "Until we get our memories back, we'll try to find out what happened. But at the same time, we have to figure out how to remember. I'm not going to just sit here and hope for my memory to come back on its own. That could take years. But we have to be faster than that."

"I agree. What do we do first?"

"I'll talk to Dora," Astrid replied immediately. She shocked herself, having a clear plan of action like that at the ready.

"Dora? Our Dora? What's she got to do with it?"

"I don't know. But she's the first person I sought out after I came back. I don't know why, but I showed up at her door. And that must mean something." It sounded a bit sillier now that Astrid said it out loud. "That day, she was with us at kindergarten, remember? Maybe she saw something. And she can help put us in touch with the witnesses. She's lived here her whole life, and unlike us, she's gotta know everything about everybody."

"Sounds like a plan," Tom said. "But before you run off, finish your tea."

Astrid gave him a look of amusement and disbelief. "You're a bit fixated on the food, aren't you?"

"I guess Mom's rubbed off on me in a few ways," Tom admitted. But even though he was able to make fun of himself, his cheeks flushed.

Astrid listened to him, bringing the mug to her lips to take a sip as Tom watched her.

"I have to tell you something," she suddenly said, all traces of relaxed laughter long gone. "I'm not doing this for myself. I mean… not *just* for myself. I have to know what happened because of Max. I have to find him. And if it's possible, I have to save him."

Tom didn't look the least bit surprised. "I know, Astrid. I'll help you."

Valeria Hattler was not happy when they told her they were going out. She looked worried, to say the least, as she tried to persuade them it would be better for them to stay home.

"At least for today. Before things settle down out there."

By "out there," she probably meant the entire village as she gestured toward the windows looking out onto the street, blinds pulled all the way down. Astrid doubted it could be as bad as the woman was implying, but she didn't say anything.

"Mom, I'm gonna have to go out eventually," Tom tried to calm her down.

"Eventually," she agreed. "But eventually doesn't have to be the very next day, does it?"

Her protectiveness amused Tom more than anything else. He reappeared in the hallway to give her a quick hug. "You don't have to worry about me every time I walk out the door. I'll come back."

Tom's mother attempted a smile. "Of course. I… know."

She smoothed down her son's hair. "Where are you going, anyway?"

"Just to get some air," Tom lied automatically.

Astrid fixed her gaze on the floor nervously. She felt out of place, as if she were curiously peeking through a crack in the door somewhere she didn't belong, but wanted to.

"Astrid," Mrs. Hattler suddenly turned her attention to the young woman. "I was thinking…" She took a canvas bag off the coatrack. "I hope you won't be offended—it's some old clothes of mine I don't wear anymore. I thought it might come in handy until you can buy some new ones. I know it's mostly men in your family, so…"

Surprised, Astrid accepted the bag. "That's so kind of you. Thank you. I don't know how…"

Tom's mother silenced her with a comforting pat on her shoulder. "It's nothing, really. Don't worry about it."

The woman walked them all the way to the front door, and they felt her gaze on their backs until they rounded the corner. On her way to the Hattlers' this morning, Astrid had been focused on which places she still recognized and which ones had changed during her absence. Only now did she begin to take in the atmosphere of the whole village. It seemed much smaller and more constricted than all those years ago.

"Can I ask you something?" Astrid blurted out.

Tom, who had looked like he had other things on his mind since they left the safety of the house, nodded. "Anything."

"Did your mom ask you? About… what happened?"

He shook his head. "No, the doctor must've told her I didn't remember anything."

Astrid nodded and continued to walk.

"And you?"

"What?"

"Did your mom ask you?"

The blank, emotionless face of Astrid's mother flashed before her eyes. Her heart felt heavy. It seemed likely that Lena Mahler would never ask anyone anything ever again.

Astrid was just thinking of how to respond when they rounded a corner and emerged onto the square, a crowd of people drawing their attention. They were all standing in front of the butcher shop around tubs full of fish, everybody shaking their heads incredulously, as though they'd never seen anything like this. Tom looked like he wanted to turn on his heel and leave, but curiosity got the best of Astrid as she took a few tentative steps toward the crowd.

The butcher, a brawny, bald man with bulky arms, stood in front of his shop, clearly dealing with unsatisfied customers.

"C'mon, folks, cut it out! I'm telling ya I dunno how it happened!"

"He sold you dead fish!"

"Where else are we gonna get carp this close to Koleda!"

Astrid pushed her way through the huddle of people. In the tubs, dozens of dead fish were floating belly up in the water, their slippery bodies piled on top of each other. Their beady eyes goggled at her, their tiny mouths comically wide open.

"Tell ya what. I'll bring a fresh batch of fish in the afternoon!" the butcher attempted to make himself heard over the din of the crowd.

"And they'll die just like these ones!" someone piped up.

Several voices joined in—some irritated, others disappointed.

"I heard the miller's mare didn't make it through the night!"

"And remember that dead cat in the bonfire! Animals are dying."

"The village is cursed," an old woman mumbled. "The gods have forsaken us."

A few others joined her lament. Several prayers echoed through the air as people clasped their hands in pleading gestures pointed skyward.

Astrid began to feel uncomfortable. She thought she saw a few heads turn in her direction. Tom caught her by the sleeve, trying to get her to leave.

"Stop it," the butcher warned the crowd impatiently. "Can ya even hear yourself, lady? What's all this bullcrap ya spewing?"

"The demons walk the earth!"

In that very moment, a bony, ice-cold hand took hold of Astrid's. She let out a shriek of surprise and was left staring into the eyes of an ancient-looking woman. At first glance, there was nothing striking about her. She looked like any other village granny. But it was her eyes that inspired terror—though the woman was clearly blind, her gaze pierced Astrid with unwavering certainty.

"It's your fault," the old woman hissed. "Wake up."

Astrid quickly jerked her hand out of the woman's grip and backed away. She let Tom drag her away, both of them stumbling as far away from the crowd as possible. They glanced back a few times, but none of the villagers paid them any mind.

"What was that?" Tom asked when they'd put sufficient distance between themselves and the crowd. "Did you see that? Those fish?"

It's your fault. Wake up.

"Astrid, are you okay?"

"Did you see that old lady?" she blurted out.

"What old lady? Who do you mean?"

"I just thought I saw something," she lied.

She lied completely unawares, surprising herself with how she didn't even feel ashamed.

The house of the Lautners belonged to the few cottages scattered along the immediate outskirts of the village. Mr. Lautner, Tom's uncle and Dora's father, worked as the gamekeeper in the Black Forest. That's why he had bought property so close to it. From one side, the house was protected by tall trees, but situated on the crest of a hill, it had to brave frequent gales of wind blowing in from the other side, the fields assaulted by whirlwinds. The house looked much more decrepit than the other ones in the village.

"I'm not sure I'm welcome," Tom announced uneasily at the gate.

"What d'you mean?"

For a while, he stared into the fields as if looking for the answer in the snowdrifts. "Aunt Lautner... Mom told me she died during childbirth, seven years ago. We were never really on good terms with my uncle, and after this... I don't think he'll be happy to see me."

Astrid recalled a hazy memory of Dora's smiling mother, who would always lift Dora up into her arms happily whenever she picked her up from kindergarten, greeting each other with nose kisses. Dora had always looked really silly while doing it.

Astrid had envied Dora her cheery mother. Astrid's mom had always looked like she'd cried away the hours they were apart. Astrid felt a pang in her chest. Her mom may be sick, but at least she was still alive.

It was as if Tom could read her mind. "Strange how many things have changed since, right?"

"Some things must've changed for the better too," Astrid proclaimed in an unwavering voice.

Tom raised his eyebrows. "Maybe. I hope you're right."

"If you don't want to go in there, I'll understand," Astrid said. If anyone knew what it was like having to deal with drawn-out family feuds that often ended in ugly fights, it was her.

"That's nice of you to say," Tom answered her with a smile, which looked much better on his face than a frown. "But we're in this together, remember? We made a pact over oatmeal."

And with those words, he walked through the gate up to the house. Astrid followed him.

"A pact?" The word made her laugh. "Sounds a bit fatal, don't you think?"

Tom gaped at her with feigned surprise. "What happened to your face?"

Her smile disappeared. "What?"

"Never mind." He smirked. "It's gone."

Astrid dismissed his joke with a shake of her head. The brief instance of happiness evaporated the moment they knocked on the door.

Dora opened the door almost immediately, as if she'd seen them coming. But one look at her shocked expression was enough to tell them she hadn't been expecting to see them at all. All three of them stood there awkwardly, staring at each other.

Astrid was the first to speak. "I wanted to apologize for dropping in on you in the middle of the night. I hope it didn't get you in troubl—"

Before she could finish the sentence, Dora caught her off guard with a hug, just like she had during their last encounter.

"Okay, it's… all good, then, I guess," Astrid mumbled uncertainly, wrapping her arms around Dora's back gingerly.

Dora pulled back after a while, her eyes glimmering with unshed tears.

"Perun's beard," she mumbled. "Astrid, it's really you! And Tom!"

He, too, received a somewhat briefer and more awkward hug.

"I can't believe it… Please, come on in."

They entered the house and Dora led them to the tiny kitchen. It looked like they'd just interrupted her in the middle of baking. Two boys were kneeling on chairs at the table, spreading jam on cookies. They both lifted their identical, fair-haired heads from their task at the same time. Judging by the smears on their cheeks, it looked like they'd eaten more cookies than they'd actually finished decorating.

"Hi," one of them fearlessly piped up.

Tom and Astrid waved at him in greeting uneasily.

"Who's this?" the other twin asked his sister.

Astrid noticed Tom tensing at the sight of his cousins, whom he'd never seen before.

"It's… They're my guests," Dora explained nervously. "How about you take a break for a while and go play? We'll finish up later, okay?"

The boys muttered an unenthusiastic agreement and climbed down from their chairs.

"Can I take the rest of the jam with me?" one of them tried their luck.

"You better not finish off the whole thing," Dora warned him before handing him the jar. His expression suggested that was exactly what he was planning to do.

"And don't bother Grandpa. You know he likes to nap until lunchtime. And stay inside the house until noon, you know that…"

"Yes, the Poludnitsa is lurking outside, we know," one of the twins finished for her in a weary tone.

She shooed both her brothers out of the kitchen, calling out a few more orders on the way regarding what they were and weren't allowed to do. When she returned, her motherly authoritative tone disappeared.

"Sorry for the mess," she blurted out. "Do you want anything? Coffee? Tea?"

"Tea would be nice," Tom answered.

"Coffee," Astrid said at the same time.

Dora nodded. "Take a seat wherever there's room."

They shrugged off their coats and sat at the table as Dora bustled about the kitchen. She was moving with her back to them, allowing Astrid and Tom enough time to look around.

In a few minutes, Dora was setting the steaming cups in front of them. Awkwardly, they all grabbed their drinks, taking tiny sips after blowing on the piping-hot liquid. Astrid grimaced almost immediately. Tom raised his eyebrows in question.

"I've never had coffee before," Astrid explained.

"Then why did you ask for it?"

"Precisely for that reason. It tastes different than I imagined." Astrid took another sip. "It's pretty good. I could get used to this."

Dora was observing them both as if they'd fallen from the heavens above.

"I don't know where to start," Astrid admitted. "I mainly came to thank you for helping me."

"That's a given," Dora assured her. "I'm sorry I didn't believe you at first. I… I was shocked. You have to understand… They told us that you were dead, that you were never coming back."

As soon as the words left her mouth, Dora bit down on her bottom lip nervously, as if she'd said something mean and wanted to take it back. "Sorry, it can't be easy to hear this."

"It's a bit crazy," Tom assured her, keeping his tone light. "But I guess we'll have to get used to it."

"Dory, we…" Astrid glanced uneasily at Tom, who gave her an almost imperceptible nod of encouragement. "We came to ask you for help. Neither of us remembers what happened. The doctor said it could be a temporary lapse of memory, but it's also possible we may never regain our memories. We wanted to talk to you about what happened after."

Dora's expression changed, becoming unreadable. She tensed, giving Astrid a hard stare. The seconds she remained silent seemed to stretch on forever.

"You remember nothing?" she finally whispered. "Nothing at all?"

Astrid and Tom exchanged a quick glance. Clearly, he didn't understand Dora's behavior any more than Astrid did.

"Nothing," Astrid confirmed. "Nothing from the past twelve years."

Dora placed her head in her hands. "Perun's beard, how could I be so stupid… Of course…"

"What's wrong?" Astrid tentatively reached for her, but then changed her mind. She didn't want to invade her personal space. "Dory?"

As if she hadn't heard a word Astrid had said, Dora lifted her head. "Not even what happened in kindergarten? Nothing…?"

Something in Dora's voice gave Astrid pause. That covert, underlying tone. Something seemed off. It didn't take long for her to understand.

"You saw something," Astrid whispered in surprise when the realization struck her. "You remember something!"

Dora shot out of her chair. "No." She shook her head in denial. "That's not true."

"Yes, it is. It is true," Astrid insisted, and with each passing second, she felt more and more certain of the fact. Dora turned so pale, her face began to blend with the snow outside the window. "You were there that day in kindergarten too. Your bed was right in between mine and Tom's. You know something, Dora. You have to tell us what—"

"No," Dora doubled down. "I didn't see anything."

"You're lying."

"Astrid," Tom butted in.

"How dare you!" Dora defended herself. "How dare you accuse me of lying! Don't ever say that again. Ever! I'm not making it up—I'm not crazy!"

Dora's words led Astrid to believe this wasn't the first time she'd had to defend herself like that. Tears glistened in Dora's eyes as she trembled with rage. Astrid felt sorry for her friend, but she also knew full well what she had to do. She had to strike her where it hurt the most. To make her tell them what had really happened.

"You sure are acting crazy."

"Astrid, that's enough," Tom hissed at her.

Rage flashed in Dora's eyes. "Don't ever, and I mean ever, tell me I'm crazy. I've spent my whole life listening to people telling me I'm not normal. And it's all your fault!"

Her voice suddenly jumped up an octave. *"That's impossible, Dora."* She was clearly mimicking someone's admonishing voice from her childhood. *"You must've been imagining things. Ghosts don't exist. You're just making it up.* I KNOW WHAT I SAW!"

Astrid may have accomplished what she set out to achieve, but she wasn't sure what to make of it. What was Dora talking about?

There were no traces left of the smiling girl who had made them tea just moments ago. "You don't know what it was like." Dora's eyes flitted from Tom to Astrid and back. "You have no idea what I've been through."

"You think we were any better off?" Astrid asked incredulously. "We went missing for twelve years! Twelve years of our life is gone, Dora. Do you know what that's like? Not to remember anything? Would you have rather disappeared along with us?"

"Yes!" Dora blurted out too quickly. "I'd rather have disappeared as well than have to stay here!"

A tense silence engulfed the room. Both of them were panting for air, as if they'd just finished a ten-mile race. Before any of them could say anything else, the door swung open, revealing Dora's father. His eyes flitted over his upset daughter to Astrid and Tom. The man did a double-take at the sight of his nephew, as if to assure himself he wasn't seeing things.

"Pa!" Dora exclaimed despondently.

"Be quiet, Dora." His sharp tone silenced her. "You two"—he pointed at Astrid and Tom—"get out of my house. Now."

"Pa…"

Rage was twisting the man's features. "I'm telling you, be quiet."

Astrid and Tom quickly scrambled from their chairs and grabbed their things, both of them unable to look Mr. Lautner in the eye. They rushed through the hallway, where the twins were watching them curiously from the stairs. Both boys were pressing against each other in fear. Astrid gave them an encouraging smile. The moment they shut the front door, they heard the shouts.

"Just how stupid are you? Bringing bad luck into the house like that! Are you out o' your damn mind?!"

A dulled blow reached their ears.

Astrid glanced over her shoulder hesitantly, but Tom grabbed her hand and led her away.

They hurried down the beaten path in the snow as fast as

possible. Only when they found themselves in the middle of the fields did they dare speak.

"Okay, that didn't exactly go well," Tom declared.

Astrid sighed. "I messed up. I shouldn't have pushed her so hard."

"Probably not."

"You're not helping."

Tom tried again. "Probably not, but we learned something."

"We did?"

"Dora saw something back then. We just need to find a way to make her confide in us. With a bit less violence next time, if possible," Tom said, giving the woman next to him a small smile.

"Okay," Astrid agreed. "Next time, I'll be quiet and you'll do the talking."

In the next few hours, there wasn't a single person in the village who hadn't seen them. Or at least that's the feeling they got as they sauntered through the village, walking past their neighbors. Tom had figured taking a walk around the old sights would do them good, would clear their heads, but after everyone began to turn their heads after them as they passed by, he started doubting it had been such a good idea.

"Looks like they have nothing better to do than stare, eh?" Tom noted in a whisper.

Astrid sighed, her expression sullen. "How are we gonna discover anything when everybody's staring at us, but nobody's talking to us?"

"I dunno. Maybe we could torture them."

"Tom…"

"Good morning," they both greeted a mother with her children they were currently passing on the sidewalk.

In such a tiny village like theirs, it had always been the custom to greet neighbors outside. But the moment the woman noticed them, she grabbed both her kids and quickly crossed the street without sparing them a second glance.

"Makes a person feel right at home," Tom grumbled loud enough for the woman to definitely hear him.

"Don't provoke them," Astrid retorted quietly.

"You're one to talk."

They found themselves standing in the street awkwardly, suddenly not really sure where they were going.

A scowl appeared on Astrid's face as the thought of Dora crossed her mind. If she had just held her tongue, they could've gotten her to talk much easier. Now, she might not tell them anything.

"We need to find another way," Astrid suggested. "At the very least, we need to reconstruct everything that happened that day. Do you think your mom will help us?"

"My mom will fly off the handle when she finds out what we're doing. We can try, of course, but get ready to receive an extra load of unnecessary information along with a couple suggestions to cut it out."

"What about your…" Astrid paused, suddenly afraid to finish the question. She wasn't sure what answer to expect, but judging by Tom's behavior and the few hints she'd picked up on, she realized it wouldn't be anything positive.

"My dad?" Tom finished for her. "He won't help us. He left Mom pretty soon after it all happened."

Astrid couldn't hear a single trace of bitterness in his voice, but she still felt like she was overstepping.

"I'm sorry, I didn't mean to..."

"You couldn't have known. Twelve years really is a long time. A lot has changed."

"I guess so."

"And what about you? Is everything... the same?"

Astrid wondered if Mrs. Hattler had told Tom something about her mother after all. Or did he actually remember what she'd told him all those years ago?

"Some miseries are... still the same miseries," she said eventually.

A merciful lie Astrid wished she could bring herself to believe too. But she couldn't very well tell him her life was even worse than before. Back then, she'd had her brother, Max. Without him, she now felt like an intruder in that house. Like a tiny, disgusting cockroach that deserved nothing more than to be squished underfoot.

"That sucks."

Astrid didn't want to dwell on it. "Let's go. I don't know about you, but I'm freezing."

They headed back to the center of the village. In front of the Hattlers' house, there was a surprise waiting for them in the form of a Guard standing outside. He was leaning on the fence, observing his surroundings like a hawk, his gaze solemn. He barely glanced at them as they passed him by. Astrid's stomach lurched. Dozens of scenarios flashed through her mind about what might have happened. She didn't find any of them the least bit appealing.

"Maybe they have a new lead," Tom thought out loud.

Astrid didn't want to dash his hopes, so she followed him, wordlessly, into the house instead. They shut the door behind them, taking off their coats and shoes. For some reason, Astrid realized that very moment that they both looked like a pair of misfits. All the clothes she was wearing were borrowed, and Tom was just pulling off his dad's old pair of boots he'd forgotten there after he left them. It was as if the world hadn't been expecting them. As if they simply weren't supposed to be here.

"Mom, I'm home," Tom announced their presence loudly from the hallway.

"We're in the living room," came the muffled reply.

Tom went in first, while Astrid clung to his back like a shadow. In the living room, it really did look like they had been waiting just for them. Tom's mother was sitting in an armchair, her back ramrod straight. The Guards who had been questioning them yesterday were sitting across from Mrs. Hattler, the presence of the militia in her house clearly making her seriously uncomfortable. Today, the chubby man was wearing a casual outfit that made him look even friendlier. His colleague still had the same unreadable and apathetic expression etched onto his face. Tom and Astrid sat down.

"We stopped by your house, Astrid," the stony-faced Guard went straight to the point. "We spoke to your family—"

"Why?" Astrid cut him off. Her aggressive tone caught him off guard. "This doesn't concern them."

"It's not just about you. It's about Max's disappearance too," the man pointed out. "We have to keep his—your—family informed about the ongoing investigation. He's still a minor."

Her heart started pounding. "Did you find him?"

"Not yet. Patrols combed through the entire village and the immediate surroundings. But they haven't found any footprints in the Black Forest. We managed to find three sets of footprints close to where you all first appeared. One set of prints—yours,

Astrid—led from the field to the Lautners' house. The only presumably male footprints led to your backyard." The Guard fixed his eyes on Tom. "The last pair belongs to Sonya Foreth and they end where they found her unconscious body. The problem is that none of the footprints begin anywhere and there isn't a fourth track to be found."

Tom's mother, who had been silent until now, spoke up. "What do you mean, they don't begin anywhere? What's that supposed to mean?"

"It looks like they just appeared out of thin air in the middle of nowhere. There must've been a strong wind that night which covered the tracks with a fresh layer of snow, destroying them, or something like that…"

Footprints leading from nowhere.

Astrid didn't recall it being windy in the forest. Quite the opposite—it had been a very calm and clear night.

"If I'm understanding this right," Astrid double-checked, "you can't retrace our tracks and follow the ones which might belong to Max."

"We've conducted a pretty thorough search of the vicinity and the forest. Astrid"—the Guard looked her straight in the eye—"we have to consider the possibility that wherever it is you came from, Max wasn't with you."

Astrid refused to believe that. It couldn't be true. Before she could respond, Tom spoke up.

"Max was definitely with us," he said. "I don't know… I don't know how I know, I have no way to prove it. But I'm positive. He was there."

He looked at Astrid, as if he wanted to encourage her. The gesture warmed her heart.

"What're you going to do next?" Astrid asked the Guards. "What're the next steps in your search for Max?"

"It's an extraordinary situation for our village. None of us have ever dealt with anything like this."

"I want to know what you're doing to save my brother."

It seemed both Astrid and the Guard were running out of patience. "We didn't know where to search for Max twelve years ago, and we're no closer to knowing where to start now…"

"In other words, you're doing nothing."

"Astrid Mahler," the tall Guard boomed out in warning. "A verbal attack on a member of the militia—"

But his colleague quickly silenced him with a raised hand. "Astrid, I understand you're worried about your brother. But you have to believe us that we're doing everything we can."

Astrid refused to accept it. She crossed her arms over her chest in silent protest.

"We wanted to talk to you about one more thing," the Guard continued. "But it only concerns you, Astrid."

"Anything that concerns me concerns Tom as well. You can speak in front of him."

The Guard's gaze flitted to Mrs. Hattler, but when she insisted, he didn't object further. He pulled a photograph out of his breast pocket, leaning over the coffee table to hand it to Astrid. The photo was yellowed with age and fairly worn around the edges.

"Do you recognize this? Do you know when and where it was taken?"

Astrid stared at the photo in surprise. The little girl in the picture was her. It looked to have been taken at one of those formal photoshoots where kids posed for professional photographers with toys in the background. She didn't recall ever having done anything like this. Her family had never had money to spare, and her mom always used to scrimp and save on precisely these types of things. Nevertheless, Astrid held the irrefutable proof in her hand that it had somehow transpired.

"I've never seen this photo before."

"But it's you, right?"

"Yes, of course it's me. But I had no idea something like this existed. Where did you find this?"

"What about this one?"

He handed her another photo, this one even grimier than the first. It was just a snapshot, blurry and with bad composition, clearly taken by an amateur photographer without the people in the photo knowing so.

"That's me," Tom breathed out as he looked over Astrid's shoulder.

They were all in the photo: Astrid, Tom, Max, Sonya, and Dora, the five friends who had once been inseparable. They were playing outside—Astrid was almost positive it was somewhere near the old quarry. They used to spend a part of summer break there.

"Where did you find this?" Astrid asked again. She was starting to get a bad feeling.

"We found these photos in the Linharts' cottage," the Guard explained. "We think they belong to Loony Gusto."

Valeria Hattler was the first to react. "My gods, so it is true…"

"Do you really think that it was him?" Tom chimed in. "That he kidnapped us?"

"Several eyewitnesses have testified against him in the past," the Guard reminded them. "If we consider he was released mere days before you three reappeared… It's making him the prime suspect."

"You have to interrogate him!" Tom's mother shrilled. "What're you waiting for?"

"Loony Gusto has been missing since Korochun. We left no stone unturned in the village, but nobody's seen him since that scuffle by the bonfire, and he didn't show up for his scheduled doctor's appointment either..."

"Nothing's changed, I see—nothing at all!" Tom's mother suddenly exploded, her voice filled with rage.

"Valeria..." the Guard warned her.

"Why won't you finally admit that you botched it those twelve years ago?"

"Mom!"

"The entire village knows! We should've called the police, but instead, the Elders put you lot in charge of the investigation! My son was already who knows where by then! In the clutches of a mentally disturbed person, no less!"

Tom's mother stood up abruptly from her armchair and began to shout accusingly at the Guards at the top of her lungs. The taller of the two defended himself in a gruff voice that demanded respect, but he was unable to stop the torrent of words flung his way. Tom stepped between the two—perhaps afraid his mother would lose her cool and lunge at the man.

Astrid was only listening to them with half an ear. She was still intently looking over the photographs, her eyes fixated on Max's face. Strangely enough, a memory suddenly sprang to mind that was so clear and lucid, it was as if it had happened only yesterday.

She saw Dora doing cartwheels in the tall grass. Tom, using his bare hands to dig out a deep waterway, which they later filled up with water from the river, creating a system of small cascades for their toy boats. Sonya, pale and tired as ever, tilting her freckled face toward the sun. And Max with a happy grin on his face, like he always got whenever she took him anywhere with her and the older kids. He felt all grown up.

Astrid, look! Look at the boat Tom made for me!

"Astrid?"

The Guard's voice drew her back into the present. "Twelve years ago, a person was charged with your kidnapping, and he did his time. We don't have any new leads indicating someone else could've been responsible for your disappearance. Especially since none of you can remember anything. If we don't manage to find Gustaw Linhart, or if none of you regain your memories, the odds of finding something new are zero."

"You're giving up, then," Astrid said. It sounded more aggressive than she wanted it to. "You won't help Max."

A telling silence engulfed the room. Astrid realized that this was the Elders' way of closing the case. They had fulfilled their duty and did what was expected of them. But the four missing children had been a nuisance back then, and they were a nuisance now. They had built them a memorial on the village green and tried to forget the whole thing ever happened.

Clearly successfully.

THE THIRD NIGHT

After the Guards left, Valeria Hattler apparently decided not to let Tom and Astrid out of her sight ever again. She involved them both in her preparations for Koleda, another significant end-of-year celebration, and didn't let them have a single undisturbed moment alone. Astrid suspected the woman had figured out their plan and this was her way of expressing what she thought of it. Tom had been right—they probably couldn't expect much help from her. Whenever they steered the conversation toward the events from twelve years ago, she would brush them off. Astrid realized that maybe Mrs. Hattler just wasn't willing to speak in front of her, and as dinnertime neared, she said her goodbyes, hoping Tom would urge his mother to talk once she left.

Outside, it was getting dark. It was barely a couple minutes' walk from the Hattlers to her house, but Astrid couldn't help feeling her courage dissipating along with the last sunrays over the horizon. When Astrid was a little girl, she believed, like all children do, in creatures that grown-ups said didn't exist. But she was convinced the grown-ups were wrong. Because her nightmares did come alive. Darkness was their domain, and Astrid had no idea how to protect herself against them.

Though what awaited her at home was a far cry from a warm welcome, her fears somewhat diminished once she found herself indoors. Standing up to her grandmother and the rest of her family suddenly seemed much easier than facing her fears.

As expected, her grandmother and aunt were in the kitchen. It was as if time had stopped in the house after her departure that morning, and they hadn't been doing anything else, trapped within the restrictive confines of their lives and everyday routines.

Without further ado, she went to join her aunt at the kitchen counter and took over chopping the meat.

"Where have ye been all day?" Grandma suddenly sprung the question at her.

"Outside."

"With that Hattler boy," the old woman filled in the blanks, her voice poisonous.

It didn't surprise Astrid that Grandma knew. Nothing escaped her notice. The woman hardly ever left the house, yet somehow, word always reached her, as if she had furtive spies at her beck and call who kept her informed of the goings-on in the village.

"If you know, why bother asking?"

"Watch yer mouth."

Astrid's hand holding the knife trembled with rage. "I can talk to whoever I want."

"His family—"

"I don't care what you think of his family."

Grandma returned her cool gaze. "Ye should."

Astrid decided to let it go and returned to the task at hand. They spent several long minutes in the kitchen when they didn't exchange a single word. The first sound to break the deafening silence was Kristian's arrival. He entered through the backdoor from the yard straight into the kitchen and made a beeline to the pantry without saying hello.

"It's almost dinnertime," Astrid's aunt said.

"So?" Kristian retorted, arrogance lacing his voice. They could hear him rummaging through the contents of the pantry. He returned with a piece of bacon, sniffing it. "Did ya hear 'bout the dead fish?"

His mother nodded. "The butcher was probably poaching them anyhow, trying to rip off his customers. Serves him right."

Kristian shrugged and shoved the bacon into his mouth. "The guys at the lumber mill said that Lautner found three dead deer in the woods. Maybe the animals are spreading some sorta plague."

"Can you imagine?" Astrid's aunt sighed. "Don't jinx it."

"I didn't jinx it," Kristian protested as he brushed past Astrid, hissing in her ear, "I didn't. Did you?"

Astrid tensed. It looked like nobody else had heard him, but when Astrid finally managed to lift her gaze from the floor, she felt Grandma's eyes on her.

She liked to imagine her family being like other families. As average and ordinary as a family could be. But some wishes were simply not meant to come true.

Dora had seen Pa furious countless times, especially after the death of her mother—the only one who had been able to console him with that extraordinarily soothing voice of hers. It's as if her presence had been the only cure for curbing the man's uncontrollable fits of rage, because after she passed away, there was nothing at all that could calm him down anymore. Dora often wished that she possessed this magical power too, especially when the twins got into trouble and she had to protect them from a beating. This was the first time, though, that Dora was nearly convinced her father was going to kill her.

As soon as the front door had closed shut after Astrid and Tom, Pa began shouting at her. He kept slamming his fist on the table-top, a decorative glass bowl ending up on the floor, shattered in pieces. Pa berated Dora for disobeying him. For being a great disappointment and disgrace to their family.

"I told you I didn't want the Mahler girl to ever show her face around here again! And whaddaya do? You drag her in along with that boy as soon as I step out the door!"

Dora determinedly kept her mouth shut. If there's one thing she'd learned, it was that timing was everything. By now, she had learned when it was better to say nothing.

"Do you want to bring misfortune upon us? Don't you know what they're saying 'round town?"

She shook her head. Her father made a face as if considering whether she was really so stupid.

"They reappeared on the day of the winter solstice. During the night, when evil spirits are at their strongest and the barrier between our worlds at its thinnest. They're harbingers of misfortune, Dora. Animals are dying in the forest and the village alike and nobody knows why."

Dora dared to speak up. "Do you think... Do you think that they're curs—"

Her father lunged at her. Dora flinched, thinking he was about to strike her, but he just shoved his hand over her mouth. "Don't say it! You're going to stay away from them, understand?"

She gave a terrified nod.

"You're not allowed to talk to them. You're not allowed to see them. And if I find out you did…"

Dora acquiesced to everything Pa asked of her. They didn't bring up the argument for the rest of the day, even though it created a palpable tension between them.

In the evening hours, Dora put her brothers to bed. It took her a bit longer than usual, as the boys, with all the excitement of the approaching Koleda, just weren't able to fall asleep. When their breathing finally evened out and it was the only thing she could hear coming from the twin beds, it was already close to midnight.

It was only when Dora settled in her bed and was finally alone for the first time all day that she allowed herself to really think about what had happened. She was angry. Not with Astrid, who had provoked her, or with her father, but mainly with herself. She'd had such high hopes.

Now that her friends were back, Dora had expected they would be able to answer all her questions and—most of all—confirm what she had seen that day. She wanted so much for the village to know she hadn't lied back then. Dora wished with all her heart that she could throw it in their faces, that for the first time in her life, they'd finally have to listen to her. Admit that she hadn't made it all up— that she wasn't crazy.

Her hope was short-lived, but Dora had clung to it all the more. That's why it was such a hard pill to swallow when that hope defini- tively evaporated today. Neither Astrid nor Tom remembered any- thing. She was still alone in all this.

Dora lay down in her bed and brought the covers all the way up to her neck. Closing her eyes, she shut them tight, firmly re- solved not to open them until the break of day. Because once upon a time, she had given in to temptation. Once upon a time, she had opened them, just barely.

And she had seen how she lost her friends.

Astrid didn't remember when or how she nodded off, but suddenly, she was absolutely certain that she was sleeping. The feeling was at once so familiar yet terrifying that she couldn't have been mistaken.

She realized she had a relatively brief amount of time, a fraction of a second, to ready herself for what was inevitably to come, with no way of protecting herself. But how exactly was Astrid supposed to ready herself for a thing like this? All her life, she hadn't managed to, and deep down, she doubted whether it was even possible.

Stiff as a board, Astrid's body tensed as if frozen in time, her arms locked by her sides and legs rooted to the mattress, while her mind remained surprisingly alert. Her lips were parted in a silent cry. She was aware she couldn't move a muscle. She hadn't lost the ability to do so, she knew that, but there was nothing she could do about it.

Astrid tried calling for help, but none of her cries made it past her lips, her voice stuck deep in her throat.

She spotted it from the corner of her eye. A presence that didn't belong. A huddling figure suspended in an unnatural position in the corner above Max's bed. It was observing Astrid, despite not having any eyes. It knew about her. It had been waiting just for her.

The figure began to move in Astrid's direction, placing its hands and feet jerkily in front of itself, one after the other. Crawling toward her, inch by inch, like a spider.

Another cry lodged itself in Astrid's throat. She wanted to escape this place—to flee far, far away. But she couldn't even budge.

The figure was now closer than ever—hovering right above her. Astrid could see its monstrosity in horrific detail. It began to lower itself toward her, as if it were hanging from an invisible thread. Slowly, stealthily, insidiously.

It was so close now that Astrid could feel its touch upon her face. It opened its black maw for a kiss of death. Astrid couldn't fight back, as she felt a smoke-like substance leaking into her throat. She began to choke on it. With horror, Astrid realized she was suffocating. This thing was going to smother her and absorb her whole.

Something was tickling the inside of her throat like fluttering butterflies desperately trying to escape to the light of day. Just as Astrid convinced herself that this was it—this was the end and she was about to die—the pressure abated.

The figure vanished, perhaps becoming one with her body, she didn't know. Astrid regained her lost breath. She shot up in bed, immediately launching into a coughing fit.

The feeling of suffocation persisted. Astrid felt something scratching her throat, trying to get out. She was coughing so hard she began to gag.

The young woman threw up in her lap, wiping her mouth with the back of her hand. A moth lay in front of her. Gray and slimy. Its wings were fluttering in one last dying effort.

"Tom, wake up. Tom!"

Tom's eyes fluttered open in confusion. It took him a while to figure out where he was and what was going on.

"You were having a nightmare."

Yes, he really had been dreaming. But he couldn't remember what about. When had it ended? Or was he still dreaming?

"Are you okay, sweetie?"

His mother was leaning over him, a deep furrow on her brow from frowning so hard.

He swallowed drily. "Don't call me *sweetie*. I'm eighteen."

She laughed, smoothing down her son's hair. "To me, you're still my baby boy. Well then, here's to a merry Koleda, Mr. All-Grown-Up."

Tom made a face, his eyes only half open. "Yeah, likewise. Can I sleep some more?"

"Okay, but just for a bit longer. No dilly-dallying."

Tom heard his mom leaving the room, closing the door behind her. Only then did he fully open his eyes. They stung and burned. He didn't need a mirror to know they were bloodshot.

Tom had barely gotten any sleep since his return. He attributed it to the things he'd gone through—the things he didn't remember—and the subsequent shock. All three nights had unfolded the same way: he got into bed and proceeded to toss and turn for hours, only succumbing to uneasy slumber in the early hours of dawn, catching a mere few hours of sleep at most. Tom didn't feel well rested, but neither did he feel exhausted. Yet.

His first thought was of Astrid. Of what she must've been feeling. There were so many things they were able to talk about together, and even more things they wanted to discuss but didn't know what they were. But he was dead sure there were also certain things they couldn't talk about. Like about how they really felt. Because Tom felt used. Somebody had stolen twelve years of his life, his memories, his identity. Tom didn't know how to come to terms with it.

131

When he finally rolled out of bed, he ate his breakfast in the kitchen and promised his mother they'd decorate their tree together. It wasn't very big, so they set it atop a low coffee table in the corner of the living room. Most of the ornaments were made of natural materials, lending the tree a sort of festive simplicity.

"Could you pass me that star?"

Tom pulled the straw ornament out of the box and handed it to his mother. She was essentially hanging up all the ornaments herself; he just assisted.

"Mom, I wanted to talk to you about something."

She pretended the task of decoration called for a lot of concentration. "Go ahead, sweetie."

"Describe to me what happened on the day we disappeared," he asked her directly.

She didn't look taken aback. Tom realized it was because she must've been expecting the question for some time now. "Why?"

"Why?" he echoed incredulously.

"Yes, Tom, why," she agreed. "What will you gain? Digging around in the past?"

He squeezed the straw donkey ornament so hard it crackled. "I need to know what happened. I need to remember."

"And what if the truth hurts you? What if your mind knows very well why it's pushed those memories out? What if you've experienced horrors you can't even begin to imagine? Are you sure you know what kind of risk you're taking?"

He didn't hesitate long to answer. "Yes, I know what I've got to lose. Nothing at all, Mom. Because I don't know who I am. And I won't figure that out until I remember what happened."

Valeria's face scrunched up in pain. "You're Tom Hattler," she whispered. "My son. Nothing else matters."

She placed her hands on his shoulders.

"I know you're trying to protect me," he said. "But that won't change what really happened. Something happened. You can't take it back, and it won't disappear if you don't talk about it."

She finally understood he wasn't about to give up on this. Her arms came to rest by her sides in defeat.

"Okay then," she said softly. She perched herself on the edge of the couch and began to speak. "It was the Monday right after Passion Sunday. Lena Mahler was taking you to kindergarten in the morning. I had to take the first morning train to the city, and the kindergarten was still closed that early."

"Why didn't Dad take me?"

"He had too much work." She looked away. "You know how he usually wasn't at home in the morning. Lena would sometimes take you, since she used to pass by our house with her children on her way to kindergarten anyway. She dropped you off at the school at seven o'clock and left you with the teacher. I was..." she faltered. "I was supposed to return from the city at noon. I wanted to pick you up after lunch so you wouldn't have to sleep there, since you'd been struggling with a cold for the past few days, and I knew you'd feel better at home, but... Oh, Tom..."

She burst into tears. Tom offered her a tissue. It took her a while to regain her breath.

"But I was late making it to the st-station and I missed the damn train and I had to w-wait until the afternoon for the next one," she confessed. One tear after another rolled down her cheeks. "I'm sorry, I'm so, so s-sorry. All these years I-I've been blaming myself. If only I'd caught that train, I would've taken you home and none of this would've happened. I want you to know how sorry I am..."

Tom walked over to the couch and sat down next to his mother. It took a while before he was able to say it out loud. Maybe he needed a few seconds to make sure he really meant it.

"It's not your fault, Mom," he reassured her. "It just happened."

"But if I—"

"If *what?* You couldn't have known. It would be easy to be mad at you, so damn easy. But you didn't do anything wrong, I was at kindergarten just like any other day."

Valeria's cries quieted into muffled sobs. It was as if her insides had crumbled completely as soon as she uttered the carefully guarded secret out loud.

"What happened afterward? When we were in kindergarten?"

"Af-After breakfast, the teacher took you all for a walk in the woods. You came back for lunch right after that, and then it was naptime. You all slept in the same classroom, there weren't many kids. She read you a story. Sometime before two o'clock, she left to go to the bathroom and left you sleeping in the classroom for a few minutes alone. When she came back... four of you were gone."

As Tom's mother spoke of the events of that day, Tom tried to imagine what the classroom looked like. He had spent three years there, but his memories were hazy. He remembered a few toys, especially his favorites. He remembered the round tabletops where he had sat for lunchtime with Astrid, Sonya, Max, and Dora. Not much sprang to mind when thinking about his kindergarten class.

"At first she thought you lot had somehow snuck out, un-noticed," she continued. "She called in the cook to come keep an eye on the rest of the kids, and went to look for you through the building and then in the garden and the vicinity. A few locals spot-ted her there and joined in on the search. Soon enough, the entire village was looking for you. I arrived by train around four, and by then everybody already knew. Before I managed to run from the station to the school, everybody knew you had disappeared…"

"Yesterday, you told the Guards that you should've called the police."

She nodded. "That's true."

"Why didn't you call them?"

Valeria tensed, taken aback. "I'm so sorry, sweetie. It's all a bit hazy. I was worried sick and I didn't know what was happening around me. Your father was the one who was really dealing with the situation. The village simply decided that the Guards would be able to solve it. Every single person here was out looking for you. They didn't leave a single stone unturned. For a few days, nothing happened. Eventually, they arrested Gusto. They handed him over to the police themselves."

Tom's heart started pounding. "Did they say why? What evidence did they have?"

"From what I know, they'd seen him that day in the vicinity of the school… And I heard somebody testified against him." She shrugged. "Apparently, he confessed during the interrogation. And you saw those photos they found at his place yourself…"

She placed the palm of her hand on his knee. "Tom… It's most likely it was him… He kept you somewhere, doing… I'm sorry."

He didn't know what to say to that. All he thought about was that he had to tell all this to Astrid.

After the unpleasantness she had experienced, Astrid didn't get any shut-eye for the rest of the night.

Toward the early hours of dawn, she could feel the exhaustion taking over, but at least she had enough time to figure out what she was going to do next. She had trapped the moth that she had regurgitated into a mason jar that she used as a little girl to store her beads. She punched a few holes in the metal lid to allow air to get in and set the jar on her nightstand. From time to time, she would look at the nocturnal creature bashing itself in confusion against the walls of its prison, searching in vain for a way out.

Why is she unconscious and you aren't? Wake her up!

In the morning Astrid's aunt put her to work on the preparations for the evening feast. She dashed between the pantry and the kitchen, tending to the stove, peeling a mountain of potatoes, and dutifully keeping watch over the mushrooms stewing in the pot. It wasn't until after noon that she managed to get away for a bit of privacy.

She snuck out of the house as quietly as possible to avoid having to answer any questions. It briefly occurred to her that maybe she should've told Tom of her plan, but she quickly stemmed that nagging voice in her head. If it led somewhere, she would tell him about it afterward.

If she's right.

If it works.

No, she shouldn't get ahead of herself.

It took her a good half-hour to reach the doctor's house. She managed to take one wrong turn along the way, but she quickly realized her mistake and retraced her steps. It scared her that her subconscious was able to recall the way instinctively, while pushing out other things. There were no other buildings surrounding the doctor's house. It had two stories—the ground floor was used for admitting and treating patients. The doctor lived with his family on the top floor. Astrid had to pound on the door several times before it opened.

When she told the doctor she wasn't looking for medical treatment and was interrupting during the holy day for another reason, he didn't look very pleased.

"Please, just a quick visit."

"I can't let you in. It's against protocol," he resolutely shut her down. "She's recovering and needs to rest."

"Please, it'll just be a moment," she begged. "Just five minutes. I want to see her..."

She wasn't expecting her voice to break like that. Clearly, her emotions weren't masked as well as she wanted them to be.

"Fine, but just for a couple minutes. I promised my kids we'd stick to tradition and pour the molten lead soon. They're eager to see what this year's shapes will tell them about their future, so be fast."

"Thank you so much, really, thank you."

"The third door on the left."

Without delay, she proceeded down the hallway according to his directions, hurrying just in case the doctor had second thoughts. She rushed along as quietly as possible. The muted conversation of the doctor's family reached her ears from the top floor. Somebody was listening to a radio play, while the stomping of children's feet resounded from elsewhere. She nimbly squeezed through the right door and found herself in a dimly lit, cramped room.

Sonya was lying in bed with an ashen face, her blonde hair sprawled across her pillow. The doctor may have thought it was an unhealthy color, but this was exactly the way Astrid remembered her. Pale and always keeping out of the sun, because her skin got painfully red after each time spent outside. She had blossomed into a beautiful young woman. She looked peaceful, as if she'd just fallen asleep.

Astrid didn't know exactly what she was doing or whether her uncertain plan made any sense. It was just a theory—a thought that occurred to her as she observed the moth trapped in the mason jar.

She shrugged her bag off her shoulder and took out everything she needed.

A bundle of herbs she had put together from the pantry and quickly tied up. She didn't manage to get all of those she needed—only valerian, thyme, and sowbread—but she had to work with what she had. She carefully lifted the corner of Sonya's pillow and placed the bundle under it, adding a head of garlic. She walked over to the window, drew the curtains open, and sprinkled the dried, ground fennel along the windowsill. Then she took a pencil and drew several tiny symbols meant to protect against nightmares and evil spirits on the wall behind Sonya's head. She did so carefully, trying to place them as low as she could. If Sonya's parents were to spot them, they'd know immediately what she'd done. The last thing she pulled out was the stub of her candle. She had to sacrifice it, it was worth a try. She struck a match and quickly lit the candle, the smell of charcoal and frankincense spreading throughout the room.

She held the candle next to Sonya's head while tracing the symbols on the wall with her fingers.

"Now I lay me down to sleep, and I shall awaken, for the evil spirits cannot reach me."

She repeated the prayer twice and then blew out the candle.

Sonya continued to lay there, still as death. Astrid gingerly squeezed her hand.

"Come back," she whispered. "We need you here."
Silence was her only answer.

On the day of Koleda, the village was unusually lively. Before it got dark and it was time for dinner, young children would go door to door caroling. Dressed in cheerful colors, they dashed around and sang carols in exchange for fruit or candy from their neighbors. On her way back from the doctor's house, Astrid encountered several of these merrymaking groups.

The closer her inevitable encounter with her grandmother drew, the tighter the knot in the pit in her stomach felt. As she entered the house, it pulled her down like a heavy stone.

To her surprise, Grandma wasn't lying in wait for her in the hallway to predictably tell her off, nor was she in the kitchen. The house actually appeared to be empty. She glanced around uneasily. A freshly baked vánočka, plaited sweet bread, was set on the table-top, while coiled wine sausages sizzled in the oven. Her aunt must've just popped out for a minute. Astrid went to check on her mother, who was lying in bed, napping. She returned to the kitchen right as her aunt appeared with a basket of eggs.

"There you are," she declared without a shred of concern in her voice.

"I'm… I apologize for leaving without saying anything." Astrid felt her face getting hot.

Her aunt was silently observing her. "Is that all?" she said.

"Well…"

"Grab that dishtowel and help me with the dishes," her aunt said after a while. "Let's set the table."

She took the dishtowel and began to polish the glasses her aunt handed her from the top shelf. When the glasses were buffed to a sparkle, she turned to the silverware. She quietly polished the knives, forks, and spoons while her aunt finished cooking the food.

"I told Grandma that I sent you to get honey from the bee-keeper," her aunt mentioned, as if in passing.

Astrid tensed. "I don't know what to say..."

Her aunt narrowed her eyes. "I'm not doing it out of sympathy," she snapped. "I just want to have peace and quiet in the house for at least one day."

The traces of affection she had suddenly begun to feel toward her aunt quickly evaporated.

"You're just like your mother," her aunt added.

The words stung Astrid like a slap to the face. She was convinced there was no way it could've been construed as well-meaning in any sense of the word.

They finished preparing the dinner together and set the table for the festive occasion, setting the food aside to keep it warm for the time being. It was starting to get dark outside, caroling children had already returned to their homes, because now the time had come when perchtas, terrifying creatures that were a menace mainly to children, would come out in the open. When a child lingered behind during caroling, adults often scared them with the threat of perchtas walking the earth, punishing dawdling children for their disobedience if they encountered them. According to legend, perchtas went from door to door, checking whether the children were obediently observing the fast. If not, they were in danger of having their stomachs cut open with a large knife and stuffed with lint and sawdust.

Astrid remembered returning late from caroling once, as it was already getting dark, when Kristian suddenly shut the door in her face, locking it. He left her standing outside crying, yelling at her through the door that a perchta was going to gut her and toss her insides to the dogs. Before her mother managed to open the door and let her in, Astrid's crying had devolved into hysteria, leaving her gasping for air. Her mother spent a long time trying to convince her that perchtas weren't real—that it was just a disguise with the appearance of an old woman with a strange, scary, box-shaped mask for a face, that it was just entertainment for adults, used to frighten children into behaving.

Astrid didn't believe her.

They sat down for dinner as soon as the clock struck six. Astrid's aunt ordered her to wear her old traditional Sunday dress—a woolen tartan skirt with a red-colored bodice, under which she had pulled on a shabby and slightly threadbare embroidered shirt. As an unmarried young woman, she was also supposed to wear her hair in a braid with a ribbon, but her aunt had cast a critical eye upon her figure and decided that it was adequate enough as is to pass her standards. Her aunt put on her Sunday best as well and tied a scarf around her head, as was the custom for married women, even though it immediately added a good ten years to her age. They both struggled together to get Astrid's mother dressed. Strangely enough, it was as if Koleda had forced them to set aside all their conflicts for a few hours and pretend for at least a little while that they were a normal family. All members of the family had dressed in their best clothes for the dinner. Astrid tried to avoid catching the eye of Grandma, who was ignoring her anyway, and Kristian, who on the contrary never took his eyes off her. Before they began to eat, they all uttered a prayer for their family's well-being. Astrid thought of her father. Her memory of him was already starting to fade. She also thought of Max, who was who knows where. She missed both of them like never before.

The festive dinner belonged to several events of the year that had their own predetermined set of rules. According to tradition, nine dishes had to be prepared and served, one of them being made of lentils, which was said to bring wealth to the household. Another custom was to have wafers slathered in garlic and honey to ensure good health. Good fortune was in store for whoever came upon a piece of stale bread. Leftovers were buried in the ground to make sure next year's soil would be fertile. The tarp covering the tabletop also held magical powers and was passed down from generation to generation. Farmers used it in spring to sow wheat, which was supposed to be spared from hail. A chain was wrapped around the table to ward off evil spirits. Nobody was allowed to get up from the table during dinner until everyone was finished eating. It was believed not only that doing so brought bad luck, but also that the one who got up first would die within a year. Astrid had long forgotten most of these rules and customs, or had simply not paid them much attention as a child. She took them with a grain of salt, but tonight, she didn't want to needlessly provoke anyone. The dinner meant a great deal to her aunt, and the last thing Astrid wanted to do was stir up more conflict. She wasn't pinning her hopes on things changing after tonight, anyway.

While in other families, men tended to be the head of the household, in their home it had always been Grandma who had the final word, as far back as Astrid could remember. It was she who led the prayers in the manner of the Elders. It was also Grandma who began to eat first and who they all had to wait on to finish.

Astrid didn't eat much, nor did she manage to feed her mother very well. She felt relieved when the others finally finished eating and they could get up from the table. She was counting down the minutes until she'd be able to leave the house to see Tom and talk to him.

They all moved into the living room to the decorated tree. Astrid wasn't counting on receiving any presents—she didn't have any for anyone either, but it seemed polite to stick it out for a while longer. She helped her mother into the armchair. She looked a bit better today, even managing to hold eye contact occasionally. Astrid stood by her side and waited patiently for the others to open their presents. She didn't pay them much attention until Kristian spoke to her.

"This one's for you, cousin—catch!"

She barely managed to lift her arms in surprise before catching a small, light package. Her eyes landed on Kristian suspiciously to see if it was some sort of joke. Her cousin smirked and held her gaze expectantly. She knew it wasn't a good idea, but what choice did she have? With trembling fingers, she ripped open the brown wrapping paper. It was the tiny body of a dead cuckoo bird. A few drops of blood had clung to the packaging.

Astrid looked into Kristian's eyes.

"Witch," he hissed angrily so that nobody else would hear.

She could feel the bile rising in her throat. She rewrapped the package, dead bird and all, and left the room before anyone could stop her.

After the families finished their meals and unwrapped their presents, they began to come out of their houses, greeting each other and wishing each other all the best. As the bell chimed eight o'clock, they gathered at the tall tree on the village green to sing carols.

Astrid took the first chance she got to grab her coat and disappear into the darkness outside. As she walked toward the tree, she couldn't get the cuckoo bird she'd buried in the backyard in the snow out of her head.

Witch.

Along the way, she passed by families, couples on their own, and large groups alike giving each other little gifts. All this merry-making was beginning to make her feel uncomfortable. It felt fake and pretentious. Sure, they could put on a face. But they couldn't fool her. She knew they were capable of stabbing each other in the back. There must've been a hundred people standing around the tree by now. She walked through the crowd, craning her neck as she looked around, but Tom was nowhere to be seen.

"Excuse me." She walked around a group of musicians she'd gotten in the way of clumsily.

Suddenly, she felt somebody's gaze upon her. She turned around, instinctively expecting to see a familiar, kind face. But it was a blind old lady standing in the crowd, the one who had spoken to her yesterday in front of the butcher's shop. Her blind eyes were fixed upon Astrid again.

Astrid headed straight for her without a second thought. She had to know what the woman had meant by her words. She pushed past the others without letting the woman out of her sight.

She pushed passersby away as if they were rag dolls until she finally came to stand a few steps in front of the old lady. She took a breath, ready to speak, but the woman beat her to it.

"I know why you've come."

THE FOURTH NIGHT

A strid didn't allow herself to be taken aback, even though her heart started pounding wildly.

"*It's your fault. Wake up.* What did you mean by that yesterday?"

The old lady's face broke into a toothless grin. "Sometimes there's no use looking for a different meaning where there is none. Can't ye see? Ye came back and dragged in the demons with ye. Perun save us all!"

Astrid felt like she only understood every other word. "How could it be my fault?"

"You attract them like light attracts moths."

"Moths come out of darkness."

"Light is best seen in the dark, don't ye forget it."

"What do you mean?"

Some of the words were like riddles.

The old woman shook her head. "If ye have to ask, ye're not yet ready for the truth."

Astrid took the bait. "What truth? What are you talking about? I don't remember anything."

"Trust your eyes," she advised her. "They won't betray you."

Astrid was about to ask another question when she heard shouting behind her.

"Astrid!"

For a split second, she glanced behind her. It was Tom, pushing his way through the crowd toward her. She turned back to the old lady, but she was gone. Astrid looked around every which way, but the old woman had vanished, as if the ground had swallowed her. Astrid began to doubt whether she was even real. What if she was starting to go crazy? What if she'd hit her head somewhere so hard she'd not only lost her memories, but her mind as well?

Trust your eyes. They won't betray you.

"Astrid?"

"Did you see her?" she asked immediately instead of a greeting.

"Who?"

"That old lady, the one who'd been in front of the butcher's shop yesterday… She was just standing here, but…"

Tom joined her in looking around. "I don't see her anywhere. Who are you talking about? Are you feeling okay, Astrid?"

She wondered how she looked. Terrified and nervous, trembling all over. "Yeah… Yeah, I am. Sorry. I haven't been getting much sleep."

Tom squeezed her arm in a comforting gesture. "You have no idea how much I understand you. Take a few deep breaths, alright?"

The cynical side of her wanted to make a face and say there was no way he could understand. But eventually, she managed to smile at him instead and tried to believe his words. The surrounding noises—snippets of conversations, screaming children, the out-of-tune melody of the band warming up—they all disappeared for a moment, leaving just the two of them, frozen in time. Inhale. Exhale.

"Better?" Tom asked her after a while, his tone cautious.

"I hate it here so much, this whole village, all these people," she blurted out instead of answering.

"That's the spirit."

They didn't join in on the festivities and merrymaking. They'd had it up to here with attention from the past few days, and they tried to blend into the background instead. They pushed through the crowds, and at times, when Tom deemed it safe, he relayed to Astrid parts of his conversation with his mom. For some reason, they both took it as a matter of course that the less people heard them, the better. Astrid patiently listened to him and didn't let on what was going through her mind. All those years ago, they had vanished during naptime after lunch. The entire village had been out looking for them, but nobody had called the police. Why?

"Astrid?"

Tom's voice brought her out of her thoughts. From the corner of her eye, she could see someone looking at her intently.

The woman looked like she'd wanted to turn her head away at the last second to break her gaze, but their eyes had already locked. Astrid didn't let her look away. Almost in unison, they both nodded politely in acknowledgement of each other. It was Mrs. Frank, their teacher, who walked up to them in the end.

"I didn't mean to stare like that," she apologized. "Nobody's been talking about anything else 'round here… I had to make sure with my very own eyes that it's really you."

Worry was etched into their teacher's face. Astrid remembered that she didn't have it easy at home, from snippets of conversations she'd overheard the mothers having at the school a long time ago while the kids were getting dressed at their lockers. The teacher's husband had worked as a coal miner, but he'd lost his leg years ago in an accident at the mine. The partial disability prevented him from working, but not from going to the pub. There were rumors of him stumbling home on his crutches every night, and heaven forbid if his wife got in his way, she'd catch a few smacks. Astrid realized the teacher's husband might've very well drunk himself to death by now, especially with twelve years gone by. But something in the woman's expression told her that no, he was still here. And he still continued to suffocate her with his presence.

It took Tom a bit longer to recognize their old teacher. Her face had aged incredibly, but her countenance still retained that familiar appearance.

They pushed their way to her. She was looking at them expectantly with that strict expression they remembered so well.

"Good evening, Mrs. Frank," Tom greeted her.

"Drop the formalities, I'm not your teacher anymore and it's been years since I last taught at the kindergarten."

Tom didn't know how to react to that.

Astrid figured they could skip the pleasantries. "Could we talk to you about what happened?"

Mrs. Frank's gaze wandered from Tom to settle on Astrid. "Everything I know I already told the Guard back then."

"But we wanted to ask you," Astrid insisted. "We want to hear your version."

"Look, girl, I'm not so young anymore and my mind ain't what it used to be either."

Astrid refused to budge. "I know this village would like nothing more than to forget this whole thing ever happened. If only it were that simple for us too. You owe us an explanation."

"Fine," the teacher eventually said. "But not here." She made a gesture as if to suggest it wasn't safe to do so here.

Astrid nodded in agreement. "Where?"

"In ten minutes behind the old mill, take the path 'round back so no one sees you."

With these words, she vanished into the crowd.

Astrid and Tom lingered in place for a while longer, perhaps to shake off the inquisitive stares that had been on them until now, and then headed out in the opposite direction than their teacher.

On their way to the old mill, Astrid told Tom of her visiting Sonya at the doctor's. She didn't mention anything about what she'd done there, just that her condition hadn't improved.

The semi-ruin of a building had always been called the old mill as far back as Astrid could remember, despite it not being an actual mill anymore. The original watermill, which was used for wheat, had fallen into disrepair decades ago. For a while the new building served as a storage place, but for the most part, it just remained abandoned. As children, they used to play in it, despite their parents forbidding them to, as it offered a number of mysterious nooks and crannies perfect for all sorts of mischief and games.

They stood there in the dark for longer than the few minutes promised. Neither of them dared express any doubts over their teacher actually coming or not. The direction of the wind changed, carrying the sound of singing toward them from the village green. Without realizing, at that very moment, they were both thinking the same thing.

"How was your Koleda at home?" Tom asked quietly, his gaze fixed in the direction from which they came.

The sound Astrid let out was a mixture of laughter and a snort. It was an apt expression of everything she was currently thinking about.

"Yeah, same here," he agreed, chuckling briefly.

Astrid glanced at him out of the corner of her eye. It was pitch dark, but she could still discern the details of his face. He was almost all grown up—and even though he was already growing facial hair, his eyes still sparkled with that same mischievous expression he used to have as a boy. She was surprised that the realization made her feel a bit nonplussed.

Just then, they both made out movement in the darkness and turned to look toward the river. Their teacher emerged from the trees, dressed in a large, thick coat. She joined them, stalling for a bit, not knowing how to begin.

"I ain't proud of what happened," she finally admitted. "But back then, I told the Guards how it went down, and I'll tell you too. We started the day with a little walk, so that you kids would get some exercise and it would tire you out for your nap later. After lunch, I put everyone to bed, read you a story, and waited for you all to actually fall asleep. Then I sneaked out back for a cigarette. I know I shouldn't have, I shouldn't have left the class without supervision during naptime. It was against the rules, but the rules also said that there should've been two teachers in charge of a class that size. But my coworker was on extended sick leave and the principal hadn't found a replacement. I'd had it up to here by then, I was sick of you kids. I couldn't even go to the bathroom during the day, not once. I told myself that since I had to supervise a classroom of kids all day every day alone, they would manage a few minutes without supervision."

Astrid and Tom didn't react to her admission.

"As I was lighting my second cigarette, I spotted a movement behind the fence of the playground. A figure soon staggered out from the bushes. It was Gustaw. The local handyman," she explained. "Everybody called him Loony Gusto. I mean, you yourself know… He's not right in the head. He never even went to school, and he had this strange way of walking, rocking from side to side. I yelled at him to get outta there. And he listened. Then I stopped by the kitchen and had a quick cup of coffee with the cook. She was talking my ear off, always complaining about something. The miserable pay, the disgusting second-rate ingredients the principal forced her to cook meals with. Village gossip. Who's fighting with who over property disputes, which family's preparing for a wedding in the spring. It was exactly two o'clock sharp that I finished my coffee and walked back to the class to wake up the kids."

Her voice began to tremble, as if she'd gone back in time. "When I left the class an hour before, there were thirteen sleeping kids. When I came back, four of the beds were empty. My blood ran cold."

With the last words she uttered, an almost imperceptible caution of sorts began to creep into her voice, as if she were carefully choosing how to relay the information. A pregnant pause followed.

"I dunno… Dunno if you want me to continue…"

Tom gave Astrid a sidelong glance, but she didn't say anything. He decided to answer. "If you can, it would be of help to us."

Their teacher nodded. "At first I thought you'd hidden somewhere… I went through the cubbyhole where we stored bigger toys and the sleeping cots. Then I went out to the hallway and asked the cook to watch over the class. I searched through the other rooms in the kindergarten, the washroom, the empty classrooms, the locker room. I ran out to the garden too, but there was no trace of you. I was calling out for you, running around the school, and then some people came up to me and asked me what had happened… Soon it was the whole village looking for you."

"The classroom had been locked," Astrid interrupted her, deep in thought.

A guilty look appeared on the woman's face. "Yes, I… It had barely been an hour. We used to do it all the time whenever we were short-staffed and had no one to keep an eye on the kids… Do you know what it's like to take care of an entire class on your own for ten hours straight every day? Sometimes, I just needed a break for a minute and…"

The woman broke off, probably realizing how empty her words sounded.

"And you're the only one who had the key?" Astrid continued without letting on what she was thinking.

"Yes."

"And there wasn't a chance that someone else could have gotten inside? A copy of the key somewhere?"

The teacher shook her head. "I had one copy, the principal had one, but she was out of town on that day, and one of my coworkers had one. Maybe you remember her?"

"The one with the short hair?" Tom recalled. "She used to look after us."

Just like Astrid, he seemed to remember they'd liked that teacher much more. She'd never raised her voice at them.

"She usually took care of the junior class," Mrs. Frank added. "But flu season was in full swing at the time and many children were sick at home, including her. That's why the principal and I had merged the two classes into one and I had to look after you on my own."

"And the windows were locked?" Astrid inquired further.

"All of them," the teacher affirmed, sounding miffed. "I'd never just leave the class without closing them…"

Astrid took a breath to snap at her, but Tom was faster.

"You left the class and locked us there, so…"

The woman's chin trembled. "I can assure you that I regret it to this day."

Tom grimaced, probably wanting to add something, but Astrid didn't let him. It seemed pointless to be looking for someone to blame or to force someone to assume responsibility for their actions after all these years, when they still didn't know what exactly had occurred.

"You mentioned seeing Gusto near the kindergarten that afternoon."

"He'd been wandering around. He did so often."

"And in the afternoon, when you ran out to look for us, you didn't see him again?"

"No." She shook her head. "You're asking the same questions the Guards did back then. They wanted to know the same things."

"Did you tell them you saw Gusto outside while we were sleeping?" Tom joined in.

"Of course I did," she assured them, as if to tell them she'd done something right. "But I wasn't the only one. If I remember correctly, his name was mentioned by several people during questioning."

"Who?" Astrid immediately latched onto the information.

"I don't know that… It's been twelve years. You'll have to ask around."

Something suddenly occurred to Astrid. "Do you remember Dora Lautner?"

"Of course."

"Dora saw something," she tried to get a reaction out of the woman. "It… had something to do with what happened."

153

The teacher shook her head. "Dora was out of it. She only imagined she saw something."

Tom cut in. "There were no other suspects apart from Gusto?"

The teacher made a vague gesture with her hand. "None that I remember... But if you want to know my opinion on the matter, then... Gusto didn't do it."

She had managed to catch Astrid off guard for the first time. This was something she definitely hadn't been expecting. "What do you mean?"

"When I told him to scram, he slunk away past the park. He definitely couldn't have gotten inside through the front door, he wouldn't have managed to circle back 'round the building. Leaving just the back entrance, but he would've had to walk directly past me as I was standing on the ramp."

"And when you were in the kitchen with the cook?" Tom didn't let up.

"I kept the door leading to the hall wide open. I was looking out that way the entire time. He'd have had to walk past right in front of my eyes."

"But it wouldn't have been impossible," Tom said, still hesitant.

The woman's eyebrows shot up. "Maybe not," she conceded. "But in that case, tell me how he could've gotten back, unnoticed, with four kids tucked in his arms?"

Nobody could answer that question twelve years ago, much less today. But there was one more thing nagging at Astrid.

"How did you manage to get me to fall asleep?" she asked. "Because it was nearly impossible to get me to sleep in kindergarten, and you know that as well as I do."

It was nearly every day that Astrid found herself lying on her cot during naptime, counting down the minutes until the others woke up. And it was every day that she'd get reprimanded for it by her teacher. When her mother would come pick her up in the afternoon, the teacher never forgot to remind her about it, throwing it in her face as a parental failure in upbringing.

She hasn't slept again, Mrs. Mahler. We don't intend to tolerate this forever. You'll have to take her home right after lunch.

Their old teacher made a face as if she were truly ashamed for the first time. "I added some brewed poppyhead to your tea. So you'd stay quiet for a while."

For Astrid, the conversation was over.

After the teacher left, Astrid and Tom stayed back for a while, quietly contemplating what they'd just learned. Astrid was more and more convinced that Gusto was innocent. Somebody had taken advantage of him to get rid of him. Maybe whoever had actually kidnapped them. Or had the entire village ganged up on the local lunatic instead? Nothing would surprise her anymore.

"You're trembling, you must be cold," Tom brought her back to reality. "We better go."

Going home meant it was late and there was another terrifying night ahead of her. Astrid wanted to confide in him just how scared she was to fall asleep, how petrifying the idea of shutting her eyes was. Maybe he'd suggest keeping her company so she wouldn't have to fall asleep alone—as soon as the thought crossed her mind, she felt embarrassed. She didn't say any of it out loud.

"Let's go," she agreed.

They set out together down a narrow side street back to the village green. People gradually began popping up here and there, evidently on their way home. The adults were talking amongst themselves, kids were excitedly exchanging details about the gifts they'd gotten.

"Mommy, look!" Some little girl whooped, shoving a doll under her mother's nose.

"She's beautiful," the woman smiled, smoothing down the little girl's hair.

"She's the bestest!"

Her father lifted the girl up into his arms. "Of course she is."

Two young boys were also walking next to the parents, their cheeks red from the cold, leftover snow from a snowball fight clinging to their coats. The whole family was heading toward a home that looked cozy at first glance.

Astrid paused in confusion as Tom suddenly froze in place.

"What's wrong?"

He had a stony expression on his face. She couldn't make sense of it.

"Tom?"

He answered without turning toward her. "That was my dad."

And suddenly, Astrid understood. She had no idea what to say, and so she stood by him silently until he gathered the strength to go on. In that moment, she wished for nothing more than to see what was going through his mind.

"Do you want to talk to him?" she asked softly.

"No," he refused resolutely and continued walking, his head hung low. "I'm nothing to him."

"You don't know that."

"He looked me in the eye, Astrid. He recognized me, but didn't say anything. I appreciate your concern, but... This isn't something that can be fixed just like that."

"Maybe he just panicked?"

"He knows. That I'm back. He's known for several days now. He just doesn't want to see me."

An evident bitterness laced Tom's voice. Sensing it would be best to keep silent, Astrid didn't speak for the rest of their walk home—neither about Tom's father nor about what was running through her head. She didn't want to burden him with additional things. They reached the Mahlers' house first. Light was shining through the top-story windows. She'd have felt better if the family were already asleep and she didn't have to see any more people today. They paused on the path leading to the front door. She was hesitant to ask him how he felt, in case it sounded nosy. Tom beat her to it.

"You look nice today," he said.

Astrid's eyes automatically dropped to the traditional dress she was wearing. She hadn't thought at all, when she'd looked in the mirror, that she could look nice. Suddenly, she felt a lot better in the uncomfortable dress than she had a moment ago.

"Good night, Astrid," he said.

"Good night."

She watched him disappear into the night before turning to the door.

She quickly did her nightly ablutions in the bathroom, changing into her sleeping clothes, and entered her room. She'd left the last remnants of the candle meant to protect her in Sonya's room. But if her weak attempt to carry out the ritual in her room worked out, then… She didn't regret it, not even at the cost of endangering herself. The other precautions would do—the mix of dried herbs warding off nightmares, garlic underneath her pillow to protect against demons, and the symbols of protection upon her wall.

According to the Elders, they had magical powers, and that's why parents used to let their children undergo a ritual during which the symbols were tattooed, burned, or carved into their skin. Traditionally, their arms were marked this way, using special mixtures of ink made from natural ingredients. However, Astrid's mother had refused to go through with a ritual that would cause pain to her children. She advocated for the traditional markings made on walls or doors, believing they would be enough. To this day, Astrid could remember the argument that her mother's decision had caused. Grandma had branded her mother a heathen, screaming at her that she was going to anger the gods. Her father had agreed, pressing her mom to change her mind. But she was stubborn in standing her ground. *I won't let anyone inject poison into my children's skin.* Astrid's father had ripped a bawling Max out of her mother's arms during the fight, carrying him to the ritual himself. Astrid stayed hidden behind her mother's back, refusing to go. The skin on her hands stayed untouched. Her parents had ended up not speaking to each other for several long weeks. Her dad thought it was her mom's fault that Astrid was unprotected. Vulnerable. At the mercy of dark forces.

If he was right, though, why hadn't Max been spared?

She didn't know.

She sprinkled the assortment of dried herbs and ground fennel along the windowsill. Her gaze landed on the jar with the moth. It was perched at the bottom, displaying its bewitchingly beautiful wings. It held a certain eerie, sublime beauty. Astrid gently tapped on the glass a few times, but the moth didn't even stir. She lifted her eyes right as something crashed into the window at eye level. The grimacing white rectangular face of a perchta flattened itself against the glass. Astrid jumped back in fright. The person behind the mask let out an uncanny cackle before disappearing into the night.

She stepped away from the window as far as she could and drew back the covers, her heart still beating wildly. On the bedsheets, there lay the curled-up dead body of the cuckoo bird she'd buried in the backyard just a few hours ago. The tiny body had begun to thaw in the warm room, creating a puddle of water beneath it.

Rage suddenly overcame Astrid. Enough. She'd had it. She walked out of her room determinedly, darting down the hall and up the stairway. She made sure to keep her steps light so she wouldn't draw the attention of the entire household to herself. She flung open the first door right across the stairway without knocking, striding into Kristian's room.

Her cousin was sprawled out on his bed only in his boxers, one hand behind his head as he held a magazine with a half-naked woman on the cover in front of his face. He tore his gaze from it and his eyes calmly locked with Astrid's.

"Don't know how to knock?"

"You think you're funny?" Astrid hissed in anger.

With a theatrical sigh, Kristian set aside his magazine and sat up. "Like in this particular moment in time? Or in general?"

His attempt at humor made her blood boil. "You're a real jerk, you know that? You don't have to keep showing me you don't want me here. What are you trying to prove, exactly?"

"Hold up," he growled, all traces of humor gone. "What the hell are you talking about?"

"You put that dead bird in my bed! Don't act like you didn't."

"You've really lost the plot, haven't ya?" Kristian rose from his bed to stand in front of her. Astrid suddenly realized just how tall and well built he was. He could overpower her with ease. "I wrapped it up nicely as a gift for you. That's it."

She paused. He didn't have any reason to lie to her when they were alone. Why would he bother pretending? But in that case, how did the animal get in her bed?

A sudden wave of unease washed over her. She decided to change tactics. "Stay away from my room."

Kristian's eyebrows shot up. "You're the one who barged into *my* room." His eyes flashed dangerously. "But I'm glad you came. At least we can have a little talk."

He was in front of her in a split second. Astrid was so taken aback she had no time to react. He used his entire body to pin her to the wall.

"Let go!"

He used his beefy forearm to press against her chest, his index finger pushing against the hollow of her neck until she couldn't catch her breath. She struggled against him, but he was much stronger.

"Wherever you were, you should've stayed there," he hissed in her ear. "You little *witch*. Nobody wants you here. If you haven't figured that out already, you should do so, and quick."

Only then did he let her go. Astrid wheezed, rubbing her bruised chest. Kristian was observing her with his piggy eyes and open disgust, as if looking at a carcass lying on the side of the road. Astrid rushed from the room, this time not caring how much noise she made. She fled to her room, locked the door behind her, and only then did she dare take a deep breath.

You little witch.

Children's voices suddenly emerged in her mind. Voices shouting at her. Flashes of blurry images. Memories long forgotten. She curled in on herself in the corner on Max's bed, as far away from the little dead bird as she could, her knees pressed against her chin.

Trembling and crying, she was dead set on not letting herself fall asleep tonight.

Although so much was racing through her mind and she had several reasons to avoid sleep, in the early hours of morning, her own mind betrayed her. Curled up in the corner of the bed, her chin tucked over her knees, she unknowingly nodded off for a while. All it took was a second, and she was waking up into a nightmare.

Her body was frozen in its unnatural position. She was looking straight ahead at her bed, her eyes wide with horror, unable to blink. In the opposite corner, five beings hovered above the floor. Their faces had a deathly pallor and were turned toward her. Taut skin stretched over their bare skulls, as if they were missing all their musculature, with only their sharp bones protruding. Floor-length, ink-black robes streamed down in place of their bodies, resembling rolling waves of smoke. Long, braided stumps resembling vines protruded where arms and legs usually grew.

She didn't know how, but all of a sudden, she was dead certain that these creatures were visiting her every night. It was just tonight that she finally saw them clearly and in all their terror.

The room was filled with the rustling of butterfly wings. The moth was frantically fluttering around in the jar, dashing its wings against the walls, but Astrid heard the sound amplified to a much higher degree and intensity than was normal. The unpleasant din was joined by an incessant whispering. Ungraspable and repetitive, as if someone kept repeating the same words over and over again, words she didn't understand. She knew it was them. They were talking to her, but their lips remained sealed.

The figures drew closer, slowly soaring through the air and stretching their claws toward her. Astrid could see their black limbs winding around her ankles, overwhelming her. She couldn't fight back, her petrified mouth emitting nothing more than a muted cry that sounded like an inhuman scream. The branches slithered up around her ankles, encircling her thighs and back, and when they constricted around her chest, she stopped breathing. The five white skulls were so close, they were almost touching her.

She knew this was the end. They had gotten her. She was going to die here.

In that very moment, the first rays of sunshine lit the room. The day was breaking. As if someone had thrown her into ice-cold water, the creatures vanished at once and Astrid jolted awake.

Her heart was pounding wildly. With trembling fingers, she drew up the pant legs of her pajamas, spotting distinct marks and bruises. This was something she couldn't have done to herself.

She didn't know how it had come to be, but her nightmares were real. Very real.

Father hadn't yet returned from his hunt in the forest, but that wasn't anything unusual during the winter months. He had to make sure the wildlife was properly fed and had suitable conditions for making it through the harsh weather. Sometimes he would spend nights and even stretches of the day in the forest before he managed to check all the feeding racks and supply of hay and fodder. When Dora was little, he often used to take her with him to the forest, letting her help him with the animals. After her mother's death, though, he told her she simply had to grow up and start taking care of the household while he was gone. There wasn't any time left to wander around the woods anymore. She returned to it at least in her thoughts and during rare occasions when she found free time.

That morning, she woke up early, tended to her grandpa and the twins, and decided to go ahead with preparing lunch. She caught a hen in the yard—it wasn't difficult. They trusted her, and she fed them and took care of their bedding every day. She grasped with both hands, quickly grabbing the hen's head with her right hand while cutting its neck with her left. She hit an artery, warm blood spurting out on the white snow, spattering Dora's feet. It took a while before the animal stopped thrashing around and bled out. She plunged it for a moment into cold water, immediately followed by hot water to scald it and make it easier to remove its feathers. She chucked it, still warm, onto the workbench behind the house and began to pluck the hen with deft fingers. The act and the stench of the scalded hen used to be nauseating. She remembered throwing up the first time she ever did it, but her father immediately forced her to keep going. Nowadays, she did it on autopilot. She proceeded to pluck the hen from head to toe. She used one hand to stretch the skin, while her other hand plucked away.

Dora was barely halfway done when a figure rounded the corner of the house. Astrid walked up, standing uncertainly just a few steps away. Dora paused in surprise. She hadn't expected to see her friend so soon after their argument. She looked even more exhausted and worn down than she had two days ago.

"You've always had a cast-iron stomach," Astrid said at the sight of Dora's bloodied hand covered in feathers.

Dora ducked down to continue working. "I had no choice."

Astrid took a hesitant step toward her. "I wanted to apologize," she said. "I didn't have any right to yell at you and say those things… It was mean of me."

Dora hesitated before answering. "You achieved what you set out to do, didn't you? You were always good at that."

"Maybe."

Dora felt her eyes begin to sting. She'd much rather ascribe it to the stench of scalded skin and feathers than admit tears were pushing their way into her eyes. Astrid stood there silently, observing her. But Dora refused to lift her head and ask her what she wanted from her. She didn't care how irrationally she might've been acting. Her whole childhood, Astrid had always come out on top. It was she who was the leader of their little group; everybody did what she said. All of a sudden, Dora didn't want to be pushed around anymore.

And then she heard something that genuinely shocked her.

"Dory, I believe you. I know you saw something that can't be rationally explained. You saw something that… nobody understands. Something that they told you couldn't possibly be real, that was just a nightmare."

Dora's head shot up. Her heart stood still. It didn't seem like Astrid was playing some sort of game.

"I know what it's like to have everyone around you think you're lying," she said, her voice unwavering. "It's not fair that nobody believed you."

"How…" Dora whispered. "How do you know about that?"

"Please tell me what you saw. I need to hear it."

It was the first time someone had said those words and actually meant it. No doubts, no disguised attempts to corner her, to point fingers and call her a liar.

Astrid believed her.

Dora hesitated, and even though she'd imagined this moment many times before, now that it was finally here, she felt an irrational fear. Because voicing something like this out loud after all those years of silence meant reopening old wounds.

Twelve years ago

Dora felt like she was too old for naptime. Her mother always let her stay up after lunch on the weekend and play instead of sleeping. This usually meant that she was more tired in the evening, but the extra hour she got to herself to play with all her toys was definitely worth it. But they were always forced to take a nap in kindergarten, even though they were supposed to go to school next year and naps weren't a thing there. And she wasn't alone—nobody in her class really wanted to nap after lunch.

That day, the teacher had taken them out for a walk until lunch. It was cold, but Dora had always found the outdoors more fun than kindergarten. For lunch they had mashed peas with sausages and stale bread. It wasn't the worst dish they could've gotten, but many of the children didn't like it and they spent lunch picking at the mash. Their teacher stood over them until every single one of them had finished it and left their plates empty. After lunch, everyone had to drink a cup of herbal tea, something that Dora had a bigger problem with than the food. It wasn't that she didn't like the taste of it. Her father had raised her not to turn her nose up at anything. But every time she drank too much of the tea, she couldn't fall asleep, because she needed to pee, and her teacher didn't allow them to get up during naptime. That's why, when the teacher wasn't looking, Dora poured half her tea into the flowerpot by the wall. After lunch, their teacher ushered them along to change into their pajamas.

While the children were having lunch, she'd laid out their cots in the classroom. Dora automatically headed for the corner where her group of friends always slept—Sonya, Tom next to her, Dora in the middle, Astrid on her right, and then little Max by the wall. Sonya dutifully spread out her blanket and pillow, smoothing down the wrinkled bed linen. It was a bad habit of hers. The teacher kept praising her for cleaning up after herself so nicely and keeping everything in order—*Children, look at Sonya here and the nice, straight pile she's folded her clothes into!* But Dora knew that in reality, there was nothing nice about it at all. It was her parents who had led Sonya to such meticulousness, and for them, no folded pile of clothes or slippers in their place were good enough. She would regularly get a smack for something that Dora considered tidied—but Sonya's mother didn't. Tom was the polar opposite. He would chuck all his clothes on the floor, pull on his pajamas inside out, and fall into bed. Dora's cousin was what the grown-ups called a miscreant. She didn't know what exactly that meant, but they probably meant to say that he misbehaved a lot. He gave the teacher a pretty hard time, and she often punished him by making him kneel in the corner as a time-out while the other children played. Sometimes, Astrid was the one kneeling in the opposite corner. And when by sheer accident they managed not to get in trouble for something they did together, she'd kneel in the corner anyway so he wouldn't be alone.

That day, Max had been cranky and sniffling since the morning. Astrid was helping him pull the pajama top over his head, speaking to him in a soothing voice. His dark, shaggy hair fell into his eyes.

"And now one arm," she urged him. "And the other one here. Awesome."

She flicked his nose, making him giggle. He crawled onto the cot, raising his arms obediently as Astrid pulled the covers all the way up to his neck. Only then did she begin to change. The teacher walked past and hurried her along nervously, telling her to get her head out of the clouds. Astrid made nothing of it and continued at her own unhurried pace. She was the last of the class to lie down.

She turned onto her right side, locking eyes with Dora. They liked to make believe that they could communicate this way with only their minds. It was nothing but a silly game, but it was fun to play. Most of the time, they'd make funny faces at each other and imitate the teacher's prissy expression when she'd read them a story. They had to cover their mouths with their hands to keep from giggling too loud and grabbing her attention.

But lately, something was different about Astrid. She didn't make silly faces at her. She didn't chuck pieces of lint from the bed linen at her. She just lay there and looked in front of her—when Dora was falling asleep, even if she woke up an hour later, Astrid was in the same exact position, her eyes staring straight ahead at something behind her, with an expression that revealed her mind was somewhere far away. Today, it was the same. She was looking right through Dora as if she weren't there. She wished she knew what her friend was thinking about.

The teacher was reading them the story about Little Red Riding Hood in that monotonous voice of hers, the excited whispers of the children gradually fading away. A quiet chitter could still be heard here and there, but one after another, they all eventually nodded off. Dora too could feel her eyelids getting heavier. Little

Red Riding Hood had just fallen into the wolf's trap when Dora let out a tired yawn and closed her eyes. The last thing she saw was Astrid's face. As Dora was falling asleep, in her mind she was wandering through the forest dressed in a little red riding hood.

It seemed like the moment she closed her eyes, something was urging her to open them again. Her mind was muddled. She hadn't slept that long, had she? She didn't feel rested yet. It was cozy and warm underneath the blanket and she definitely didn't want to get up. She blinked several times. It took her a while to understand what she was seeing.

She must've turned onto her other side in her sleep, and she saw that Tom and Sonya's beds were empty. She found that strange. Could she really have been asleep for so long, the others already having left for snack time? She turned over on her side, freezing in terror. Tall, black figures were leaning over the beds of Astrid and Max—boogeymen that were wrapping themselves around the kids' bodies. Dora couldn't utter a single sound, petrified as she was into silence. They were stretching their large arms toward Astrid and Max, their gaping mouths swallowing them as if they were just little bite-sized crackers.

Dora knew she should start screaming for help. But she couldn't do it; her voice got stuck in her throat. In that moment, one of the specters turned its head, as if it had heard her shaky gasp.

Dora screwed her eyes shut immediately. She clutched the blanket up around her neck in a viselike grip, praying to any and all of the gods out there for the boogeymen not to notice her, to leave her be.

She lay there and pretended to be asleep until the teacher came, calling for the class to wake up.

She kept pretending, even after their teacher started to shriek, yelling for Astrid, Max, Tom, and Sonya, looking for them everywhere. Dora sat up, a warm, wet puddle surrounding her. She'd peed herself out of fear. There were two empty beds to either side of her.

When the teacher shook her shoulders, asking where the others had disappeared to, she said the big bad wolf had swallowed them.

The present day

Even though Astrid had heard various versions of the events that had transpired in the past few days, none of them had affected her as much as Dora's. Perhaps because it was told through the eyes of a small, frightened child, or because Dora was visibly trembling at the mere memory.

"I know how it sounds," Dora whispered.

Astrid shook her head. "No... I... It's not like I don't believe you."

She did, she believed every word. But that didn't mean she was able to come to terms with reality. How could her nightmares have come alive? How come the others were able to see them too?

"Obviously I know it wasn't a real wolf," Dora blurted out, a blush creeping up her throat. "It was... I just remembered the fairytale, and I dunno, I was so young, and everybody was yelling at me, as if it were my fault..."

"What... What was it then?" Astrid urged her, trying to ignore the dull pain of the headache that suddenly overwhelmed her. "Describe it to me."

Her voice trembled. "It was... big, black... I think it was hovering over you, it had a big, long nose, or... I dunno, a beak, maybe?

And there were two of them. Maybe just one. It emitted this sound… this deafening sound, like…"

"Like the rustle of wings," Astrid finished for her.

"Yes!" Dora concurred. "The rustle of wings! You… You remember?"

Astrid massaged her temples. Black dots swam in front of her face. "I don't know, maybe…"

"You've gone pale as a ghost. You don't feel good?"

Dora grabbed Astrid's hands and led her to sit on a rickety old chair by the cowshed where Astrid remembered Dora's grandpa spent his summers, sitting and observing the animals. Astrid sat down, her eyes screwed shut. She tried to imagine what Dora had described to her, but her mind refused to.

"What happened next?"

"Astrid, you look terrible…"

"Just—go on."

Dora didn't push her. "When the teacher couldn't find you anywhere, she came back to the school and started to question us. I told her, I told her what I saw. But she kept claiming that I'd just been imagining things, that it was a dream, and that I'd gotten it all mixed up in my mind. My mom picked me up and took me home, and Auntie Hattler came in the evening. She was a sobbing mess, and she kept asking me what happened that day at school. I dunno why I did it, but if I could take it all back, I would."

Astrid began to get a feeling she knew what happened next.

"I told her what I saw. I described it to her. Mom and Pa were looking at me like I was crazy. Auntie latched onto it, she believed me. She wanted me to describe what happened again and again, she kept asking for details… And I was so scared, it got dark outside and I was terrified they'd come for me too. And as I kept having to repeat all of it, I… I peed myself again and started sobbing, too, until Pa started yelling, telling Auntie to shut up at once, saying she was just messing with my head. Auntie started to argue with him while Mom stood between them and then everybody was yelling at once. Pa threw her out and said that if she believed such nonsense, she wasn't welcome in the house ever again. Then he took me and beat me with a cane so hard I couldn't sit down for days. He said he'd beat the nonsense out of me if I didn't stop."

Astrid opened her eyes and squeezed her friend's hand with her own trembling one. But Dora didn't stop talking. It seemed the injustice had been eating away at her for too long and was clawing its way out.

"Then the Guards came to our house, I don't remember if it was the first day or not… Maybe later, and they asked me about what I had seen. Astrid… I'm so sorry, I really am. But Pa was sitting right next to me the entire time, and I couldn't bring myself to say anything, I was so scared he'd beat me again and kill me, and… If only you'd seen how the other kids treated me in kindergarten. They laughed at me that I was a bed-wetter, that I believed in ghosts, and… I just couldn't bring myself to tell the Guards…"

Dora wiped the tears from her cheeks with her bloodied hand covered in feathers.

"I'm so, so sorry… If I had told them what I really saw…"

"Then they wouldn't have found us anyway. Don't apologize—you were a terrified little girl."

"The entire village looked down on me. They would badmouth me, even in front of my parents. Saying I had lost my marbles. Batty Dory, they called me. I couldn't sleep at night. I would wake up every night from a nightmare, screaming, and for each sleepless night, I'd get a beating.

"And then, a few weeks later on a Saturday, my mother sent me in secret, behind Pa's back, to take some eggs and vegetables to the Hattlers. I took the long way, out back over the fields, hoping nobody would see me and tell my father at the pub. I didn't want him to get angry with Mom.

"As I was coming back, I ran into a group of older boys behind the cemetery. They were already in elementary school. I wanted to avoid them and pretended not to see them. But they called out, telling me to come over where they were, saying that they had... found something there—that I definitely had to see it, that surely I wasn't a scaredy cat.

"I knew that I should've avoided them, that the older boys were just making fun of me, but... by that point, I'd had it up to here. Everybody thought I was a liar and a crybaby. I had to prove—to myself especially—that I wasn't afraid.

"So I approached them. They were standing in a huddle, staring at something on the ground. I realized too late that I had made a mistake. They weren't looking at the ground, but into it—into an open grave. When I leaned over to look at what they'd found, one of them pushed me and I... fell in.

"I hit my head and landed on my back, knocking the wind out of me. I came to in a few moments. They were... standing over me, laughing in my face. 'Batty Dory. You see any ghosts down there? Maybe they'll come for you after dark and take you away.' I couldn't stand up on my leg, it hurt like crazy. It hurt like crazy because it was broken.

"And so I just lay there. They kept laughing, and began shoveling dirt and stones over me, and one of them... one of them pulled down his pants and peed all over me."

"Dory..." Astrid didn't know what to say.

"I begged them to pull me out of there. Instead, they covered the dug-out hole with a wooden lid and left me there. As I lay there in the freezing cold, in the dark, my mouth full of dirt, I was terrified that if I called out for help, they'd come back and it would be even worse.

"It wasn't until the next morning that they finally found me. I could hear people walking around, calling out my name, but I couldn't bring myself to respond. It's as if someone had stolen my voice. It wasn't until it occurred to the gravedigger to lift the wooden lid the next day that they found me. I was suffering from hypothermia, and I spent several weeks in bed with a broken leg and pneumonia. The entire village knew who had done this to me. But they acted as if nothing had happened. As if I deserved it for saying the things I said.

"And so I stopped talking. Completely. For a long time. And the others thought I had gone insane for good, but at least they finally left me alone."

Astrid had listened to the whole, hair-raising story with goose-bumps prickling her arms. All the words Dora had uttered during their fight a few days ago suddenly made so much sense. *I'd rather have disappeared as well than have to stay here!*

"I can't imagine what you've been through. I'm so sorry," Astrid eventually said, though she couldn't shake the feeling that they were just empty words.

Dora didn't react, just stared off into the woods, absorbed in thought.

"Well, I can't imagine what all of you have been through."

"The worst part is that a part of me doesn't even want to re-member," Astrid admitted out loud. "But I have to. For Max."

Something that Astrid had said convinced Dora to glance at her. "What do you mean?"

"If I manage to find out what happened to us, then… I want to find him, no matter where he is."

"What can I do to help?"

Dora really meant it, too, and said it automatically, as if it were a given. It almost made Astrid cry.

"I'm serious," Dora assured her. "I'll help you find Max, wherever he is. I know that if it were the other way around, if one of my brothers… You'd do the same for me."

"I… I know it sounds weird, but you might be the only one who won't be looking down on me, especially after what you just told me." Astrid drew in a shaky breath. "What you saw… It was my nightmares. I've had sleep paralysis since I was just a kid. And those… creatures… appear to me. But I'm afraid they're not just a figment of my imagination, they're real… And every night, they prevent me from remembering what happened all those years ago. I can't… fall asleep. And I think the key to all this is in my mind, in my memories."

And then Dora, hands on her hips, uttered something that ignited hope in Astrid: "You could try bypassing your mind. You could try hypnosis."

"If none of you are gonna say it, I will. This is insane."

Tom was perched on the windowsill in his room, his eyes darting from Astrid to Dora and back again, as if he couldn't believe what his two friends had just told him.

Astrid had insisted on Dora coming with her. She didn't force her to tell the story in its entirety, so she wouldn't have to relive those horrors again. Together, they managed to recount the bare essentials.

"You mean you don't believe me?" Dora asked softly.

"I didn't mean it that way." Tom shook his head. "I mean that... Maybe it makes sense but also doesn't at the same time."

A confused expression appeared on Dora's face. She looked at Astrid, as if she'd have the explanation. For it being only noon, Astrid's fatigue was growing, and she felt more tired by the minute.

When her friend provided no answer, Dora admitted defeat. "I don't know what you mean, Tom."

He started tapping his fingers against the windowsill, perhaps to put his own thoughts in order. "I... I don't remember much, just flashes... But whatever it was, it keeps coming back to me in my dreams at night, so..."

That caught Astrid's attention. "You have nightmares?"

He shrugged uneasily. "Can't fall asleep, more like. I have weird dreams that I don't remember in the morning. That hypnosis plan just might work out. But it's insane. How can you know which of the things you see are real?"

"You don't have to do it," Astrid immediately countered.

"Are you crazy? Of course I'll do it."

Tom's resolve warmed Astrid's heart, but she couldn't help but start to have doubts. Tom wasn't willing to admit what Astrid was giving more and more consideration. He didn't see, or didn't want to see, what was absolutely evident—that neither Gusto nor any other person had been the cause of their disappearance. It was rather something that couldn't be described with reason.

"Do we have a plan?" Tom asked. "Or...?"

Astrid spoke up. "I thought we could go see the doctor that was tending to us. He could help us with the hypnosis, right? Or recommend someone else."

Tom looked doubtful. "I guess. But he didn't seem to me like someone who really recognizes hypnosis as a legit medical discipline. He was all facts and dictionary entries. And I don't know about you, but there was something off about him."

Astrid wanted to object to that, but then she recalled the doctor's tone when he'd spoken to her. Tom was probably right. She didn't like the thought of him putting her through any more tests.

"Any other ideas?" she asked instead. "How is this done normally? Do we just look in the classifieds for a local hypnotist...?"

She almost laughed at her poor attempt at a joke.

"You think there's one out there?" Tom said with an amused smirk. "In the circus performance section? Right below the palm readers?"

"I'm glad you find this so funny."

"I might... I might have a solution," Dora suddenly piped up, interrupting their joking around. "When... that thing... happened and I stopped speaking, Mom tried everything, and I mean everything. She took me to see someone like that... some woman," she explained. "That's why it crossed my mind."

"Are you joking?" Tom asked.

"No." She shook her head. "Just... It wasn't any use. Which wasn't her fault. I just didn't *want* to speak. That's what the problem was. I could speak if I wanted to, they didn't have to look for any other cause. It was my decision."

"Do you remember where she lived?" Astrid blurted out. "We could go visit her!"

Dora shrugged, a sheepish expression on her face. "It was so long ago..."

"Is there any way to find out who it was?" Tom chose his words carefully, clearly not wanting to broach any touchy subject.

"I don't know. I don't think Mom ever told anyone about it.

There's no way she told my father. But she must've learned about her somehow."

"Maybe she was recommended to your mom by someone in the village," Astrid suggested. "She must've gone to someone for advice…"

"She wasn't on speaking terms with most people here." Dora obviously had her doubts. "Back then, everyone saw her as having that weird kid at home that everyone avoided. Except for—"

"My mom," Tom completed the sentence for her, looking just as surprised as she was as they both arrived at the same conclusion. "My mom kept talking to her."

"It would make sense." Dora nodded in agreement. "But it's still just a guess, of course."

Astrid locked eyes with Tom. She didn't have to say anything. They were on the same page.

"I'll talk to her," Tom promised. "She should be back any minute now. She just stopped by to visit the neighbors."

"I have to get back home," Dora sighed uneasily. "If Pa found out… Well, you saw yourself what he's like."

"I'll go with you," Astrid offered. "And I don't mean home," she quickly added when she saw the confusion on Dora's face. "I'll just walk with you."

Astrid felt that Tom would rather speak to his mom alone. She didn't want to put him in an awkward position by sticking around.

"We'll meet up in the afternoon?"

"Yeah, I'll come to your house."

Astrid wondered whether she should warn him about her family, but she finally figured words couldn't prepare someone for the likes of her grandmother. They said their goodbyes, and Astrid headed out with Dora into the blindingly sunny day.

"My father…" Dora started in a shaky voice after they'd been walking alone for some time. "He wasn't… After my mom…"

The rest of her sentence disappeared as she got lost in her own thoughts.

"Don't apologize for your family," Astrid interrupted. "You don't choose your family."

"Sometimes I feel like it's not family that's to blame," Dora said as she pulled her coat closer to her body, as if to protect herself. "But this place. This village."

Astrid understood what she meant. "People retain the values they're born into. The problem is that the values here have always been pretty skewed, and not all of us are willing to blindly adhere to them. And that's punished here."

Dora gave her a weak smile. "Astrid… I want to help you. If there's anything I can do for you…"

A thought suddenly struck Astrid. "Do you know all the people who live in the village well?"

"Pretty much," she replied. "I help out in the store on the weekends. Almost everybody shops there."

"I'm looking for someone. I don't know their name. An old lady, petite, barely able to walk. She's blind and has glass eyes, both of them are."

Dora thought for a second, but she didn't react the way Astrid had hoped she would. "I've never seen anybody like that…"

"That's okay. Thanks anyway."

"Maybe she just doesn't go to town," Dora tried to assure her. "I can try to ask tomorrow at work."

"That would be great."

They split up at the main road, and Dora continued in the opposite direction into the fields, while Astrid's house was just a stone's throw away. With head bowed, she walked past the memorial the village had erected in their memory. She was almost home when she suddenly glimpsed a flash of movement in one of the side alleys. She turned to look and saw someone she wasn't expecting. As soon as the man saw her, he turned on his heel, his coat swirling with the movement, and disappeared among the dumpsters.

"Hey!" Astrid shouted. "Wait!"

She picked up her pace. The alley between the houses was cramped and dirty. Astrid squeezed between dumpsters and old junk just lying around and found herself in a spot where the corners of four old houses met, forming a sort of small crossroads. The man stood underneath one of the gutters, the collar of his coat pulled up to his nose.

Astrid stopped a good ways away from him. She wasn't sure how the man was going to react, and she wanted to keep a clear path ahead of her, just in case she needed to make a getaway.

"You're Gusto, right?"

The right side of the man's face twitched. She couldn't tell whether it was to signal confirmation or it was a nervous tic. He wouldn't look her directly in the eye, and his restless gaze flitted every which way. Astrid was immediately able to remember what had seemed so disturbing about him when she was a kid. The past years hadn't been kind to him, and he was gaunt and unkempt. He looked much older than he probably really was.

"I'm Astrid." She gestured toward him uncertainly. What was the proper way to speak to someone accused of your abduction?

Gusto suddenly turned on his heel and started to walk along between the houses.

"Wait!" she shouted. "I know you didn't do it!"

He stopped but didn't look back. She couldn't be sure he was listening to her, but she hoped he was.

"I know that you didn't hurt those kids, that you didn't kidnap them."

He turned his head a fraction to the side. And all of a sudden, he spoke in a husky voice. "It wasn't human."

Astrid tensed. "What d'you mean?"

His head jerked several times, a tic pulling his neck in one direction. "It wasn't… It wasn't human."

"You know who did it?"

He was silent for so long that Astrid thought he might not have understood her.

But then, he replied with a question. "Where do we go when we fall asleep?"

"What—"

Astrid was cut off by a bang. She whipped around, spotting a trashcan on its side in the alleyway. It must've keeled over suddenly. The metal lid rolled away to her feet. It all happened in a flash, but by the time she looked back, Gusto was gone.

"Don't just stand there. Come help me."

Valeria Hattler was lying on the bathroom tiles, grappling with the metal hatch on the side of the bathtub, trying to pry it open. The floor was flooded with water. Tom entered the bathroom, his socks immediately drenched.

"What happened?"

"It's been acting up again."

Together, they managed to pry the hatch open after several tries.

A putrid stench assaulted their noses. The drainpipe was all rusted and leaky. And it clearly wasn't a new issue—in several places, all that was holding it all together was duct tape. Valeria obviously noticed the look Tom was giving her.

"I can't afford a new one. I'll call for someone later to come take a look at it."

She grabbed the duct tape and scissors from the sink and began to wrap the drainpipe in a fresh layer of the temporary fix. Tom knew this wasn't the best occasion, but he doubted one would present itself today.

"Can I ask you something?"

"Of course," she said.

Tom could hear the slight hesitance in her voice, as if she wasn't sure in which direction the conversation was going to go and how that uncertainty made her feel.

"When we disappeared, Dora stopped speaking for some time."

"That's true." She nodded. "But that's not a question."

Tom gave her a faint smile. "She told us that Auntie Lautner took her to see a hypnotist."

Tom's mother tore off another piece of duct tape before speaking. "She tried everything... even this."

"Do you remember how she found her? Where did she live?"

She lifted her head, locking eyes with him. "Why?"

"We think she might help us remember. We want to go see her."

A silence filled the room, interrupted only by the repetitive dripping. Tom shifted his weight uneasily, the water squelching under his feet.

"That's not a good idea," his mother finally said.

He was expecting a reaction like this. "I know it's hard for you to get used to, but I'm an adult. I decide for myself now."

She let out a disdainful chuckle. "You don't know anything about being an adult. You're still a child. You haven't matured a single day from the moment you disappeared. Don't you get it, Tom? It's experience that makes you an adult, not age."

Her words hurt him. "Maybe you're right," he admitted. "But at the end of the day, it's my decision."

"Yours or Astrid's?"

"What's that supposed to mean?"

"That it seems like that girl's a bad influence."

Tom gritted his teeth. "I can make my own decisions. Mom, I know you're worried about me. But I'm gonna go through with the hypnosis, whether you like it or not. I'd appreciate your help and support. I have to find out what really happened, but I understand if you don't."

She hunched back over the pipes again, fiddling around. "Fine, if that's what you want... The charlatan my sister sought out wasn't any sort of doctor. She was a regular farmwife, a rozhanitsa."

Tom felt his whole chest swell with excitement. He'd heard about rozhanitsy as a boy, and it was said they had special magical powers. His mother, though, saw them as tricksters who boiled tea from poisonous mushrooms and passed off their hallucinations as prophecies. Even so, Tom remembered the respect with which the others had regarded the rozhanitsy. It couldn't have just been the magic mushrooms.

"Does she still live in the village?"

She mumbled something, but he didn't catch what. It sounded like a muffled invective and a sigh all at once.

"Mom?"

"Maybe," she replied reluctantly. "But I'm warning you it's not a good idea, and I'm telling you I don't approve."

Something in her voice convinced him that she wanted him to change his mind at the last minute. But it was already too late for that.

"Tell me everything," he requested.

When Astrid, Dora, and Tom were still kids, the Elders were the ones who dictated the rules for the whole village, and everybody knew that. The Elders were the ones to settle disputes between neighbors. The ones who decided whether to tear down the old mill when it was in serious disrepair, a danger to passersby. The ones who sanctioned marriages and blessed newborns. They were made up of midwives and experienced healers, while some were said to foresee the future. Girls came to them to find out if and when they'd get married, while farmers received advice on what kind of crops to expect. They initiated all the village rituals and customs, they led all the communal ceremonies, and they had always had a higher social status than the others—more estates and property, nicer houses. The Elders were the unappointed rulers of not only the village, but also the surrounding settlements.

According to the legends, they were the descendants of the original seven families that had built the first houses here so many years ago and begun living by the rules that were respected and observed to this day. Many generations later, though, newcomers arrived and began to question the faith. Only a very few individuals remained whom the others called the Elders out of habit and respect. But with each passing year, their control gradually grew weaker and weaker. Or at least most of the villagers believed so.

It was despite or because of this that Astrid couldn't help feeling slightly nervous. Naturally, she felt scared that they might be a mere small step away from discovering the truth. But also concerned that the Elder might turn them away and they might lose their chance. Both emotions grappled with each other inside her as Tom tentatively reached for the ancient doorknocker. Even he was nervous, and she could see his hand trembling. But there were other circumstances playing a role in this for him.

"Are you okay?" she asked him.

Instead of answering, he went ahead and knocked. The sun, stained a bright red, was slowly setting behind the rooftops. Astrid gazed into the last of its rays, which were, to her, both terrifying and beautiful at once, as they symbolized the approaching nighttime.

The door slowly swung open, a tall man appearing in the doorway. His bushy, dark eyebrows converged into a single line above his nose, and when he spotted them, it jumped from a suspicious frown into a surprised arch. He looked like he was completely caught off guard.

"Hi Dad," Tom broke the silence.

His father tensed at the expression and didn't respond. Astrid didn't know where to look. She felt awkward, and could imagine how much more so it was for Tom.

"Don't worry, I'm not here to see you," her friend continued. "We came to see your wife. We want to make use of the talents of a rozhanitsa."

He scrutinized them as if he were expecting some sort of funny business. His eyes flitted from Tom to Astrid and back, glancing behind them at the street to see if anyone could see them.

"Whaddaya want from 'er?" he finally asked in a harsh voice.

"That's between us and her."

"I'll have to ask 'er first. Come in so nobody sees ya."

They squeezed into a small hallway. Tom's father left them standing there in the gloom and disappeared somewhere into the house. Astrid didn't dare say anything. She wasn't sure if or who could be listening, so she decided it was better not to risk it. It didn't take long for the sound of voices to reach them from the back of the house—the muted voices of a man and a woman. They were clearly discussing something, but she couldn't make out a single word. Astrid could feel how Tom was squirming beside her. She wanted to calm him down somehow, but couldn't think of the right words. After several never-ending minutes, a young woman appeared in the hallway. They'd spotted her the day before on the street—the wife of Tom's father. She looked furious, her cheeks aflame. Several strands of her hair had fallen out of her bun and were now hanging around her shoulders every which way. Astrid couldn't get the impression that she looked like a younger copy of Tom's mother out of her head.

"So you're looking for the help of a rozhanitsa." The way she said it made it sound more like an attack than a question.

Tom kept quiet, his jaw locked. He looked like he was doing all he could to hold back. Astrid realized he must've noticed the similarities as well.

She decided to take matters into her own hands. "We want to undergo hypnosis, and that's something that the rozhanitsy can do, right?"

The woman narrowed her eyes. "You've come for someone else then," she said. "You're lookin' for my ma. She's the one who devotes herself to the advanced teachings of the rozhanitsy. My abilities aren't enough for what you need, I'm still a novice."

"And will your mother see us?"

"Ya got money?"

"Yes," Astrid lied. In reality, she didn't have any money, but she refused to give up now that she was so close. She'd pay with her own blood if she had to.

"My ma's upstairs. She'll decide herself if you're worth her time."

The woman began to ascend a steep, wooden staircase, and they were right behind her. They had to walk up one by one, holding onto the banister, because they wouldn't otherwise fit. On the first floor, they walked down a hallway. The door to the room at the very end of the hall was slightly ajar.

The woman knocked and opened the door.

"A client here to see ya, Ma."

Astrid and Tom stood hesitantly in the doorway. The bedroom was small and murky, with dark, heavy drapes covering the window. A wooden table stood in the middle of the room, upon it a burning candle. An older woman was sitting at the table, observing them intently, as if she'd been expecting them this whole time.

"They're just kids," she rasped without looking at them too closely.

Her daughter nodded. "I know, but they say they got money."

"They're lying."

Astrid had heard many things about the rozhanitsy, half of which were probably made-up stories. But one thing was always the same—they were women born with the divine gift of clairvoyance who could foresee the future or predict the weather. They were happy to lend their services to their neighbors for a small fee. Without exception, the rozhanitsy brought up their firstborn daughters to follow the teachings of their mothers, as sons didn't inherit their gift. Together, these women would go offer their blessings to newborn children in the village, wishing them all the best in life. But the measure of the favorability of their fate rested on how much money the new parents paid.

Everybody knew it wasn't good to antagonize or anger the rozhanitsy in any way. So Astrid decided it would be easier to just tell the truth.

"I lied. I don't have any money."

She could feel Tom's eyes on her. Even his stepmother was looking at her with reproach, any traces of politeness long gone.

But the rozhanitsa didn't yell at her or cast her immediately out of the house.

"You're the daughter of Lena Kwiatkowska," she said instead.

Astrid nodded. "That was my mother's maiden name."

It was strange that the woman remembered her mom's name like that. Her mother had hardly been of age when she got married, and it wasn't until after the wedding that she moved to the village from a nearby settlement.

"My name is Astrid Mahler."

The woman raised her hand. "I know who you are. I know who he is too." She pointed to Tom.

Tom's stepmother fidgeted in the doorway. Clearly, she wasn't thrilled by the presence of her husband's son from his first marriage.

"I'll receive you," the rozhanitsa declared eventually.

"But Ma—"

One look was all it took for the woman to fall silent. She bowed her head obediently and left. In a moment, they could hear her footsteps upon the creaking stairs. The rozhanitsa gestured for Astrid and Tom to enter the room.

"Take a seat."

They both sat down dutifully on the rickety wooden chairs in front of the table. In that exact moment, the door behind their backs clicked shut. Tom started and glanced over his shoulder, but Astrid's eyes stayed warily fixed upon the old woman.

"You came for help but don't have any money to pay for my services. Tell me, are ye that stupid, or just bold?"

"Neither," Astrid assured her.

"We're desperate, if anything," Tom added.

The rozhanitsa clicked her tongue. Astrid noticed that she was rolling around some herbs in her nearly toothless mouth. In the dim light of the room, she looked older than she really was, and the unflattering flicker of candlelight made her wrinkles all the more noticeable. She looked like she'd lived dozens of lives.

"Where are the others?" she asked.

"The others?"

"Four children vanished." She held up four fingers. "But I only see the two of you."

"Sonya's at the doctor's place and still hasn't woken up," Astrid said. "My younger brother didn't reappear with us."

The woman finished chewing the herbs and then spit out the contents of her mouth into a chipped porcelain cup. Astrid had to hold back from shuddering in disgust.

"The Foreth girl is awake," the woman calmly informed them. "She woke up this morning."

"What?" Tom couldn't hide his surprise.

"How do you know that?" Astrid added.

The woman didn't answer. Instead, she asked her own question. "Why did you come here?"

Astrid didn't know where to start. Whether to ask about Sonya or the things that had led them here.

"They say the rozhanitsy can delve into people's minds," she started to speak in general. "Neither of us can really remember what happened to us. The doctor said it might just be temporary memory loss. But it could also be permanent. We need to remember. We want to get our memories back by means of hypnosis."

"You do?"

"Yes." Astrid nodded.

The woman leaned in closer to her. "Do you really want to, lass?"

She sensed a warning in the question, as if, unlike them, the woman could see and realize some sort of intangible threat, but couldn't warn them of it directly.

"I'm positive," Astrid replied, her tone now less assured.

The woman got up from the table, slowly walked over to a small cupboard in the corner of the room, and began preparing something, facing away from them. Astrid couldn't see what she was doing. But soon, the fragrance of herbs and flowers was wafting through the room. She heard the hiss of water right before it reached its boiling point on the stove, and the crack of an egg. A few seconds later, the woman returned to the table, carrying a small enameled saucepan. She poured boiling water over the chewed-up contents of the cup she'd spit in earlier. An unpleasant smell spread throughout the room. The rozhanitsa then pulled a pair of scissors out of her apron and drew closer to Astrid's face. She didn't budge, though she felt the urge to. The old woman snipped off a lock of Astrid's dark hair. She deftly tied it up with red string and positioned it over the burning candle. While she looked on as the hair burned, she began repeatedly mumbling something unintelligible. The lock of hair went up in flames almost at once. Only when the very end was still intact and she was in danger of getting burned did the woman throw it into the cup. She took a spoon and stirred the liquid inside the cup several times—first clockwise, then counterclockwise.

"Here, drink this." She handed Astrid the cup.

Astrid looked at its contents with suspicion. It resembled sludge. Though the liquid was no longer boiling, bubbles kept breaking through to the surface as if it were. She didn't even have to lean in to smell how it stank. It was making her stomach churn.

"Drink," the woman urged her once more.

Astrid's eyes locked with Tom's. He didn't look like he wanted to switch places. She decided it would be better to just get it over with. She opened her mouth and drank the contents of the cup in two gulps. She could feel the sludge sliding down her throat and started to cough.

"Swallow it."

When Astrid swallowed the last of the concoction, she began to feel woozy.

The woman placed her arms on the table. Her sleeves were rolled up, revealing the ancient, intricate symbols tattooed into her old, wrinkled skin—symbols that Astrid hadn't seen for ages, only on the Elders. The rozhanitsa turned over her arms and grasped Astrid by the palms of her hands. Her touch was like ice. She examined Astrid's hands in hers, and soon began to act strangely, as if she'd detected something that she couldn't tell her—and didn't even want to. The silence that fell over them stretched on until it was almost unbearable. With each passing minute, Astrid felt more and more exhausted. Her eyelids grew heavier. When the rozhanitsa finally spoke out loud, she almost jumped up in alarm.

"Is your brother worth it?" the woman asked.

Astrid replied without a second thought. "He's my brother."

"Maybe he doesn't want you to find him."

"I have to."

The woman ran her fingers over Astrid's palms repeatedly, as if she were rippling the water's surface in an attempt to peer through to the bottom of a pond, but the more she probed, the more impervious the darkness grew.

"Even at the cost of getting yourself killed?"

Tom whispered her name. Astrid didn't know whether it was a silent plea or a warning. She ignored him.

"No matter the cost."

In that moment, Astrid felt a strangely wet warmth spreading over the back of her neck. Her head started to droop. Whatever it was the woman had made her drink, it was starting to kick in.

"Hypnosis isn't sleep, dear. You don't have to be afraid," the woman told her.

Astrid didn't even bother asking how she knew about her fear. That's just the way the rozhanitsy were.

"Heed my words. Focus on what I'm saying. If your thoughts begin to stray, bring yourself back to what I'm saying. Allow everything that's about to happen to run its course. Close your eyes, lass. Take a deep breath. And now breathe out."

Her voice was compelling, and soon, it filled every crevice of Astrid's mind, leaving no room for anything else. She listened to it and slowly began to fall asleep, even though she didn't want to. But for once, her fear of falling asleep was less than her desire to sleep.

"Try to relax more. Focus on relieving the tension in your muscles. Start with your right leg. You feel the tension leaving you… Now your left leg…"

Any sort of self-defense was futile, and she gradually stopped fighting it. Her body was growing slack, and she felt like a rag doll that had slumped into the chair, slouching there powerlessly.

"Inhale into every single particle of your body... Hold the air in as long as you can... And slowly exhale... Until you expel it all..."

Astrid's consciousness was falling in on itself, deep into an unknown world where she had buried her greatest fears and worst memories.

"Recall that fateful day, lass... What do you see?"

All of a sudden, Astrid was standing in the pitch dark. Gradually, images began to emerge from the darkness like out of a fog—people were growing up out of the ground around her, their features sharpening with each passing moment. But she still didn't see anything clearly. Except for...

"The white rabbit," she muttered in surprise as the creature appeared at her feet. *Where did it come from?*

"*Ān*... Follow the white rabbit, Astrid... Go after it... *Tu*."

She took a step forward. The small rabbit was leaping its way through impassable brushwood too slowly, constantly coming across more and more obstacles, as if disoriented. She was crouching behind an uprooted tree, her fingers digging into the tree bark as she fixed her eyes on the rabbit.

"You're falling into a deep slumber... *Þrēo*... *Fēoper*... *Fīf*... Deeper and deeper."

She could catch it with her bare hands if she wanted to. All she'd have to do was jump over the tree trunk, take two, maybe three quick steps, and grab it by its silky fur. She tensed in anticipation when she suddenly heard a sharp cry.

She glanced over her shoulder. "Max?"

"*Seox*... *Seofon*... *Eahta*... You're now asleep. In a moment, you will go back to being six years old. Everything that happened

192

afterward is gone. As soon as I touch your forehead, you will be a child once more. You'll return to the moment right before you vanished. *Nigon... Tien.*"

Astrid was standing in the middle of nowhere. The rabbit was gone.

"You won't wake up until I tell you to."

It was as if someone had launched her through the air to twelve years ago. She landed back in the moment that she hadn't remembered until now, or that she thought she'd forgotten, but it emerged nevertheless like a perfect photograph.

"Astrid... What do you see...?"

She couldn't tell where the voice of the rozhanitsa was coming from—she could've been standing right next to her, or speaking to her from the heavens like Svarog, or whispering inside her head—Astrid had no idea.

"It's Passion Sunday," she answered. "I see smierć. Death."

Words she hadn't used for years naturally rolled off her tongue once more.

She was outside, in the village. It was getting dark. But she wasn't afraid. More than anything else, her feelings resembled irrepressible excitement. She was allowed to be outside after dark. It was the first time her mother had let her. And she was taking part in the procession. She had never been allowed to before, even though this celebration had always belonged to the young. The older girls would always use thatch to put together an effigy of Death—Morana, as she was called in these parts. Singing traditional songs, they would ceremoniously dress Morana in the shirt of the last person to have died in the village and adorn her with the bridal veil from the most recent wedding. The girl who was deemed the most robust then received the honor of carrying the effigy of Morana at the head of the procession.

To Astrid, this custom seemed humiliating—it wasn't an honor. The others usually picked a girl who was too tall, too hefty, or simply unattractive. They'd single her out from the community this way, letting her know just what it was they thought of her. She wouldn't want to be in her place.

"Astrid... What can you hear?"

She perked her ears.

"Singing."

Astrid joined in on the traditional folk song with the others.

"We carry out Death, we bring in the spring, just as Passion Sunday begins..."

People came out of their houses and stood by the road. They stood there in silence, intently watching the procession pass by. Side by side, they formed a long, endless line that seemed to show the procession the way to go, out of the village.

The girl carrying Morana was walking a few dozen feet ahead of the procession. All of a sudden, the first stone was flung from the crowd of spectators, followed by another. Even though Astrid was ready for it, the brutishness of the act caught her off guard every single time. The villagers threw sticks and rocks at Morana, showing their aversion toward her. *Winter, begone! Death, begone!* Sometimes, a rock would miss its mark, and instead of hitting the effigy would hit the girl carrying it. Her task, however, was to persevere, no matter how painful the blows got.

For the villagers, casting Death out of the village symbolized not only the beginning of a new season, but also the purging of all the old and evil in anticipation of new life. It also had the role of protection—from human and animal sickness alike, from fires and droughts.

"We carry out Death. Summer's in town. Welcome, sweet summer, with your green crown."

"Who's there with you, Astrid?"

She looked around. The girls in the procession were dressed in brown tartan skirts and coats, their braided hair crowned with wreaths made of dried lichen, berries, and pine cones. The boys marched in attire that resembled a uniform. Their headdress was somewhat less ornate, a twine of dried willow sprigs adorned by the antlers shed by young stags. The youngest children carried long, white candles that illuminated their excited faces. As the procession passed, the onlookers gradually began to join in, creating a second procession in the wake of the children. In a few minutes, the entire village was walking side by side in the parade.

"Max."

Astrid clutched her candle with one hand while the other held onto her brother, who could barely keep up with the others. Unlike the others, she wasn't singing, just pretending to as she opened her mouth from time to time. The crowd genuinely fascinated her. They were marching along like soldiers going to war. Suddenly, Max tripped over his own feet and stumbled for a moment. They would've almost fallen out of formation if it weren't for someone catching them from behind at the last minute. Astrid looked over her shoulder. Tom, her savior, gave her a small smile. An image of them immediately crossed her mind, the memory of them secretly climbing a tree in kindergarten a few days ago to hide from their teacher, who combed the garden for them in vain. When she finally found them, they both had to kneel in the corner all afternoon as punishment. There was always fun to be had with Tom, who never cared about being punished for misbehaving. Astrid returned his smile and quickly looked ahead once more.

"Describe what's happening…"

The procession left the village and was now walking over the field. The soil underneath their feet was still hardened and frozen. When they reached the valley with the river, they formed a line along the riverbank. Their singing echoed off of the surrounding cliffs. The flickering candlelight created fantastic images as the sun set, scaring the youngest children. The ravine wasn't very deep, but even so, Astrid realized with awe just how dangerous the rushing water of the river was. The singing ceased. The girl at the head of the line lifted the effigy of Morana a bit higher and began to recite something.

"Nobody's noticed her," Astrid said, surprised.

"Noticed who?"

Astrid's mother had explained to her that throwing Morana into the river didn't annihilate Death and winter, but merely sent them back to the underworld, to which the water served as a portal.

"Morana. Nobody's noticed that she's really here among us."

Astrid was absolutely certain of this. She could see her on the opposite bank. A woman in black, fixing them with an unwavering gaze.

The crowd yelled out as one—to the children, it sounded like the roar of a mighty dragon. The effigy of Morana soared through the air and landed in the river. The current immediately carried her away. People pulled rocks out of their pockets and threw them at Death floating by, attempting to drown her. Even Max joined in on the efforts, but his pebble barely made it over the bank into the water.

The excitement grew. Morana floated by the last remaining villagers lining the riverbank and disappeared under the bridge. The wind picked up. The flames of the candles flickered wildly for a second, lighting up the pale, anxious faces of the villagers, before suddenly leaving them at the mercy of darkness. The sound of a tolling bell from a far-off village reached their ears, announcing the evening prayers. As soon as the last candle flickered out, everyone turned and broke into a run back to the village. The uneasy calmness suddenly evaporated.

"Come on, hurry!" Astrid urged her baby brother along.

But the sudden mass hysteria of the crowd had startled Max. He was frozen to the spot and didn't understand what was happening. People were coming at them from all sides.

"Max!"

"Astrid… Talk to me… What's going on?"

Astrid, who had managed to take a few steps, quickly rushed back for him. She wasn't strong enough to pick Max up, he was too heavy for her, so she just grabbed his hand.

"Come on, we gotta hurry! Or we'll be left behind!"

"But why?"

She didn't waste any time explaining. They stumbled along after the others. Already, the crowd was dispersing into smaller groups and lone runners. The more able-bodied individuals were already long gone over the hill, while many parents were helping their younger children along, running with them in their arms. Astrid didn't see her mother anywhere, so they had no choice but to help each other and hope it would be enough.

"I can't," Max started to whine after a while.

Their feet were sinking deep into the trodden furrows of the field.

"Just a bit farther! Come on, you can do it!"

In the meantime, darkness had descended upon the land. Astrid's heart was in her mouth, pounding wildly. She didn't know if it was because of physical exertion or fear. The others had disappeared out of sight. They ran as fast as they could. At the forefront of Astrid's mind was the saying that whoever made it to the village last, Morana would take them away within the next year.

And suddenly, Astrid felt—knew—that Morana had caught up with them.

"Astrid!"

Max's hand slipped out of her grip as Astrid fell to the ground on her hands and knees. She whipped around immediately. A tall figure in black was leaning over her, hair streaming wildly, limbs tightly wrapped around Max's body. She picked him up from the ground, tightening her grip on him.

"Max!"

Astrid scrambled to her feet and grasped her brother's hands, which were stretched toward her, as he cried hysterically.

"Let him go!" she screamed.

She planted her feet into the ground in a naïve, blind belief that it would be enough. But the figure began to drag them both along.

"Give in, Astrid," a thousand voices were whispering in her ear.

"Never!"

The ground beneath their feet trembled and split open. With Max in its arms, the specter began to disappear into the bowels of the earth. Astrid could feel her brother's small hands slipping out of her sweaty grasp. She knew she was a moment away from losing her brother forever. She fell to her knees in the mud, her knees quivering with exertion.

"He's ours."

No!

Right before the ground swallowed the both of them, Astrid could feel someone grabbing her coat and pulling her back, so she wouldn't end up in the ground too. The figure screeched. She took advantage of the distraction and grabbed Max by the collar as someone pulled them both out. They all fell on the ground in one big heap.

Astrid, a blubbering Max, Tom Hattler, and Sonya Foreth. All four of them were gasping for air and staring at the spot where the specter had vanished not a moment ago in total shock.

"What was that?" Sonya cried out. "What happened?"

"We gotta go," Tom decided at once. "Come on. Get up. We gotta get to the village before the sun sets completely."

He helped Astrid to her feet, they both grabbed Max by the hand, and all four of them, petrified, dashed off toward the village.

"Astrid. Astrid… Wake up… Before I count to ten, you're going to wake up."

The rozhanitsa's voice was getting clearer by the minute.

"Astrid!" Max tugged on her sleeve. "Don't leave me here! Astrid!"

"*Ān… tu… Þrēo… fēoper… fīf…* You're slowly waking up… *seox… seofon… eahta…* You're coming to. *Nigon… tīen.* Wake up."

Astrid shot up in her chair so abruptly that her hands crashed into the table and overturned the candle, which rolled onto the floor, spilling hot wax on both her and the rozhanitsa.

"Astrid, you're okay, you're safe!"

Tom was by her side in a flash, laying a comforting hand on her arm.

"W-What happened?"

Her heart was trying to burst out of her chest and she had a splitting headache, as if she'd been holding her breath the entire time, her lungs screaming for oxygen.

"You were…" Tom glanced nervously at the rozhanitsa. "You were… I'm not actually sure…"

"You're very hypnotizable," the old woman murmured, lost in thought. "It's rare for hypnosis to work right away like that, but in your case, it did… What did you see?"

Astrid blinked. The room was blurry, as if submerged in fog. "I…"

"You weren't answering my questions. You were ignoring my voice. You pushed me out of your mind. I've never seen anything like it."

Give in, Astrid.

She looked over her shoulder. The voice brushed her ear like the rustle of butterfly wings. It was like someone was standing right behind her.

"What did you put in my mind?" she answered with a question. "What did you make me see?"

The rozhanitsa narrowed her eyes. "The truth, lass. Only the truth."

Chaos exploded in her mind. It was as if someone had turned a key in a lock and opened some hidden door. One memory after another began to flood in.

"Astrid." Tom sounded worried. "What's going on?"

"It doesn't make sense," she blurted out. "What… What I saw. It doesn't make any sense."

And yet she was sure that's how it had really happened all those years ago. But what did the events of the ceremony have to do with their disappearance? Did Morana really come for them the very next day?

"I want to go back!" Astrid said in a resolute tone. "Let me go back, right now!"

"No." The rozhanitsa shook her head. "Your mind has to rest."

"But I have to!" She slammed the palms of her hands onto the table a bit more aggressively than she'd intended to.

The rozhanitsa gave her a meaningful look. "No, Astrid. That's enough for today. Leave my house."

Tom tried to lift her from the chair gently, but Astrid kept sitting in her spot, a stubborn look upon her face. She refused to give up so easily.

"Please, you don't understand... I have to go back, I have to know what happened..."

But the woman didn't move a muscle, making it known that she had no intention of discussing it further.

Eventually, Astrid had no choice but to let Tom pull her to her feet and lead her first out of the room and then out of the house itself. She stumbled on the steep stairway several times, and before they stepped over the threshold, she glimpsed two curious children's faces peeking into the hallway.

In the meantime, complete darkness had fallen outside. Tom grabbed Astrid's hand and led her toward her house. If he wasn't supporting her, she'd definitely collapse to the ground. Her legs were like rubber.

"What happened?" he asked when they were mere steps away from their houses.

"Do you remember what happened on Passion Sunday back then? The day before we disappeared?"

Tom thought hard about it for a minute before shaking his head. "No, I don't remember."

"We were running across the field. Max and I. And then

a figure appeared and wanted to take Max away. Because…" Her voice broke and her eyes filled with tears. "Because he was the last one left behind… Remember? Whoever was the last one to make it back to the village, Morana would take them away within a year… I think it was her."

Tom was looking at her with an inscrutable expression on his face.

"She wanted Max for herself, I tried to rip him out of her clutches… And then you appeared with Sonya and you helped me and we managed to escape together."

Her sniffles were the only thing to pierce the icy silence. It took a while for Tom to respond.

"Don't take this the wrong way, but… you really believe all this?"

It felt as if Astrid's heart, which had been pounding like crazy until now, suddenly stood still.

"What?"

"Astrid… For Perun's sake! Who knows what that crackpot of a lady put in your tea," he pressed on. "All she did was make more of a muddle in your mind than you had before. Maybe it was her way of getting back at us for not paying her…"

"You don't believe me," Astrid whispered incredulously. She ripped her hand out of his. "You think I'm lying."

"No." Tom shook his head. "I think the rozhanitsa did her hocus pocus on you and made you see something to, I dunno, scare you off…"

"I just underwent hypnosis. You saw it, you were there. It wasn't magic…"

"You don't believe in magic, but you're claiming that it was Morana, the goddess of death herself, who kidnapped us?"

Tom took great care to make sure the question didn't sound like he was attacking her. But Astrid didn't see it that way, or didn't want to see it that way, as she began to defend herself.

"You didn't believe Dora either..." she whispered. "You didn't believe what she saw, and now you don't believe me."

"No, Astrid. Listen to me. It's not like that. I just want you to hear this... You want to believe it, so you're instinctively filtering information that supports your version of the story."

Astrid froze mid-motion, as if lightning had struck her.

"You told me that we were in this together. That we'd figure it out. Together."

Tom let out a heavy sigh. "Yes, that's true."

"But you don't believe me."

Astrid didn't wait for him to explain his behavior. She turned on her heel and marched in the direction of her house. She was convinced that he would call after her, that he would catch up to her and apologize. But he didn't, and with each step Astrid took, the more the emotional turmoil of anger, pain, and fear inside her grew, making her feel powerless.

Astrid didn't go home straightway. She stepped off the path leading up to the front door and slipped, unnoticed, into the alleyways behind the houses. It seemed to her that weeks, not just hours, had passed since she last ran into Gusto at this very spot. In a few minutes, she was already trekking up the hill behind the chapel. She needed a moment to herself, to be as far away from curious faces and nosy questions as possible—and as far away as possible from her uncle, Grandma, and Kristian too.

That's why with the approaching evening, she found herself standing over her father's tombstone in the middle of the small cemetery atop the hill. A piercing wind that blew from the mountains tangled her hair and bored through her clothes. The place reeked of damp soil, and wherever she looked, all she saw were lit candles casting terrifying shadows. There was an unearthly calm up here. She crouched down, her fingers ghosting over the engraved name of her father, as if it would allow her to caress his cheek for real. Life had been easier with him there. Or at least that was how she'd remembered it being. Her mother used to be happy. Grandma didn't dare say things that could hurt them. They were more of a family. But his death brought with it a string of unfortunate events that couldn't be stopped. She genuinely missed him—especially now that she'd found herself alone and didn't know what to do.

After ruminating over his grave for a while, she stood up and walked between the tombstones toward the cemetery gate. She was just about to exit when she noticed the cemetery wasn't as empty as she'd initially thought. Someone stood underneath the tall willow tree, and although Astrid couldn't see their face, she knew almost at once that it was the blind old woman. She headed toward her without hesitation.

"Have you come to honor the dead, Astrid?" the woman asked her as soon as she was close enough.

"How come you always recognize who I am?"

A hint of a smile appeared on the old woman's face. "Because you're the only one who can see me."

She was speaking in riddles again. Astrid had had enough.

"What do you mean by that? Who are you?"

The old woman pointed to her feet. A name, barely legible, was carved on a low gravestone.

"Who is that?" Astrid asked. The name was unfamiliar to her.

"It's me," the old woman replied.

Astrid's eyes shot up to the woman in confusion before glancing back at the gravestone. The date of death was over sixty years ago.

"I don't understand. What are you saying, that you're…?"

"Dead," the woman finished for her. "Yes. My spirit returns to the places it used to frequent when alive."

The determination with which the old woman uttered the words left Astrid dumbstruck. It only added to the confusion already present in her mind.

"To speak to the dead is a sign of bad luck."

"They want you to believe that."

"Who?"

"The Elders. They gradually started to put all their hopes in the gods, forgetting that the root of our faith lies in respecting our ancestors. How could the dead hurt you, Astrid?"

She didn't know. "How come it's only me who can see you? Why not anyone else?"

"Only my own flesh and blood can see me. I'm not the only one who returns. Others, too, visit their offspring and watch over them. But people have stopped observing their surroundings. They don't see us. Seldom can someone even sense our presence. Like you. You have the power."

"I don't have any power." Astrid shook her head.

The old woman turned her head toward her a fraction. The whites of her unseeing eyes shone in the darkness.

"What do you know about the winter solstice, about Korochun?"

Astrid thought for a moment. "It's when the shortest day is followed by the longest night of the year. According to the Elders, it's on this day when the power of the life-giving sun is at its weakest, the influence of dark forces upon the earthly realm culminates, and the barriers between our world and the underworld disappear."

"Ye still don't understand?"

Astrid shrugged, unsure, but then she went numb. The pieces of the puzzle in her mind were finally starting to fall into place.

"It's no coincidence that you all reappeared during this time. A portal is opened during the solstice, and for the next twelve nights, when the barrier is at its weakest, when the demons and the dead roam the earth, almost nothing is impossible. The fathers of our fathers return to bless their descendants. The nights belong to ghosts and evil spirits you call demons. The seemingly impossible is made possible, and that which has been lost returns."

Astrid's mind was abuzz. "But why now? Why this particular solstice? Why not the one last year or five years ago? Why didn't we return then?"

The old woman raised a finger into the air. "You're asking the wrong person the right questions. Something's different this time around. The darkness is stronger. Beware, evil forces are gathering around you. Especially at night, when you're at your most vulnerable. You have to fight them, or else the portal will close behind you and you'll never be able to come back."

"But what about my brother? Where's Max? How can I get him back?"

The expression that appeared on the old woman's face was similar to the one the rozhanitsa had had as she grasped Astrid's hands. As if she knew much more than she was letting on.

"Your brother hasn't come through the portal," she eventually said. "Don't go back for him."

"So it can be done?" Astrid blurted out. "It is possible? I can bring him back!"

The old woman nodded, albeit reluctantly. "As long as the gateway remains open."

For the first time in the last couple of days, Astrid could feel optimism spreading through her veins. Even if it all sounded completely crazy, her obsessive need to keep poking at it and rubbing salt in her own wounds had been warranted. Everyone around her could pretend that nothing had happened. And maybe even Tom wanted to suddenly forget, but not her. Max was alive. She could save him. She was positive she could do it, even if she had to walk straight into Nav, the underworld, itself. She was willing to do anything.

It was only when she suddenly felt prepared for anything, her chest bursting with hope, that she fully realized the significance of the old woman's words.

As long as the gateway remains open. For twelve nights, when the barriers are at their weakest, and then there's no way back.

It only took her a fraction of a second to calculate that it was the fifth night that was just commencing.

There were only seven nights left.

THE FIFTH NIGHT

D ora learned, fairly quickly, to just accept the way things were in her life. She didn't ask too many questions, she never complained—at least not out loud or in front of her parents. As a little girl, she felt wronged for one thing, and one thing only, which her parents begrudged her: she had always wanted to have a sibling. Someone she could play with, someone who would understand her and not look down on her like the others. And that desire grew, especially after she lost her friends and the villagers turned their backs on her. To her, a sibling was first and foremost a good friend you acquired practically for free. If she had a sibling, her life would be much easier.

But the older she got, the less it began to matter to her. Partly because she'd long grown used to the loneliness, and partly because she had started to feel guilty toward her parents. She knew her mother longed for a second child but just couldn't get pregnant. Back when Dora was a little girl and her mother was certain that she wouldn't remember any of it, that she wouldn't understand at her age, Dora had seen her crying because of it. But her mother had been wrong—the memory of her broken and unhappy

208

mother got lodged in her mind. And whenever it surfaced unexpectedly to the forefront of her mind, Dora acutely felt all of her mother's pain.

When her mother finally got pregnant again, Dora was already on the cusp of puberty, and she had long given up her desire for a sibling. She didn't remember how her father had reacted to the news, but her mother underwent a complete transformation—she was glowing with happiness. Even though half the village was whispering behind her back that she was too old to have another baby, she didn't pay them any mind. As her belly grew and her pregnancy became more noticeable, she radiated a tangible positive energy all around her that had an effect on Dora too. She began to get excited as well. She was going to have a new sibling, someone she could take care of!

Her mother went into labor so suddenly, weeks before her due date. Dora could remember it as if it were yesterday. Her father woke her up in the middle of the night. The midwife was already there, and screams were coming from the bedroom. Dora rushed down to the village to get Auntie Hattler—that's what they'd decided on. Her father didn't like to see her visiting in other circumstances, but this time, he didn't have any objections. She should've suspected something. She didn't realize that something bad was happening until they sent for the doctor at dawn. He examined her mother before demanding, in a stone-cold tone, to call for an ambulance at once—the delivery was going to be complicated. By the time the ambulance arrived, Oleg had already been brought into this world, the umbilical cord wrapped around his neck. Anton was born twenty minutes later. He was so tiny he could fit into the palm of her father's hand. It was Dora's job to swaddle him and keep him warm and close until the paramedics could take over.

She remembered her heart being in her mouth, she was so scared she might hurt him by accident. He didn't look anything like the dolls she played with—he was ugly, messy, and wrinkly. Neither of the twins cried. She cradled them in the kitchen by the heat of the stove as muffled sounds came from the bedroom. When the ambulance arrived, Dora's mother suffered massive bleeding, and neither the doctor nor the midwife could staunch it. She was already unconscious when they moved her to the ambulance. Before the ambulance had even arrived at the hospital, she was gone.

Dora removed the bloody bed linen from the bed, feeling her desire for siblings was to blame for her mother's death. Disgusted with herself, she knelt on the mattress, trying to get out the bloodstains, which symbolized both the birth of her siblings and the destruction of the one person she loved most in the world. It was as if they'd simply taken their mother's place, as if Dora didn't have the right to keep all her loved ones together at once.

She took on her mother's role. She took care of her baby brothers and tried to give them as much love as she could. She brought them up, defended them, and tried to cover up the fact that their father could never really love them as much as they deserved. He may never have said it aloud, but Dora remembered well the look he gave them when they returned home from the hospital weeks later. Love, anger, and aversion all mixed into one. Dora knew he blamed the twins for the death of his wife. That wasn't something she was able to do, so she blamed herself instead. She was the first-born, and whether she felt ready for it or not, her job now was to take care of her brothers.

That's why she understood Astrid. She understood her friend's incentive perfectly, her desire to figure out what had happened, her persistence on the complicated journey toward saving Max. Dora would do the same for her own brothers, because that's what older siblings do for the younger ones, that's the way they are, that's their job—protecting them, taking care of them, and passing on life values to them.

She thankfully managed to return home that afternoon before her father did. Oleg and Anton were a bit cranky that she'd left them at home for most of the day with their grumpy grandpa, who demanded constant attention. To appease them and ensure they wouldn't tattle on her, she quickly baked them a sponge cake. Her father came home long after dark. Dora had learned not to worry about him, though it was only a few years back when she'd still get terrified by the thought of something bad happening to him in the woods, leaving her to take care of two children and an aging grandfather on her own in a rundown house, and her not even having finished school or having a proper job. He came back in a foul mood, and with a couple astutely placed questions during dinner, Dora managed to inconspicuously wheedle out of him what was going on.

It turned out that the Guards hadn't exactly conducted themselves in a considerate manner during their investigation in the woods, and their brash conduct had interrupted the wildlife out of their hibernation. Consequentially—or for some inexplicable reason—animals were dying left and right. Her father spent most of the day tracking the herds of wildlife in order to calculate the damages, and then clearing away the carcasses. They had to be incinerated too, in case some rampant disease was spreading.

"Is there any way we can help?" Dora asked during dinner. Over the years, she'd learned some things about gamekeeping from her father. And she knew parts of the woods like the back of her hand, at least the ones where he used to take her as a child.

"I don't want you going into the woods," he ordered all his children.

"Why not?" Oleg asked instantly.

"Because I said so."

An impish grin appeared on each of the boys' faces as they elbowed each other. But Dora recognized the evident warning in her father's expression. He was genuinely worried.

"I'm dead serious," he warned them. "If I catch you so much as glancing toward the forest, you'll get a beating you won't forget."

After that, they didn't dare lift their eyes from their plates.

Dora wordlessly cleared the table, and it was only after the rest of the household had retired that she allowed herself to unwind. She slid down into her armchair in her room and automatically reached for a book, but ended up merely resting it on her lap.

She began to think about everything that had happened that day. Deep down, she had always imagined that Astrid would return one day, that she'd fix those fathomless, dark eyes on her and tell her it was all just another one of her games. But although her friend really had returned, she was still lost.

Dora couldn't shake the uneasy feeling that her friend hadn't been completely honest with her. Thoughts like this just made her mad at herself, and she chalked it up to her frustrating, unfulfilled expectations. She'd spent years imagining what it'd be like to finally confide to somebody about everything she'd gone through. What it'd be like when somebody finally believed her. By all accounts, Astrid did believe her, but Dora didn't feel relieved whatsoever. That boulder she'd been lugging along all this time hadn't changed a bit. She very well might've been angry with herself rather than with Astrid.

In fact, it was something else completely that was bothering her much more. She sat in her armchair, legs folded underneath her, and tried to rid herself of her feelings of jealousy. It had emerged at some point during the afternoon, catching her completely unawares. She'd thought she had rid herself of it ages ago.

When they'd been little kids, she and Astrid, they always used to only play with each other—whether it be with dolls or somewhere outdoors. Astrid had always been the one to come up with the games they'd play, and Dora always went along with whatever she was told to do—not because Astrid was bossy, but because she always had the best ideas.

But then, sometime between their fifth and sixth birthday, Tom suddenly appeared out of nowhere. Till then, they'd always seen boys as dummies who only thought of sports and cars and constantly made fun of girls, which they in turn readily reciprocated. In general, they were just impossible to play with.

For some inexplicable reason, Astrid decided to take pity on Tom, and almost immediately, they became an inseparable duo. Dora felt left out, especially once they brought in Sonya and Max as well. It was no longer just the two of them.

Now, Astrid was making up games for their whole group, and even though Dora liked the others and eventually got used to them, the jealousy remained. It reared its ugly head especially at times when Astrid and Tom would be huddled together, whispering things to each other and refusing to tell the others what they were talking about. It was as if her best friend had gone and replaced her.

The feeling used to bother her back then and it had suddenly returned after all those years. It was Astrid who Dora wanted to confide in, not Tom. She wanted to go with her to the hypnotist, to be there as support and help her figure out what had happened.

But unlike Tom, she couldn't. She spent the whole evening wondering whether they had managed to locate the hypnotist. What did they find out? And will they even tell her? She felt like some unwanted piece of junk left in the corner.

A dull thud interrupted her train of thought. She jumped in fright, whipping around. The remnants of a snowball were trickling down the windowpane. Just then, another snowball hit the glass. Dora got up, her heart pounding, and tiptoed over to the window. She couldn't make out anything in the darkness for all the light in her room. She had no choice but to open the window and lean out.

A figure was huddling beneath the tree in a too-large coat. Astrid.

She wasn't sure if Dora would even still be awake, but when she saw the light coming from the top-floor windows, she decided to try her luck. Dora peeked out of the window and let her inside without a second thought. They snuck up to her room, and a few minutes later, they were already sitting on top of Dora's bed while Astrid described to her in a whisper just how it'd gone with the rozhanitsa. Dora listened to Astrid silently and patiently, not interrupting her once. She didn't even stir when Astrid spoke of Morana. She didn't imply in any way that her story might sound like a lie.

Even so, Astrid felt the urge to justify herself. "I know it sounds crazy…"

"It doesn't. Why did you come?" Dora asked her when Astrid was done talking.

Astrid thought about it. Frankly, she had no idea why. She had just acted on impulse. All she knew was that she needed to talk to someone about it. And the only person she knew had turned his back on her.

"Because Tom doesn't believe me," she admitted, feeling that it had in fact affected her more than she'd initially thought.

Betrayal. A tiny, treacherous pang at her heart. One side of her knew it wasn't fair to condemn him like this for it, but her other, more emotional side disagreed.

Dora nodded. "I believe you. Because you believed me. Do you think Morana is behind all this?"

"Maybe." Astrid pulled her legs up to her chin, resting her head against her knees. "Maybe she's got something to do with it. Maybe not. I don't know. All I know is that it wasn't a hallucination. That figure... It was real. Whoever was hiding beneath that cape was real."

A shadow of terror flitted across Dora's face. "Do you know what that means?"

"What?"

Dora was whispering so softly Astrid could barely understand her. "That all those creatures they always scared us with as kids... actually exist."

Astrid was quiet for a long time. They were staring into each other's eyes intently, and Astrid could only guess if her friend, like her, was trying to figure out what she was thinking about. Astrid wanted to tell Dora about the old blind woman who had appeared to her. About what she'd said to her and the vague guidance. But one part of her was convinced that at this point in time, it wasn't important. And anyway, wouldn't it just drive Dora away? Finding out Astrid was talking to the dead? Wasn't that just a little too much?

"I came here because I need your help," Astrid eventually said. Dora didn't hesitate to answer. "I'm listening."

Astrid recalled her always having been this way—loyal and selfless. She felt guilty.

"I know it sounds weird, but… I can't fall asleep. I need you to stay awake with me until the morning and not let me nod off for a second. No matter what."

Astrid was relieved when Dory agreed and didn't ask any more questions. She still wanted to keep some things to herself, so she was glad she didn't have to explain them.

They said a prayer together. "Now I lay me down to sleep, and I shall awaken, for the evil spirits cannot reach me," they recited. Dora was tracing her tattoos, while Astrid at least moved her fingers through the air around her. "At this nightly hallowed hour, we call upon the ancient powers," Dora continued. "Protect us till the light of day from Notsnitsa's evil sway."

They completed the prayer by crossing their index and middle fingers and placing them first on their brow, then their lips.

"I didn't know the full version of it." Astrid was surprised. "I must've forgotten it."

"This is how my mom taught it to me," Dora explained. "She always rushed me to get in bed to fall asleep before the witching hour.

They sat in bed, wrapped in blankets, and chatted away to keep from falling asleep. It was mainly Dory who told stories. She opened up about the village, and what it's like to go to school and study. At first, Astrid listened to her with great attention, but when the clock struck midnight, exhaustion slowly overcame her. Dora tried to involve her in the conversation and began to reminisce about their childhood. For some time, they quietly walked across the room, there and back, they lounged and they stretched. In the latter part of the night, however, the fatigue really came to a head.

"Do you remember when Sonya shoved a crayon up her nose and the teacher almost lost it because the tip had broken off?"

Astrid laughed mid-yawn. "Yeah, a pink one."

"She only did it because you'd bet whether she'd be able to stuff the whole thing in or not. Remember?"

Astrid nodded. She yawned again. Her eyes fluttered shut.

"Astrid. Stay awake."

The fatigue crashed over Dora as well, and she rested her head on Astrid's shoulder.

"And remember when…"

But Astrid didn't hear the rest. Before she fell asleep completely, she wanted to answer her friend, but her tongue had turned to wood and her lips were sealed shut. She was just too tired. Her chin fell onto her chest.

Dora fell asleep not long after. Astrid realized this because when she woke up a few seconds later, her friend's head was resting against her shoulder like a weight.

But Astrid hadn't really fallen asleep. She immediately jolted awake, or so she thought. The nightmare was back. She was petrified. The only thing she could control was the movement of her eyes and her breathing; otherwise she felt completely paralyzed. She started to breathe through her nose rapidly, but a feeling as if she couldn't inhale properly was suffocating her. She knew what was coming next—and her panic felt that much worse for it. She tried realizing that she was safe, but the surge of the worst of her fears that she couldn't influence was inevitable, and the terrible pressure she felt pressing down on her chest just intensified the feeling that she was definitely going to suffocate. Goosebumps spread over her entire body, from the tips of her ears down to her toes. It felt like someone was scrutinizing her intently, but she didn't see anybody at first. The unpleasant experience was amplified by a constant buzzing in her ears that almost split her head open. She wanted to scream, but she couldn't even crack her lips open.

Her eyes were flitting frantically around the room, when she suddenly made out the outline of a figure outside the window that was looking at her. Astrid's fear skyrocketed, becoming almost unbearable as she thought of only one thing.

Let me wake up. Please, let me wake up.

But deliverance was not coming. The window creaked open. The creature first stuck its hand inside—tapping its long, bony fingers against the windowpane and grating them on the glass. Its fingers turned into creeping vines. And then it appeared in all its glory. Though it wasn't the first time Astrid had seen the creature, its stare always utterly terrified her.

The figure was already inside the room, drawing nearer and nearer as it floated through the air. Astrid tried to scream again in hopes of waking up Dora, but she was out like a light. The buzzing sounds were getting louder, along with the thumping of butterfly wings in her head.

How come Dora couldn't hear it? Was she ever going to wake up?

The creature wrapped its hands around Astrid's neck and squeezed. Now she really couldn't catch her breath and began gasping for air. Astrid kept repeating a mantra in her head.

Now I lay me down to sleep, and I shall awaken…

She could see dark spots obscuring her vision. She was about to lose consciousness.

"Astrid!"

The pressure eased off. Astrid woke up lying on her back on

the bed, her clothes drenched with sweat. She sucked in a breath of air and cried out. Dora, who had been leaning over her, put her palm over her mouth.

"Shhh, Astrid, it's me," she whispered urgently. "Please, calm down, or you'll wake everybody up."

Astrid's heart was thundering in her ears as tears began to flow down her cheeks.

"You're safe. Everything's okay," Dora comforted her. "I'm here. You're not alone."

Astrid didn't cry out again. Dora figured it was now okay to let her go. She drew in a shaky breath.

"Perun's beard, Astrid," Dora blurted out as her gaze fixed upon Astrid's neck. "What happened to you?"

Astrid couldn't find her voice and just let out an uncertain wheeze. Dora climbed down from the bed and returned with a pocket mirror. Her hands were shaking, as if she'd endured the paralysis along with Astrid. She tilted the mirror so that Astrid could see the black bruises lining her neck. Evident proof of strangulation.

"They just showed up on their own," Dora whispered. "I woke up and you were sitting and twitching beside me. Your eyes were closed and you were mumbling something. I tried, but I couldn't get you to wake up. Then you fell on your back and they just appeared, the fingerprints. You didn't do it yourself..."

Astrid finally regained her voice. "It was... It was just... a nightmare."

"A nightmare that attempted to kill you?" Dora retorted.

"I think I know where it is we disappeared to all those years ago," Astrid finally admitted out loud—something she still refused to believe herself. "We were captured by nightmares. And imprisoned for twelve years."

She waited for Dora to call her words into question. But she just kept staring at her wordlessly, and Astrid realized that like her, her friend didn't want to believe it, but the longer she thought about it, the more evident it was.

"That's why you don't want to fall asleep."

"I'm scared that one day, I'm just not gonna wake up."

As the new day dawned, Astrid almost began to cry with relief. Last night was again a bit more exhausting than the one before, but above all, it was terrifying—not because of the nightmares themselves, but because of the moment when they disappeared. Because if the blind old woman was telling the truth, Astrid had only seven days and seven nights to rescue her brother. And all she'd done so far was stand idly by as time ticked by. How could she possibly make it in a week's time, when she didn't even know where to start?

With the first rays of the rising sun, Dora walked her friend to the backdoor, so she'd avoid passing under her father's bedroom window. Astrid crept through the backyard and continued part of the way along the tree line toward the horizon to really make sure nobody saw her from any top-floor windows. Only then did she head toward the village.

It was a crisp, bright December morning. The snow underneath her feet was crunching rhythmically, her legs unpleasantly numb with cold. Fatigue was taking more and more of a toll on her. She tried her best to think rationally, but she would always lose the thread soon and couldn't retain a single thought.

Twelve days during which demons walk the earth. Nightmares becoming reality. Memories that cannot be found.

Whoever makes it back last...

Astrid began to formulate a plan. She didn't know whether it was because she had barely gotten any sleep, or because everything happening was starting to make her go crazy—but suddenly, the plan made perfect sense.

She got home in the early hours of the morning. She snuck past her grandmother's bedroom, but if she were to guess, she'd definitely say Grandma heard her. It was almost certain that she also knew Astrid hadn't been home all night long. And Astrid wouldn't have been surprised in the least if Grandma knew where she had spent the night instead. She didn't know how her grandmother did it, and it used to both fascinate and terrify her as a little kid. But Hedda Mahler had always had a gift for exposing every one of Astrid's lies and for showing up at the right time in the most unlikely of places.

Astrid washed up and went to her room to change into fresh clothes. Then she helped get her mother clean in the bathroom and, despite the unspoken rule she'd adhered to till now, she guided her to the kitchen. Astrid didn't care what the other family members would say on the matter. She refused to shut herself with her mom in a gloomy room where she spent her days like an animal forced to gnaw furtively at leftover pieces of bread in the corner, away from the others.

She began to prepare breakfast. Her mother sat at the table, her fingers pushing around crumbs left over from dinner as she rocked back and forth in a rhythmic motion. Sounds began to echo through the house as its inhabitants slowly woke up, one by one. As Astrid was about to pour boiling water into two chipped mugs of tea, she heard banging on the door. She set the kettle back on the corner and took a few hesitant steps toward the hallway.

Her aunt was faster, though, as she must've just walked down the stairs from the top floor. She reached the front door first and opened it. Tom was standing in the doorway. When he saw Astrid's aunt, he looked surprised, but his eyes immediately sought out Astrid standing in the hallway. It flashed through her mind that he probably wasn't there so early in the morning to apologize. He looked impatient and nervous.

"I came to see..." Tom didn't even bother to finish the sentence for her aunt's sake and made a gesture as if to wave her off. "Astrid," he blurted out when he saw her. "Did you hear about...?"

"What?"

"Do you realize what time it is, young man?" Astrid's aunt butted in, sounding displeased.

"They found Loony Gusto last night. He hanged himself from a tree," Tom explained, ignoring the woman. "He killed himself. Apparently, he'd already been hanging from the tree for a few days. The Elders consider it his confession."

A shiver ran down Astrid's spine. "A few days? That's impossible. Yesterday afternoon I..." She promptly swallowed the rest of her sentence. "I mean... I thought I saw him."

If Gusto really was dead, then who was it that she talked to yesterday? Could it have been an apparition? Another ghost? Like the old woman? Astrid was slowly starting to recognize that the old woman really hadn't been lying to her. But why did the dead appear only to her?

"Good riddance. He deserved it," her aunt commented on the situation. She left them standing in the hallway and entered the kitchen. When it was just the two of them left, an awkward silence overtook them.

"Astrid, about yesterday, I wanted to—"

"We have to go see Sonya," she interrupted him. "If the rozha-nitsa was right and she's woken up, she might be home by now. We have to find out what she knows. I'll explain everything afterward."

She immediately put on her shoes, grabbed her coat, and headed out. Tom followed close behind, not daring to say anything else.

It only took them a few minutes of brisk walking to arrive at the Foreths' house. Sonya's mother was still sleepy as she opened the door, with only a knitted shawl thrown over her nightgown. She wasn't pleased by the early callers.

"Sonya is very upset," she told them. "She ain't in a state where she could talk 'bout stuff... The doctor gave us some medicine, but it ain't helping."

"It'll just be a minute," Astrid insisted, trying not to sound too impatient. "We just wanted to... to just welcome her back and wish her a speedy recovery."

After some more urging, she relented and let them in. The family must've been having breakfast in the dining room, as the sound of children's voices reached their ears. She led them to the tiny kitchen right next door before disappearing down the hallway. When she came back, Sonya was with her. She looked so fragile that Astrid's heart constricted. Her pale skin was almost translucent. Sonya's mother shut the door behind her, leaving the trio alone.

"We're glad you've woken up," Tom spoke up politely. "That's good news—"

"Sonya, listen, I know it's hard," Astrid interjected eagerly. "I know it's unfair, because we've already had a few days to get used to it all, but... we need to talk to you. About what you re-member. Because we're suffering a blackout and trying to remem-ber. We want to know what happened. So that we can find Max, who didn't come back with us."

223

"We were hoping you'd help us," Tom added amiably.

"Help you?" she echoed, looking baffled. Even her voice was feeble.

Tom exchanged a look with Astrid, who took over again. "Yes, to remember what happened…"

"You don't remember anything?" Sonya assured herself.

They both shook their heads.

"Why? You do?"

"What do you know, Sonya?"

It looked like Sonya was about to faint. "There's no way I'm helping you two," she declared firmly. "Forget it."

"What d'you mean?"

"It's all your fault." She pointed at Astrid. "Your fault that we ended up where we did. That we went missing for twelve years. You're to blame. They were your nightmares. And you're to blame for what happened to Max as well. I won't help you. I don't want anything to do with you."

Tom was the first to recover. Astrid stood there, completely dumbstruck, unable to utter a sound. It wasn't so much Sonya's words that shocked her; it was the hatred she infused them with. Like someone who was absolutely certain of their truthfulness. Like someone who didn't just want to hurt them, but also considered them the root of all evil.

"I understand this is a sensitive matter to all of us," Tom attempted to say in a sensible voice. "But there's no need to accuse each other and—"

"I'm not accusing her," Sonya cut him off, driving her fingers into her ruffled blonde hair in an act of despair. "I'm saying it's her fault."

"Well… Sounds the exact same to me," Astrid hissed aggressively.

Sonya frowned. "You're unbelievable. Seriously, unbelievable. As long as you don't have to assume any responsibility…"

"Calm down," Tom asked them. "Both of you. Let's all just…"

A chilly silence filled the kitchen, interrupted only by the loud ticking of the clock.

"Sonya, could you… could you please tell us what you remember? Please?"

For some completely incomprehensible reason, Sonya's gaze darted over to the corner, as if she were locking eyes with someone they couldn't see. Astrid turned a fraction to look over her shoulder, but there was nothing there, except for a cupboard.

"You cursed us," Sonya whispered urgently as she focused all her attention on Astrid once more. "You brought bad luck upon us, angering the gods. Mom told me that I should stay away from you, that you're just like your mother. A witch…"

Sonya almost spit out the last word at Astrid. A shiver ran down Astrid's spine. Sonya was talking about her the same way Kristian had. What terrible thing could she have done to them, all those years ago? They were only kids, after all.

She could feel Tom tense beside her. After all this, there was no way he was going to believe her anymore.

"What did I do?" Astrid asked, her voice cracking several times. "What was it that I did?"

But it was like Sonya had lost the last remnants of sanity. She began to mumble something to herself. To pull at her hair. To wave her hands around her head, as if warding something off. Her eyes kept straying to the corner behind Astrid's back.

"You angered… You summoned them… They haunted me in my dreams for weeks… They were under my bed… Behind the window… I heard them scratching at the glass… Nobody believed me then, nobody believes me now… They were here…"

Inconsolable, she burst into tears.

"Calm down, Sonya. We're here with you." Tom took a few hesitant steps toward her, but she backed away in a panic, her back hitting the kitchen counter.

Tom stopped in his tracks, leaving enough distance between them. "Who is this *they* you were talking about?"

Sonya flailed her hand by her ear again. In that moment, Astrid recognized the gesture. She had done the same before too. The buzzing that jolted every single facial muscle she had. The intense pounding of butterfly wings in her eardrum. Sounds so loud they drowned out everything else.

"They would show up at my bedside..." Sonya whimpered miserably. "Every night. They whispered things in my ear for weeks on end. And then we fell asleep and... they dragged all of us off... You really don't remember?"

Astrid began to put the pieces together, the fragments of her memories with Sonya's words. What had transpired was becoming clearer and clearer.

Whisperers. That's what they called them. Faceless creatures with claws for hands. They dragged people into nightmares they spun themselves. How could they have forgotten about them?

"I can't." Sonya clenched her fists, hitting her temples repeatedly. "I can't stop thinking about it. It's driving me crazy..."

Her sobs were getting louder. The kitchen door suddenly flew open, with Mrs. Foreth appearing in the doorway. One look at her expression and they knew they were no longer welcome there.

"Get out, now." She left no room for argument. "And I don't want to see you here again."

Astrid took one last look at Sonya. It looked like she was no longer aware of where she was as she writhed with her head in her hands.

They exited the house, feeling the stern gaze of Sonya's mother on their backs. As they were standing in the doorway on their way out, she hissed in their direction, "Don't come here anymore. Don't you see what you did to her? Sonya is sick. You're just pointlessly reminding her of those awful things. Our family's trying to get over our hardship."

Before she could rethink whether it was appropriate or not, Astrid snapped back at her, "You got over it pretty quickly, didn't you? When you declared Sonya dead all those years ago."

She knew she had broached a sensitive topic. But she was fed up with everyone around her constantly hurting her while she just let it happen.

Mrs. Foreth turned even paler than usual. Her features tensed. "Get out of my house!"

Tom grasped Astrid's elbow and began to pull her away. Astrid was shaking with anger.

"You better watch out!" Mrs. Foreth yelled after her. "Or you might end up like yer ma!"

With those words, she slammed the door shut. Astrid bristled at that, and was just taking a breath to yell back at the woman at the top of her lungs.

"Forget it," Tom reasoned with her. "Let's go. Come on, Astrid, look at me."

She reluctantly obeyed, her eyes finding his. Tom's eyes were completely calm. "Breathe," he demanded.

Astrid took a deep breath and slowly expelled the air from her lungs. Her rage abated, fractionally.

"There. That's better. Now, let's go."

A few minutes later, they were sitting in Tom's room on the carpet. Both clutching a cup of tea, and while Tom was gratefully gulping it down, it was enough for Astrid to have something to keep her numb fingers warm.

"What made you change your mind?" she asked him suddenly.

The question had been at the forefront of her mind since that morning, when Tom had shown up on her doorstep. Just the day before, he had refused to believe her. A few hours later, he was standing in her kitchen, pretending like nothing had happened.

Tom grimaced. He gulped down some more tea, as if to buy a bit more time to think it over.

"I went home yesterday and thought about everything you said. It didn't make sense, but in its own way it did actually explain everything. I had to talk to Mom. And after a while, she let slip that in the weeks before we disappeared, I'd been suffering from nightmares."

Astrid got goosebumps. This time, it wasn't caused by fear but by an unpleasant feeling of excitement.

"She said that... I described to her what the boogeymen that visited me night after night in my sleep looked like. The nightmares would wake me up. I was sleepwalking. I have... My body's covered in scars from scratching myself in my sleep out of fear. I had completely forgotten all about it." Tom set aside his cup, got up, and pulled some papers out of his desk drawer. "Mom kept these old drawings of mine," he explained, handing them to Astrid.

She looked closely at them. On the one hand, they were cute, childish drawings, but what they depicted was far from pleasant. Whisperers. Black shadows. Elongated limbs. Eyes hidden in the dark underneath the bed, lying in wait for a chance to pull you down by the ankle.

"They look like what Dora was describing to us. And how Sonya did today too," he sighed. "All of you were right. We were taken... taken by something unnatural. Something that doesn't belong here but that we all know has always been here. You know what I mean?"

"Demons," Astrid said in a whisper, her eyes fixed upon the kid drawing.

"Yes, that's the word for it," Tom agreed, sitting back down next to her. "Demons."

Astrid placed the drawing on the floor and looked at Tom. "I've seen them every night ever since we came back. I have proof that they're real."

She unwound her scarf from around her neck, uncovering the bruises she'd obtained during the night.

"Astrid..."

"They're everywhere," she whispered, pulling up her pant legs. The bruises were gleaming in contrast to her pale skin.

"I had no idea... Why didn't you tell me? Astrid, let me help you."

"Could I see your old scars?" She felt stupid as soon as the words were out of her mouth.

Tom grew solemn, but eventually nodded. He slowly unbuttoned the first few buttons of his shirt, almost all the way down to his stomach. Astrid tried hard to keep her features steady, suppressing through sheer willpower the blush threatening to emerge. It was strange how quickly their serious conversation veered toward an intimate moment—even though she had no idea if Tom felt the same way, and she suddenly wished with all her heart that she knew. But all thoughts of his physical proximity vanished as soon as they appeared when Tom finished unbuttoning his shirt and revealed his chest. Astrid immediately forgot about her own bruises, because these were real scars—deep, symmetrical lacerations covering his stomach.

"Tom, a six-year-old boy isn't capable of doing this to himself," she whispered. "This was done…"

"By them."

Astrid hesitantly reached for his exposed chest. Perhaps she wanted to touch the scars, but she pulled her hand back at the last second. Like an echo, Sonya's voice filled her head with all those accusations she had spewed at her in anger.

You cursed us. You brought bad luck upon us, angering the gods.

Astrid let her hand fall back to her side. Tom looked into her eyes, searching for what was on her mind. Like several times before, he managed to puzzle it out fairly easily.

"I don't believe anything Sonya was saying before," he assured her.

Astrid took a breath, ready to argue, but Tom didn't let her.

"I believe she saw those things she described to us. But I don't think it's your fault, Astrid."

"How?" she whispered. "How can you be sure?"

"Because no six-year-old girl is capable of causing such misfortune."

But Astrid couldn't smile. There was still another heavy stone weighing her down.

"I have to tell you something." She bit her lip.

"I'm listening."

She took a deep breath before launching into describing the old blind woman, the twelve magical nights following the winter solstice, and her fear that they only had a week left to save Max. Opening up to Tom was much easier than she'd expected. Even so, she felt uneasy, as if someone had cornered her.

When she finished, Tom didn't say anything for a long time. It was starting to make her nervous.

"What's on your mind?" she asked after a while. "Do you think that I'm crazy? That I've lost my marbles?"

"No, nothing like that," Tom stopped her train of thought immediately. "I'm thinking about where to start."

Astrid wrapped her fingers around her cup of tea again. It'd long gone cold.

"I think we should go back to see the rozhanitsa," she thought out loud. "To try the hypnosis again. But this time the both of us, together. To recall those events, to somehow... push through the barrier. We have to remember the way to where they were keeping us. Maybe I'm unable to do it myself, but if we work together, at least us two, then it might just work..."

"Do you really think Sonya won't help us? She clearly remembers much more than we do. I wonder why."·

Astrid shook her head. "You saw the way she looked at me. I don't have enough time to try to persuade her to get it together. I'm pretty sure she won't help us. Unless..."

"Unless?"

"Unless she didn't know that she was helping us," it occurred to Astrid. "We could send Dora to see her. To gain her trust and try to get something out of her..."

"Astrid Mahler, you're a born manipulator." Tom crinkled his eyes in amusement.

She knew it was a joke, but she almost got offended. "Excuse me? D'you have any better ideas?!"

"I was just kidding." Tom raised his hands defensively. "I actually do think it's a good idea. If anyone'll be able to win her over, it's doe-eyed Dory."

Astrid smiled. "That's what I'm counting on."

Dora knew she was playing with fire when she secretly let Astrid sleep over at her house. It was just a matter of time before her father would happen upon people talking in the village, and then she'd really be in for it. Especially after Astrid and Tom showed up at the shop after noon, wanting to talk to her. She saw the suspicious look Mrs. Lesovska threw her way from behind the counter, it was a wonder the display case full of sausages didn't crack under her gaze. Dora asked for permission to go on the break she was entitled to, and then left through the back behind the store where the duo was already waiting for her. Astrid briefly laid out her plan and Dora agreed.

After her break, Dora went back to work, trying to act completely casual. She could feel the shopkeeper's prying gaze following her every step. When they finally closed the shop, she managed to smuggle out a couple bruised apples and a chocolate bar past its sell-by date in her bag before setting out straightaway for the Foreths' house.

She had to knock five times before Sonya's mother finally opened the door for her. She merely cracked the door open, looking her up and down suspiciously.

"Whaddaya want?"

Dora had never seen her like this. The Foreths had always presented themselves in public as respectable people no matter what, always greeting their neighbors across the road, heaven forbid they should think something bad about them. They attended Mass several times per week and they helped the needy, even though they themselves had little. It was almost suspicious how inconspicuous they managed to stay in everybody's eyes, when old Mrs. Kober wasn't provoking them with her prattling at the cemetery.

"I came to visit Sonya," Dora explained amicably, lifting up her bag full of apples and chocolate. "I just wanted to say hi, and then I'll be on my way."

"Sonya's exhausted," Mrs. Foreth rebuffed her. "She's had more than enough visits today."

She tried to slam the door shut, but Dora didn't let it discourage her. "I understand. I don't want to bother her. I just wanted to welcome her so she'll know that if she needs anything, she can rely on me."

"Bless your heart. Why don't you stop by another time?"

The door slammed shut in Dora's face.

"Mrs. Foreth!" Dora pounded on the door again.

The woman was reluctant to open the door. "Didn't you hear what I said?"

"It gives me no pleasure to bring this up," Dora said, her tone turning serious, "but Mrs. Lesovska asked me to remind you that you still haven't paid your December shopping bill. She feels a bit awkward, but she understands you've got other things on your mind at the moment..."

Mrs. Foreth's face turned red. Dora managed to put her on the spot, as nobody in the village was aware that the Foreths had to buy things on credit. *Too many mouths to feed, should've thought twice,* Mrs. Lesovska always muttered to herself when Mrs. Foreth asked her to delay payment for a couple days. She obliged her every time, but it wasn't without a string of comments that Dora had to listen to. Personally, she felt sorry for the Foreths. They really did have more children than they could feed. She felt a bit lousy now for standing at their door, trying to guilt-trip them.

"I'll pay it as soon as my husband gets his paycheck," Mrs. Foreth mumbled, obviously ashamed.

"I know." Dora nodded. "I'll let Mrs. Lesovska know, as long as…"

She left it open-ended. As Mrs. Foreth caught on, her expression changed in a flash. She suddenly opened the door all the way, as if she were welcoming her.

"I guess you can come see her for a little bit."

"You're too kind."

A few moments later, Dora found herself standing in the bedroom a mere few feet away from Sonya, who was observing her with suspicion in her eyes. Or at least that was the impression Dora got. She hardly recognized Sonya. Slim with fair hair down to her back, she may have looked like a carbon copy of her mother, but everything else had changed. Her features and the vigor that used to radiate off her were both gone. Her expression was unreadable, her gestures lifeless. She looked like a body devoid of a soul. Dora was surprised to even see her standing on her own two feet.

It must've been cosmic irony that made Sonya utter: "You haven't changed a bit."

Dora attempted to smile. She didn't have the heart to lie to her friend, but she wasn't really sure how she'd react to honesty either. Astrid and Tom had warned her to proceed with caution when it came to Sonya.

"It's nice to see you," she said instead.

Sonya narrowed her eyes. "Really?"

Dora could make out the underlying aggression in her voice.

"Really."

"That makes you the only one, in this house at least."

Dora decided to venture out onto thin ice. "What do you mean?"

Sonya turned her back on her and climbed back into her bed. She sat back on her covers, pulling her knees up to her chin. She let out a long sigh.

"I feel like a parasite here."

Dora slowly approached her. When Sonya didn't react in any way, she gingerly sat down on the edge of the bed beside her.

"I've always felt the same way, living in this town. It's never gotten any better."

Sonya fixed her eyes on her. Dora felt strangely exposed underneath her penetrating stare, but she held her gaze, fighting through the discomfort.

"How come you got to stay here and we didn't?" Sonya asked out of the blue. "What makes you so special? They were gonna take you away too... I saw them reaching for you."

A shiver ran down Dora's spine. "I've been asking the same thing for the past twelve years."

"It's not fair."

"Yeah, it's not."

"I didn't ask for any of this," Sonya blurted out, her aggressive tone morphing into sheer despair.

"Of course you didn't," Dora agreed.

"It's all Astrid's fault," Sonya said, tears welling in her eyes. "She brought bad luck on us."

Dora didn't know how to react, so she placed her hand on her arm in a comforting gesture. "It must be so incredibly hard for you. I can't even imagine what you're dealing with."

"Twelve years, Dory. How am I supposed to make up for twelve years?"

"You're not alone. You've got your family, friends. We're here to help you, if you'll let us."

Sonya lifted her tearful eyes to look at Dora. "You don't understand. I don't have anyone. I've only got myself. My family wrote me off, and Mom decided to deal with it by having a bunch of babies to compensate. The doctor thinks I'm insane."

"Why would you be insane?"

Sonya bit her lip and curled in on herself. Dora realized she had just touched upon some imaginary boundary that her friend didn't want to cross.

"When you four disappeared," Dora tried again, "I went through hell. And I'm not downplaying what happened to you, not in the slightest," she quickly added when she saw Sonya opening her mouth to reply. "But I was left here all alone, and nobody believed that I saw what I was trying to describe. Everybody looked down on me. Everybody ridiculed me. They made me change my statement and deny what I claimed to have seen. I guess what I'm trying to say is, I know the feeling. The feeling that it's just you against the world."

"Thanks," Sonya whispered, sniffling.

Dora nodded, feeling like she was closer than ever. "Maybe it would help you to open up about it… to tell me what you remember happening."

Sonya's expression changed again. This time, she went pale as she started to quiver.

"N–No," she whispered while shaking her head. "I c-can't…"

"Why not?"

"I can't," she repeated, this time even more quietly. "They can hear me."

A feeling of unease tingled down the back of Dora's neck. "Who can?"

Sonya lifted her hand, pointing to the corner on the opposite side of the room. It took Dora a moment to understand she was pointing under the other bed.

"They're here." Her lips were trembling. "They're lying in wait for it to get dark so they can come out. They came back here with us."

At first, fear petrified Dora, but the next thing she knew, she was shooting up. Sonya tried to grab her hand and pull her back, but her fingers barely grazed the sleeve of Dora's sweater. Dora took a few steps toward the opposite side of the room. The wooden floorboards were creaking with every step as she cautiously approached the bed. She rested her hands on the mattress as she knelt beside the bed. Her heart was pounding in her ears so loudly it drowned out everything else. She took a deep breath, convinced she wouldn't see anything underneath the bed, yet unable to shake the dreadful anticipation.

Dora slowly bent down and looked into the pitch dark. Astonished, she found herself staring into gleaming eyes.

Before she could even let out a startled scream, the creature's hand reached for her.

This time, it was the rozhanitsa herself who came to the door, as if she'd been expecting them, appearing on the doorstep even before Astrid had managed to knock. She crossed her arms over her chest and narrowed her eyes at them.

"Ye must be incredibly stupid to come back here," she said.

"I prefer the term *brave*," Tom countered.

"Maybe both," Astrid agreed. "But I'm not gonna give up. We want to undergo hypnosis again," she announced. "The both of us this time. Together."

The rozhanitsa raised her chin at them. "This time, it's gonna cost ye."

"We have money," Tom assured her, pulling two bills out of his pocket. Earlier, he told Astrid that he had stolen them from his mom's secret stash in the kitchen cupboard, hidden in a sugar bowl, positive she wouldn't have let him borrow any money if he'd asked. She was evidently still angry with him for visiting his father's house despite her pleas not to do so.

The old woman snatched the money from his hand with her dirty fingers, shoving it into the pocket of her apron. "Let's go then."

They entered the house and followed the rozhanitsa up the rickety stairs to her room. She hobbled along slowly, Astrid's impatience growing with every step.

When they finally reached the top of the stairs, Tom's stepmother stepped out of one of the rooms into the cramped hallway, carrying a load of laundry. She frowned the moment she recognized them.

"You've dragged them back here?" she hissed at her mother. "I told you that Tomas is against that boy coming here."

"This is my house," the old woman countered, bristling with confidence. "Yer husband had no right to tell me who I can and can't bring here. As long as I'm still breathing, I'm the one in charge."

They both stared at each other defiantly, but the younger woman eventually bowed her head in defeat.

"And ye shouldn't obey his every word either," the rozhanitsa advised her.

The younger woman pressed her lips into a thin line before descending the stairway.

"Let's go," the rozhanitsa urged them once again.

Today, the room was filled with heavy, stale air once more, with a hardly identifiable sweetish smell penetrating their senses. Astrid and Tom hung their coats over the backs of their chairs before sitting down. The rozhanitsa began to walk around the room, preparing the concoction. While she chewed up the mixture of herbs, she cut off a lock of hair from each of them. Tom gave Astrid a reassuring smile, but she could tell he was nervous.

"Combined hypnosis of two people at once is demanding," she informed them. "It might not work out. Either of ye could wake up at any point, losing the other. I can't guarantee ye'll encounter each other in the hypnotic realm. Do ye understand?"

"Yes." They nodded.

"Drink this." She poured each of them a cup of the concoction.

Astrid was slightly more prepared for the disgusting taste than Tom, who choked on it a bit.

"Place your hands on the table, grab each other's hands, and place your other hand in mine."

They obeyed. Astrid felt Tom squeezing her hand in encouragement, as well as feeling the fatigue that was suddenly spreading through her entire body. The rozhanitsa took out a ball of red yarn, and with a few deft movements, she bound their hands together.

"Heed my words. If your thoughts begin to stray, bring yourself back to what I'm saying. Allow everything that's about to happen to run its course. Close your eyes. Take a deep breath. And now breathe out."

Astrid fell under the hypnotic spell much faster than the day before. Her body was too exhausted.

"You feel the tension leaving your muscles. One after the other. Start with your right leg. You feel the tension leaving you. Now your left leg. Moving on to your arms…"

Astrid could feel Tom's grip loosening, though he kept holding her hand. Astrid's consciousness was gradually falling in on itself. This time, the white rabbit began to lead her almost immediately, and she set out after it without hesitation.

"Give into the feeling," the rozhanitsa's voice reached her ears from a distance.

"Ān... Tu... What do you see?"

She was standing in the middle of a white room. Right next to her, the outlines of a shadow gradually began to get clearer—she recognized it to be Tom.

"You're falling into a deep slumber... *Þrēo... Fēoper... Fīf...* Deeper and deeper."

She felt movement behind her and heard a shout. *Astrid!*

"*Max?*"

"*Seox... Seofon... Eahta...* You're now asleep. In a moment, you will go back to being six years old. Everything that happened afterward is gone. You'll return to the moment right before you vanished. In a few moments' time. *Nigon... Tīen.*"

The details of the white room were becoming clearer. Astrid suddenly found herself standing in the middle of her kindergarten classroom, and it was as if someone had cranked up the volume on a radio. All around her, kids were chittering away and roughhousing as they got dressed in their pajamas, getting ready for their afternoon nap. Their heads barely reached Astrid's waist, but she was certain that she was one of them, that she too was six years old again and was also getting ready for her nap with the others. As she stood there, she noticed that the sharp edges of objects and the outlines of the children's faces were slightly blurry, as if a mist were enveloping them all.

She fully realized that she was observing her own memory while reliving it.

"Astrid, can you help me?"

She looked down and met the eyes of her little brother, Max. Her heart leapt with joy. Her brother stood there, tangled up unhappily in his small turtleneck, which he was trying to get out of by himself to no avail. His dark hair sticking up every which way, his eyes shining with tears.

"Let me," she said soothingly. Astrid brought his hands up over his head, and with one deft movement, she freed him from the turtleneck. "Hand me your PJs."

Max turned to his bed and rummaged through the covers for a minute. In the meantime, Astrid took a look around. On her right, little ponytailed Dora was just pulling back her covers for her doll and herself. On her other side, Sonya was sitting ramrod straight on the edge of her bed, dressed immaculately in her pajamas, observing the others haughtily. And then Astrid finally noticed Tom. But it was no longer the small six-year-old boy from her memory. It was an adult Tom—her Tom—with whom she was currently being hypnotized. He was standing next to his tiny bed, wearing adult-sized kid pajamas and the same confused expression as herself.

"Here," Max interrupted Astrid with PJs in hand.

She resisted the urge to pull his tiny body into hers to give him a great big hug. Some invisible power was keeping her from doing so. She was forced to act exactly the same way as back then, and it was as if someone were putting the words in her mouth.

Astrid helped her baby brother into his PJs.

"And now one arm," she urged him. "And the other one here. Awesome."

Max let out a giggle as she flicked his nose. He crawled into his bed, lifted up his arms dutifully, and Astrid pulled the blanket all the way up to his neck. When she leaned over him, he placed his palms on her cheeks to pull her closer, whispering softly so nobody else could hear, "I'm scared, Astrid."

She could hear his little heart pounding wildly, like a baby bird.

"I'm here with you. Nothing's gonna happen to you, okay?"

"You promise?"

"I promise."

Only then did Max nod his head, seemingly pacified.

"Now I lay me down to sleep," she murmured, and Max was quick to join in. "And I shall awaken, for the evil spirits cannot reach me."

Astrid returned to her bed and pulled out her pajamas from under her pillow.

"Come on, Astrid, hurry up," the teacher rushed her along impatiently. She had a distant look in her eye again. Astrid suspected that she sometimes didn't even know what day of the week it was, or whether she was at work or at home. She felt sorry for her teacher, even though she often found herself at the receiving end of her yelling. Her mom had explained to her that the woman was unhappy, having to deal with much hardship.

Astrid was the last one to get in bed—even though it was a tiny bed and she had no idea how she was going to fit, it was as if it suddenly lengthened to accommodate her adult body. She let her hand fall from her bed and grasped Max's, though she was facing away from him. She locked eyes with Dora, who reciprocated her gaze.

Their teacher sat down on a chair in the middle of the classroom and began to read the story of Little Red Riding Hood. Astrid was only half-listening to her. For one, she knew the story well and didn't care to listen to the same story over and over again, and the teacher didn't put much emotion into reading the story either. Unlike her mother, she didn't even put on voices or make dramatic pauses. With her, the fairytales just weren't exciting enough.

In the past few weeks, Astrid hadn't gotten much sleep in kindergarten. She suffered from terrifying nightmares and didn't want her classmates to know about it. Whenever the teacher would do her rounds walking past the little beds, Astrid always screwed her eyes shut and pretended to be asleep. But as soon as she'd walked past her, her eyes would shoot open. And then she would stare at the wall for minutes on end, waiting for everybody to wake up.

But that day, Astrid felt uncharacteristically tired and weary. Whenever Dora yawned, so did she. Her eyes were slowly falling shut on their own. She always managed to catch herself in time, opening her eyes, but all it took were a few seconds for her eyelids to start drooping again.

Astrid suddenly got scared she might not be able to stick it out this time around. The fear of six-year-old Astrid filled the mind of the eighteen-year-old version. Memories that were twelve years old were suddenly flashing through her mind. And then, while Little Red Riding Hood fell into the Big Bad Wolf's trap, Astrid succumbed to sleep.

But even though she was asleep, some part of her managed to stay somewhat conscious. She got the feeling that as she was falling asleep, she could still hear everything happening around her. She was aware that the story had ended. That the teacher had shut the door, locking it behind her. And all of a sudden, the rustle of butterfly wings reached her ears, and she knew that everything was about to go wrong.

"Astrid… Astrid…"

Her eyes shot open. Though she had been lying on her right side as she fell asleep, she was now lying on her back, an invisible weight bearing down on her chest. The first thing she realized was that she was no longer holding Max's hand. Immediately afterward, she grasped just what had materialized right in front of her eyes— her nightmares, tangible and real.

The rustling of butterfly wings transformed into an almost imperceptible whisper, coming from them.

"Give in, Astrid. Give in…"

She could hear them right inside her head. They were talking to her. Whisperers.

She couldn't budge, she couldn't cry out. Astrid tried turning her head to look at Max, but it was impossible. A whisperer was leaning toward her, closer and closer. It opened its gaping mouth resembling a fathomless hole, reaching for her with its fingers, wrapping them around her body like a long black shawl.

"Close your eyes and sleep, Astrid… Lose yourself in your dreams…"

In the corner of her eye, she could make out a creature picking up Max on her left. Her brother was suspended midair, strangely paralyzed, his eyes wide with fear. She had to help him!

"I wonder if you know… Where do we go when we fall asleep?"

They were whispering, laying their words into her brain like maggots into fruit. Poisoning her mind.

Her lips froze in a silent scream that nobody heard.

And then the creature opened its mouth and swallowed her whole. Astrid dissolved into black nothingness.

She couldn't even see the tip of her nose in the pitch dark. But someone was holding her hand. It was Tom. She recognized his gentle touch. Knowing he was there with her was reassuring.

They were nowhere.

Never.

With nobody.

The only thing she could hear were their own breathing and the echo of Max's cry for help.

"Max!" she called for him desperately. "Max!"

"Astrid, don't do anything stupid," Tom warned her. "Don't let go of me or we'll never find our way back to each other here again."

The red thread held them tied together snugly.

"Hold on, Max!"

Suddenly, after a long span of silence, the voice of the rozhanitsa reached their ears. *"You're too far out… I can't keep a hold on you, you have to come back…"*

"No!" Astrid refused in a flash.

And all of a sudden, she knew where she was, where she had found herself at that moment in time—she was standing at the portal. At the very border between the land of the living and the land of the dead, between the real world and the magical world, between reality and the land of dreams. A mere few steps separated her from the place where Max was being held.

"Ān… Tu… Þrēo… Fēoþer… Fīf… You're slowly waking up…"

"No!" Astrid resisted. "I have to keep going."

"It's dangerous!" Tom warned her. "Let's go back…"

The wind was picking up all around them, and they suddenly found themselves smack in the middle of a strong whirlwind. Their ears were assaulted by the shrieks of invisible enemies. Dozens of hands were reaching for them, dragging them away through the portal.

"Seox... Seofon... Eahta... You're coming to."

The red thread snapped, and they lost each other in the dark.

"Tom!"

"Astrid!"

"Nigon... Tīen! Wake up."

What Astrid was feeling could be compared to someone shoving their hands into the core of her being, crushing all her ribs, and tearing out her very soul through the shards of her bones. And when an endless amount of time had passed, during which her body languished and her heart nearly ceased beating, and her soul was roughly shoved back into her body, they made sure that the wound was even bigger and more painful than before and that she'd feel, in every single particle of her flesh, that she had escaped death by a hair's breadth.

Astrid came back—and this time, it wasn't just an awakening from a deep trance, but a reconfiguration of her own self. An invisible force slammed her back into her own body, shot out of her chest like a shock wave, and rushed through the room. The candles set on the table were snuffed out immediately. The cups still holding some of the undrunk liquid crashed to the floor. The heavy drapes along the walls began to flutter. An inhumane shriek burst out of Astrid's mouth, nearly scaring her to death.

And that *something* swept through the room.

A muted crackle could be heard, followed immediately by a loud crack as the windowpane behind their backs shattered, the glass shards crashing out into the street.

The rozhanitsa let go of Astrid's hand in shock, as if it had burned her. She crossed her index and middle fingers, placing them first upon her brow and then her lips as she quickly muttered a prayer in the old tongue. Her words were indiscernible. Astrid was slowly coming to. She glanced over at Tom, who was sitting in his chair, broken, his chin lolling on his chest, eyes still shut.

"Tom!" She quickly flung herself at him, grabbing his face in her hands. His head lolled limply in her grasp, and he was deathly pale. "Tom, wake up!" She slapped his cheeks lightly. "What happened to him?" She rounded on the rozhanitsa in despair.

But the woman looked at her, as she later realized upon reflection, with a mixture of repulsion and sheer terror. "What've you done? What've you let in here, you stupid girl?"

"What are you talking about?" Astrid snapped, confusion lacing her voice. "What happened to Tom?"

A door slammed down below in the house. They could hear voices echoing toward them, and in no time, heavy, quick footsteps were thundering up the stairs.

"Get out of my house," the rozhanitsa told Astrid. "Get out, and take what you've so recklessly released into this world with you."

Baffled beyond belief, Astrid gaped at the woman. "What are you talking about?"

Tom was finally starting to come to. He groaned in confusion, his eyes flitting around. "What... What happened?" he mumbled.

"Thank the gods," Astrid let out a sigh of relief. "You're awake!"

The door flew open. Tomas Hattler stormed into the room, his face red with anger. "I don't care how much they paid you," he shouted at his mother-in-law, "but they're getting out of my house, now. Come on, scram!" He snapped at his son and Astrid as if they were nothing more than mangy rats. "Get the hell out of here!"

The rozhanitsa didn't protest, merely staring down at her old, wrinkled hands resting on the tabletop.

"Let's go," Astrid urged Tom. "We're leaving."

Thankfully, he didn't object. Perhaps he was still out of it or wanted to avoid a conflict with his father, but he slowly rose from his chair.

Astrid felt the need to smooth things over somehow. "I… I don't know what happened…"

"Get out," Mr. Hattler growled impatiently. "Right now."

"You didn't heed my words," the rozhanitsa told off Astrid in plain terms. "Our deal is off. You've gone farther than I can take you."

"But I need you…" Astrid blurted out as she gathered her things. "I need to go back."

"I warned you," the rozhanitsa said. "You can forget about me helping you. I'm not going to put you to sleep again. Didn't you feel it? Don't you realize what's gotten out?"

"Mother," Mr. Hattler interjected, his tone insistent. "They'll bring bad luck upon us."

He entered the room and grabbed Astrid and Tom by their sleeves, dragging them out. He had incredible strength.

"Let go of me!" Tom rounded on him. "Don't touch me!"

Astrid was nearly already in the hallway when she managed to glance back. "But who will help me?" she pleaded desperately.

"Find someone else," the woman advised her.

"But I don't know anybody else!"

The rozhanitsa cast her gaze down to her hands. "During the days when all is white, when the barriers between Nav and our mortal realm are removed, the dead can speak to the living. Your foremother has appeared to you. Ask her for the truth."

That was the last exchange of words they managed. Tom's father literally shoved them down the stairs and out of the house, wordlessly slamming and locking the door behind them. They both fell onto all fours into the snow. Neither of them could get up for a long time, and they just lay there, trying to figure out what had just happened.

It was Tom who spoke first, after what seemed like an eternity of silence.

"There were hundreds of them," he mumbled incredulously. "There *are* hundreds of them. You saw them too. We don't stand a chance against them."

Astrid stared at the night sky. She knew almost everything she needed to know.

"I think we used to call them Whisperers when we were kids. Remember? Because they always emitted this strange whispering murmur that infiltrated our dreams. I think that's how they managed to lure us away all those years ago. And that's why they spared Dora."

Tom looked at her with a confused expression.

"She couldn't hear them. She was lying on her right side," Astrid smiled sadly. "Her injured ear saved her. They weren't able to lure her in."

"So it was a coincidence? What about the incident from the night before we vanished? What about Morana?"

She hesitated. "I think you were partially right when you said my mind was messing with me. That thing in the field… It happened, something really was trying to drag off Max, but it wasn't Morana that I saw. I merged two things into one. I had come to see the holiday as the actual banishing of death so much that I daydreamed Morana into being. But it was one of them—one of the

Whisperers. He appeared when it got dark. Like so many times before in my dreams. He was lying in wait for us. Or for one of us, at least."

It had nothing to do with kidnapping or with Gusto, who had been innocent all along. The false accusations and shortsightedness of the villagers had driven him to take his own life.

The truth was much more terrifying.

They finally knew what they were up against. All they needed to do now was figure out how to outsmart them and how to find Max without running straight into their clutches.

Dora screamed at the same moment that the unnaturally pitch-black fingers wrapped around her wrist. For a fraction of a second, a warm tingle shot through her tattoo, like when a sip of hot tea spreads through a body numbed with cold. With surprising strength she didn't know she had, Dora yanked her hand away before the creature could pull her down under the bed. She banged the joints of her wrist against the edge of the bed, her hand emitting an unpleasant crunch, but she managed to escape. She scooted back frantically, shoving herself away from the bed as far as possible. She didn't stop until her back hit the bed that Sonya was sitting in.

But there was nothing chasing after her. She gasped for air, cradling her bruised hand unnaturally in her lap.

"What... What is that?" she whispered, completely terrified, her voice rising in pitch.

"Nightmares," Sonya whispered back. "They've come for us. They're waiting for us to fall asleep before dragging us back. The Notsnitsa has cursed us. Astrid has cursed us all."

Dora whirled back, staring at Sonya in shock. Her friend was trembling—from her eyelids to her lips—her shoulders visibly shaking in her fit of panic. Sweat broke out on her brow, as if she were in the throes of fever.

Dora was afraid to ask, but she realized this was precisely why Astrid had sent her here. "What do you know, Sonya? What aren't you telling me?"

The sweat was dripping into her friend's lashes, but she didn't utter a sound.

"You have to get out of here," Dora decided, her eyes fixed on the blackness under the bed, though she couldn't make out anything from so far away. "It's not safe here. Come with me. We'll tell your parents... Look, we'll think of something."

To Dora's surprise, Sonya shook her head. "Don't you get it? There's nowhere to go. They're everywhere, and if they're not, it's just a matter of time before they show up for me. I have no place to escape them."

Dora didn't know what to say. Her mouth fell open, but she promptly closed it again. She knew there were no words that would comfort her friend.

"You should go," Sonya said. It didn't sound like she was worried—she was merely stating the facts as they were. "I'm telling you, don't get mixed up in this. You don't know what... The less you know, the better."

"But..."

"Run, Dora," she warned her. "Run while you still can."

Dora tried to get Sonya to keep talking to her, but she just sat there curled up in her bed, a distant look in her eye. After a few minutes of her trying in vain, Dora got up and left. She headed straight home as it began to get dark outside. With what she'd seen under the bed and with the sun setting fast, anxiety was beginning to bloom within her. What if Sonya was right? And they'd come for her no matter where she was?

Astrid had a plan for the coming night, and the hypnosis she had undergone had changed nothing. On the contrary, the unpleasant experience increased her desire to hurry the whole thing along. The rozhanitsa had been right. They had both felt it. Something had crossed over during Astrid's journey into her own memories and subconscious, or wherever it was that she'd ended up. Something that didn't belong here. Maybe Sonya had actually been right after all. Maybe it had really been her who had damned them all.

Astrid tried to stay cool, calm, and collected. Judging by what she'd relived in her hypnotic state that afternoon, Dora truly remembered the circumstances of their disappearance with remarkable accuracy for a little girl. When Astrid had been lying in her kid bed again in the middle of her kindergarten classroom, a sense of having seen, heard, and experienced it all before overcame her right then and there. Not only because she had slowly begun to recall the events of the day of her disappearance, but also because it resembled many days and nights preceding the whole tragedy. Always those same nightmares about pitch-black fingers wrapping around her neck to strangle her. And then one day, the Whisperers crossed over—they transcended the barrier to get what they came for. They had been shadowing her for years, until they finally managed to whisk them all away. But to where? And most importantly, how was she going to get there?

The answer to this last question seemed crucial. Without it, she'd never be able to find Max.

Tom and Astrid had split up on their way back from the rozhanitsa's house. If her plan was to work out tonight, they needed a few things that she sent him off to get a hold of. No sooner had they gone their separate ways than Astrid got a sinking feeling in her gut. She was walking down the street alone, but she felt eyes on her, as if she were trapped inside a stifling bubble that clung to her wherever she went. She kept looking over her shoulder nervously, but she didn't see anyone peering at her through the windows of the surrounding houses either. Where was this feeling of a hundred eyes on her coming from? What was her subconscious trying to tell her?

A man was standing in his driveway, barely paying attention to anything beyond scraping the ice from the sidewalk. A stray cat crossed her path, bestowing a disdainful look upon her, as cats were wont to do, before continuing on its way. The neighbors across the road were in the middle of saying goodbye to someone in front of their house. The group went quiet as their eyes met, fixing their gazes on her until Astrid looked away, bowing her head.

She was mere steps away from her house when out of the blue, the bells began to toll. Extremely loudly and much differently than when they were keeping time or summoning worshipers for Mass. The bells were ringing like crazy, as if in alarm, sounding like a warning. Astrid paused for a moment, her hand resting on the gate to her house.

"What is it? What's going on?" A terrified voice could be heard from between the houses.

The neighbors across the street hastily said their goodbyes, grabbing their kids and quickly disappearing into their homes.

"Come on, hurry up!"

With each passing second, it seemed the bells were getting louder and louder.

A neighbor dashed out of her house on the corner of the street. Astrid didn't remember her name, but the woman began to scream hysterically at the children sledding down the hill near the cemetery. "Nora! Edgar!"

There was no way they could possibly hear her. She ran out, half-dressed and wearing only her slippers, straight for the hill, and continued yelling at her kids.

Doors were slamming shut left and right. Some people didn't think twice before bolting down their aging window shutters too. Astrid walked up to her house and closed the door behind her with mixed feelings. No sooner had she entered the hallway than she came face to face with her grandmother, who must've been lying in wait for her behind the door.

"Where've ye been all day?" she rounded on her, her tone unpleasant. She shoved Astrid to the side and slammed the door shut herself, as if her granddaughter was incapable of doing so properly. She turned the key twice in the lock and deadbolted the door.

Astrid swallowed her pride and forgot her rule of avoiding conversations with her grandmother. "What's all the fuss? What's up with the bells?"

Grandma pressed her lips into a thin line and sauntered off with a slow shuffle back to the kitchen.

"Could you answer me?" Astrid asked her impatiently. "What's going on?"

"A curfew's been imposed," she finally replied. "Everybody's got to be home by nightfall, and nobody's allowed to go outside before first light."

Taken aback, Astrid found herself standing in the kitchen

doorway. Her aunt was sitting at the table, darning the men's overalls. Grandma returned to the stove where the pots were bubbling away. Both acted as if the sounded alarm was an everyday occurrence and the curfew didn't bother them. She didn't get it.

"Why the curfew? On whose orders?"

Her aunt lifted her gaze from her task and glanced at Grandma. She waited to see whether she would respond, but when she stayed quiet, she went ahead and answered her. "The Elders met today to discuss last night's incident and decided on these temporary safety measures."

"What incident?" Astrid didn't understand. "Because of Gusto?"

Her aunt set aside her sewing for a minute. "Didn't you hear? Half the village's chickens were throttled to death during the night. The ill omens are piling up."

Astrid felt a sinking feeling in her gut. "Wolves?" she tried.

Her aunt's eyes flitted over to her grandmother again. But she kept stirring something in the pot with her back to them, as if unaware of their conversation. "Couldn't be wolves. All the chickens were strangled. Wolves would've torn them to pieces."

"The Elders can't possibly forbid people from going out because of a bunch of chickens," Astrid said in a doubtful voice.

"It ain't just because of the chickens," Grandma snarled from the stove.

"Then what is it? Why don't the Elders tell it like it is?"

She got no reply to that. Astrid felt like there was something hanging in the air that everybody knew about but was pretending didn't exist.

"Is it because of the demons?"

Grandma slammed a pot lid down on the counter. "Shut up. Don't summon them into this house!"

"Or what? You can't lock me in the cellar. I'm not five anymore."

Astrid turned on her heel and left to go to her mom's room. She needed to calm down. She hated her body for reacting to her grandmother's presence every time—how anxiety always surged within her and wrapped around her organs, how scared she felt, as she remembered spending hours on end in the dark, damp cellar as punishment. She was an adult. That woman no longer had any power over her, she couldn't hurt her anymore, and yet her voice still trembled whenever she spoke to her, and she was afraid of every one of her blunt words.

"How was your day, Mom?"

Lena Mahler was sitting by the window, looking out. She was wholly unaware of curfews and strangled chickens. She just observed the world around her, no longer in touch with it.

Astrid sat down next to her. When she was just a little girl, her mother had encouraged her to pray to the gods every night before going to bed.

"Everybody should believe in something, Astrid," she used to tell her when her daughter refused to participate in the evening prayer.

Being six years old, Astrid didn't understand faith all that much, but it seemed that if the gods truly did exist, then surely they'd never allow her to feel so useless so often, as if she were nothing, a mere smudge of dirt she'd forgotten to mop up and gotten a thrashing for it from her grandmother. Surely, the gods would never let her grandmother lock her in the cellar, even as she sobbed and begged to be let go. Surely, the gods would've helped her whenever Kristian and his brother stuffed straw down her pants and smeared chicken poop all over her hair before locking her in the chicken coop. The gods wouldn't allow her nightmares to become real and steal them away to who knows where.

"Are you hungry?" Astrid asked her mother a bit pointlessly.

More than anything, her mother had picked at her breakfast and barely even touched lunch, which was spread around her plate in pieces.

"Come on, I'll help you wash yourself."

She led her mother to the bathroom, where she helped her get undressed and get in the bathtub. While she rinsed her gently, she wondered whether her mom mourned both her children the same. She may have never said it out loud, but Astrid knew that her mother loved Max more. He was the baby of the family. The one she had always embraced first—not because he was younger or because he needed it, but simply because she wanted to. She didn't treat them as differently as Grandma did, but children can tell these things anyway. Astrid had always felt that her mother pushed her away, that she blamed her for something she herself couldn't put into words and probably never would, because she'd never again have the opportunity to ask. Astrid had always felt that her mother's hugs were colder, that she sometimes glanced at her from the corner of her eye as if she were a stranger. Astrid was certain that if ice broke under herself and her brother, her mother would jump to pull out Max first—even if he were the better swimmer.

The despair that took hold of Lena after their disappearance was mainly caused by the loss of her beloved Max. And perhaps partly due to guilt that she couldn't feel the same for her firstborn child.

"Careful," Astrid said as she helped her mother step out of the bathtub. "Take small steps."

She slowly toweled her off and changed her into her nightgown. They returned to the room. Astrid pulled back the covers on her mother's bed and helped her lay down. As she was covering her with the blanket, something unexpected occurred.

All of a sudden, Lena grabbed Astrid's hand. Astrid jerked back in shock.

"I… I should've told you," she wheezed out in a hoarse whisper. "I should've told you the truth. I should've told you where we go when we fall asleep."

"Mom!" Astrid gasped, shocked to hear her mother's voice after so many years. "What are you talking about? What is it you should've told me?"

The rare moment disappeared just as quickly as it arrived, the light in Lena's eyes dimmed, her hand fell back down upon the blanket, and once again, her mother was gone, her eyes staring into space. Astrid kept talking to her, but her voice broke after a while.

She was too far gone.

Astrid was wary of one thing only—that her plan, despite being foolishly risky, would ultimately be thwarted by something as banal as a curfew. She hoped that Tom was still on the same page as her and wouldn't back out and leave her to go through with it on her own.

Sneaking out of the locked house without her grandmother noticing actually proved to be much harder than she had expected. It was as if nobody wanted to go to sleep tonight, as everybody kept walking through the house. And as if suspecting her plan, her grandmother remained sitting in the kitchen after dinner for an unusually long time, and Astrid eventually began to run out of excuses as to why she urgently needed to go into the kitchen and pantry right at that hour. She knew how conspicuous her feigned cough must've seemed as she desperately tried to stuff a sachet of dried herbs down her front, trying to cover the rustling noises. She rummaged around the shelves blindly in the dark, sniffing at the individual boxes, scared that if she turned on the light, her grandmother would catch her stealing. It was a paradox—in reality, she could hardly steal something that belonged to her. It had been her mom who had grown, picked, and dried all the herbs and flowers, and Astrid had the right to use them. But when it came to her grandmother, one never knew what to expect.

Astrid packed the essentials into her backpack. She couldn't wait any longer. They had agreed to meet at ten o'clock, but as the clock struck ten, her uncle was still wide awake, pacing up and down the hallway. Astrid found herself sitting motionlessly on her bed, watching another half-hour go by. Her eyes sometimes flitted to the moth fluttering around its glass prison. It was still alive. She didn't even want to know how that was possible. It wasn't until almost eleven, as she nodded off with fatigue, that the house finally fell silent. She tiptoed out of her room, heading to the front door. She had almost made it into the hallway when she heard a rustle behind her. She expected to come face to face with her grandmother, who had been shooting her furtive looks all evening, but it was Kristian instead. Astrid had been avoiding him since that incident in his room.

"You think the curfew doesn't apply to you or something?" He narrowed his piggy eyes at her.

She didn't allow herself to be intimidated by him. "Thought you said you didn't want to be under one roof with someone like me."

Kristian stepped off the last stair into the hall, reducing the space between them. Astrid automatically took a step back, but her back clumsily made contact with the old sideboard. Kristian noticed her startled expression when the silverware rattled.

"Afraid granny's gonna catch you sneaking out?"

"What's it to you?"

"Everything. When the Elders ordered us not to leave the house, it was with good reason. I don't want you bringing more of a curse on this house than you already have, *cuckoo bird*."

"I'm getting tired of all of you talking to me in riddles. Acting like you know more than me," she hissed and turned around to leave. "Just try to stop me."

She pulled on her boots and coat in record time, just in case Kristian decided to take her up on her dare, but he didn't budge. "You're running around with that dipshit Hattler Jr. and Batty Dory?" he taunted her. "With the pale one from that penniless family to complete the gang, right? Oh, sorry… apart from your brother, that is."

Astrid whipped around. "Don't you dare mention my brother."

"What did you do to him, Astrid? Did you leave him there because everybody liked him better than you?"

Astrid wanted to punch him. To break that bulbous nose of his. To sink her nails into his eyes. To scream at the top of her lungs that if she could, she'd give her life for Max and trade places with him. But Kristian wasn't worth all that. He just wanted to provoke her. To strike a sensitive spot.

But she knew his secret.

"It was you who pushed Dory into that grave, wasn't it?" she whispered. "You, your brother, and your little pals from school. I know you used to go behind the cemetery to dig up old graves. I saw you there many times."

Kristian didn't even bat an eyelid. "You want to pin some stupid prank on me?"

"Prank? Dora could've frozen to death. That fall could've broken her neck. That was no prank—it was an assault."

260

"She was hysterical and made a scene," Kristian shrugged arrogantly. "And then whimpered about it like a little kitten. She was asking for it."

Astrid stared at him incredulously. "You make me sick. You better believe you're gonna pay for what you did to Dora."

With those words, she unlatched and unlocked the door, walking out into the night. She wasn't going to let anyone intimidate her anymore. She wasn't a little girl anymore that Kristian could bully around.

The dogs were barking their heads off again. Maybe they had never stopped in the first place. When she thought about it, she'd heard their incessant barking for the past few days. It subsided a bit during the day, but was in full force at night. As if the darkness somehow nettled the animals until they couldn't take it anymore.

Dora took the imposed curfew very seriously. But when the boiler started acting up again, and rusty, foul-smelling water began pouring from the kitchen faucet, she had no choice but to take a pail and go fetch some water from the well in the yard.

She bundled up in layers and went out through the backdoor into the yard. It was peculiarly quiet outside, apart from the barking. She set the pail under the spout of the water pump and began pumping. Rhythmic creaking, the water jetting out sporadically, and the teenage girl's accelerated breathing cut through the silence.

A pail of fresh water would be enough. They'd have to do without a bath, but her brothers were always acting up every night before bed anyway, whining that they didn't want to take a bath, so she'd be making them happy for once. But the pail was too heavy for her to lift due to her injured hand. She took it in her arms, and a bit of the water splashed out on her shoe when an inhuman shriek pierced the night. Dora dropped the pail on the ground, her hands shooting up to cover her ears. The shriek was unbearable, penetrating every particle of her body and sowing a coldness within. She abandoned the pail and dashed back toward the house as fast as she could. Dora had almost reached the doorstep when such a terrible chill suddenly overtook her, she found herself gasping for air. The wind picked up, and something resembling an invisible storm hurtled through the dark from the east. Dora grabbed for the doorknob as a wave of something rushed at her. But this time, the cold gust penetrated deeper, and Dora could feel it wrapping around her heart, which suddenly felt like it was no longer a part of her body. It almost scared her to death. She began to grapple with the door, which suddenly wouldn't budge, and pray to all the gods out there. The shock wave was gathering strength and rushing through the forest toward her, bending the entire length of the trees down to the ground.

Dora finally managed to get inside. She quickly locked and deadbolted the door behind her, backing away from it in alarm. Something slammed into the door with a thunderous thud.

Again. And again. As if the something was knocking on the door.

"Dory! What's going on?" one of her brothers cried out. "I'm scared!"

"Dory!"

She wasn't able to answer. She crossed her trembling fingers, pressing them to her forehead and then her lips, rattling off one prayer after another as they sprang to mind.

The pounding on the door ceased. Dora waited with anticipation for what was going to happen. Had they given up? Or would they attack with even greater strength than before?

Something collided with the window. Giant clawed hands scraped along the windowpane with a screech until her blood ran cold. She cried out.

Sonya had been right. They had found her.

Valeria Hattler, sleepy and in her dressing gown, didn't look too thrilled to see Astrid on her doorstep around eleven o'clock, despite the curfew, especially when Tom tried to talk her into letting his friend sleep over. She might've even started to suspect that the girl was a bad influence on her son but kept it to herself. After a while of negotiations, she finally offered to put her up on the couch in the living room. But Tom insisted she sleep in his room.

"It'll be better this way, Mom," he whispered to her around the corner while Astrid waited by the door. "She suffers from nightmares. I can't just leave her alone like that."

Tom's negotiation tactics almost made Astrid smile. He was basically telling his mom the truth. She did suffer from nightmares. But if Mrs. Hattler knew the full extent of what that meant in her case, there's no way she'd have allowed her to stay the night.

"Your room is too small."

"I'll let Astrid take the bed and sleep on the ground," he countered, his mind made up.

Mrs. Hattler was still hesitant. "I don't know what you two are up to, but…"

"Nothing, Mom," Tom assured her. "We… We just don't want to be alone, you know? After everything that happened."

"You're not alone," she comforted him. The tenderness in her voice warmed Astrid's heart. What she wouldn't give to hear something like that from her own mom.

"I know I'm not. But Astrid is."

The warmth she felt immediately vanished, replaced by a feeling of being doused in ice-cold water. Of course, Astrid was able to distance herself from his words, and she knew that he'd say anything to get his mother to agree while assuring her just enough to make sure she wouldn't suspect anything. Nevertheless, the truth hurt.

But there was no time to feel sorry for herself. They'd already lost a few precious hours when she was unable to sneak out of her house. Mrs. Hattler brought out an extra blanket and pillow while Tom carried the sofa cushions into his room. He set up a makeshift bed on the ground. Once his mother looked it over with a critical eye and deemed it far enough from where Astrid was going to sleep, she went off to bed. Tom left to go to the kitchen to make Astrid the large cup of tea that she'd requested. In the meantime, she prepared everything they needed—positioning the candles consecrated to Dazhbog and sprinkling dried fennel along the windowsill and doorstep to protect them from any evil entering the house. She drew the symbols of protection with chalk on the wall and the inner part of the door. Tom returned to his room with a large mug. A blend of lemon balm, passionflower, and valerian, traditionally used as a sleep aid, wafted through the air.

"Are you sure?" he asked.

"I'm sure."

Astrid took the mug from him and took several gulps of the tea. She scalded her throat and tongue, but she didn't care. She'd spent the last five days fighting sleep. Tonight, she would face it head-on.

There was another mug in Tom's hand, this one even bigger than hers. Astrid shot him a questioning glance.

"Coffee," he explained. "To help me stay awake."

"Thanks for doing this for me."

Tom smiled. "Don't thank me. You'd go ahead with it, with or without me. You're too stubborn and I don't have what it takes to talk you out of it anyway."

"That you don't."

"Better to stay on your good side, then," he joked. "And I meant what I said. Take my bed. I'm not gonna be lying down anyway. I'll sit next to you on the floor and—"

"Or you could... you could stay here, next to me," Astrid blurted out before she even realized what she was saying. She quickly glanced away so he wouldn't see how her face had turned red.

"Sure," Tom's response was immediate.

Her back facing him, Astrid smiled to herself. Tom was the first to crawl into bed and sat back against the wall, huddling in the corner. Astrid curled up next to him, carefully resting her head on his shoulder. Neither of them said anything, but Tom lifted his arm in such a way as to allow Astrid to cuddle into his embrace. She lay there with her head on his chest and closed her eyes. Suddenly, she knew that there wasn't a safer place on earth.

"If you start to feel that..." she started to say, but almost immediately yawned.

"I'll wake you up," he assured her in a firm tone. "No matter what happens, I'll wake you up in time. I'll be right here."

Sleep overcame her unexpectedly quickly. She didn't even have enough time to wonder whether Tom felt her racing heart. She hoped he did. She wished he could tell that it wasn't caused by fear but by his close proximity.

Astrid was ready to offer herself up to the Whisperers like a piece of meat. It was finally time to stop resisting it. She hoped they would take her away, far away. Deep into dreamland, where Max was waiting for her. There was no other option for her to start searching than this one. She prayed that it wasn't also the last.

THE SIXTH NIGHT

This time, something was different. Astrid couldn't pinpoint what it was, but the moment she fell asleep, she knew.

Tom's soft, warm embrace was gone, and even though her body was still in his arms, Astrid couldn't feel a thing—as if it were only herself and herself alone, curled up and paralyzed, that existed.

Two Whisperers were sitting in the opposite corner of the room. She couldn't see them, couldn't turn her head their way, but she felt their presence. They began to draw nearer.

It was impossible to switch off the fear she felt in that moment. Astrid couldn't detach herself from it, no matter how much she wanted to. She knew what was coming, she had wanted it this way, but was still unable to convince herself that everything was going to be okay. Astrid realized that the fear wasn't coming from her, from her inner self, but it was these creatures who were sowing fear all around them, emitting it like vibrations that she couldn't fight off.

The intense rustling of butterfly wings was getting louder and louder. Astrid already knew that it was their whispering—words meant to poison her mind and escalate her fear to an absurd degree. The Whisperers drew closer, wrapping their fingers around her hands entwined with Tom's. They moved up the bed, higher and higher, engulfing her in their darkness. This time, Astrid didn't try to wake up, didn't try to escape them. Inwardly, she was screaming, kicking, fighting them off—but with the same tenacity she had fought them in her mind, she plunged headfirst into the endless darkness.

Suddenly, Astrid found herself standing in the midst of grayish fog. The Whisperers were nowhere to be seen, and she was completely alone. No matter which way she looked, the gray nothingness was spread out everywhere in the form of hovering, identical clouds. She could throw herself in any direction, it didn't matter.

Before long, the fog parted, creating a narrow opening that resembled a gorge. A small cloud morphed into a white rabbit, dashing past Astrid's feet and into the distance. And so she broke into a run. She ran, because she felt she had to. Though Astrid had no idea where she was going, she ploughed through the fog, the sounds of her footsteps fading into silence.

She ran and ran for minutes, maybe hours. Her legs were starting to give out, she had a stitch in her side, but she didn't stop. The white rabbit vanished, the fog parted, and Astrid found herself in a narrow, dungeon-like room, lit only by two torches on opposite walls.

Suddenly, Astrid heard something moving behind her. She lifted her arms up defensively, ready to fight, but there was nobody there. She swiveled her head back to face the room and jerked back in shock. Right in front of her was her brother.

"Max!" she cried out with relief and ran to him. But something in his expression made Astrid stop in her tracks. Her smile froze on her lips as she realized her brother was looking at her in a way he never had before—with repulsion and hatred.

"What happened?" she asked him warily.

"How could you do this to me, Astrid?"

"I don't understand what you're—"

"Why did you leave me here? I thought I was your little brother! I thought you loved me, I thought we did everything together! You promised Dad you'd always look out for me. But those were all just empty promises. You left me here and saved yourself. You're a bad person."

"Max, this isn't the best time or place," Astrid protested weakly. Her usual levelheadedness was replaced by panic. "Come on, we gotta get out of here. I came back for you, and right now, we need to run. I'll explain everything once I get you somewhere safe."

She reached out for him, but Max brushed her off.

"You know what I think, Astrid? I think you're lying to me again. You told me that I was safe—that nothing would happen to me. But look where we are right now! Where I ended up! Where you abandoned me! I trusted you! It's all your fault!"

"That's not true!" Astrid's voice trembled with fear.

"You're nothing but a monster, Astrid. You lie to everyone around you, but I know what you're really like. I saw you doing witchcraft. You brought evil down on us. You're to blame for what happened to us."

"No," Astrid whispered, tears welling in her eyes. She tried to convince herself that this was just an illusion, but the fear that was currently eating away at her insides was stronger. Two figures suddenly appeared behind Max. They stepped out of the shadows, and to her horror, Astrid realized she was now face to face with her parents.

"How many times have I told you to act normal?! You were supposed to fit in. Why can't you be like other children?" her mother scolded her. "Why couldn't you just listen to me and not stick your nose where it doesn't belong? And instead take care of your brother?"

"I tried, I really did," Astrid whispered.

"You're my biggest disappointment," her father hissed at her. "How could I have trusted you to keep your promises?"

"Dad…"

"I don't want your help," Max added. "It's too late, anyway. I'm stuck here forever. And you should be too. You belong here. Stay here with me, Astrid."

"It'll be better that way for everybody," her mother agreed. "You won't be able to hurt anyone else if you stay here."

"No, please," Astrid pleaded, falling down to her knees.

Their voices grew louder and louder as they spoke over each other, each word as painful as a punch to the stomach. The words Astrid had always been most afraid to hear were falling from their lips.

Astrid had fallen asleep incredibly quickly. Tom wasn't surprised— she had looked utterly exhausted. No sooner had she rested her head on his chest than her breathing evened out. He was on ten- terhooks, waiting to see what would happen, but for the first hour, nothing at all occurred. Astrid slept soundly, curled up so close he could smell her hair. Tom had pins and needles in his arm, and soon he couldn't feel his hand, but he didn't dare move an inch, lest he wake her up by accident.

In her sleep, Astrid's features were relaxed—the mask of an un-approachable Astrid was gone—and she suddenly looked much younger and more vulnerable. Tom wanted to touch her, to caress her hair to let her know he was there with her, no matter what internal struggle she was going through. But something prevented him from doing so, some sense of shame or embarrassment that he was going behind her back like a coward.

The night dragged on. Tom lay in bed, embracing an unmoving Astrid, and wondered what it would've been like if they hadn't vanished back then. Would their childhood friendship have lasted? Was a friendship between a girl and a boy even possible? Wouldn't they have grown apart over the years?

It seemed strange to him that they last spoke as six-year-old kids, then a chunk of their lives had been stolen from them, and now they'd barely spent more than a few days together as adults. And yet, during those few days, Tom felt somewhere deep inside that Astrid was the closest person he had in this world, that he could talk to her about anything, and that every hour they spent apart was somehow devoid of meaning. No matter where they had been for the past twelve years—remembering nothing, for whatever reason—they had been together. He was sure of it, with every par-ticle of his being. They had spent over a decade together, and no memory loss could take that away from them.

Around midnight, the witching hour, Astrid finally stirred. At first Tom thought she had only gotten a cramp in her leg—he was all sorts of sore and stiff himself—but after her leg jerked, her en-tire body tensed from head to toe.

"Astrid?" he whispered warily.

She didn't answer and she didn't wake up. Her whole body was drawn tight as a string. Some inner drama was unfolding just behind her eyelids—her eyes flitting from side to side frantically. A muted whimper pushed past Astrid's lips. In the corner of his eye, Tom registered movement. He lifted his head a fraction and came face to face with the creatures he'd seen in his hypnotic state not several hours ago.

They were here and they were real.

Tom didn't bat an eyelid as they began to draw near.

The nightmare changed.

Her mom, her dad, and Max all suddenly froze mid-motion, turning into statues as Grandma appeared right above Astrid's kneeling form. But Hedda Mahler wasn't the old and tired woman she was in the present day. She looked like she did back when Astrid was still a little girl. Suddenly, she grabbed Astrid by the hair with such force that the girl cried out.

"What're ye crying about this time? I'll give ye something to cry about!"

With incredible strength, she jerked Astrid forward. The girl fell to the ground, and Hedda proceeded to drag her along by her hair.

"That hurts!" Astrid shouted, her arms and legs flailing.

"Everything in our house always revolves 'round this brat. I've had enough," Hedda spit out in a spiteful tone.

"Dad!" Astrid cried out desperately. But her dad didn't budge, staring blankly ahead of himself as if carved out of stone.

"My son may have been yer saving grace, but he's not here to protect you anymore," her grandmother snarled. "Ye won't get away with any more o' yer nonsense. Those days are over."

The woman dragged her along the ground like a ragdoll as tears of pain sprang into Astrid's eyes.

"Gonna get that nonsense out o' yer head once and for all."

"Grandma, please. It hurts! Grandma!"

Hedda stopped in front of a stone wall, where a door suddenly sprang into existence. Astrid yelped. The door looked exactly like the one leading to their cellar.

"Don't do this, Grandma! I'll be good, I promise, I'll start behaving!"

But Hedda didn't pay her any mind as she yanked the door open and kicked Astrid inside. The girl collapsed right past the threshold as her grandmother began leaning full force into the door. Astrid managed to latch onto the doorframe—but in that instance, the door slammed shut, catching her fingers. Something crackled in her bones. The girl yelled out.

"Stop fighting it! Ye deserve to be locked away, ye deserve to rot in the cellar where ye belong, ye brat. Ye're nothing but a burden."

The door finally shut, Astrid found herself engulfed in darkness. The putrid stench of rot and dampness assaulted her nose head-on. The girl sat on the cold ground, her eyes straining to adapt to the impenetrable darkness. Astrid's heart was in her mouth as she desperately tried to stop thinking about the cramped space she was in. With each passing second, it grew more and more difficult to catch her breath. She didn't know what was lurking in the pitch dark. She didn't *want* to know.

It's just a dream, it's just a nightmare, it's not real, she kept repeating to herself.

But Astrid couldn't convince her mind to accept the truth of her own words. An alarm kept going off in her brain. She would be stuck here in the dark forever. The Whisperers would slowly suffocate her. There would be nothing left of her.

Astrid placed her head on her knees, trying to take a deep breath. She felt a panic attack coming on.

She'd been sitting here for hours. Or was it mere seconds?

There was no way out of here. She could very well be stuck here for ages…

Astrid knew it was only a game. They were likely trying to break her down mentally to her very core. To induce the utmost terror. Astrid wanted so much to believe that she could overcome her own self. She wanted so much to convince herself that this was just a dream. But in this instance, it just seemed impossible.

The Whisperers were back. They surrounded her from all sides.

"What do you want from me?" Astrid cried out. "What do you want? Why am I here?"

They didn't answer. Their whispers grew louder.

"Where is my brother?" she managed to get out in between sobs. "What did you do to him? You hear?"

Stop fighting us, they whispered. *Come join us.*

Something touched Astrid's head. Pain shot through her temples, as if someone had pressed a red-hot poker to her skin.

And then, an image of a desolate forest full of tall larch trees flashed through her mind.

Finally, *finally*, Astrid knew where to start looking.

"Astrid!"

She heard screaming, and it took her a long time to realize that the person screaming was her. She couldn't bring herself to stop.

"Wake up, Astrid! It's me. You're okay!"

Tom shook her. Astrid opened her eyes, and it was only when she recognized the face in front of her that she stopped yelling. Even then, she couldn't catch her breath.

"You're okay. I'm here," Tom soothed her.

Astrid was cold. She glanced around in confusion, noticing she was no longer lying in bed, but in the bathtub, ice-cold water gushing out of the faucet at full blast. Her hair and pajamas were drenched. She was clutching Tom's arms in a viselike grip as he held her tight.

"I'm gonna let you go for a second, okay? Just need to shut off the water," Tom explained before he quickly switched off the faucet and grabbed her again. "Everything's okay. I've got you."

"Wh-What happened?" Astrid managed to get out.

"I couldn't get you to wake up," Tom said, his face despondent. "You began thrashing around. I had no idea what was going on. You didn't react to my words, I tried shaking you awake, but… no reaction. Then I got the idea to try waking you up with cold water, so I dragged you in here…"

Astrid stared at him incredulously.

"Come on, let's get you out or you'll catch a cold."

He helped Astrid up to her feet, leaving her standing up to her ankles in ice-cold water. In that instance, Tom's mother appeared in the doorway. Her jaw dropped in shock.

"For Perun's sake! What's going on here?" the woman asked in a panic. "I heard screams…" Her gaze fell from Tom to a drenched Astrid, who began to shiver with cold.

"She had a nightmare," Tom explained, his voice surprisingly steady. "I couldn't wake her up…"

"So you stuck her in the bathtub? And flooded half the bathroom while you were at it?"

With shaky legs, Astrid stepped out onto the bathroom tiles. Tom handed her a towel, which she wrapped around herself.

"I'll clean it up, Mom," he assured her. "Go back to sleep."

But Valeria Hattler didn't look like she believed them. She lingered in the doorway, staring down her son. But, for some reason, Tom won the silent battle of wills.

"We'll be talking about this in the morning," she promised him before leaving for her bedroom.

Astrid and Tom found themselves alone in the bathroom, standing next to each other in a puddle of water. Neither knowing where to start, they both spoke at the same time.

"I saw the Whisperers. They were in the room," Tom said.

"I know where to start looking," Astrid blurted out.

Tom froze in shock. "Okay, you win. You go first."

"It wasn't a competition!" Astrid cried out, feigning offense. "And if it was, then winning brings me no joy."

"I was just kidding," Tom assured her. "Go on, talk. I'm listening."

"I..." Astrid searched for the right words. "I think I finally get it. Our dreams are the key to this whole thing... They're the way to getting back to that place. But does it mean that all we have to do is fall asleep? I doubt it. That'd be too easy. Just now, I was on the precipice. I didn't cross over into the dream, I didn't get far enough, deep enough... All this time, I've been going about it wrong."

"I don't understand. What're you getting at?"

"That place we came from isn't just something in our heads, in our subconscious. Think about it—it wasn't only our minds that were gone, like when we fall asleep or are hypnotized. We disappeared, bodies and all. That means that we have to be able to get *there* physically. The dreams are just the key to finding the way, not the actual gateway. The portal we passed through is somewhere deep in the Black Forest... I saw the trees again, sharp and clear this time, and the way there—I think I've been to that spot before as a kid. That's why we all turned up covered in mud and dirt... The Black Forest is where we need to go."

"But the Guards have already searched the woods." Tom clearly had his doubts. "They said the tracks led as if from nowhere, and they didn't find anything else beyond the borders of the village."

"I don't trust them. I don't trust the Guards, and I don't trust the Elders either. Think about it. Nobody was really looking for us. They didn't care about it twelve years ago, and they don't care about it now, about what happened to Max. They just want their peace and quiet. To appease the village, as if everything's fine. To rattle off their prayers, bow down to their gods, and wait until it all blows over."

"But everything's not fine. If they announced the curfew today, then it means..."

Astrid nodded. "It means they know what's going on. They know that this year, during the nights of the demons, demons really have crossed over to our world and now walk among us. And if that portal is anywhere, it's gotta be close by. Tom, think about it. The curfew and the claims that they found nothing in the forest. They're just trying to keep us away from it."

"Astrid, you do realize that the Black Forest is huge, right? That even the most experienced trackers get lost in there? It's a wild, treacherous place. Few people have ever seen all of it in a single lifetime. Not to mention—if a portal really is hidden somewhere in there, it might be guarded by creatures I don't even want to think about. Finding the exact spot could take... weeks."

277

Astrid didn't dare look at him. Perhaps so he couldn't read the fear in her eyes.

"I know. But we only have six days left."

That morning, the temperature dropped deep below the freezing point. It was so cold that ice flowers bloomed on the crooked, shabby kitchen ceiling. Dora observed them from the stove as she made scrambled eggs for breakfast. The family ate in silence. She walked her father to the door, and before his silhouette merged with the shadows of trees beyond the edge of the forest, she had already pulled on her boots and was dressing herself in warm layers.

"Where're you going?" A sleepy Oleg appeared in the hallway, rubbing the sleep out of his eyes with his little fists.

"I have to go to town," Dora answered him vaguely. "I don't know when I'll be back. There's food in the kitchen. Will you look after yourselves while I'm gone?"

"We're not kids!"

Dora forced a smile on her face and kissed the top of her brother's head. "You know what Pa said…"

"We won't go anywhere," her brother assured her in a tone that insinuated he wasn't going to suffer her lecturing. "Who'd wanna go outside in this weather anyway? Only a total nincompoop."

Dora shoved her winter hat over her ears and headed out. The icy wind whipped at her entire body and cut into her exposed cheeks like a thousand tiny needles. Before Dora had made it halfway down the hill to the village, she was already frozen to the bone. As her heart pounded in her ears, her increased heart rate warmed her, protecting her from the cold. She only met a few sullen neighbors along the way, their hands buried deep in their pockets, the collars of their coats turned up high.

Dora knocked on the door of the Hattlers' house with urgency. Almost at once, Astrid appeared in the doorway.

"What're you doing here?" Dora blurted out in surprise.

Astrid gestured impatiently by way of an answer, quickly ushering her friend inside. She shut the door behind her with a soft click. Dora took a breath to ask what was going on, but in that moment, she heard Tom and Auntie Hattler arguing in the other room.

"I don't like whatever it is you two have been up to. I don't like that you're keeping things from me and I have no idea what's going on. I understand that your shared trauma has brought you together, but Astrid can't just show up for a sleepover out of the blue, Tom. She can't be here screaming in her sleep all night. You can't be taking care of her. I don't know what you two found out during the hypnosis, but I forbid you—"

"You can't tell me what to do, Mom," Tom interrupted her. "I'm an adult."

The fight made Astrid bow her head in shame.

"You're living under my roof, and I don't want there to be a repeat of last night."

"We're just trying to figure out what happened to us!"

"Gustaw Linhart kidnapped you, that's what happened! He kidnapped you and released you when they let him out of the nuthouse. Maybe his bad conscience finally got to him. And now he's dead, and good riddance. End of story."

"Mom, what are you so afraid of? What do you think will happen?"

"I'm worried about you, Tom. I'm scared you'll get hurt. Is it really so hard to understand that I don't want to lose you again?"

"Why are you playing this game, along with everyone else? Why can't you just admit that something totally crazy is going on here?"

"Tom, what are you talking about?"

Silence cut through the room. Astrid gestured to Dora that they better go to Tom's room. Just then, the door flew open and Valeria Hattler stepped into the hallway.

"I have my shift at the doctor's today. I'll be back in the evening," she muttered at her son over her shoulder. Noticing the two young women standing in the hallway, she came to a halt.

"Hi, Auntie," Dora piped up.

Auntie Hattler didn't smile back, an angry look on her face. "Your father will tan your hide if he catches you here."

With those words she left, slamming the front door harder than usual. Dora and Astrid made their way to the living room. Tom was standing with his back to them, looking out of the window. He probably just needed to calm down.

"I'm sorry," Astrid spoke first.

"You have nothing to be sorry about," Tom assured her, turning to look at them. He forced a smile onto his face. "Mom's just being hysterical. She'll calm down. We have more important things to deal with right now. Dory, what did you find out when you visited Sonya?"

Dora began to recount the bizarre encounter with their friend, taking off her outer layers as she talked. For some reason, the heating in the house was turned on full blast. They all sat down on the couch. Both her friends listened to her closely and didn't interrupt her once. Part of Dora enjoyed the feeling of someone finally hearing her out after all these years.

"It was there in the light of day?" Astrid made sure, feeling shocked. "One of the Whisperers?"

"Right underneath the bed, hidden in the dark." As proof, Dora pulled up the sleeve of her sweater, showing them the bruise left by the creature's touch. It looked like the ones that littered Astrid's body. "I think my tattoos saved me. I felt this tingling all over my skin, and the creature let me go right after. It recoiled from me."

"So what does this mean? That they can hide in the dark even during the day?" Tom asked with worry. "Are they getting stronger? Are there more of them? Can they attack us during the day too?"

"Hard to say," Astrid frowned. "It could be because we're running out of time. There's only a measly six nights left. The tattoos definitely work as protection, to a certain degree," she mused. "But Dora, it was something else that saved you twelve years ago."

Dora's pulse accelerated upon hearing those words. All these years, she'd hoped that someone could shed light on that mystery. She'd almost stopped believing it would ever happen. "What?"

Astrid carefully cupped the palm of her hand over Dora's deaf ear. Dora's body broke out in goosebumps.

"What do you mean?"

"You didn't hear them. They were whispering into your deaf ear while you lay sleeping on your side. Remember? That's what protected you from the Whisperers."

So it had been... a coincidence that saved her? That's all it was? But then Dora realized that wasn't the whole truth. It wasn't just *coincidence*. She always lay down on that side, every day, so that she and Astrid could see and make faces at each other. It was Astrid who had saved her.

"And what about the hypnosis? Did it work?" Dora asked quickly in hopes of hiding the blush blooming on her cheeks.

Astrid frowned. "Yes and no. We got further than last time, but not far enough."

"We think the key to finding that place is in the Black Forest," Tom explained.

Dora immediately thought of her father. Her heart clenched in fear. He usually spent his days and nights in that forest. What if something were to happen to him?

"Your dad knows that forest better than anyone else around here," Astrid said.

"No. Don't even think about it," Dora replied, barely stopping herself from bursting into desperate laughter. "He'd skin us alive, all three of us. Pa would never take us there. I'm not even allowed to speak to you. It's a no."

"But he could tell us something at least?" Tom tried.

"All I know is that in the past few days, something… weird has been going on in the forest," Dora admitted reluctantly. "Animals are dying for no apparent reason. Whole herds have vanished. He's worried about it."

Astrid and Tom exchanged a glance. It seemed that once again, they were back to communicating without words.

"Dory, think. Is there any spot in the forest that nobody speaks about? That everyone avoids? Something your dad might've warned you about?"

Dora thought about it. When she was young, when her mother was alive and her brothers hadn't been born yet, her father would sometimes take her with him to the forest. She was allowed to tag along to observe the wildlife, to pick wild berries and mushrooms to later dry at home. Pa used to tell her about the ravine where bears lived and warn her about the pack of wolves that roamed higher up in the mountains. He used to tell her the forest was much more dangerous than people thought.

"Nothing comes to mind." Dora shook her head. "I'm sorry."

"That's okay," Astrid assured her. "Either way, we have to go in there."

"You want to go into the Black Forest?" Dora made sure she hadn't heard wrong.

"Yes."

"Tonight," Tom added.

"We want you to come with us," Astrid proposed. "It's dangerous, but you know the forest better than any of us."

Dora was used to automatically agreeing with anything Astrid said. But this time, she had a harder time answering her friend. Dora had promised her father to steer clear of that place. She had promised to take care of her brothers. She'd had to swear on it. The gods punished oath breakers.

Astrid could sense her friend's hesitation. "I know it's risky..."

"I'll do it," Dora heard herself agreeing. "I'll come with you."

Astrid squeezed her hand in encouragement. "Dory, I want to ask one more thing of you. We're gonna need Sonya to come with us too."

Dora shot up from the couch. "Have you gone insane? Haven't you seen her? She's completely out of her mind. For Perun's sake, she's afraid of her own shadow. You'll never get her to step foot in that forest."

"She's the only one of us who remembers something," Tom interjected. "She knows more than she's letting on. She might know the way back there."

"That is, if there really is any *there* to speak of," Astrid added.

Dora felt as if neither of them had heard her—as if they already saw themselves in the forest. Didn't they realize just what was at stake? What all could happen?

And then Dora remembered poor Max, and the promise she made Astrid to help her get him back. The only problem was, it went directly against the promise she'd made her father. How was she to know what the right thing to do was?

"How on earth am I gonna persuade Sonya to come with us?" Dora finally said.

THE SEVENTH NIGHT

Though they had spent the whole day getting ready for their expedition into the forest, with the night fast approaching, even Astrid was starting to doubt whether this was a good idea. She knew fear was threatening to overcome her. The utter exhaustion and fatigue she felt were doing nothing to improve her mood either. Astrid didn't even know how many nights it had already been since she had last slept soundly. Her eyes kept drifting shut on their own. It was getting hard to focus her eyes on things, and she couldn't concentrate. Everything took longer. Astrid felt that even talking was gradually turning into an insurmountable task. The only reason she managed to stay awake at all was due to the coffee Tom diligently supplied her with at regular intervals.

They left the village before the sun set to avoid the night patrols, which were overseeing that the curfew was being upheld. On their way across the field toward the forest, they didn't exchange a single word. Astrid knew that like her, Tom too was wondering whether this was the right course of action or sheer lunacy. They had agreed to meet Dora at seven o'clock sharp at the crossroads not far from her house. But it got dark a bit earlier than that, and the two ended up spending more time than they would've liked at the crossroads before the agreed-upon rendezvous.

As the sun set, a deeper chill was creeping in on them, hand in hand with the approaching darkness.

Once the last rays of sunlight disappeared behind the mountaintops, Tom and Astrid were soon engulfed in a darkness so impenetrable that they couldn't even see each other. They stood there side by side, teeth chattering with cold, not daring to move a muscle.

Astrid caught herself nodding off several times, her head falling onto her chest. She was so exhausted, she felt like she might fall asleep standing up.

After waiting for what seemed like an eternity, two beams of light appeared nearby.

"Wait," Tom warned her in a whisper, but Astrid went ahead and signaled with her flashlight the way they had agreed to beforehand.

The lights began to draw closer, and the crunching snow was the only sound cutting through the eerie silence. And then Dora appeared in the clearing, with Sonya right behind her. Astrid couldn't believe it. Dora had actually pulled it off.

"Sorry we're late," Dora apologized, sounding a bit embarrassed. "It took Pa a bit longer than usual to leave for the pub."

"He won't notice you're gone, right?" Astrid made sure. She didn't want her friend getting into even more trouble because of her.

"I told him I wasn't feeling very well and was gonna go to bed early."

"What if he comes to check up on you?"

"All I have to do is say I'm on my period and he steers clear of me as if I were a leper," Dora blushed. "He doesn't know how to talk to me about it, so he pretends it doesn't exist and even allows me to stay in bed for two days while forgetting all about it."

The conversation between the two was just an attempt to mask the tension caused by Sonya's presence. As a matter of fact, Astrid hadn't expected Dora to succeed in persuading Sonya to come at all. Astrid was itching to ask how her friend had pulled it off, but she knew now was not the right time. They all exchanged awkward glances.

It was Sonya, however, who spoke first. "My parents have so many of us kids they'll barely notice one is missing."

Nobody knew if it was a joke, and they didn't dare laugh.

"I'm only here because I owe Dora," Sonya added. "I don't trust you guys. I don't trust you," she looked defiantly into Astrid's eyes. "And this is the last time I'm ever speaking to you."

Her words were met with silence.

"I think that's a fair deal," Tom eventually said. "What do you say, Astrid?"

"Let's go," Astrid said by way of an answer and led the way into the forest behind her.

They stuck close together, and as they made their way deeper into the forest, the distance between them diminished even more. Left and right, they were surrounded by dark woods, the pitch dark, and endless silence. They walked down a trodden path. Astrid hoped that sooner or later, she would remember something. She had to. Maybe she'd spot something familiar—a boulder, an uprooted tree… Where had she been before she found herself knocking on Dora's door? Which way had she run? Was it down this path? And did she run from the east? Or from the opposite direction?

After a while, Sonya took over leading the group—claiming, rather convincingly, to remember the way to the place they'd come from. But she didn't answer any of the questions Tom and Dora asked her after that. Astrid stayed quiet. She didn't want to risk upsetting Sonya again with her own questions. But it took her much effort to refrain from doing so.

The deeper they made their way into the forest, the less life surrounded them. The wind died out. The trees were bare and forlorn.

"Did you hear that?" Dora suddenly asked.

Everybody froze.

"What is it?" Tom whispered.

"Now I lay me down to sleep, and I shall awaken, for the evil spirits cannot reach me," Sonya mumbled, utterly terrified. "At this nightly hallowed hour, I call upon the ancient powers. Protect us till the light of day from Notsnitsa's evil sway."

"Shhh," Astrid hissed at her with irritation. She couldn't hear anything over the girl's praying.

But Sonya ignored her. "Now I lay me down to sleep, and I shall awaken, for the evil spirits cannot reach me. At this nightly hallowed hour, I call upon the ancient powers. Protect us till the light of day from Notsnitsa's evil sway. For Perun's sake, I shouldn't have come here. I should not have come here."

"Sonya," Dora pleaded with her urgently. "Try to keep it down…"

"Now I lay me down to sleep, and I shall awaken, for the evil spirits cannot reach me," Sonya repeated out loud for the third time in a row. "I can't keep it down. The gods have to hear my prayers to protect me. You have no power over me, Notsnitsa." She pointed at Astrid with fear.

"Calm down, Sonya," Dora implored. "They'll find us here."

"They don't have to look for us, don't you get it?" Sonya cried out hysterically. Her pale face looked terrifying in the shadows cast by the flashlight. "They're everywhere. Always. They're here because of her. Astrid has cursed us. She's a Notsnitsa."

"What?" Astrid couldn't contain herself any longer and raised her voice. She was starting to get fed up with all the accusations.

"Perun's beard," Dora whispered fearfully.

"She's a what?" Tom clearly didn't understand.

Sonya began to beat her temples with her fists. It looked like she was conducting some inner battle. Dora tried to hold Sonya's arms at her sides.

"Notsnitsas are demons of night and nightmares," Dora explained. "You remember, don't you, how our parents used them to scare us when we were kids? Saying how if we didn't go to bed early, they'd come for us during the witching hour. Something like the poludnitsas, who kidnap children to punish farmers for working the fields at high noon when they're supposed to be resting. The third type are the klekanitsas, twilight witches, who roam the land after dusk, chasing stragglers that are late for the evening prayers. Three sisters—a story told to misbehaving children to make them respect the rules of their elders…"

"But they aren't real, right?" Astrid was taken aback when she saw the way Tom was looking at her.

"You don't actually believe that I'm some demon of the night, do you?" she protested. "For Perun's sake, Tom, I'm afraid of the dark! So how could I be?"

"No, I didn't mean it like that," he assured her. "But think about it. Where did all the Whisperers come from? Did they just appear out of nowhere? Maybe. But what if somebody summoned them?"

Suddenly, Sonya screamed. She collapsed onto her knees, her hands pressing against her temples. The girl looked like she was having a fit.

"Help me with her," Dora wailed. "Sonya, can you hear me? We've got you, you're safe. Nothing's gonna happen to you."

Sonya's sobs grew louder and louder.

"She can't hear me. Come on, Sonya! Sonya, it's me, Dory."

Astrid stood frozen in place, unable to move or speak. *A story told to misbehaving children to make them respect the rules of their elders. But what if it's more than that?*

"If Sonya's telling the truth," Astrid blurted out, "and the Whisperers are just the servants of the Notsnitsa, then is Max being held captive by the demon of night?"

Astrid's words caused both Dora and Tom to turn to her, and for a crucial split second, they took their eyes off Sonya.

"For Perun's sake, this is bad," Dora was the first to react. "This is much worse than I thought, and I thought it couldn't *get* much worse."

"It just did," Tom suddenly piped up—the first to realize it was now just the three of them standing there. "Sonya! Sonya, come back!"

"Where did she go?"

They rushed off in the direction of her fading footsteps. Astrid snatched up the flashlight their friend had dropped mid-run. Sonya had flung herself headfirst into the pitch-black darkness. What kind of despair must've driven her to do such a thing? Astrid couldn't even imagine.

"Sonya!"

None of them was trying to keep quiet anymore. It didn't matter if their footsteps echoed through the hushed forest in all directions. The light beams of their flashlights bounced off the tree trunks, bringing to life a terrifying shadow play. Astrid tried to ignore the fact that it might not be an optical illusion at all, but that the Whisperers could be watching their every move, just waiting for the right moment to pounce and drag them away.

"Sonya, stop!"

The distance between the trio began to increase. Tom being the fastest runner and Dory much more agile than one might've thought, it was ultimately Astrid who lagged behind. She wondered whether she had been running down this very path a few days ago too. Did they stick together at first but lose track of each other later? Did they forget about each other the moment they stepped through the portal, or was it their frantic getaway that caused them to leave their memories behind?

The forest was thinning out, and before they realized that the darkness was growing lighter, they found themselves back on the crossroads where they had initially met. Astrid froze. This was bad. They shouldn't have ended up back here. Not now, when they finally managed to get inside the forest. This was their chance to save Max. She had to go back.

"Astrid?" Some instinct made Dora stop and glance over her shoulder. Her eyes locked with Astrid's. "Don't go back there by yourself, you hear me?"

"But…"

Dora didn't stick around for her response and kept running. Tom and Sonya were slowly receding in the distance. Astrid had promised herself she'd do anything to save Max. This was her chance. What if this was her only chance for gods know how long? But her friends needed her help. She owed them that, after they'd risked everything for her. And she owed it to Sonya, whose mind was apparently damaged for good.

"To hell with it," Astrid cursed before running after the others.

"Sonya! Sonya, stop!"

The young woman was running across the field toward the village. It was apparent now that they were in big trouble. They wouldn't be able to stop Sonya in time. The closest patrol was going to spot her, and they'd never be able to lie their way out of it after that.

The ploughed field was like a minefield of pitfalls and potholes that Astrid blundered through, almost spraining her ankle as she ran on. In the meantime, Sonya had reached the edge of the village and fallen to her knees in exhaustion, as if she didn't have the will to keep running anymore. Tom was right on her tail. He collapsed to the ground next to her, wrapping his arms around her—a superfluous gesture at this point—so she wouldn't run off again.

Dora and Astrid were mere steps behind them when two men—Guards—stepped out of the darkness, blocking their path.

"You've violated the orders of the Elders," one of them informed them in a formal tone. "It's forbidden to be outside after dark."

Sonya was sobbing loudly. Dora and Astrid were frozen in place.

"We're sorry," Tom tried to reason with the Guards. He could barely catch his breath. "We—we were just…"

"The sun set hours ago," the man cut him off. "You'll have to answer to the Elders for your transgression."

Tom and Astrid managed to exchange a brief glance. She knew what he was thinking.

Run, he mouthed at her. Without a second thought, Astrid turned on her heel and broke into a run. Dora did the same.

"Hey, stop!" The Guard lunged at Astrid, but she slipped out of his clutches. His massive paw of a hand missed her just barely, glancing off her back. She dashed off frantically with no sense of direction, zigzagging between buildings like a startled rabbit. Astrid couldn't let him catch her. It was more than just her agility that was spurring her on. She was driven by unimaginable fear.

"You little…!" the Guard wheezed out somewhere behind her.

Shouts of warning and the sound of a whistle were resounding all through the village. The patrols already knew about them.

The locals reacted to the sounding of the alarm by immediately gathering outside. Almost the entire village showed up. There was no pushing ahead or neck-straining. Everybody just stood there quietly, keeping their distance from the others, and waited.

Tom felt like he was about to be pilloried. Sonya was still lying next to him, pressing her face into the dirt as she mumbled incomprehensibly. They caught Dora just a few yards away. One of the Guards dragged her back roughly, chucking her toward the two.

A man Tom didn't recognize began to speak. "The signs we've come across in the village over the past few days, along with the strange occurrences, all point to this year's nights of the demons being more powerful than ever before. Our village isn't protected. We didn't manage to secure it against the dark forces that roam the earth at night, and these children here, with their irresponsible behavior, have put us in even more danger."

A murmur ran through the crowd. A woman gasped. Most villagers placed their crossed fingers on their brows and lips in prayer.

"The demons have never attacked us without cause!" someone shouted from the crowd. "We've kept them at bay for generations!"

Several of the villagers grumbled in agreement.

And then a voice from the back swept over the crowd. "Those three kids are to blame. We've had peace for twelve years!"

"That's right!"

"Why, we were doin' just fine till they showed up!"

A frightened whimper escaped Dora's lips. The way the others were looking at them was starting to make Tom feel uncomfortable. He could feel their anger.

"We didn't do anything," he defended himself.

The whispers were getting louder and louder.

"You've brought bad luck upon us all!" A woman pointed her finger at them.

Just then, Tom's mother pushed her way through the riled-up crowd to stand before the trio. At first, she seemed visibly relieved to see Tom, but her relief was immediately replaced by fury. She stood in front of him as if willing to protect him with her own body. "I won't allow you to accuse my son like this! He's done nothing to you! Do you even hear yourself? You want to lynch children now? After everything they've been through—their families have been through?"

"Shut up, Valeria," someone shouted at her from the crowd. "What do you know about what's best for the village? You've been nothin' but a blasphemer for years."

Somebody laughed.

"Don't hide in the crowd like a coward. Come say it to my face!" she snapped back.

The crowd parted again. "Dora?!" a gruff voice cut through the silence.

Tom felt Dora shiver beside him. "Pa," she mumbled.

Without waiting for an explanation, her father grabbed her coat and began dragging her away, just like he dragged his quarry from the forest.

"Lautner! They must answer to the Elders! They broke curfew."

Dora's father turned around, looking like fury incarnate. "You all are breaking curfew." He pointed at those closest to him. "I'll handle this myself. She's my kid."

Nobody dared defy him. When the Lautners left, a brief silence fell over the crowd as everyone realized they were currently standing outside in the middle of the night, unprotected.

"You're right!" Sonya suddenly cried out, a surprised murmur rumbling through the crowd. "It might be our fault!"

"Sonya!" Tom reproached her pleadingly.

"Open your eyes!" she yelled at the top of her lungs. "The village is cursed! Demons walk among us! Save your souls!"

Somebody screamed. The volume of the crowd increased. Soon, the sound of children crying cut through the din.

Loud voices emerged from the crowd. "A thundering heard all night long, cries on the streets, demons running around in human guise," a few people recited in unison. "Verily, whoever stepped out of their home soon found themselves dead…"

Panic broke out, and almost at once, everyone forgot all about Tom and Sonya.

Astrid managed to shake off the Guard the moment another patrol ran right into him. As if suddenly forgetting he was chasing her, he ran back with the others. The village bell was sounding the alarm. People began to emerge from their homes, craning their necks to see what was going on.

Astrid slowed down and blended in with the others. She pretended to look over her shoulder with everyone else, but slowly backed away toward the cemetery instead. Astrid slipped through the gate behind her back and found herself standing there quietly. It was almost pitch dark in the cemetery that night. Not a single lit candle in sight, which was peculiar. She couldn't even see her hand in front of her face. Astrid heard a few people passing by, but nobody dared visit the dead at this hour.

She did. They owed her answers.

"Hark, o spirit of the dead, upon the threshold of our worlds, your true purpose, now unfurled, show your mortal guise instead," Astrid mumbled into the quiet. She wasn't even sure this was going to work—she just strung a few choice words together, traced a symbol of veneration for the dead through the air, and hoped for the best. Like someone drowning in rapids, Astrid was latching onto anything that could help her.

A gentle, icy breeze caressed her face. She was no longer alone.

"For the first time, we're on an even footing, zduhać," the old blind woman said. "Your eyes now see nothing but darkness, and you can only focus on my voice. Darkness is no longer your enemy, methinks. You've learned to make it your ally."

"You told me to summon you when I'm ready to face the truth," Astrid went straight to the point. "I think the time has come."

"You think or you know, zduhać?"

"I know," she corrected herself. "If this'll help me save Max, then I'm ready to hear it, no matter what it is. What was it you called me? A zduhać?"

The old woman reached for her, as if wanting to touch her. "It's better to see it as a gift, not a curse. The zduhaći are individuals whose spirits leave their bodies at night to fight evil beings and demons," she explained.

"In ancient times, some were gifted with limited powers, allowing them to fight for fair weather and a rich harvest for their settlement, while others fought off werewolves, vampires, water sprites, and other demons that were a menace to villages.

"Centuries ago, our forefathers respected the zduhaći, because they valued the sacrifice these protectors undertook for their folk, night after night. But as faith in gods slowly waned, anyone who possessed even a smidgen of gods-given magic was suddenly seen as an advocate of evil and was persecuted. From then on, fewer and fewer zduhaći were born, and some never even found out what powers they'd been gifted with. They were born and they died without ever remembering they had set out on their nightly journeys."

"But why me? How did I come to be a zduhać? Our family is ordinary."

"You're not ordinary," the old woman assured her. "You were born with a caul—a membrane covering your head. It's a sign of exceptional good luck bestowed by the gods. A sign of the zduhaći."

Astrid was about to protest that her life bore no signs of good luck whatsoever. But it was as if the old woman could read her mind.

"Every test and obstacle makes you who you are," she said. "If you hadn't suffered so much hardship, you wouldn't be able to be a good zduhać."

"But I'm not…"

"As a rule, the zduhaći come into their power when they turn seven years old," she continued. "It's then that their ventures into dreams begin to intensify and they gain awareness of their gift. Because you vanished, you've been robbed of these years, that's why you're so reluctant to believe my words."

Astrid's head was spinning. She believed that the rozhanitsy had always been more skillful herbalists and manipulators than bearers of any actual powers. She believed that prayers and attributing certain meanings to symbols were nothing more than shared rituals passed down from generation to generation and didn't wield actual power. But if she were to accept the fact that all her dreams were real, did the old woman just give her the answer to what had been going on all this time? Was Astrid really a zduhać?

"The Notsnitsa has cursed us, right? Sonya… she said that it was me."

"It's not you, dear. You were born as the exact opposite of that demoniac being."

"How come you know so much? Are you also one of…?" Astrid faltered.

"In my lifetime, I never met a zduhać in the flesh."

"So how do you know they're real?"

"I may be blind, but that doesn't mean I'm unaware of what goes on around me."

"If the Notsnitsa trapped us in a nightmare for twelve years, it means Max is still stuck there. How can I stand up to her? Where will I find her? How am I supposed to get him out of there?"

"Use your gift."

"But how?" Astrid almost yelled. "How should I do that? I don't wanna fight anybody. I just want to find my brother and get him to safety. I wasn't destined to be some sort of redeemer of this village. I don't want to fight for people who'd burn me at the stake given the chance. How can I fight for someone who doesn't believe in me?"

"First you have to believe in yourself in order for others to believe in you."

Astrid opened her mouth to respond but changed her mind at the last minute, asking something else instead. "Who are you really? Are you my relative, and that's why I can see you? The dead appear during the nights of the demons to visit their kin. Are you my mother's ancestor? And why are you helping me?"

But the old woman didn't answer any of her questions. Instead, she asked one herself. "What did I tell you to do when we first met?"

Astrid searched through her memory. She recalled their encounter on the village green, where the butcher was selling fish. "To wake up."

"And you really did. You followed my advice. I have one last piece of advice for you, zduhać."

Astrid's heart was pounding in her ears. Was she finally going to find out how to get through the forest to Max? Was that it? Would the old woman tell her the way?

"When the time comes, follow the white rabbit."

With those parting words, the old woman vanished into thin air, leaving Astrid standing alone in the middle of the cemetery. More questions were now swirling in her mind than ever before.

The Guards dragged a half-conscious Sonya all the way to her house. Her father came to the door. When he spotted his daughter, he froze. What followed once the door closed behind her, Sonya wouldn't have been able to imagine in her wildest dreams. Her mother stood in the doorway, a sibling hanging off each arm, as they all gaped at him.

"How dare you defy my orders! How dare you embarrass us in front of the others! Isn't all your mother and I do for you enough? Don't you appreciate all we've sacrificed for you?"

"Sacrificed?" Sonya didn't understand. "What are you talking about? You left me for dead! You consigned me to an empty grave without a second thought!"

"Without a second thought?" he retorted coldly. "You think it was easy for us?"

Sonya felt tears welling in her eyes. "I don't care what it was like for you! Try to imagine what it must've been like for me. I was gone for twelve years, and in the meantime, you substituted me with half a dozen mini-me's! And when I came back, you started treating me like some distant relative who was gone on a trip somewhere for a couple years and is now suddenly a burden to you!"

The slap landed so quickly and with such strength that she didn't even have time to flinch. As her father's palm smacked her face, Sonya lost her balance and was thrown into the wall.

"Let her be!" Her mother ran into the hallway and squeezed between her husband and her oldest child, protecting Sonya with her own body.

"She doesn't get to talk to me like that!"

Sonya's mother stood her ground. "It ain't easy for any of us!" she cried out, her voice verging on the hysterical. "But we don't beat our kids!"

As they were shouting at each other, Sonya slipped away, heading straight for her room. Her father yelled after her to come back. She didn't listen. She slammed the door, immediately locking it. No sooner had the key turned in the lock than her father rattled the doorknob.

"Sonya, open this door!"

He pounded on it several times. She backed away in fright.

"Open the door right this minute!"

Sonya didn't answer. She grabbed a pair of tailor's shears from her desk, crawled into bed, and pulled up her blanket. Being much more afraid of the approaching night, she was able to filter out her raging father's voice in no time. Her heart was pounding wildly in her chest. Sonya's mouth went so dry it felt like thumbtacks were lodged in her throat every time she swallowed.

Sonya sat with her knees drawn up to her chin with the light on, her eyes fixed on the dark corner underneath the bed across the room, holding up the shears in front of her defensively like a weapon. Every few seconds, she pinched the skin of her forearm to reassure herself she wasn't asleep.

It felt like she was still trapped in a nightmare. And what if she really was? The torment was unbearable.

"Now I lay me down to sleep, and I shall awaken," Sonya mumbled to herself softly, "for the evil spirits cannot reach me."

She stifled a scream when she spotted a clawed hand emerging from underneath the bed.

"Leave me... Leave me alone," Sonya pleaded. "Now I lay me down to sleep. And I shall awaken," she kept repeating to herself, "for the evil spirits cannot reach me."

She was shaking from head to toe.

"Sonya! I'm breaking the door down if you don't open up this very second!"

The Whisperer was drawing closer and closer. It slithered over the wooden floor, scrapping its fingernails along the floorboards, the sound assaulting Sonya's ears. Its movements were jerky but surprisingly fast.

"Leave me alone!"

"Who are you talking to in there?!"

The Whisperer raised its clawed hand and grabbed her wrist in a viselike grip. Its touch burned like a red-hot iron poker. With brute force, it began to press her hand back toward her body.

"Please," Sonya sobbed. "Please…"

The tip of the shears grazed her snow-white skin.

When Sonya's father finally broke down the door, he found Sonya lying in bed, her throat slit open.

There was no helping her anymore.

THE ELEVENTH NIGHT

Astrid spent the four days following Sonya's death in a haze. She couldn't believe what had happened. The days merged into one endless moment of shock, shattered only by the strongest of emotions.

Tom tried his best to spend every waking moment with her, but it was as if the death of their friend had put a stop to whatever had been budding between them.

And Dora's father basically kept his daughter under house arrest. He even marched right into Mrs. Lesovska's shop to tell her that Dora needed to take a few days off on account of being sick. But Astrid knew that a cold wouldn't keep Dora indoors. Her dad just wanted to keep a close eye on her. And it didn't surprise Astrid either—a palpable fear was taking over the village. Everyone could sense the presence of evil, grazing the thoroughly locked windows and doors after dark. What if it came for them next? What if it tore open their throats too?

But the three friends figured out a system that allowed them to stay in touch. Every morning, one of Dora's brothers always went shopping in town, and he would always take a message from Astrid or Tom to deliver to Dora. And she'd send her reply the same way. It was Dora's job to keep an eye on her father and find out as much as possible about the Black Forest.

Sonya's death didn't shock the village to its core. It simply happened, and those who weren't directly involved seemed relieved by the fact it didn't concern them, feeling they were safe. At least for now.

"The Foreths had too many kids to take care of, anyhow. S'just one less mouth to feed," Astrid's grandma appraised the whole situation the next day during lunchtime. And that was that. Astrid rose from the table, and from then on, she refused to sit in her grandmother's presence during meals.

Instead, Astrid became a ghost in her own house—creeping, unnoticed, from room to room, learning to discern the creaks and groans of the house, and keeping her eyes open. She spent four days in her mother's room, leafing through old books. She had stumbled upon them by chance—a volume her mother had been holding in her hands one day when she fell asleep. Astrid had wanted to place it on the bedside table when she suddenly noticed what it was—an old herbarium that her mother had put together herself many years ago. Apart from facts about herbs and flowers, the book also contained hand-drawn sketches and notes on preserving dried plants and on the properties these herbs possessed, according to folklore. This led Astrid to believe that the books she'd blatantly ignored could possibly contain answers to many of her questions. She delved into the books during the day and at night, when she would try to stay awake. She was so exhausted that it seemed as if time stood still.

Whenever she couldn't hold out any longer, whenever she did end up falling asleep for a while, the Whisperers would trap her in their viselike grip, and with each passing night, it became harder and harder to escape their clutches. Astrid was worried she wouldn't be able to withstand their attacks for much longer. She didn't know what being a zduhać actually entailed. Nobody had ever taught her anything.

How was she supposed to leave her body and fight off demons and evil spirits when the mere thought of falling asleep made her tremble in fear? What kind of powers could she, of all people, possibly have? Astrid doubted she was capable of anything. The blind old woman must've been mistaken.

They doubled the number of patrols in the village. Everybody now knew that the warnings of the Elders were not to be taken lightly. People were afraid to go outside. The Guards patrolled the streets day and night, bedecked with amulets to ward off evil and trained to be ready to attack at any sign of someone breaking curfew. What Astrid found most ironic of all was the fact that her cousin and uncle joined the patrols voluntarily. The thought that her safety lay in the hands of someone so selfish and mean terrified her.

The year was drawing to a close faster than ever. Only two more nights remained. Astrid was terrified that any chance of getting back to the Black Forest was now gone forever.

Sonya's funeral became the catalyst for everything else that was to come. It all started when the Elders refused to allow the memorial service to take place in the chapel, a decision that divided the village into two camps. According to the old faith, man did not bestow life upon himself and neither did he have the right to take it. Life was a mission bestowed upon mortals by the gods, and this mission could involve hardships along the way that one simply had to suffer through.

Astrid had always found this part of religion barbaric. Sonya had failed in the eyes of the Elders. She had taken her own life, and that meant her mortal remains couldn't rest in the ground conse-crated to the gods.

"It's all a bunch of nonsense." Mrs. Lesovska shook her head in disbelief behind the cash register, a few customers agreeing with her. "Poor girl, barely out of her teenage years, she couldn't have even known what she was doing. A pure soul like that should be allowed a proper burial."

"What with her mother havin' a headstone made fer the girl all those years ago," the butcher's wife interjected in a loud whisper. "On the hallowed ground of the cemetery, no less. And now they ain't even allowed to bury their daughter there?"

"Poor Zoya. Hardly had any time to come to terms with get-ting her daughter back before losing her again."

"And now nothing will bring her back."

A can of peas slipped out of Astrid's grasp onto the floor. She picked it up quickly, but the racket silenced the women's conver-sation. When she rounded the corner and the women spotted her, they looked at each other knowingly. Astrid fled the shop in such a hurry she forgot her groceries, her shopping basket abandoned somewhere in the aisles.

Sonya's funeral took place behind the cemetery wall in the plot reserved for newborns and suicides. Astrid stood further back, as far as possible from Sonya's family. Just seeing Sonya's mother on the verge of a breakdown made her heart clench painfully. If it weren't for one of her children holding her up on either side, the woman probably would've thrown herself right into the open grave after her oldest daughter.

"The ground was so hard the gravedigger broke his shovel," Tom suddenly said right in Astrid's ear. "It took five guys to even get it to yield."

She didn't respond. The goosebumps that appeared on the back of her neck had nothing to do with the chilly weather.

"I was... I also helped a bit," Tom mumbled. "It was the least I could do for her."

"That's..." What was she supposed to say? Nice of him? How can digging your own friend's grave be nice? Astrid could taste the bile in her throat.

Tom guessed what she was trying to say and gave her an encouraging smile. "Do you want to go closer?"

Astrid shook her head. "It's safe here."

He didn't question her fear of getting too close to the mourning family of their dead friend. They stood by at a considerable distance, the chilly wind whipping around them and carrying every other word uttered over Sonya's grave.

Through her frozen eyelashes, Astrid spotted Dora on the other side. Like a personal bodyguard, her father stood over her in a protective stance, while her brothers were glued to her sides, clutching either of her hands. Dora met Astrid's eye briefly before bowing her head again.

The time came for the prayers to be uttered in the old tongue. Astrid and Tom didn't join in.

"Do you think Sonya believed in the gods?" she asked him quietly.

Tom shrugged. "I think as a child she didn't know what to believe. And as an adult, well... She didn't have enough time to figure it out for herself."

He was probably right. Faith was intangible. And it was intimate. Each and every person had to know for themselves how strong their faith was. But in these parts, children were born into a world where faith was thrust upon them. It was the parents who decided whether or not symbols of protection would be burned into their children's skin during the ancient ritual.

"And you? Do you believe in the gods?" Tom suddenly asked Astrid what she had just been asking herself.

"After everything that's happened, is it possible not to?"

"Precisely because of that fact. Are the gods really that all-powerful? And if they are, why do they allow demons to walk the earth, hurting others?"

"I'm afraid of the gods, if that's what you're asking," Astrid answered. "Of what's waiting on the other side. Even if it is nothing-ness."

"I understand."

Astrid turned to look at him. "It's all my fault, Tom," she whispered.

He sighed, a puff of condensed air escaping his lips. "You always say that, Astrid. Stop blaming yourself for everything that's wrong in the world. It's not your burden to bear. It's not your fault that—"

"It was me who woke her up," Astrid interrupted him. "I came to see her at the doctor's house. I used some herbs to perform a rit-ual in the ancient tongue that's used for"—she squirmed uneasily—"for summoning the spring. I just thought it was worth a try. I didn't actually expect it to work... It doesn't matter now. I woke her up from her coma. It's my fault. Her body couldn't take the strain, that's why she was having those fits. She should've been sleeping instead. Getting better."

Before Tom could reply, the funeral drew to a close.

"Sonya Foreth." The man officiating the ceremony raised his hand into the air. "Leave in peace. Your debts are settled. Do not linger among the living. Find rest with the gods."

Four men began to lower the coffin into the ground. Zoya Foreth was the first to scoop up a handful of dirt and throw it into the grave, followed by her husband and children. Then they all stepped aside to allow the others to express their condolences. As the funeral-goers approached from all sides, two lines formed that met over the grave.

The moment arrived that Astrid had been dreading this whole time. The line kept getting shorter, and she wished she could just run away. The smell of fresh soil and incense brought to mind another funeral Astrid had attended. The only other one. Her father had died so long ago, it was a wonder she remembered it at all. But she did. Every second of it was engraved in her memory.

Astrid dug her fingers into the dirt and picked up a handful, waiting for the man in front of her to leave. Hesitantly, she approached the grave, gazing at the simple coffin down below. Sonya was in there. Cold, vulnerable, alone. The dirt rained down upon the coffin lid.

As Astrid moved away to make room for the next person in line, Dora appeared in the line winding toward the grave from the opposite side. Before Astrid could react, her friend approached her quickly, squeezing her hand briefly in a gesture of comfort.

Astrid felt the note her friend slipped into the palm of her hand. Dora didn't offer a word of explanation as she stepped over the grave, throwing in her handful of dirt. Dora's father was watching them both like a hawk, a suspicious expression on his face. Astrid shoved her hand clutching the note into the pocket of her coat and stepped aside to wait for Tom. His mother, who'd been standing with the others, appeared next to them as well. All three of them joined the line for offering condolences to the bereaved.

This line was advancing much slower than the other one had.

People seemed to want to talk with the grieving family and offer words of consolation longer than they spared a thought over the grave of the deceased. Astrid just wanted to get it over with. She wanted to run away from it all and find a moment to read Dora's message. The note was burning in her pocket like a hot ember.

When her turn finally came, Astrid suddenly found herself face to face with Sonya's father. He stayed calm as ever, but his expression changed. Even a blind person could tell he wasn't happy to see her. He shook Astrid's hand, briefly.

"My condolences," Astrid mumbled quietly.

She stepped to the right, reaching out her hand to Sonya's mother. The woman's hand lay limp in hers. Unlike her husband, Zoya Foreth didn't even try to mask her hatred. Suddenly, she grabbed Astrid by her elbow and pulled her close, until they were almost nose to nose.

"I told you to stay away from my little girl. You bring bad luck everywhere you go, just like that mother of yours!"

Astrid recovered from the initial shock. "What are you talking about?"

"Everybody knows she was a hussy," she hissed at Astrid. "She bewitched so many men in her day! Thank goodness your father didn't live to see it."

"That's enough." Zoya's husband yanked her away from Astrid. "Let her go, Zoya."

"Let everyone hear it!" she screamed hysterically. "Let everyone hear that this is all her fault! That the Mahler girl is to blame for what happened to our Sonya!"

Astrid was at a loss for words. What could she say in her defense? She kind of agreed with the woman, after all. She felt everybody's eyes on her. Unexpectedly, Tom's mother intervened.

"That was unnecessary, Zoya," the woman raised her voice, speaking in an authoritative tone. "You've suffered a great loss and don't know what you're saying. Stop blaming the children."

One of Sonya's younger siblings burst into tears, but nobody paid him any mind.

"I do know!" Sonya's mother countered. "From the bottom of my heart, damn her! Damn her to hell!"

"Zoya!" her husband yelled at her. "Stop acting like a blasphemous wretch!"

But Sonya's mother was already on the verge of a nervous breakdown. She was screaming at the top of her lungs now, allowing everyone to hear her. "I don't care about the gods! Where were they when our little girl disappeared? Where were they the past twelve years we spent mourning her? Where were they when she went astray? Well? Where were the gods then?"

Chaos erupted. Tom grabbed Astrid by the hand and led her away. She let him, incapable of any other reaction. Tom's mother was arguing loudly with the others. It was only once they were far enough away from the cemetery that Astrid allowed herself to take a deep breath.

"It's just the grief talking," Tom tried to console her.

"Maybe," Astrid replied absently. She pulled out Dora's note from her pocket and read it. Her friend insisted they meet after dusk that evening. She had even detailed a plan for how to go about doing it without getting caught. The whole thing seemed, at the very least, unwise.

"What? What is it?"

Wordlessly, she shoved the note into Tom's hand just as his mother suddenly popped up right beside them. He hid it in his pocket and smiled at his mom.

"Thanks for sticking up for Astrid."

"Let's go," the woman hurried them along in a dry tone. "They're not going to invite us to the reception anyway."

Astrid was drumming her fingers against the tabletop. Tom had to rest his hand on her thigh to stop her jittering knee, which was shaking the entire table, causing the cups of coffee to spill over onto the tablecloth. Tom's mother had insisted on not letting them be alone, asking them to sit in the kitchen with her.

Both of them would have preferred a moment in Tom's room to discuss how to carry out Dora's plan that evening, but Valeria insisted they have coffee together. Astrid was expecting another lecture to discourage them from their activities as Mrs. Hattler sat down opposite them, her face unreadable. "I don't know where to begin," she let out a long sigh.

Both Tom and Astrid became alert. Tom placed his hand on his mother's forearm resting on the tabletop.

"Mom, did something happen?"

But Valeria's eyes were trained on Astrid. "I once made a promise to your mother, but I can't keep quiet any longer. Not after what happened today."

Astrid could tell the promise was important to Mrs. Hattler. She chose her next words carefully. "I'm sure my mother confided in you to protect me, to help me. But telling me her secret might end up helping me more in the long run."

Tom's mother nodded.

"Zoya Foreth had no right to say those things, not to mention the way she did it—out in the open in front of everybody. Your mother has had enough troubles of her own. To become a widow at such a young age and then lose both her children… Who wouldn't go crazy? I admire her for how long she managed to hold her head up high despite it all."

Astrid felt tears welling in her eyes.

"Listen to me closely." Valeria leaned toward her. "When Lena, your mother, was your age… She showed up on our doorstep one night. She begged my mother—gods rest her soul—who had been a midwife back then, to rid her of her… mistake."

"I'm not sure what you're trying to say. What did my mom want from your mother?"

"To get rid of an unwanted baby. She wouldn't be the first or last person to get herself pregnant before marriage."

Astrid froze. Her mother had wanted to get an abortion?

"Don't look at me like that," Valeria begged her, the look on her face betraying how sorry she felt.

"My mother was a midwife her entire life. The number of babies she delivered far outweighed those she aborted. She just did her best to help those in need. My mother used to bring me with her when I was a girl so I'd learn. And she never judged anyone who came to her for an abortion.

"But with Lena, it was already too late. She was already too many weeks along, and nothing could be done. So my mother sent her home. I felt so sorry for her—I remember how much she cried. She was a few years younger than me, barely an adult.

"The poor girl then tried to get rid of the baby herself. She toiled in the field till she dropped. She carried things too heavy for her. In a moment of desperation, she even threw herself down a flight of stairs. A few weeks later, she got married with a sprained ankle. A limping, tainted bride."

313

"But why would she…" Astrid couldn't even finish her thought. "Why… when she was getting married anyway…?"

Valeria tilted her head to the side, as if considering her reply. "You really can't think of a reason?"

"No," Astrid said. But somewhere deep inside, she knew. She just didn't want to admit it.

"Because the baby wasn't her fiancé's," Valeria said, confirming to Astrid that all those feelings of displacement and not belonging she struggled with her whole life had always been justified.

"Nobody found it suspicious that you were born seven months after the wedding," Valeria continued. "You were tiny—a preemie, born early. But you were born with a caul, and that has always been a sign of good luck. My mother used to say that children blessed in that way were born lucky."

Astrid couldn't wrap her head around it. Quite unexpectedly, the blind old woman came to mind.

Tom asked a question instead. "Born with a caul? What does that mean, exactly?"

The words of the blind woman came back to her. *Zduhać*.

"On rare occasions, children are born with a membrane covering their heads. I myself have never witnessed any such birth—and before you, neither had my mother. You were the only one," Valeria explained. "It's a membrane that usually tears during birth. If not, though, it has to be removed, or the baby could suffocate. They say that children born with the caul are fated to become individuals gifted with supernatural powers. In any case, it's exceptionally rare. They told your mother that you were born under a lucky star."

But Astrid could only think of one thing. "She wanted to get rid of me?"

Could she really have been born out of wedlock? Was her mother having some secret affair? Why hadn't she married the other man, then? And did her father know?

"Oh, my dear, surely you must've figured it out ages ago." Valeria threw her hands up, no trace of sympathy to be found. "That's why Hedda Mahler has hated you all your life. She knew. She knew you weren't her own flesh and blood. Everyone and their mother knew. It's just that nobody was willing to say it out loud."

Astrid swallowed drily. She was just a cuckoo bird. Merely someone's bastard child.

A deafening silence filled the kitchen. Tom's mother looked like she'd just set down a heavy burden she'd been hauling uphill for ages. Astrid felt irrationally angry with Mrs. Hattler. What was the purpose of telling her this? Now, of all times? When it wasn't at all relevant—when all that mattered was getting Max back during the last two nights she had left?

Astrid had nothing to say. Even Tom, for the first time in ages, couldn't bring himself to ask her what she needed. Maybe he sensed it was best to stay quiet this time. Astrid's mind was working overtime. But the longer she tried to convince herself, the more the clues that had always been there were coming to light.

Everyone had always said that Max had those trademark Mahler looks. But not her. Astrid never really resembled anyone in the family. Did Kristian know? Is that why for her entire childhood, he and his brother kept tormenting her? During the Koleda, he *had* gifted her a dead cuckoo bird—a traditional symbol of parasitic children.

It should've dawned on Astrid sooner. *Bastard,* her grandmother used to call her. *Ye ungrateful little bastard.* And with what gusto she used to single her out from Max to give a thrashing to, time and time again. The woman had been punishing her for not being her own flesh and blood.

"Did my dad know about this?" Astrid just went ahead and asked. "I mean… Mahler?"

Suddenly, her family name sounded strange and unfamiliar.

"I don't know," Valeria admitted. "He probably did."

If the entire village was talking about it behind their backs, it must've reached him eventually, Astrid reasoned. And even so, he never insinuated to her in any way that he loved her any less than he loved her brother. Unlike others.

Astrid willed herself to thank Mrs. Hattler. And with that, she considered her decorum-dictated obligation to stay for coffee as fulfilled and rose from the table. Valeria didn't try to stop the two as she sat there, gazing into her cup, her mind far away.

Tom didn't speak until his bedroom door was shut securely behind them. Or rather, he opened his mouth to speak, but Astrid cut him off.

"It doesn't matter. Not right now. We have to focus on tonight's plan. I have to go home and pack a few things before coming back here."

"The sun's setting in half an hour," Tom warned her. "If you get held up, we won't manage to leave before the first patrols show up in the streets. Let's meet in twenty minutes in your backyard. We'll take the path out back along the cemetery wall up to the hill. That's where Dory will be waiting for us. It's longer, but much safer."

"Okay, I'll meet you behind my house," she agreed.

With no time to lose, Astrid set out for her house straightaway. The village was almost deserted. Astrid saw a few of the funeral-goers exit the local pub, but she hadn't spotted a single patrol so far. A few minutes later, she was already closing her front door behind her as she stepped into the hallway.

"Lock the door properly. Latch it," a voice suddenly rang out behind her.

Astrid broke out in a cold sweat. It was incredible how just the sound of that voice caused her to have such a reaction. How many times had Astrid begged, sobbing until she had no more tears to cry, to be let out of the cellar! And how many times had the woman silenced her with a similar, bone-chilling command. But not this time. Those days of cowering in terror were over.

Astrid locked the door as her grandmother demanded. She took off her shoes and coat and entered the kitchen. For the first time in a long while, Astrid wasn't afraid. What she wasn't expecting, however, was her entire family to be in the kitchen. Grandma was sitting by the stove, gazing out of the window into the darkness beyond. Kristian and her uncle were sprawled out at the table, waiting for dinner to be served.

"You're on time," her aunt said matter-of-factly as she eyed the young woman. Astrid was still wearing the simple black dress Tom's mother had let her borrow for the funeral.

"She's late," Grandma snapped in her direction.

"Astrid has always done whatever she wanted to, anyway," Kristian interjected mockingly, narrowing his piggy eyes at his cousin.

Astrid's aunt picked up Kristian's plate to serve him a helping of mashed peas. Her uncle just continued pretending that his niece didn't exist. After all these years, Astrid perhaps finally understood the reason why he couldn't even look her in the eye. It was because she wasn't his brother's daughter. He despised her.

Astrid walked over to the empty spot at the table, but didn't sit down. She waited until her aunt finished serving dinner to everyone. Kristian didn't bother to wait and immediately began scarfing down the food in front of him. The others were trying to figure out Astrid's intentions.

"Sit down," Grandma ordered her in a steely voice.

"No."

It was forbidden to talk back to Grandma. Kristian chuckled snidely, but fell quiet as soon as his father shot him a warning look.

"I don't know what kind of scene ye're trying to cause here, but either sit down or get out o' my house," Grandma said unflinchingly.

Astrid didn't let the woman intimidate her. "For once in your life, I want you to listen to me."

Grandma lifted her wrinkled face to pierce Astrid with her gaze. "Why should I?"

"Because I deserve at least that much."

The old woman observed her without a trace of concern. "Is that all?"

Astrid didn't allow herself to lose her cool. She had to keep her distance. Just this once. This woman didn't deserve to see her vulnerable side.

"You didn't come to the funeral."

"Why would we?" Grandma retorted. "The girl's already been buried once. What does it matter that she was back for a few days? Once pronounced dead, she should've stayed dead."

Astrid felt like jumping over the table and screaming in the old woman's face at the top of her lungs. Where did all this bitterness come from?

"Were you glad when everyone considered *me* dead?" Astrid whispered. "When you finally managed to get rid of me after all those years? The bastard child that will never be your granddaughter?"

Astrid's words startled her aunt, who accidentally knocked over her glass, water spilling onto the white tablecloth. Even her uncle finally spared Astrid a glance, as if finally acknowledging her existence.

But all of Astrid's attention was directed toward her grandmother. The woman's eyes flashed dangerously.

"Who told you? Let me guess, that Foreth woman? Did she go running her mouth? I always suspected that lying chatterbox of a woman knew the truth. She just kept it to herself till she could use it to her advantage."

"Clearly, everybody but me knew about it."

This time, it was Kristian who interrupted the silence. "Took ya long enough."

"Shut up, boy," Grandma silenced him abruptly, turning back to Astrid. "So what is it ye actually want from me? Ye've made a show of yerself. Happy now?"

"What do I want from you?" Astrid repeated her grandmother's words incredulously. "Is it so hard to believe that I just wanted an explanation? That I just wanted to know if this was the reason you've hated me all these years?"

"Haven't ye just answered yer own question? Or are ye so stupid? Yer mother was nothing but a tramp that bewitched my poor son with her charms! She cast her spell over him and caused him to completely lose his mind. That woman brought nothing but bad luck into this house. And then I lost my poor son for good, and ye're to blame for that!"

After so many years of those words being unspoken, they were finally out in the open. And that was that. Once upon a time, they would've caused Astrid pain. But not anymore.

"Why didn't you just kick me out?" Astrid asked. "When I came back?"

Her grandmother looked at her with open disgust. She didn't have to pretend anymore—it was as if she had set aside her mask and revealed her true self. The silence that engulfed them spoke volumes.

"Because you can't," Astrid suddenly realized. "Dad left me and Mom his part of the house in his will. You can't kick us out because we have a right to be here."

She took her grandmother's silence as a yes.

"Is that what all this has been about? An attempt to get rid of my mom? If I hadn't come back, you were planning to torment her to death so that all this could be yours again? Does it make you feel good, knowing you broke her spirit?"

"Enough!"

A resounding, masculine voice cut through the room and took everyone by surprise. Her uncle slammed his fist on the tabletop so hard the plates rattled. They all turned their attention to him.

"You will not talk to my mother like that!" He pointed in Astrid's face. "Nothing in the world gives you the right to disrespect your elders. Apologize."

Only her aunt kept her head bowed down, while the others were staring at Astrid. Kristian was clearly taking great pleasure in the situation. His eyes flitted between his enraged father and Astrid, waiting to see who would back down first.

This was the first time that Astrid's uncle had shown any sort of authority. It was the first time he paradoxically reminded Astrid of her own father. Both brothers usually regarded Grandma as the head of the family, but personality-wise, they couldn't have been more different. But it seemed that even her uncle sometimes reached his limit.

Astrid didn't care. He could threaten her all he wanted. This was between her and Grandma, and she didn't take her eyes off her. "You've tormented Mom into the state she's in today. And if I hadn't disappeared, you would've done the same to me."

Her uncle rose from the table. "Get the hell out! Get out of my sight!"

Astrid began to back away to the door. With a calm expression, Grandma kept her eyes trained on her, not bothering to confirm or deny her accusations. "It's going to be a long night," the woman eventually said. "For some, maybe too long."

In that moment, Astrid decided that she was done with this family for good—the same way they must've been done with her too.

"Pack your stuff and get out of here, the both of you. You and your mother," her uncle decided in a resolute voice. "We're done here. Come morning, I want to see you out of the house."

"You will," Astrid assured him before exiting the kitchen.

Though anger coursed through her veins, Astrid made sure not to slam any doors. She entered her mother's room, shutting the door behind her. Glancing at her watch, Astrid saw she had ten minutes left. Her legs were shaking from exhaustion, but all it took was a single glance at her mom to regain her strength.

As usual, Lena Mahler was sitting in her armchair, her hands wrapped around a cup of tea that had gone cold hours ago, her eyes cast down into her lap. On the table lay the untouched meal Astrid had prepared for her earlier. Astrid lifted the piece of cold toast and held it right in front of her mother's face as if she were a toddler.

"Take a bite."

Her mother shook her head, her hair sticking to the jam slathered on the bread.

"Fine then," Astrid sighed in resignation. "Go hungry. It's time for bed. Give me the cup."

She tried pulling it out of her mother's grasp, but she wouldn't budge.

"Mom, give me the cup. I'm not in the mood and I don't have time for games," Astrid demanded impatiently. "Come on, give it to me already!"

Suddenly, all of Astrid's frustration and anger came pouring out. She wrenched the cup with all her might. It flew into the air, cold tea spilling all over Astrid's legs as the cup shattered on the floor into several pieces.

"Look what you've done! Can't you just do as I say for once? At least once you could finish your damn food! You could keep your shirt from getting dirty from every meal! For once you could make it to the bathroom on time! Is that really so much to ask?"

But her mother just kept staring apathetically into the distance, which ended up angering Astrid even more.

"You could act like a mom for once and comfort me, tell me that everything's gonna be alright, because I don't know how to be an adult. Nobody's taught me how to be an adult, and I haven't had time to figure it out on my own. I haven't had anybody to look up to, and if this is what being a grown-up is like, then it sucks." Astrid's voice broke into sobs. "Damn it, Mom, what happened that made you see me as a disappointment before I was even born? Why did you want to get rid of me?"

All Astrid got in response was more silence. What was she thinking? That her mom would suddenly start talking again? That everything would go back to normal, just because she asked for it? Fat chance.

Astrid slowly started to calm down. There was no use hoping for miracles. She forced herself to think of Max. Max needed her. She would bring him back and everything would be okay again.

"I have to go, Mom," Astrid whispered urgently. "I have to try to rescue Max. We'll leave this place in the morning, and then all three of us will be together again, okay?"

Astrid kissed the top of her mother's head before pulling her backpack from under the bed. For the past few days, she'd been secretly packing her things into it. She had no idea what awaited her in the forest, but reason dictated she should be prepared for anything.

Without looking back, Astrid snuck through the house into her own room. She quickly took off her funeral dress and pulled on the warmest clothing she could find. She pried open the floorboard that hid her casket of amulets and artifacts for warding off nightmares and shoved it into her backpack. The moment Astrid turned to leave her room, the door swung open on its own.

Her grandmother stood in the doorway.

"It's getting dark soon. Where do ye think ye're going? I won't allow ye to put this family in danger by breaking the rules. Do ye want to turn the Elders against us?"

"Try to stop me," Astrid snapped at her defiantly.

She expected Grandma to step into the room and grab her like a little girl by the hair. But the old woman just shifted her weight and didn't move from her position in the doorway. Astrid considered her options. She could walk past Grandma and push her old, wrinkled body out of the way, but for some reason, the thought of having to touch her filled Astrid with loathing.

Astrid decided to go for option number two. She turned on her heel and made for the window.

"Don't ye dare!"

In a flash, Astrid opened the window, pulled herself up into it nimbly, and jumped into the snow below. She could hear her grandmother yelling after her, but she broke into a run along the house without a backward glance. Astrid snuck along the perimeter of the house as quietly as she could, avoiding the backyard. She rounded the corner, running into something soft.

Tom's hand shot up to cover Astrid's mouth to keep her from yelling out. Soon, they were creeping from fence to fence, terrified that one of their neighbors would spot them from a window and alert the patrols. The animals in the front yards they passed were restless. For eleven days straight, the dogs had been barking incessantly from the moment the sun began to take on a darker hue, so none of the inhabitants paid the noise any mind.

Before Tom and Astrid had made it to the field behind the cemetery, dusk was falling—fast. As soon as they left the village behind them, they allowed themselves to take a deep breath, picking up their pace. As promised, Dora was waiting for them in front of her house. Dressed in her father's gamekeeper attire, she looked more grown up than usual. She even had his hunting rifle slung over her shoulder.

"I like this new Dora." Tom's voice was the first to cut through the silence.

Dora gave him a nervous smile. "Pa's gonna be gone all night long. He's guarding Sonya's grave for the first night. He drew the shortest straw."

According to tradition, someone always had to keep vigil over the deceased's grave for seven straight days after the funeral, to assure the soul of the deceased person wouldn't wander the mortal realm for too long and could find peace.

"We have until dawn," Dora added.

The Black Forest swallowed and drew them in as if they had been a part of it forever. Astrid led the way, lighting the path ahead with their biggest lantern. Tom kept an eye on the needle of his compass while Dora occasionally checked the map. Their plan depended on many variables.

"Getting anything past Pa was hell," Dora broke the silence. "I swear he's been watching my every move. I had to make up excuses to go to the pantry so he would get off my case for one second. But thanks to Anton and Oleg, I managed to check almost all the maps of the forest. Thankfully, I was at least allowed to go to the bathroom by myself, so that's where I had time to look over them all. You were right, Astrid. They all had one thing in common."

"Uncharted territory," they all said in unison.

The idea had popped into Astrid's head when she was reading through her mother's old books. In the olden days, cartographers and explorers used to mark unexplored areas on maps with the phrase *Here There Be Dragons*. If a gateway leading to another world existed somewhere in the Black Forest, Astrid wasn't naïve enough to think that the cartographers would've marked it down. But they definitely had to account for it. And hence her theory—that all the local maps had to have one spot that somehow stood out from the rest.

"One of the maps just showed an empty white blot," Dora recounted. "Another one had an area marked as the valley of wolves situated in the same spot. On the third map, there was just a red cross, and the fourth contained a warning about the dangers lying in wait there. The area differs in size, but it's always marked eastward in the direction of the mountains. And every time, a swamp is located close by."

Another bullseye—in the freezing cold of winter, they couldn't have gotten mud and dirt all over their bodies, unless they had dragged themselves through some sort of marshland.

Astrid suspected Dora kept talking just to drown out the terrifying silence surrounding them. But she didn't blame her, as she was feeling antsy herself. If only she could lie down for a minute... Close her eyes and sleep for a while. Astrid was dying to get some sleep. Every particle of her body was screaming for it.

"We have to get off this path," Tom suddenly told them. "It's leading us down this hillside."

None of them wanted to abandon the safe path, but they had no choice. The forest undergrowth began to change. Tall bushes replaced the trodden dirt and bare trees. The three friends picked up branches, using them to break through the dense shrubbery. Tiny twigs clawed at their faces, scratching their exposed skin. They had to close their eyes to keep them safe from the branches.

Astrid had never felt so weak and powerless. Every swing she took with her branch was tougher than the last. Their clothes caught on the prickling thorns as their feet stumbled over exposed roots. They couldn't stop, they couldn't take a break. Dora was whimpering somewhere behind her. Astrid felt like crying.

After what felt like an eternity, the thicket finally thinned out. Astrid pushed the last branch out of her way and suddenly found herself standing right in the middle of a swamp. She felt the icy water filling up her shoes.

"Be careful, it's—"

Before Astrid could warn the others, Tom let out a surprised yelp. He managed to catch Dora just in time as she sank waist-deep into the water.

"Perun's beard, that's cold. That is damn cold." Dora's teeth began to chatter.

The marsh was spread out all around them as far as they could see in the light cast by the lantern. Tom pulled out his compass to check their course. Astrid sunk her branch in front of her into the bottom of the swamp. Only then did she take a hesitant step forward.

They advanced at a snail's pace, gingerly testing the depth of the waters ahead of them with their branches. It happened more than once that one of them almost sunk into the swamp. The water reached their ankles, but in the deepest parts, it was waist-deep. Tom, because he was the tallest, carried Astrid's backpack and Dora's rifle to make sure they wouldn't get wet. Fear didn't allow them to dwell on how cold they were. Eventually, tiny blue lights began to appear over some parts of the water's surface.

"Don't look at them," Astrid warned the others. "They might pull us down into the waters."

"Do you think it's fairies?" Dora yelped.

"I've read too much about water demons in the past few days to believe we're alone in these waters," Astrid replied. "It might just be bugs, but it could very well be tiny demons that want to drown us."

Tom froze mid-step, as if he'd just decided this whole excursion of theirs wasn't worth the risk. "So the vodyanoy might live here?" he whispered in awe.

"Probably not here," Dora guessed. "He's the protector of fish, right? You won't find those here. He might be up by the river near the old quarry. But you've heard that fairytale about the miller, right? It says that the vodyanoy sleeps in the winter and in the spring, he's the one who breaks the ice."

"Well, if that's what the fairytale says…" Tom mocked.

They continued on in silence, trying to synchronize their steps to avoid rippling the water too much. Astrid would pause from time to time to shine the light in front of them.

"Look, there's the shore!"

She sighed in relief. There were only a few more steps dividing them from dry ground. Astrid abandoned all caution as she took off toward the shore as fast as possible. But with her very last step, she lost the ground beneath her feet, and before she could let out a scream, she plunged straight into the water.

The icy cold engulfed her, and she could taste the stinging water in her throat. She was falling fast into the pitch-black. A silent scream escaped her lips, her mouth immediately filling up with water. Astrid didn't know how to swim. She'd never learned how. She kicked around and flailed her arms furiously through the water until she actually began to rise up.

I can't die here. Not here and not now that I'm so, so close.

Astrid began to kick her legs with even more effort, forcing herself not to inhale, not to give in to the all-consuming water. But something was preventing her from swimming up, some invisible force was pulling her down—not up to the surface. Astrid's brain was slowly running out of oxygen. An unpleasant pounding was hammering her temples and the only thing her lungs yearned for at that moment was to take a deep breath. She gave up the futile fight, letting the water take her.

In that moment, Astrid felt hands grabbing her wrists and pulling her upward.

Astrid's head broke through the surface, and she landed back-first on the cold hard ground. She began coughing like crazy to get the water out of her lungs. The whole world was spinning.

"Astrid, are you okay?" Tom appeared right next to her.

She nodded. His face disappeared out of her sight. Astrid pushed herself up by her elbows, shaking all over, and rolled over into a sitting position. Dora was lying close by on the ground, drenched to the bone, coughing up water everywhere too. Tom was gently slapping her on her back.

"It's okay, get it all out."

"You saved my life," Astrid whispered gratefully.

Dora tried to smile. "Because I'm the only one of us who can swim, you weirdos."

Having to walk on in their drenched clothes was an incredibly un-pleasant experience. At first, the icy garments clung to her skin uncomfortably, and with each movement, Astrid just wanted to tear them off. Half an hour later, though, it only got worse as the clothes began to freeze. Dora didn't say anything, but Astrid could feel her friend's identically desperate gaze on her back. If they didn't stop to change into warm dry clothes right away, they were going to freeze to death.

"The compass must be broken or something," Tom suddenly said desperately.

"Broken how?"

"It keeps changing direction, it's acting... I dunno, unpredict-ably. I'm not sure we're going the right way."

"I'll check the map," Dora decided. Her hands were visibly shaking.

Astrid's heart sank. They were lost. They didn't have a fighting chance of finding the place. They were never going to get out of here and were probably simply going to freeze to death by morning. She shook her head to clear away the gloomy thoughts.

"It's gotta be close by," Dora mumbled under her breath as she peered at the unfolded map. "Shine your light over here."

A twig crackled somewhere behind them. First one, then another. They all froze in place.

Astrid saw them before the others. "You were right, Dory," she hissed. "We're close."

The Whisperers began to emerge from the shadows. Dozens of them.

"Run!"

They all broke into a run at the same time. One of the Whisperers had managed to creep up, unnoticed, dangerously close to them, taking advantage of their momentary distraction and grabbing Tom by the ankle. It yanked him to the ground.

"Tom!"

Astrid and Dora immediately whipped around and hurried to help their friend as the Whisperer dragged him into the shadows. Astrid leapt and landed on her stomach, reaching out her hand to grasp Tom's. They barely managed to latch onto each other's fingers. But doing so presented no obstacle to the Whisperer, who continued to drag them both away with ease.

Without a second thought, Dora slung off her hunting rifle, pulled out two cartridges, and loaded the gun with unfaltering precision. She aimed and fired twice right at the Whisperer. An inhuman shriek echoed through the forest as the creature released Tom. Astrid quickly clambered to her feet, offering her friend a helping hand. His leg was injured, blood seeping through his pant leg.

"I'll be okay," he assured Astrid stubbornly. "Run."

"No. We're all in this together."

Astrid propped up Tom the best she could, and all three of them ran into the night. His leg was slowing him down and making him lose his balance, but Tom gritted his teeth and continued to hurtle onward. Dora was right on their tail, her rifle at the ready—no trace left of the once scared, fragile girl.

The forest in front of them got denser and denser, the trees growing much closer together. Astrid stared straight ahead, trying to ignore the movement in her peripheral vision. They might already be surrounded. Maybe it was all over for them.

And then, all of a sudden, Astrid spotted a white hopping blur near the ground that bore an uncanny resemblance to a rabbit. Instinctively, she changed course and set out after it.

Dora fired her rifle again, meaning the Whisperers were dangerously close. Tom began to lean more and more of his weight onto Astrid's shoulder. They were both running out of energy. The rabbit stopped suddenly, turned its head, and looked straight into Astrid's eyes. It was only in the light cast by the lantern that she finally noticed the rabbit's eye sockets were empty. It was blind.

They staggered toward it, and the animal vanished in a puff of dust. Astrid, Tom, and Dora squeezed through the tree trunks where the rabbit had disappeared, finding themselves in a small, empty clearing, with large round rocks lining its circular perimeter.

The moment they stepped onto the trodden dirt and into the middle of the circle, the Whisperers stopped in their tracks. They stayed frozen in place, as if the rocks were a barrier they couldn't cross.

"This is it," Astrid sighed in awe. "This is the place."

In the middle of the clearing stood a single tree—an old, twisted yew tree whose massive trunk formed a sort of gateway through which they could see the other side.

"Any ideas why the creatures aren't following us here?" Dora asked warily.

"I don't intend to find out. The main thing is they're far away enough from us."

Tom suddenly cried out in pain as his leg gave way. Astrid and Dora grabbed him from both sides and helped him sit down. He leaned back against one of the rocks.

"This doesn't look good." Dora frowned as she pulled up the tattered leg of his pants.

"I don't feel very good either," Tom mumbled.

Sweat had broken out on Tom's brow. His injured leg really did look ugly. The wound was deep and gaping, the skin around it inflamed. Astrid didn't know much about injuries, but this was definitely not what a fresh wound looked like. This looked like a mess left untended for hours. If Tom didn't get it cleaned properly within the next few hours, he was definitely in danger of blood poisoning.

Dora began to look around them. "We have to stop the bleeding."

"Wait."

Astrid slung off her backpack and rummaged through it for a second. She pulled out several sachets of herbs and a tiny mortar, asking Dora to help her.

"Tighten the wound, there's a rope in there." Astrid nodded toward her backpack. In the meantime, she used the mortar to crush the contents of the two sachets.

Dora did as she asked, pulling out a piece of rope and constricting Tom's ankle. In a makeshift bowl made of tree bark, Astrid crushed several herbs, adding tincture. She chewed up several leaves of sorrel to better release their acidity, spitting them into the concoction.

Astrid applied the mixture with her freezing fingers onto Tom's wound. He hissed in pain at every touch.

"Sorry, almost done."

Together with Dora, they covered his leg with the herbs and bandaged it with a clean piece of cloth.

"It's no miracle, but it's the best I could do," Astrid admitted with defeat.

"It's perfect. Thank you." Tom squeezed her hand in gratitude.

Astrid stood up and turned to look at the portal behind her. She still couldn't believe that they had actually found it.

"We gotta go. We're running out of time."

"Astrid…" Dora whispered urgently.

"What?"

Her friend gave her a meaningful look. "Tom's not gonna be able to make the journey."

Astrid's heart clenched. Of course he wouldn't be able to. How could she be so stupid? She faltered, unsure what to do. Tom noticed her indecision.

"Go. What're you waiting for?" he urged them. "Go on without me. I'll wait here for you."

Astrid shook her head. "I'm not going anywhere without you."

"Astrid, stop it," Tom pleaded. "Dora's right. I can barely stand up, let alone walk. You can't drag me with you. Go and save Max. We've come so far. This is what you wanted, after all. I won't allow you to just throw your one chance away like this. I won't be the one to stand in your way. Go and save your brother."

Astrid wanted to say so much to him. The words were stuck in her throat, and they didn't make it past her lips. Instead, she ran her fingers down his cold cheek. Tom's eyes were bright from the pain and fever taking hold of him.

"I know," Tom whispered.

The two women began to gather their things. "Okay, I'll leave these things for the protection prayer here with you in case the demons come any closer," Astrid handed Tom her casket. "It's not much, but make sure to use all of it."

"Don't worry."

"I could leave the rifle here," Dora offered.

"No." Tom shook his head, drawing a shaky breath. "I'll feel much calmer knowing you have it with you."

Astrid pulled out an envelope from her pocket and handed it to Tom. He looked at her questioningly.

"I wrote down a few notes and pointers in case we return and lose our memories again," she explained warily. "It'll be easier having me read that than trying to explain everything to us."

Dora jerked in alarm at Astrid's words. Apparently, she hadn't considered the possibility of losing her memories.

"You've thought of everything," Tom admitted.

Instead of answering, Astrid stuck her hand in the backpack one more time, pulling out a ball of red yarn, not unlike the one the rozhanitsa had wrapped around their wrists when they underwent hypnosis. She tied one end around her forearm and placed the ball of yarn in Tom's lap.

"So we'll be able to find our way back to you," Astrid explained. "One tug means we're okay. Two tugs indicate danger. And three tugs mean you can slowly start reeling us back."

"I understand. Be careful in there," Tom said in parting.

The girls set out for the portal. Astrid didn't have time to think about how scared she was, or about what she was about to do. The only thing she was aware of was the soft whispering coming out of the shadows, and Astrid wondered whether she would finally be reunited with her brother.

It was like walking through a veil. The darkness around them clustered into black clouds, which soon transformed into a gray, impenetrable fog. Dora and Astrid were standing on the other side. They made it. And with all their memories intact—at least for now.

Astrid gently pulled on the red yarn. Within moments, Tom—however far away he was from this place—tugged back in answer.

"Is this it?" Dora whispered in awe. "Is this the realm of dreams?"

Astrid nodded. "Or at the very least, it's the place I see in my dreams. Whatever it's called."

"Where do we go now?"

As if in answer, the white rabbit appeared out of nowhere, showing them the way. They followed closely behind.

"Astrid?" Dora whispered. "What's the deal with this rabbit? How d'you know it's safe to follow it?"

"How do you know it's safe *not* to?"

Dora had no argument for that.

"I just trust it," Astrid added in a conciliatory tone after a while. "What choice do I have?"

The fog engulfing them was strange. It didn't allow them to see beyond their outstretched hands, and yet the outlines of shapes were filtering through at the same time. Astrid soon realized the shapes were actually figures. Tall, black shadows, walking there and back, back and forth—some almost within reach, others farther away. They never approached the two—it seemed they weren't aware of their presence. Astrid and Dora couldn't see their faces—they couldn't see anything but dark outlines, but they could hear the figures mumbling under their breath.

"What do you think it is?" Dora asked nervously. "Ghosts?"

"Sleeping people," Astrid voiced her assumption out loud. "Their dreams make up the fog. This is where we go when we fall asleep."

"They're just dreaming?" Dora released a breath in surprise.

The rabbit sped up, and so did they. The fog began to cluster into smaller and smaller clouds that eventually thinned out. They suddenly found themselves in a space that brought to mind a vast cathedral with no floor and no ceiling, adorned with countless identical columns.

"We're in deep, Dora. I've never gotten this far before. This is it!" Astrid was unable to control the excitement in her voice.

"Astrid?"

The tone in which Dora said her name rattled Astrid. She spun around. Dora was standing two paces behind her, blood gushing out of her nose. She was unnaturally pale, turning almost translucent.

"What's going on?" Dora mumbled in fear. "I can't feel my body… I…"

"Dora, back away!" Astrid shouted. "Take a step back, quick!"

Dora listened and retreated into the fog. Her nose stopped bleeding. Shocked, she wiped the blood away with her sleeve.

"What was that? What happened?"

"Don't take another step," Astrid warned her. "You probably can't go so deep into the dream world. You'd hurt yourself. You have to stay in the fog."

"And let you go on by yourself? Are you crazy?"

Her friend's loyalty warmed Astrid's heart. "Hold onto the yarn. I'll be on one end, Tom on the other. If I don't come back for a long time, give the yarn three tugs and Tom will reel you back out. And the rabbit will watch over you." Astrid nodded toward the animal at Dora's feet.

"Astrid, I don't like this plan at all. What's going on here? How come you can go on and I can't?"

"Dora, it wasn't a request. I'll explain everything later."

They led a silent battle of wills for a while. "Fine," Dora eventually gave in. "Be careful. And come back with Max as soon as you can."

Astrid set forth without a second thought. She crept along the massive columns, running her fingers down the cool marble as she crouched in the shadows. Whenever she noticed movement in her peripheral vision, she pressed herself up against the columns as if trying to melt into the marble.

The Whisperers were near. Astrid felt their presence—that alone was much more terrifying than when she actually spotted one of them in the shadows. It felt like they were everywhere, surrounding her. Like if she glanced over her shoulder quickly enough, they'd be hovering right behind her. And maybe they really were. They were definitely watching her. And waiting for the right moment to pounce? Or trying to corner her, trap her? Astrid focused all her energy into a single objective. She knew she wouldn't get any more opportunities. She had to act now.

Max. Max, where are you?

This was her last chance. The endless hall resembled a labyrinth and, with an ache in her heart, Astrid realized she was probably walking around in circles. She tried to spark some sort of connection with Max—to call him to her, like she'd managed to do in her dreams. But all her efforts were in vain.

"Come on, come on," Astrid whispered desperately, rubbing her temples.

Her head splitting open like never before, Astrid was close to bursting into tears. What if the entire night had already gone by? What if Tom had frozen to death out there, with Dora lost in the fog forever? Sonya was dead, and Astrid's two closest friends had risked their lives to get her here.

But how was she supposed to find Max? How was she supposed to rescue him? It could take years before she found him here. Everything was all wrong. She'd never make it happen. She'd never find him. If anything, the Whisperers would probably find her first.

And then, after an endless stretch of silence, Astrid heard something—swift footsteps.

Somebody grabbed her by the waist from behind, wrapping a hand over her mouth. Astrid didn't dare let out a sound, fear constricting her throat. It wasn't a Whisperer—she could feel the warm breath of a human being on the back of her neck. They moved past several more columns, stepping into a hallway with stone walls and alcoves. Her kidnapper stopped.

"Don't scream," he asked of her, his voice quiet.

Astrid nodded to show she understood. He let her go so she could turn around. All it took was a fraction of a second for Astrid to recognize him. It was Max. An older Max, on the threshold of adulthood. The twelve years had gone by for him, too, and he'd grown into a young man. He was tall, taller than Astrid. And he resembled his father so much! Her baby brother.

"Is it really you?" Astrid whispered. "The real you?"

He smiled. "Yes, it's me."

"Oh, Max!" She pulled him into a hug. "I'm so sorry I left you here. I didn't want to. I don't know how it happened…"

"Astrid." Max pulled away from her gently. "What are you talking about?"

"I… I guess you're unaware, but since our disappearance, since the moment we found ourselves trapped here… It's been twelve years," Astrid began explaining hastily. "A few days ago, me, Tom, and Sonya managed to get back. You didn't. We left you here. I left you… I didn't want to, I—"

"Wait," Max interrupted her. Even his voice sounded like his father. "Don't you remember?"

Astrid faltered. "I lost a lot of my memories… Bits and pieces are slowly coming back to me, but I'm missing the bigger picture. Why? What happened? Why are you looking at me like that?"

Even in the dim light, she noticed Max turning pale. He reeled back, running his fingers through his hair. "I can't believe… You really don't remember…"

"What happened?" She got a sinking feeling in the pit of her stomach. "What am I supposed to know?"

"Astrid." Max grabbed her hands in his. "I'm so sorry that I have to tell you this… That you have to experience this all over again, but… You didn't leave me here. You didn't forget about me. I *had* to stay here.

"That nightmare that we ended up stuck here because of—it wasn't yours. It was mine. It was me who caused it, Astrid. All those rituals before bedtime, the prayers, the symbols of protection on our bedroom door—we were doing all that because of me.

"That day in kindergarten… you launched yourself at those monsters to protect me, but with your abilities too shaky and volatile, you accidentally took Tom and Sonya with you. We ended up trapped here for twelve years, looking for a way out." Max's eyes filled with tears. "You never wanted to give up, you kept insisting it was possible. And you were right, the portal really did appear. It was our chance to escape, but I couldn't get through. The

Notsnitsa's curse wouldn't allow me to. I'm trapped in this dream world as long as the curse lasts."

Astrid gaped at her brother. His words drove out all the air from her lungs. She suddenly couldn't breathe.

"So... So all this time that I've been..."

Max's face fell. "If you came here with the intention of rescuing me and bringing me back... It can't be done. I didn't know you were trying to get here. In the past few days, I kept hearing your voice coming out of the fog, but I could never see you clearly. You always disappeared too quickly. I thought that I would try waiting for you in that great hall, that you'd show up again eventually, and we'd be able to at least talk to each other in your dreams for a while."

Astrid felt the tears rolling down her face. "There has to be a way to get you home. There has to."

"I can never make it past the columns. I can't even step into the fog—I don't know what's beyond it, what it looks like. My body"—Max stared at his hands—"or whatever this is, dissolves, and I end up back at the beginning. And believe me, that's a place I don't want to end up in again."

"The beginning?"

"This world has several stages," he clarified. "For you, the fog is the beginning, but for me, it's the end. It's the place from where you can wake up the easiest and get back to the real world. It's made up of the everyday dreams of mortals. That hall where we met is something like a transfer station—the second stage. That's where those monsters that kidnapped us dwell. The ones who used to appear in our room. The Whisperers. Some are weaker than others, while some are super sensitive to any movement. Tom always thought it depended on how well they'd just fed off their sleeping victims. I think they patrol the place to make sure nobody gets where they're not supposed to be. Then there's these hallways between the great hall and other places." Max looked around. "It's basically a labyrinth with no way out. You could spend years wandering around here."

"That's terrible. And the third place?"

Max shuddered. "Just the thought of it makes me feel sick. Don't make me relive it."

"I'm sorry." Astrid squeezed his hand in comfort. "There must be a way to get you out of here. You can't stay here forever. You just can't. We can defeat the Notsnitsa. Every demon can be defeated somehow."

Max was dumbstruck.

"You really have lost all your memories, haven't you?" he realized. "You don't remember anything. Not even what occurred right before we vanished? The secret you confided to me the night before this all happened?"

Astrid shook her head. "Just bits and pieces."

Max grabbed her hands in his. His hands were warm to the touch. "Astrid... you had a theory that it was our grandma who was behind all the nightmares and bad dreams. You believed that she was the Notsnitsa."

Astrid drew in a sharp breath, only for her incredulous response to catch in her throat.

"She hated you so much. All those punishments when she'd lock you in the cellar... Trying to convince you that you were making it all up—the things you saw in the dark. She thought that by plaguing you with nightmares, she'd be able to get rid of you for good. Back then I didn't see it; I was too young to understand what she was trying to do. She knew you were special. You never let her break you, though. That's why you can move between both worlds. But I'll be stuck here unless she revokes the curse."

"But it doesn't make sense," Astrid replied, doubt lacing her voice. "Grandma loved you. Why would she leave you here? She wouldn't allow any harm to come to you. And if she wanted to get rid of me, she could've just drowned me in the well like a newborn kitten. I mean…"

"She wanted you to suffer, Astrid. To never find peace. Death would be too easy a punishment."

"But she could've called off the spell after I came back. She could've gotten you out of here. Why didn't she?"

"I don't know," Max admitted. "You said twelve years have gone by? Wow."

Astrid nodded with pity.

"I don't know why, but it's hard to imagine. Time passes differently here. Twelve years…"

They fell silent. Astrid's mind was in a whirl. Try as she might, she couldn't think of a solution. Except for one.

"I'm gonna go back and confront Grandma," Astrid announced resolutely. "I'll make her revoke the curse and come back for you. We still have one night left before the portal closes."

Max squared his jaw. "You've really lost your mind. Do you even hear yourself, Astrid?"

"Loud and clear," she confirmed. "I'm gonna get you out of here. I promised I would, and as long as I'm still breathing, I won't stop trying."

Max was staring at his sister as if considering how seriously she meant what she'd just said. He eventually realized Astrid was dead serious.

"You're just as crazy as ever," he sighed.

"I know—that's why you love me. At least I hope so."

Max opened his arms and embraced her. It was the first time

Astrid felt as if he were the older sibling, there to protect *her*. He was no longer a little boy running to her for help. Twelve years in this place had turned Max into a self-sufficient, grown-up man. Astrid held him close to her the same way their mother had always done. The eighteen-year-old poured all her love into the hug—all her concern for him and hope that everything would turn out okay in the end.

Astrid didn't know how long they stood there hugging each other, but when they pulled away, both of them had tears in their eyes. No words were necessary—no special bond to communicate what they were feeling in that moment. They just knew.

If I'm lucky… If we're both lucky… We'll soon see each other again.

Max walked his sister back to the spot where the fog began. Dora was nowhere to be found. Astrid got a sinking feeling in the pit of her stomach. Something terrible must've happened to her friend. She took a step forward, disappearing into the little clouds.

"Dory?"

The figures she'd previously seen in the fog were suddenly gone. Astrid found herself alone, and it didn't make her feel calm in the slightest.

"Dory?"

In desperation, Astrid pulled on the red yarn tied around her hand. It fell slack. At what point had that even happened? And how come she hadn't noticed? Astrid began to reel in the string frantically, succumbing quickly to her hysteria. She pulled and pulled, scrunching it up into a tangled mass. After several breathless minutes, she came across the end. The string was brutally torn in two.

"Dory? Dory!"

Astrid's voice echoed through the fog. She broke into a run straight ahead. Suddenly, the fog seemed much more treacherous and endless than ever before. Astrid knew she should try to keep her head, but she panicked, making the worst possible mistake she could've made. She stopped paying attention to where she was going.

She called out Dora's name. No answer. She even called out for that damn rabbit, but for the first time, the animal decided not to show up. This was it. Astrid stopped being aware of her surroundings. What if she didn't get out of here on time? What if she got stuck in here with Max? Surely she couldn't be so stupid as to get lost. She dashed from one place to another, sobbing and crying for her friend until her voice grew hoarse. Astrid didn't know how long she ran around in circles, and as her strength gradually left her, she fell to the ground on all fours.

"I'm sorry," she whispered. "I'm sorry, Max."

Astrid couldn't stop the surge of tears that poured down her face. And then, as if through a veil, she suddenly spotted a flash of red. She threw herself forward, her fingers coming across the other end of the yarn. With her heart pounding frantically, she pulled on it three times.

In a flash, Astrid felt something reeling in the string from the other side. She wrapped the string tightly around her wrist before setting forth. Soon after, the gray fog turned into black smoke, and a moment later, Astrid found herself on the clearing, stumbling right into the arms of a surprised Dora.

"Astrid! I thought you'd never come back!" Dora shouted. "I'm so relieved. I almost lost my mind I was so scared. For Perun's sake, tell me you remember me, tell me you didn't lose your memory again."

"I remember. *You* almost scared *me* to death!" Astrid replied. "I found the string torn in two. What—What happened? What happened to your face? And where's Tom?"

The clearing was empty, and it was only the two of them standing there. Astrid's stomach flipped. "Dora, where's Tom?"

"He's okay," Dora quickly assured her as Astrid gaped at her friend's torn lip, her face covered in bruises. "Didn't you feel the tugging? It almost tore my arm off. You were in there for so long, and then Tom started pulling on the string like crazy, reeling it in. I had to keep a hold of it in order not to get lost. I called out for you, but you didn't answer. I ended up all the way back at the portal and had to go through. We'd been gone for too long. The day was already breaking, and Tom was afraid that if we didn't come back, we'd get stuck in there. But you didn't manage to pass through in time, and the portal closed."

Astrid looked at her friend in confusion. "What're you talking about? It's still nighttime!"

Dora bit her lip nervously. "You were in there for too long. It's the first of January already, Astrid. It's the New Year. The twelfth night of the demons."

Astrid's heart sank. "I was in there the whole day?"

Dora nodded. "I'm so sorry. I helped Tom get down to the village. The doctor said he'd be all right, and I came back here right away. Pa… flew into a bit of a rage." Dora gestured vaguely at her face, which spoke for itself. "But it doesn't matter. What happened in there, Astrid? And how come we can still remember everything?"

"I promise I'll explain everything," Astrid assured her. "But I have to get home, right this minute. I have to talk to my grandma. Immediately."

THE TWELFTH NIGHT

I t took them a bit less time to get through the forest than the night before. It was Dora's fourth time around in the span of a couple hours, after all, and she was already aware of the biggest pitfalls they could encounter along the way.

This time, it was Dora who waded through the swamp first. She'd put on much better-suited boots, leading the way through the spots where the water level was at its lowest. She had even chopped a path through the brushwood with an ax. After that, weaving their way through the trees was easy, and before they knew it, they were out of the woods, heading down to the village. Even so, Astrid couldn't help feeling they weren't moving fast enough.

"You don't have to go with me the rest of the way," Astrid told her friend. She could see the confusion and hurt reflected in Dora's expression.

"What I mean is… This is a family matter," Astrid added in a friendlier tone. "I have to square a few things with Grandma. If it all goes well, I'm coming back for Max tonight."

"And if it doesn't?"

Astrid left her friend's question unanswered. "Go home, Dory.

Don't let the patrols see you. You're already in enough trouble as it is."

"I'll wait for you at the forest's edge," Dora decided, "until you come back."

Astrid couldn't find the right words to convey how grateful she was to her friend, so she just nodded before heading out into the night by herself. She came across the first Guards when she was still a ways away from the borders of the village.

"Hey! You there! Stay where you are!"

Astrid stopped in her tracks. The figures ran in her direction, and almost immediately, she recognized the prying, piggy eyes that were currently observing her eagerly in the light of a lantern. She considered it a great irony that it was none other than Kristian who had caught her breaking curfew.

"Well, well, well." He smirked with amusement. "If it ain't our little Astrid! What happened to you? You smell like you just climbed outta the sewer. Grab her," he ordered the two other Guards. "We'll take her to our house. I'll deal with her myself."

Kristian didn't have a clue just how much he was playing into her hands. Astrid allowed the Guards to grab her from each side by the arm, lugging her off to the Mahlers. She didn't resist, and she didn't bother reacting to Kristian's provocations. There was only one thing on her mind.

They led her all the way to the front door of her house. Kristian took over from there, managing to boast to the others how he'd *beat the living daylights outta this lil' witch,* brutally shoving her inside the house. Astrid figured she only had one chance to overpower Kristian. And that chance depended wholly on the element of surprise. As he shoved her through the door, she pretended to lose her balance and slid down along the wall into a half-crouching position. She let her backpack slide from her shoulder, slipping her hand inside.

"What're ya doing, you little—"

Astrid swung her arm back with all her might, slamming the handle of her ax right into Kristian's teeth. Blood gushed down the man's chin, his mouth agape in a gruesome grimace. He tried to say something—an angry swear word, most likely—but only a rasp escaped his lips.

She swung again, this time switching her grip, hitting Kristian in the temple with the butt of the ax blade. He immediately toppled to the floor, unconscious. Astrid stared down at his limp body in total shock for several seconds, hoping she hadn't killed him.

Gripping her ax, Astrid entered the kitchen, but it was empty. The clock had long chimed the witching hour. The house was asleep. She returned to the hallway and cautiously began to open the door to Grandma's room. Enough moonlight was streaming into the room from the window that she didn't even have to switch on the light. Grandma's bed was empty.

There was only one place left to check. Even now, the door leading to the cellar struck terror into Astrid's heart. She grabbed the door handle with one hand, her other hand clutching the ax close.

The door creaked open. Astrid could see the flickering candlelight all the way to the top of the stairs. She took the first hesitant step forward and slowly descended the stairs.

Astrid remembered the cellar underneath the house being spacious, but even so, the place fascinated and terrified her all at once.

Dozens of candles were flickering everywhere, and the room was filled with the stench of mustiness and decay. Hedda Mahler sat in the middle of it all, an open book laid out before her, softly reciting something in the ancient tongue. As Astrid descended the last stair and stepped into the room, her grandmother opened her eyes, turning her head to gaze straight at her.

The old woman didn't look surprised to see her.

"This whole time, it's been you," Astrid said. "You're the Notsnitsa, the demon of nightmares. Twelve years ago, we vanished because of you. It was you who cursed us."

Astrid wasn't sure whether it was because of the light or the fact that she'd figured out just who her grandmother really was—but suddenly, the woman seemed even more terrifying to her than ever before. And for the first time, Astrid was forced to admit to herself that the old woman looked dangerous.

"Why?" Astrid asked in as calm a voice as she could muster. "Why did you do all this? Because I'm not your own flesh and blood?"

Hedda Mahler didn't answer. Astrid didn't know if the woman was merely contemplating her response or simply didn't see her worthy of one.

"I know you hate me, but tell me, why did you drag the others into this? Why Tom? Sonya? How could you hurt Max? I thought you loved him."

"The only person who hurt Max was you," her grandmother replied in a raspy voice.

"It was you who cursed him, though!"

The accusation provoked Hedda into responding. "I was trying to curse *you*, idiot child! But for a six-year-old, ye turned out to be a precocious zduhać. Try as I might, I couldn't break you.

Locking ye in the cellar, day after day. Sending all manners of boogeymen after you. But ye always managed to get out of it, as if nothing had happened. Ye had no weakness. Except for…"

"Max," Astrid finished for her, shocked. "You sent a nightmare to capture Max to get me to go rescue him? You sacrificed your own grandson!"

"But unlike you, Max was supposed to return! All along, the plan was to get rid of you and you only. But the curse backfired. Ye had too strong a protective barrier surrounding you, and what's more, ye managed to drag those other kids with you, like the fool ye are."

"Max was supposed to come back and not remember anything? To forget about me?"

"It would've been best for everyone."

"But your plan didn't work out. I went back to that place for him, and now I remember everything. I'm going to report you to the Elders. They'll finally know who's really harming the village."

Her grandmother began to laugh. "Ye'll do no such thing. Ye won't be saying a word to anyone. I'll make sure o' that."

Astrid swallowed the lump in her throat. "If you did all this out of hatred toward me, why didn't you just get rid of me some easier way? You could've smothered me with a pillow in my sleep, pushed me into the river… anything! Instead, you chose the evilest way possible."

Hedda Mahler had a wild glint in her eye. "Yer wretched mother was smarter than I thought. She probably realized I was planning to do something. She paid the local rozhanitsa to cast a spell of protection over you. I couldn't hurt ye physically. It barely allowed me to lay a hand on you. Pushing ye off the stairs? Impossible. The final straw was when she taught ye to do the rituals of protection yerself, that sly little shrew. She would put garlic under yer pillow, sprinkle fennel along the door and windowsill. I couldn't cross the barrier."

Even though last night, Astrid had been angry with her mother for wanting to get an abortion all those years ago, now she felt guilty. All this time, she had actually been protecting her.

"How did you become the Notsnitsa?"

Hedda started to laugh, her voice filling up the cellar. "So many questions, and ye ask me the least important one! I'm disappointed at how stupid ye are. Wherever a zduhać is born, a Notsnitsa will always manifest and live close by—and vice versa. It's simple. One cannot exist without the other. The Notsnitsa spins out nightmares while the zduhać blocks them.

"They keep the world in balance, just like the rozhanitsy and witches that draw from light or dark magic. Ye were born as my counterpart, and I was born so that one day, ye would have to stand up to me. That's the way it's been destined to be from the days of old."

"I wouldn't have become a zduhać if you hadn't caused me to have nightmares. It's you who made me who I am!"

"Don't ye get it? This is precisely the meaning of life. All things are constantly forming, affecting, and determining one another. What came first? Good? Or evil? And how can we determine which is which, without the existence o' the other? Without them existing at the same time? Who decides what is wrong and what is right? And why even distinguish between the two? Good and evil mean different things to different people. What gives ye the right to judge?"

Astrid clenched her fists. "The point of your existence is to create nightmares that you use to manipulate people. To terrorize

351

them. To awaken fear in them. You kidnap six-year-old children and imprison them for no reason. *That* is evil."

"So ye say," the woman replied.

"I have one last question. Why haven't you revoked the curse and let Max come back? He can't leave the realm of dreams because he's bound to the place by your spell. Recant it."

"No," her grandmother refused her coldly. "Ye can't just take back the Notsnitsa's magic. It can only be redeemed by one's own blood."

Astrid sneered at Hedda in disdain. "And I guess your grandson just isn't worth it, right? How could you just leave him there? You're loathsome and weak, and you disgust me."

She didn't know what was about to happen, but Astrid could instinctively tell that it was going to be bad. Her grandmother lifted her arms, crossing them in front of her face. She began to recite a spell. Thick black smoke poured out of her fingertips. Astrid was quick to react. She took a few steps back, pulling a piece of chalk out of her pocket to draw a circle on the ground, deftly stepping into it.

"These cheap tricks won't save ye," her grandmother warned her.

Indeed, the smoke broke through the circle, wrapping around Astrid's ankles and yanking her to the floor. It knocked the wind out of her, as Astrid's ax was torn out of her hand and flung into a distant corner of the cellar.

Grandma rose from her spot. She towered over Astrid, who could barely catch her breath.

"What has awoken from a dream must again fall into a deep slumber," Hedda uttered. She mumbled a few words in the ancient tongue, words that Astrid didn't understand. Almost at once, she felt a strong urge to doze off. Sleep began to overcome her.

For the evil spirits cannot reach me, Astrid kept repeating to herself, again and again. Her hand fumbled across the floor, managing to pull on a piece of cloth underneath one of the tall, lit candles. The hot wax spilled on Grandma's skirt. The woman yelped in surprise, taking a step back.

Astrid immediately took advantage of this and sprung to her feet. She had only taken a few steps forward when a strong gust of airless wind slammed into her. Astrid flew through the air helplessly, crashing into a shelf full of tools and old paint cans, several of which tipped over. She fell to the floor, hard, face-planting right into the spilled paint. Blood filled her mouth from her busted lip.

What on earth did she think would happen when she came here? That she could convince Hedda to let Max go, easy as that?

Astrid's fingers brushed against a bunch of long nails. For a second, dark spots obscured her vision, but she managed to scramble back onto her feet and come face to face with her grandmother.

"Ye still haven't had enough, ye little brat?"

Even before Hedda finished uttering the words, a blast of dark energy burst from her palms. Without a second thought, Astrid launched herself behind a tall, wooden table. The spell hit the edge of the tabletop, splinters flying in all directions.

"Stop hiding from me, Astrid."

Grandma rounded the table, the spilled paint squelching beneath her boots. Astrid crawled on all fours along the table to put distance between them, allowing her grandmother to take only as many steps closer to her as she could afford. Their eyes met. Astrid swallowed the lump in her throat.

"Let's finish this, once and for all."

"Yes, let's," Astrid retorted, confidence lacing her voice.

She only had one try to get it right. Hedda began to conjure a spell, her fingers tracing symbols through the air. Astrid threw herself under the table, deftly crawling to the other side of it, ending up right behind her grandmother's back. In the candlelight, she could distinctly make out Hedda's footprints, having tracked through the spilled paint. Astrid grabbed the first heavy thing she could get her hands on, which happened to be an old, hefty book. With all her might, Astrid used the book to drive several of the nails she had into her grandmother's tracks through the dirt floor.

Hedda Mahler cried out.

Without hesitating, Astrid drove the rest of the nails into her grandmother's other footprint on the ground and backed away in alarm. But Hedda didn't budge. Unmoving, she stayed glued to the spot. It had worked.

Astrid clambered back to her feet and hurried to face her grandmother, hardly able to believe it. The old woman was standing there, frozen in time and space, her crazy eyes goggling at her.

"The easiest way to stop a demon is to drive nails into its tracks," Astrid hissed right at Hedda's face. "Maybe you shouldn't have left me alone with my mother's books. All that advice in them sure came in handy."

Astrid reached into her coat pocket and pulled out a small penknife she'd stolen some time ago from her uncle's toolshed in the backyard. She took a step closer to Hedda, making sure the woman could see the blade.

"You won't ever hurt me again. Or Mom. Or Max. Or anyone else. You're finished."

Astrid was dashing through the forest, running on fumes, sheer willpower spurring her on. Tree branches and brushwood whipped at her face as she ran by, but nothing could stop her. The day would be breaking any moment now. The birds were already gathering and starting their song to herald the approaching dawn.

Astrid was barreling toward the portal as if completely out of her senses. She knew Dora was somewhere behind her, but she didn't wait for her and didn't look back. Astrid plunged into the swamp. This time, she didn't have time to scout out the safest path. She just ran on, hoping luck would be on her side. Her legs kept sinking through, sometimes falling knee-deep into the swampy waters. At one point, she was sure she'd drown, but the water mercifully stopped at her chest as she went down. Astrid finally waded through to the other side, scrambling to reach dry land and pulling herself up with her arms.

She had a stitch in her side. It felt like her lungs and heart were about to give out any second. Through the trees, Astrid spotted movement. The Whisperers were floating by the bare tree trunks, but didn't pay her any mind. That unsettled her. They were drawing back to where they came from. They could sense it. The portal was closing.

Astrid had the feeling she could see the first light through the trees in the distance.

Not yet, Dazhbog. Let the sun sleep for just a little longer, Astrid pleaded to the god of the sun.

She forced her way through the last of the thicket, spotting the familiar clearing ahead.

"Max!" she cried out, unable to stop herself. "I'm coming for you, Max!"

In a tiny flask hidden in the palm of her hand, Astrid was

clutching the most precious thing of all—the Notsnitsa's blood, which was supposed to possess the power to break the curse. As she hurtled forward, the tree in the midst of the clearing suddenly began to move, right in front of her eyes. The branches began to entwine with one another, slowly growing over the portal from top to bottom, making it slowly disappear out of sight.

"No, please! Not yet!"

Astrid was a mere few feet away. Just a little bit farther. She was going to make it, she had to...

But fate dealt her a cruel blow. With the last of the branches weaving into one another, the portal definitely closed up for the year to come. Astrid's hand slid down the bark of the twisted yew tree in a last, desperate gesture, as she sank to her knees in utter exhaustion.

It was over. She had failed.

The sun came up, illuminating the clearing with the first rays of sunshine. A new day began.

THE FIRST NIGHT

One year later

For the first time ever, Dora finally felt in control of her life. Twelve months ago, when she had emerged from the forest at dawn, dragging a bedraggled Astrid behind her, her father had already been waiting for her at home, and it was the first time he hadn't raised his voice at her. He helped her put Astrid to bed, even going into the village to fetch the doctor to check up on her. Dora wasn't sure what convinced him to do so. Perhaps seeing the utterly broken and sobbing girl, or the authoritative tone Dora used to tell him what to do.

The truth was that from that moment on, Pa started seeing her in a different light. He was angry with her—without a doubt. And he grounded her for several weeks as punishment. But that spring, for the first time since her mother's death, he allowed Dora to accompany him to the forest to help him look after the wildlife. Dora felt as if she'd passed some sort of test.

That winter solstice, as she observed her brothers during dinnertime, roughhousing and joking around, Dora couldn't help but think back to last year's Korochun—the bonfire that went out and the misfortune it brought with it, but also all the good that came of it. She got back her friends. She finally felt like she fit in somewhere again.

In the past year, her brothers had grown up so much. They were on their way to becoming young men, and Dora was painfully aware that soon, they would no longer need her.

"Bedtime, let's go," Dora urged them in vain, long after dinner. "Don't you know you have to be in bed before the witching hour?"

"Yeah, yeah," Oleg groaned in annoyance.

"Will you read us a story, please?" Anton implored.

"Just a short one this time," Dora agreed. "I don't have much time. I have to leave soon."

"During the witching hour? Don't you know you should be asleep by then?" Oleg mimicked—fairly accurately—his sister's admonishing tone, making them all burst into giggles.

The twins got into bed and began listening to Dora's storytelling. Some time ago, she had stopped reading them fairytales and had switched to stories about heroes and malevolent creatures that lurked in the dark. It wasn't Dora's intention to scare them, but just in case... they should be better prepared than she had been.

"All right." She shut the book after a good half-hour. "Time for bed. No backtalk."

Almost in unison, both brothers pulled out their arms from under the covers so they could pray together.

"Ready?"

Astrid smiled, facing away from Tom. "Like never before in my life."

She pulled her hair into a ponytail, pausing for a minute as she glanced at herself in the mirror. Astrid still couldn't get used to the new tattoos that now covered her arms. Dora had helped her pick them out and ink them into her skin. Maybe the symbols couldn't protect her from all the evil spirits and demons, but they helped Astrid define herself, where she belonged, and where she came from.

After last winter's events, Astrid and her mother had found a temporary haven at the Hattlers. At first she thought it would only be for a few weeks, but Tom's mother offered them the choice to stay as long as they needed. Astrid refused to return to her own house, not if it were the last option on earth.

She never did find out what happened to Hedda. The only thing Astrid knew was that after she ran away from the woman's motionless body into the forest to save Max, she was still alive. The Mahlers never officially held a funeral in Hedda's name, but from that night on, Astrid never spotted her grandmother in the village again. Whenever she had to walk past their old house, she deliberately looked the other way, as if the place didn't exist. Sometimes, an uneasy feeling would overtake her, as if Hedda's eyes were intently watching her every move from behind the heavy curtains. But it must've just been Astrid's imagination playing tricks on her.

She never really got rid of the nightmares either. After the nights of the demons, they may have abated somewhat, but Astrid would still sometimes wake up with a scream, her nightgown drenched in sweat. Night after night, Astrid learned what being a zduhać entailed. She had no one to really guide her through it, but she started visiting the local rozhanitsa, who, taking pity on the young woman, offered her basic advice. At the very least, the woman helped her overcome the difficult beginnings. Later on, Astrid learned to listen to her subconscious intuitively. And even though she fought it at first, she gradually stopped fearing her own powers.

That evening, Astrid, her mother, and the Hattlers joined the other villagers in lighting the traditional protective bonfire. The winter solstice came earlier than the inhabitants would've liked—this meant they were in for another long, harsh winter. But to Astrid, it felt as if time had dragged on at a snail's pace this past year. She couldn't wait for Korochun to arrive. Every particle of her body called out for it. To her, it was the light in the darkness.

After dinner, like always, Astrid helped her mother pull on her coat, taking her out for their daily walk. The routine and fresh air did her mother good. They would stroll along, arm in arm, with Astrid telling her what was new and how much she had to study to catch up in school. Unlike Tom, Astrid actually enjoyed trying to catch up on everything they'd missed. And she couldn't say she didn't enjoy competing with Tom, just a little bit, either.

Most of the time, her mother remained apathetic, showing no reaction to Astrid's words. Not even that time when Astrid confessed to figuring out who her real father was. She'd just needed to get it off her chest, once and for all, and to say his name out loud.

"That's why he had my photograph on him—he knew about me too, right? He knew I was his daughter. That's why he kept following us all the time. That's why I could talk to him, even after his death. After the solstice, the dead can connect only with their blood relatives. And I was able to talk to him, long after he was already hanging dead from a tree."

Her mother stayed silent.

"I don't know whether you loved him, or whether I'm the outcome of something you'd rather forget, but I wanted to tell you that I forgive you. I forgive you for not telling me."

Her mother squeezed her arm tightly, as did Astrid in return. A year ago, she had promised her mother that she would bring Max back, and she was determined to keep her word.

She had waited the entire year to do so.

Astrid set out with Tom before midnight. She walked toward the forest, much more nervous than she'd been last year. Only this time, it was a pleasant nervousness spreading through her veins, along with the anticipation that everything would turn out well.

Dora joined them beyond the borders of the village. She was waiting there in the shadows as if she had been born for adventure.

"Well, this is it," Dora said, her voice trembling. She couldn't mask her excitement either.

"We're bringing Max home," Tom said, squeezing Astrid's hand.

"We're bringing Max home," Astrid confirmed his words.

They all entered the forest together. The only sound to be heard on that chilly, December night, the longest night of the year, was the rhythmic crunching of the snow underneath their feet.

When Astrid was a child, she had been afraid of falling asleep because her nightmares came alive. But as soon as she came face to face with her fears and demons, as soon as she confronted them, she realized that nothing was as terrifying as it seemed.

Because as Astrid realized soon thereafter, she was never really completely alone in the dark.

ACKNOWLEDGEMENTS

Like every book, this one, too, needed a little push forward in certain stages of its creation to draw out the very best that was hidden within it (or perhaps within me). The person most deserving of credit for making this book a reality is Vojta Záleský. Many thanks for his work as editor, proofreader, nitpicker, and untangler of all my chaotic ideas. It was he who publicly encouraged me to write my second novel, persevered in constantly testing the stability of the foundations of the plot, and helped move the story forward with his constructive criticism.

I'd like to thank Štěpánka Coufalová for breathing life into the characters and scenes with her illustrations, which have, by far, surpassed my own imagination. Gorgeous work!

Infinite thanks to Markéta Trefná, the first reader of this story, stories past, and all those to come.

Last but not least, I'd like to express my gratitude to my colleagues at work and in my department, who for several months had to pretend—time and time again—not to see how desperately behind I was on everything, who covered for me and my chaos, and who always waited patiently for me to tear myself away from my manuscript and get to the task at hand.

But I owe my greatest thanks, as ever, to my loved ones. You know who you are. For me, writing will always take precedence over everything else; there is no middle ground—and never has been. And I'm grateful to you for respecting me whenever the first option wins out over the other. I couldn't do it without you.

Kateřina Šardická
I Shall Awaken

© Albatros Media Group, 2022.
5. května 22, Prague 4, Czech Republic.
Text © Kateřina Šardická, 2020
Translation © Tereza Novická, 2021
Editing: Scott Alexander Jones, 2021
Cover & Illustrations © Štěpánka Coufalová, 2021
Printed in Czech Republic by TNM Print, s.r.o.
www.albatrosbooks.com

ISBN: 978-80-00-06347-8